A POUND
OF FLESH:
Surviving the Zombie
Apocalypse

SHAWN CHESSER

ACKNOWLEDGMENTS

For Mo, Raven, and Caden, you three mean the world
to me… love you. And thanks for putting up with me clacking away
at all hours. I owe everything to my parents for bringing me up the
right way. Mom, thanks for reading… although it is not your genre.
Dad, aka Mountain Man Dan, thanks for your ear and influence. Cliff
Kane, RIP. Daymon, thanks for taking me all over the slopes in
Jackson Hole! Thanks to all of the men and women in the military,
past and present, especially those of you in harm's way. Thanks to all
LE personnel for your service. To the people in the U.K. who have
been in touch, thanks for reading! Beta readers, you rock and you
know who you are. Thanks George Romero for introducing me to
zombies. Steve H. thanks for listening. All of my friends and fellows
at S@N, thanks as well. Lastly, thanks to Bill W. and Dr. Bob… you
helped make this possible. I am going to sign up for another 24.
Cover designed by Jason Swarr of Straight 8 Photography.
Thank you sir! Thanks to Steve and Ken at International Harvester
Scout Parts in Portland. www.scoutparts.com
Special thanks to Craig DiLouie, Gary Mountjoy, John O'Brien, and
Mark Tufo. One way or another all of you have helped me and
provided me with invaluable advice.
Once again, extra special thanks to Monique Happy for taking "A
Pound of Flesh" and giving it some special attention and TLC while
polishing its rough edges. I am glad to have met you Mo! Working
with you has been a seamless experience and nothing but a pleasure.
You are the best! If I have accidentally left anyone out…
I am truly sorry.
*****

Edited by Monique Happy Editorial Services
http://www.indiebookauthors.com

ACKNOWLEDGMENTS

TABLE OF CONTENTS

Prologue
Outbreak - Day 10
Jackson Hole, Wyoming

The trilling Iridium satellite phone nearly failed to rouse Robert Christian from a black, two Ambien aided sleep. With his head still banging from the night's festivities, he reached blindly, probing the nightstand for the annoyance. Upon recognizing the glowing green numbers on the readout for what they meant, a spike of adrenaline surged through his body. He stabbed the talk button on the third ring, anxious for an update. "Yes," he said.

"Your man made it inside," the male voice said.

"Did you make contact?"

After a slight pause the disembodied voice answered, "Affirmative."

"*And!*" the President of New America pressed.

"The man you sent *did not* follow your orders. He *did not* wait for her."

The billionaire king maker and self-appointed New America President Robert Christian wasn't used to dealing directly with people. Usually his head of security Ian Bishop mined the information first then presented *only* the useful nuggets. Christian's time was valuable, he always demanded bullet points—information presented promptly and succinctly. He could feel the first spikes of white hot rage forming behind his eyes. *Pull it together Robert,* he silently told himself. He knew if he lost it now the woman lying next to him would be the first victim of his legendary temper, and there was no telling what the unbridled rage would make him do. As President he had found had many perks, but the major downfall was that no one was brave enough to intervene when he went on a rampage.

His anger subsiding, Christian reluctantly resumed the conversation. "Please tell me *exactly* what Francis did."

"At the agreed upon dead drop I left your man a timeline detailing *every* one of the President's visits. I also sketched a map showing where her Osprey lands at the airbase. When and where she typically went when she was here, as well as how many secret service agents she traveled with, and what kind of weaponry they were openly carrying..."

"*I didn't ask you for a rundown of your day!*" Christian bellowed. The blonde next to him rolled over and mumbled something unintelligible. "I want to know *exactly* what happened last night. Start from the beginning."

"Instead of watching and waiting for her return, your man went off on a tangent."

"*A tangent?*" Christian screamed, spittle flying. Then suddenly he went silent as he realized exactly what had happened. *Oh no,* he thought to himself. *Pug had shown up instead of Francis.*

"I guess *tangent* is a little bit of an understatement. Your guy is a one man *wrecking crew*... killed six or seven people and started a couple of fires. The President *cannot* be touched now... *no way*. I did my part. I *swear* it wasn't me who dropped the ball, Mr. Christian."

"I want details. Not *blather.*"

"Two doctors were brought here from the CDC in Atlanta..."

The veins snaking across Robert Christian's temple began to pulse. "I know where the *fucking* CDC is. Stop waffling and get to the point."

"The doctors apparently had engineered a drug to counter the effects of the virus."

Robert Christian's heart fluttered. "Can you *confirm* that?"

"Not with firm, eyes-on intelligence. The point is moot though... your man *killed* the doctors. I've overheard base personnel; your man did a good job destroying their lab. Took them an hour just to put out the fire."

A wide, Grinchlike smile blossomed on Robert Christian's face as he caressed the woman under the sheets with his free hand. "What happened to *Pug?*"

"You mean *Francis?*" the man said, sounding confused.

Silence.

"No, I misspoke," Christian lied. "*Somehow...* *Pug* showed up instead of *Francis.*"

"At any rate," the voice on the other end stated, "they rolled someone up."

"So he's in custody," Robert Christian said, thinking out loud. He pondered this for a moment before adding, "The question is... *will he talk?* And the answer... if I know Pug like I think I do. Mums the word."

"I hope so, because they have him locked up in an area which is off limits to civilians."

"*Valerie Clay* has to make an appearance at the base," Christian said, hopeful sounding words spilling forth. "She has got to come and see the damage first hand with her own eyes."

"There is *no* chance of the President coming here now. I presume she's inside of Cheyenne Mountain just in case the wind shifts..."

"Wait a moment," Christian said slowly. "What do you mean, in case the wind shifts?"

The blonde rolled over onto her back causing the sheer silk sheet to cascade from her body, leaving her pert breasts fully exposed. She was seemingly too out of it to care.

Christian took advantage as he listened to the man explain himself.

"A klaxon sounded last night... long... like a warning, and then a few minutes later I heard a very loud explosion... rumbled my bones like thunder. I even felt the ground move... like an earthquake. Rumor that's flying around is they set off a couple of nukes to kill a huge herd of those creatures."

Christian tightened his grip on the blonde's breast, waking her abruptly from her drugged stupor. His mind spun as he disseminated the information. If Valerie Clay would be so cavalier as to use nuclear weapons so close to home, he reasoned, what would stop her from using them against him?

"What do you want me to do now?" the voice asked.

"Carry on with your task." Then, unsure how to channel his conflicted emotions, he killed the connection, rolled over and turned his full attention to the blonde.

Chapter 1
Outbreak - Day 10
Schriever Air Force Base
Colorado Springs, Colorado

The seconds seemingly turned to hours as everything around her slowed. The last few feet seemed like a marathon, but to survive she had to keep running. With a burst of newfound energy, Brook wrenched the screen door open, her free hand propelling Raven ahead of her and into the room. Acrid gunpowder clung to their clothes; the smell of death was close behind. Mother and daughter reached the shadows as the zombie stopped and abruptly aboutfaced. The young woman wavered on unsteady bare feet, rheumy eyes searching for prey. She had obviously endured a horrible death at the hands and teeth of the infected. Scraps of blood-soaked clothing hung from her gaunt form, while the fistful of flesh absent between her jawbone and clavicle told of the viciousness of her attackers. Like silken stockings fluttering on a clothesline, thin ribbons of alabaster dermis dangled where her carotid used to reside.

Brook ejected the magazine from the carbine, confirmed it held thirty rounds, then deliberately replaced it in the well where it seated with a soft *snick*. Next, she pulled the M4's charging handle. The military rifle was now hot—its safety off.

"Why didn't the bombs work?" Raven whimpered. "Daddy said he would keep us safe."

"Shhh... you *have* to be quiet," Brook whispered, backpedaling deeper into the shadowy room and pulling Raven along with her. *Go away. Go away. Go away,* Brook chanted in her head, hoping somehow the creature would telepathically get the message and move along.

As if in response to the absurd notion, a rasp, like wind weaving through dry corn stalks, emanated from the creature's azure lips.

Brook risked another quick look, peering around the bunk with one eye. The monster was one of the *first turns* as the soldiers had taken to calling the living dead that were more than a week old. Mottled ashen skin, distended gas-filled abdomen, and maggot infestation—all telltale signs of the age of the walking corpse. *The only good thing about the first turns,* Brook reminded herself, *was that they usually didn't moan the same as the newly reanimated.* The newer turns moaned incessantly at the first sight of the living, their eerie call inviting other dead, thus creating a daisy chain of followers in pursuit of the warm meat.

Although Brook was a nurse and not a medical examiner, she did have her own theory. She guessed the differing sounds had something to do with the first turns' vocal cords having dried up over time, and her one hope was that this walker at the door didn't already have a following. That hope was quashed as the shambling throng of dead collided with the first turn, forcing her through the flimsy screen door; the surge of carrion followed, pouring into the barracks in search of their quarry.

"*Run Raven. Run and don't you dare look back!*" Brook cried as the first rounds erupted from her M4 carbine. She had already sprayed a quick full auto burst at the leering white faces before Cade's words filtered into her head. "*Controlled single shots. You must make every round count.*" His voice calmed her. Brook switched the rifle's selector from full auto to single shot. Then, using the remaining ten rounds much more effectively, she dropped eight of the walkers just inside the entrance.

Just as the bolt on the smoking Colt locked open, more of the horde surged through the splintered doorway. Without looking, Brook hit the release on the right side of the rifle's lower receiver, sending the spent magazine tumbling to the ground. Then, in one fluid motion, she jammed a fully loaded mag home and pulled the charging handle, racking a round into the chamber. "*Die fuckers!*" she cried, pouring lead into the approaching zombies. A crazy grin appeared on her face and she couldn't help but laugh inwardly at her choice of words. The walking corpses had already died once. She couldn't use *"Die again fuckers"*—it didn't have the same ring to it.

Slipping and sliding on a crimson lake of bodily fluids and spilled entrails, the crush of putrid bodies closed in on all sides as Brook used up the last of her ammo. *"You can't have her!"* she screamed, swinging the useless rifle at the encroaching knot of tooth and nail.

Before the gnarled hands could rip Raven from her grasp, Brook's upper body exploded from beneath the sheets. Her chest heaved and her ripped abdomen glistened slick with sweat. Still running on the very impulses that had been jumping synapses milliseconds earlier, her right hand frantically searched the bed, not for her husband Cade, but for the M4 rifle that she had wielded in her nightmare.

Gradually coming to her senses, Brook inhaled fully, held the air in her lungs for a tick, and then gently exhaled—willing her heart rate to slow. Then she pulled the strands of sweat-dampened hair behind her ears and listened to the rhythm of Raven's breathing.

Brook knew without a doubt that this latest nightmare was a direct manifestation of her subconscious fears—the very fears that she kept stuffing, the ones she was neither fully ready, nor willing to deal with.

She shuddered. This macabre masterpiece had been the most vivid and horrifying to date. Though she wasn't overly superstitious or into psychic phenomenon, she couldn't help but think these recurring "creature features" in her brain were somehow premonitions of things to come.

At that moment as she lay in the dark trying to analyze the nightmare which was becoming more distant with each elapsed second, the realization that her brother was dead, his murder not conjured up by some cruel part of her subconscious, rippled through her like a 9.0 earthquake. Then the reality that she was now essentially an orphan clawed for her attention. It had been only ten days since she had shotgunned her mother and father in the house that she had been raised in, and now, further compounding that loss, her brother

Carl had just been murdered in cold blood by an unhinged lunatic whose motives still remained a mystery. Getting her mind around this, let alone telling Raven everything that had transpired, was going to be a monumental task.

Brook felt another cramp forming. The pain attacked in short bursts, radiating from within like menstrual cramping, only markedly more intense. In response she rubbed the tender area above her pubic bone, trying to stave it off. Being a nurse, she knew the human body had its own way of taking care of a defective pregnancy, and her body was doing just that.

Shuffling slightly hunched over, the tiny porcelain tiles chilling the bottoms of her bare feet, she made her way to the toilet. The nondescript room smelled of chlorine bleach and the rank wild flower smell of piss-coated urinal cake. The bathroom, which had been designed when men predominantly made up the Air Force ranks, had a long row of stand-up urinals and only half a dozen toilets. The lack of doors on the sit downs made her feel more than a little exposed. It wouldn't have been an issue if she was only *going* to the bathroom. That she was losing her baby made her long for a half-inch thick piece of wood for privacy. Sitting alone, feet hovering above the real and imagined microbes that made the floor their home, she fought the overwhelming urge to bawl out loud.

A bout of diarrhea, she had told herself convincingly. *Maybe you're hungry*, another voice chided. All the while, *You are losing your baby*, is what the recurring spasms in her abdomen were screaming. The hope that she had been privately clinging to for half a day disintegrated when she looked in the toilet water between her legs. Gossamer strands of bloody discharge confirmed her worst fears— she had just lost her baby. That Cade was gone again made the loss even harder to accept.

Still sitting on the commode, Brook hailed her daughter in the other room. "Raven... wake up. We've got to leave in a few minutes. Annie is going to need your help today with Junior and the twins."

"Ok... Ok. I'm up," Raven grumbled from the other room.

The sound of her daughter's dainty feet hitting the floor spread a half smile across Brook's face. *Be grateful*, she told herself, fighting to stand erect and pull on her pants. On a scale of one to ten the pain was about a six. This Brook could handle. She put her game face on, retrieved the M4, and greeted her sleepyhead. "Sweetie... did you get enough shuteye? Did you have any nightmares?"

"Yes Mom... no Mom," Raven answered, the irritation from being prematurely roused now absent from her voice. Then, rubbing her eyes, she asked, "Where's Dad?"

"Out saving the world I presume," Brook said dramatically. Instantly she wished she could take it back. Cade was Raven's Super Man, King Arthur and Robin Hood all rolled into one. She adored her dad and remarkably her world still revolved around him—he still had the "dad mystique" that usually disappears around the time a girl turns thirteen. *One more year Mr. Grayson*, Brook thought to herself.

"I've got to pee like a racehorse," Raven declared, making a beeline for the toilets.

"Where in the heck did you hear that young lady?" Brook asked, suppressing a smile.

"Duh... Dad, of course."

"Wait a minute... I forgot to flush," Brook said, cutting Raven off at the pass.

She didn't want to have to explain all of the blood. And it wasn't the right time to further traumatize her by letting her know that her sibling had just died.

When the shit hit the fan the previous night, Cade had been away on yet another mission with his Delta team, leaving her and Raven alone to fend for themselves. During a deployment in the old world the only life in jeopardy had been Cade's. But thanks to the deadly rampage, it had become evident to Brook that she and her daughter were no safer inside the wire than out. Since her flight from Fort Bragg she had become extremely capable of protecting her family, but she still longed to have all three of them together again for good. The fifteen months prior to the Omega outbreak had been, hands down, the best stretch of family time she could remember since Raven was born. That she had given Cade her blessing to rejoin the Unit and embark on another mission didn't soften the blow of losing her brother Carl. The silver lining to the very dark and brooding cloud hanging over her world was that Raven hadn't been murdered along with the others. The big man up above had been looking out for her daughter, who had somehow missed crossing paths with the killer by only a few seconds. *Timing is everything*, Brook thought to herself. By the time she found Raven, sitting on the curb sobbing, the infirmary was already fully engulfed in flames and there was nothing she could do to save Carl.

As Brook sat with her arm around Raven watching the building burn with her brother trapped inside, she could think of only one thing: it was about time she started getting her way. The Unit, the Country, President Clay, and the myriad other forces pulling her husband away were going to have to take the back seat. Maybe losing the baby now was a blessing, some sort of sign, she thought. Bottom line, after her family was together again for good, she *would* be bringing another Grayson into the world—crawling with dead or not—this she would not be denied.

Brook found her way back to the tiny slab of fabric the military called a bed. The side of the lumpy mattress Cade had fallen asleep on hours ago was now lonely and cold. She knew her man— either he was jogging around the base or the Delta operator was at the mess hall filling up on coffee. He rarely slept the day before an operation, spending every spare moment checking and rechecking weapons and equipment, poring over Intel and endlessly running scenarios through his head. He did everything he could to keep the talented Mr. Murphy (of Murphy's Law fame) from worming his way into the equation. One missed detail would be all it would take to make the upcoming operation go sideways—and spoil everyone's day.

She also allowed Cade all the breathing room he needed during his after-action decompression, when sleep became especially elusive for the Delta Force operator.

Brook knew that her husband had been on one constant *operation* since the day the dead began to walk and that he was running on sporadic bursts of adrenaline and dangerous levels of caffeine. Whether he was on base or away on a mission, she wasn't going to let her resentment build. And considering the events of the night before, she was determined to be as supportive as possible, even if that meant not talking about *her* loss. Cade would eventually open up and grieve for his friend Mike Desantos, in his own way, and when he did she would be there for him, all ears, eagerly awaiting her turn to be heard.

***

Three hours earlier

It was one of the rare instances when Brook had failed to read her man correctly. Cade couldn't sleep. The thoughts of revenge, very graphic in nature, looped through his mind like a snuff film. It was as if the killer's face was tattooed on the insides of his eyelids and the flat-faced mongrel taunted him every time he closed them.

Cade dressed and laced his boots in the dark, being careful not to wake his wife and daughter. He gazed at the woman he loved before leaving to confront the man he truly hated.

Brook snorted and then grimaced in her sleep. No doubt she was having a whopper of a survival dream. Cade had stopped referring to the nocturnal horror movies in his mind as nightmares. He now referred to them as survival dreams, figuring it was his mind's way of staying on the razor's edge even when it was supposed to be at rest. At any rate, he hoped Brook was learning a thing or two from hers.

Easing the door shut behind him, he made doubly sure the lock was engaged. The fact that there might be other killers roving freely about Schriever made it entirely necessary.

Chapter 2
Outbreak - Day 10
Schriever AFB
Colorado Springs, Colorado

Security Pod
Senior Airman E-4 Croswell snapped to attention, a crisp salute merging with his blue beret the second he recognized Captain Cade Grayson's approach. The leather-bound ledger that had been used dutifully to document the time and identity of anyone coming into contact with General Mike Desantos' killer launched off of the E-4's lap and slapped the floor perfectly flat, issuing a loud report.

"At ease, Airman Croswell," Cade ordered.

The E-4 relaxed slightly, scooped up the fumbled log book, and plunged his arm under the gray folding chair blindly searching for his only pen.

"No need for formalities. Colonel Shrill sent me... *under the radar*," Cade lied. "This visit stays off the record," he continued, glaring at the younger man. Cade didn't receive the response he was hoping for. Unlike most enlisted personnel, Croswell didn't melt. He gamely deflected the Delta operator's attempt at persuasion by saying, "I have orders to follow. I *cannot* allow you entry without signing in."

Doubling down on the bullshit, Cade persisted. "That man in there murdered my friend General Desantos..." Cade paused in order to let his words sink in. "That waste of skin also murdered my wife's brother, and three other helpless people in the infirmary. And to cap it all off... that monster killed the doctors and destroyed the lab containing the antiserum that everyone on this base has been buzzing about."

"I wasn't told what the man did to get thrown in here. I knew it had something to do with the fires... I had no idea how bad it was," said the E-4, his glare softening.

Sensing he was almost home, Cade put on a full court press. "It's way too late for me to go back... wake up the Colonel just to satisfy you. Listen, you didn't achieve the rank of Senior Airman because you couldn't follow orders... I get that. You received that patch because of your ability to make decisions, the correct decisions, on the fly," Cade said, locking eyes with the cleancut young man.

Adam's apple bobbing like a rowboat in the ocean, the airman's heavily lidded eyes broke from Cade's and looked at the clock and then back, settling on the two silver bars pinned to Cade's beret. "Go on in Captain. You were never here."

After exchanging salutes with the airman, Cade went through the inner door and stood directly in front of the glass separating him from the murderer.

The man calling himself Pug lifted his head and stared daggers of rage through the observation glass. A shudder traced up Cade's spine; it was as if the seated and manacled prisoner on the other side of the one way mirror could see him, head shifting, seemingly following, as the operator paced back and forth. If he didn't know any better he would have thought that the flat-faced mongrel had x-ray vision—or at the very least the olfactory senses of his canine namesake.

Cade paused outside of the steel door and tried to quiet his inner voice—the repetitious droning chant that demanded revenge, all the while valiantly fighting the desire to march in and end it all here and now. Standing there with E-4 Croswell's eyes burning a hole in his back, he came to the conclusion that he would be battling these urges until Pug had drawn his last stolen breath. That he had lied to keep his name off of the ledger baffled the hell out of him. *What the hell was I thinking? Just kill the fucker and waltz right out, hoping the anal E-4 wouldn't intervene. What then, Grayson...kill him too to cover it up?* Trying to distance himself from his momentary character shift and mental lapse of judgment, he opened the heavy steel security door. Cade's entrance elicited a wan smile from the man who called himself Pug. The two were far from strangers. The night before, after the man had been captured, Cade had been given immediate access to him. Back-to-back fifteen second waterboarding sessions had failed to elicit any information, not his real name, not where he came from, who sent him, nor if there were more saboteurs or agents inside of Schriever. After Pug's third introduction to simulated drowning, he divulged only his name and that he had left Jackson Hole two days prior—the rest of his story still remained a mystery.

The fact that the prisoner had weaseled his way onto the base in the company of four other survivors, with a hidden weapon, pointed to some semblance of intelligence. That the man nonchalantly walked back to the civilian tents after his murderous rampage, leaving a perfect trail of wet footprints for the security personnel to follow, was, to say the least, very hard to fathom. *Was it a mental lapse on the killer's part,* Cade asked himself, *or had he wanted to be caught*

Pug had spent the last few hours marinating under the sterile white light bulbs. By design, the air was frigid due to the constantly running air conditioner. Comfort was now a thing of the past for the murderer, and Cade was going to see to it that the man would spend each minute from here on out wishing he were dead.

"I have a question for you, big man. Why did you intervene and save the other survivors?" Cade said, letting the question hang.

Manacles clanking, Pug shifted in his seat. Then he bent at the waist, stretching across the table to massage his swollen face with his cuffed hands.

"Did you save those people because you like teen girls? Or do you like 'em younger? I have a daughter, she's eleven... gonna be twelve real soon." Cade paused, again waiting for a response. He wanted to find a crack. Anything to get the dialogue flowing. The *real* physical pain would be applied as a last resort. Cade had a promise to keep and he knew that once he started, nothing was going to keep him from finishing the job.

The killer slowly moved the chain along the affixed bar that bisected the center of the table top as he stared at his blurred reflection in the brushed stainless steel. *Don't talk*, the voice counseled.

"Too bad the prison system isn't what it used to be. They'd adopt a *Short Eyes* like you in a New York second. You're a small guy... you'd be real easy to pass around. Like a party favor. They'd have their way with you until you were worn out and broken. You would enjoy that wouldn't you?"

Don't let him talk to you like that Pug. Stepdad did that to me... we would never hurt a kid. Don't let the fucker call you Short Eyes. Bash his face in.

Cade waited for a response.

Nothing.

"I know you came here with a group... but you were really alone. The redhead and her brother... they told us that they met you for the first time on I-25. Said you came out of nowhere, gun blazing. Said that you saved them like some kind of super hero."

Cade was no dummy. This Pug bastard was crafty—he'd give him that. Stalking them and watching from afar. Waiting for the opportune moment to insert himself into the equation—brilliant.

As soon as Pug heard the words *super hero* the demon lurking in his brain couldn't resist the urge to sing its theme song. *Here I come to save the dayyy.*

"I know who sent you." Cade crouched on his haunches to look the man in the eye. "Pug... Robert Christian sent you here."

No recognition. Cade had hoped to see some sort of expression, however small. He kept probing.

"I want to know who helped you after you got here. Little runt like you couldn't have pulled the whole thing off by yourself. Someone on this base provided you with the gun." He already knew how the gun had been smuggled in; the security personnel had found the ruptured Camelbak bladder in Pug's tent. He was trying to chip away at the man's self-esteem, which from the looks of him was probably on the low side. A person like that, Cade knew, could be malleable and easily persuaded with the proper motivation.

Pug smiled and said, "I'm just a traveler—a survivor." *Here I come to save the day.*

The arrogance masked behind the smile wasn't lost on Cade. He walked behind the prisoner, and after counting to ten Mississippi delivered an open handed roundhouse to the left side of Pug's head. "Wipe the fucking smile off of your face. The kids' stories match up—no

discrepancies. Their names are in the Denver yellow pages," Cade bellowed. "Then we looked into Ted Keller's background. He lived in the same building as the siblings. His name is also in the phone book like the others. It turns out you killed Ted's partner in the infirmary."

"I knew they were *fags*," Pug sneered. *That wasn't in the script*, the voice cried.

Cade lashed out with another open handed roundhouse, catching Pug across the opposite ear and starting it bleeding. The blow produced a stark white hand print.

A look of shock lit up the prisoner's flat face.

"I didn't do it," he croaked. "I'm just a traveler trying to survive." Then he spat. The bloody globule slapped the floor near Cade's boots. *Get us out of here*, the all too familiar voice urged.

"Very few people on this base even know you're here, and once you talk—*because you will talk*, everyone does *eventually*—I'm going to *kill* you."

Pug opened his good eye and said, "Francis is already dead. Dad killed him." *You don't tell him anything.*

"Pug or whatever the fuck your name is, I'm going to Jackson Hole and I *will* find out who you really are. I'm going to find out who sent you here, bring them back with me—have a little fun—and then kill them too."

Pug launched out of his seat as far as the restraints allowed and bellowed, neck veins bulging, "Good luck with that!" *Calm down and wait. Have faith. We will get out of here,* one of the more rational voices soothed. In a moment of clarity Pug suddenly doubted the familiar voices in his head. He wished that he hadn't left his pills in the obscene marble bathroom in the dead Denver Nugget's mansion. It was too late for wishing now.

For a schizo like Pug, once the voices took over, short of a medical intervention there was no going back.

Cade was pissed to say the least. He wanted to glean all he could so he might start the wheels of justice grinding. Secure some vengeance for his dead friend Mike Desantos. Not only had this waste of skin murdered Carl, he had also killed Doctor Fuentes and Jessica Hanson and then burned the entire research tent to the ground along with all of the equipment—including the computers and the data stored on their hard drives. Cloud storage and the Internet were things of the past in this zombie-plagued world. The few doses of effective lifesaving antiserum that remained went up in the inferno. Pug's actions had effectively signed General Desantos' death warrant, depriving Annie Desantos of a husband, his three kids of a father and Cade of his best friend. He wanted more than anything to put a boot to the fucker and a blade in his black heart, and after the trail of death and destruction the man calling himself Pug had left in his wake the night before, a good beating and a quick death would be letting him off easy. As a matter of fact he deserved no less than a million lifetimes of agony as payback for the innocents he had murdered in cold blood and the lives he had forever altered.

Pug's face never changed from the expression of detached amusement he had been wearing since the second brutal slap, and he didn't move a muscle as Cade's mouth hovered inches from his ear. "After I'm finished with the vermin in Wyoming I am coming back here to exterminate you."

Cade exited the room without a backward glance. He snatched the ledger out of Croswell's hands, signed in and then promptly signed out.

Airman Croswell shot the operator a quizzical look.

"That fucker in there... he's still breathing. And that means it's no longer our secret that I dropped by," Cade said as he stalked out of the room.

Croswell watched the door slam shut behind the captain and then waited until he was certain that the pissed off officer wasn't returning. Then he peered in the window to confirm the captain's claim. The scene inside caused him to drop the clipboard once again and bolt into the interrogation room.

Chapter 3
Outbreak - Day 10
NORAD Complex
Cheyenne Mountain, Colorado

The living dead pressing against the razor wire-topped fence began arriving days ago, shortly after the President's Osprey landed for the first time just outside the entrance to the old NORAD facility.

Located within Cheyenne Mountain, the super secure complex consisted of tunnels and bunkers which were carved into the solid granite deep enough to withstand a direct nuclear blast. Cheyenne Mountain had originally been selected to house the North American Air Defense Command because of its structural integrity and its close proximity to both Schriever Air Force Base, twenty miles to the northeast, and downtown Colorado Springs, just a stone's throw to the North.

After having its command and control transferred to Peterson Air Force Base, the Cheyenne Mountain Complex had been placed on a warm standby status. Luckily for the President, the Air Force personnel had the dusty facility up and running hours after she had reclaimed it as her own.

Valerie Clay sat alone in the darkened war room watching the grisly image splashed across the eight wall-mounted flat panels. The combat command center had once been filled with airmen and officers whose sole job it was to monitor the entire northern hemisphere and provide an early warning in case of a Soviet Union nuclear first strike.

Clay watched as the monsters in the front of the crush were being slowly compressed through the heavy gauge wire fencing. Jostling for position behind them, the hundred plus zombies were driven by one impulse—to get at the meat they knew was somehow associated with the noisy machine.

The President sat in the dimly lit room not at all concerned about the abominations assembled outside—it was the untold millions of migrating dead that the satellites had been tracking from space with their high powered cameras that caused her the greatest concern. If the fence failed—and it would eventually— the second line of defense would contain them long enough for her protection detail to hustle her out to Marine One and away to safety. In the days since the facility was chosen to serve as the new White House, Clay's secret service detail, with the help of soldiers from Fort Carson, had brought in the twenty shipping containers which now encircled the makeshift grass landing pad. Stacked two high, the two-ton steel rectangular boxes weighed enough to keep the throng of dead from displacing them and were too tall for the creatures to climb over. Although a tight fit because of the Osprey's twin tilt rotors, the President's bird still had sufficient clearance for takeoff and landings.

President Clay ran her fingers through her shoulder length black hair. The last time she dared look in a mirror she had noticed an abundance of new 'grays' no doubt brought on by her rapid ascension to the office of President and the toll two short weeks of hell had taken on her.

Mount Saint Helens, Mount Rainier and the Gifford Pinchot wilderness area of her home state of Washington had been on her mind all morning. Missed were the fragrant tall pines, clean air, and abundant wildlife.

Screw the radiation, she said to herself. This was no way to live; cooped up with a million tons of rock parked directly over her head made her feel no different than one of those things on the monitor. No—she was still alive—and she had made up her mind.

She called in her senior Secret Service Agent Adam Cross. The former Special Forces operator, with multiple combat deployments under his belt, had been on her protection detail since she was Speaker of the House. Now as President of the United States her armed entourage had doubled in size, surrounding her everywhere she went. Agent Cross was fiercely loyal. He would not only take a bullet for her, the tall blonde shooter would also get in the way of a Z bite for her.

The President sprang her ambush the second Agent Cross entered the low-ceilinged war room. "I've thought this over six ways from Sunday," she said confidently. "I'm going to go... I can still make it in time if we hustle. Get the flight crew ready, I want to be wheels up in five—*that is an order.*"

Cross hailed the Osprey crew who were suited up and standing by on Alert 5—which meant they were ready to go and could be airborne in less than five minutes. The Marine Major and the rest of her four-man crew jumped at once and were in the elevator heading to the surface in under a minute.

"With all due respect, Madam President, I recommend you stay inside until we have a better handle on the effects of the blasts."

Silence.

Cross bent at the waist to get the willful President's eye. "Valerie..." The agent instantly regretted using the President's first name. They were close—but not that close. "Madam President, will you at least give us a chance to take a few more hourly readings?"

President Clay said nothing. She stood and stretched, popping several vertebras in the process then asked, "What did the latest readings tell us?"

Before answering, Cross briefly glanced at the lower right corner of the flat screen display where, topside, the crew of the Osprey was busy scurrying about the flat black aircraft performing routine preflight inspections. Then after a few seconds the dual thirty-eight foot rotors started to spin. "The rad levels outside have inched up a bit since last night's reading. But keep in mind the location is static... it's on top of the mountain and subject to deviation. To get a better idea of the radiation levels north and east of Cheyenne and most importantly so that I can ensure your safety, I recommend that an advance team be sent out."

The President made a face. "You crossed your T's and dotted your I's... your concern is duly noted, Adam. I do appreciate the fact that you have your job to do—"

"I sense there is a *but* coming," Cross said with a grimace.

Silence.

As if she were about to pray, the President placed her palms together on the darkened glass-topped control panel. "I'm going to make an appearance—even if it ultimately kills me."

It might kill us all, Agent Cross thought to himself. He shifted his weight uncomfortably, causing his concealed MP7 to brush against his ribs, a subtle reminder of the predicament he was in. *'The principal must be protected at all times from each and every threat'*—went through his head. His instructors at the James J. Rowley training center in Maryland had repeated the mantra during every waking moment of his training. Hell, for all he knew they probably played it through hidden speakers as he and the other recruits slept. And each time he had been forced to compromise this basic tenet—which rarely happened—he was left questioning everything he stood for. That the radiation was invisible and odorless elevated it to a level of danger on par with the creatures outside of the wire.

But, orders were orders and *Valerie* was the Commander in Chief and he would follow her orders to a T.

Cross snapped to attention and adding a positive spin on their departure said, "At least the prevailing winds are cooperating." After pausing for a beat he finished, "They're tracking strongly from West to East which is stellar news for anyone this side of ground zero."

After an affirming nod the President grabbed her olive drab flight jacket and, with a satisfied look on her face, pushed past her six-foot-three inch body guard and strode purposefully through the doorway.

"President Clay," Cross said, calling after her. "I have to insist that you put on your vest."

Silence answered him, so he grabbed the vest and hastened after her.

Chapter 4
Outbreak - Day 10
Schriever AFB
Colorado Springs, Colorado

As Cade traversed the base, his thoughts quickly turned to Annie Desantos and her kids. He had already fulfilled Mike's first request, and that final act, difficult as it was, had stopped his friend from reanimating and coming back as a zombie. The second promise had been mutually decided upon years ago after one especially deadly firefight in Afghanistan. Both men had vowed to take care of the other's family should one of them go MIA or fall in battle. Desantos fulfilled his part of the bargain while Cade was travelling from Portland, Oregon on his desperate search for Brook and Raven during those first days of the Omega outbreak. Now, with Desantos' passing, it was Cade's turn to step up and reciprocate.

***

Desantos' family billet

Annie yanked open the door before Cade could announce his presence, wrapped her arms around the startled operator and began to sob. For several long minutes he returned the embrace as a soul wrenching sound emanated from deep within the new widow.

Annie finally released her grip and Cade spoke first. "I'm sorry Annie. I did everything in my power to help Mike." He stopped in order to compose himself. With tears wetting his cheeks he continued. "Mike was gone the second he got bit. He mentioned the girls as soon as it happened... *all* of you were on his mind when he succumbed to the virus."

"Did he mention Mike Jr.?" Annie asked, probing for fresh memories of Mike Senior to pass on to his only son.

"This is for him," Cade said, handing Annie her husband's Luminox wristwatch. "And these are for the girls."

Annie held her palm out and received the two well-worn dog tags.

"He *always* had good things to say about his family. When I settle down... no idea when that'll be," Cade said, shaking his head slowly while looking directly in Annie's eyes. "I'll sit down and put my recollections on paper. Mike Jr. and the twins will know who their Dad was and how the sacrifices he made saved their lives and the countless lives of others."

Annie stretched her shirt sleeve and dried her eyes with the rumpled cuff. "What now...?"

Cade spoke softly. "We take things one day at a time. If you need anything just ask. Brook and Raven could take care of the kids... to give you some time to think things through... or you might move closer to our billet. Whatever works."

"How am I going to break it to the twins?"

"Be honest. They will thank you later. That's not coming from me... that's Mike talking. At least that's what he said to me more times than I can count."

"When can I see him?"

"He didn't want anyone to see him in that bad a shape, especially his loved ones." Cade paused, made eye contact, then continued speaking. "The virus... it does awful things to the human body... it shuts down the organs first. Mike was suffering horribly. That's the stage he was going through when I... when I..." Cade sighed. "I didn't think I had it in me."

Annie intuitively knew what Cade had been forced to do. "Shhh, it's all right Cade," she said softly, pulling him down to her level and cradling his head with the crook of her arm. "He had nothing but the utmost respect for you. In fact he loved you like a son, Cade. My Mike would've done the same thing for you... without hesitation"

The words sounded good but did little to assuage the guilt he carried. Cade had been manning the top machinegun and was turned around watching their six when Desantos was attacked. Cade felt that somehow, in a small way, he had let his commander down and having this conversation with Annie Desantos made him feel lower than a snake's belly. Furthermore, he hated the idea of watching the kids grow up without a dad.

He checked his emotions. "Brook and Raven will be by within the hour to escort you and the kids to the funeral."

Annie was on the verge of breaking down again when the troop of raucous kids blew into the room. Sierra and Serena led the pack, with the young Russian boy Dmitri close on their heels.

Raven filed in last cradling Mike Jr. protectively. She beamed and bounced at the knees, up and down rhythmically, soothing the swaddled infant. "See Aunt Annie, I'm supporting his head. Take notes 'cause I'm gonna be ready when my little brother or sister gets here."

"Raven, give Junior to Aunt Annie and come along. You too Dmitri..." Cade barked.

Annie needed some time alone with her kids. And what she did with that time was hers alone to decide.

***

A remote corner of Schriever Air Force Base

In the early morning hours the day after his death, Mike Desantos was put into the earth. The newly promoted General Ronnie Gaines, Cade and the remaining two members of Mike's Delta team, Lopez and Maddox, took turns carving the grave into the near bulletproof high plains soil.

Cade had singled out the site which was near Schriever's southwestern perimeter for its commanding views of Cheyenne Mountain, Pikes Peak and the rest of the Rockies rambling further off to the north.

Half a dozen Zs, mostly first turns, loitered on the other side of the twelve-foot tall chain link fence. Pacing back and forth, the monsters emitted their raspy cat calls coveting the meat just out of reach.

Annie Desantos tried her best to ignore the abominations as she comforted the fussing Mike Jr. Although impossible, it seemed the newborn somehow knew his dad was gone, or, more than likely, he could sense his mom's growing unease. Sierra and Serena stood, shoulders touching and heads bowed. The eight-year-old twins knew what the word die meant; they just hadn't yet grasped death's finality. Raven pressed against Brook, holding tight, one arm wrapped around her waist. Brook stood beside Annie, ready to provide emotional support and lend a shoulder to cry on if needed.

By the time the grave was six feet deep, Ari Silver, Durant, Hicks and a handful of other operators from the 10th Special Forces had all logged shovel time.

As the soldiers lowered the stainless steel coffin into the shadowy gash hewn in the red earth, a noise like a million buzzing ceiling fans reverberated from the general direction of downtown Springs.

At once the low murmur of respectful voices ceased and all eyes cast across the desert towards the southwest.

Cade squinted, trying to identify the approaching black speck on the horizon.

"Looks like POTUS had a change of heart," Shrill yelled over the cacophony of the rapidly approaching aircraft. Then his right hand snapped up and he held the crisp salute. *Lady sure knows how to make an entrance*, he thought to himself.

Surrounded by a tempest of swirling dust and airborne debris, Major Ripley settled Marine One on a plat of sand and coarse rock a safe distance from the funeral goers. Ripley spied the brass and cursed—sandblasting a General, a Colonel, and a Major with rotor wash was the last thing she needed.

"Wheels down Madam President," she said over the intercom as the rear deck motored down.

Silenced MP7s materialized from under windbreakers as Agent Cross and three other Secret Service agents went out ahead of the President. Puffs of dust marked their footsteps and they closed the distance to the pack of walkers.

***

"Cover your eyes girls," Annie said to the twins. Knowing their innocence was the only thing remaining from their old lives, she vowed to preserve it at all costs.

Following their mom's orders, Sierra and Serena put hands to face without complaint.

Raven angled for a good view of the men who had just emerged from the strange hybrid helicopter. As she looked on, the agents efficiently put down the zombies with near silent rapid-fire double taps to the head.

"Efficient," Brook noted quietly to herself.

***

Colonel Shrill unlocked both access gates and let the President and her detail inside. Then after pausing to exchange salutes with the assembled soldiers, airmen, and brass, President Clay made her way around the open grave and approached the grieving families.

She offered her condolences to Brook, then stopped in front of Annie and the girls. After matching the widow's gaze for a few silent moments, the President felt her composure begin to crumble. Although she had ordered herself not to cry, once she saw the sorrow reflected in Annie's and her girls' eyes she had no defense and the tears started flowing. She wiped her eyes, calmed herself, and then took a spot near Annie's elbow.

Alongside Mike's well-worn combat boots, his M4 stood at attention, barrel pointed ground ward, bayonet piercing the earth. The operator's desert tan tactical helmet and goggles appeared abandoned, resting atop the rifle's fully collapsed butt stock.

Colonel Cornelius Shrill saluted first. His white gloved right hand snapped crisply to the spit polished black visor on his service cap. Major Freda Nash and the rest of the soldiers followed suit with crisp textbook salutes of their own.

The remainder of the final Delta team which Cowboy had led into battle, along with the Ghost Hawk crew that had ferried them into hell's maw, seven men in all, hoisted black SCAR rifles to their shoulders and fired a single volley. After repeating the ritual three consecutive times the solemn twenty-one gun salute concluded, leaving the lonely corner of the airbase cloaked in silence. And then quietly, each lost in their own thoughts, the soldiers took turns shoveling dirt onto the coffin.

"Cowboy deserves more than this anonymous patch of dirt in the corner of a *fucking* Air Force base," Lopez stated angrily. "*Vaquero* deserves a *grande* statue in his honor."

"I agree with you Lopez. But you and I both know that no one's going to be laid to rest in Arlington *anytime* soon," Cade stressed. "This is the best that *I* could do on such short notice."

"I concur Boss, I saw Washington D.C. with my own eyes from a Black Hawk at five hundred feet. Nothing but walking *demonios* there now," Lopez said as he performed the sign of the cross.

Drawn in by the Osprey's arrival and the ritual gunfire, two more walkers arrived outside the wire. As the chaplain began his only prayer, one of the Zs emitted a low plaintive wail as if to protest the Catholic ritual.

Leaving Brook's side, Cade broke ranks and double-timed it to the fence, drawing his Glock along the way. Then with his arm outstretched, the semiautomatic pistol bucked rapidly four times. Before the sharp reports subsided, the two rotting interlopers hinged over and crashed to the desert floor dead for the second time.

Cade trudged the twenty yards and regained his spot between his wife and daughter.

The chaplain surveyed those in attendance before reciting the final petition prayer. "May his soul and the souls of all the faithful departed through the mercy of God rest in peace."

Cade closed his eyes in order to reflect on the events that had occurred over the last few days. Adhering to Mike's wishes by not allowing Annie and the twins a chance to see his corpse was one the most difficult and conflicting orders Cade had ever been asked to follow. That he did so without hesitation was a testament to the high regard he held the man even in death.

Mike Desantos abhorred attention, shunned the limelight, and never accepted accolades; instead he deflected any praise onto his men. It was his opinion that war stories were for drunks and liars. He told Annie he didn't want the words of warriors spoken at his funeral and she made it known ahead of time to everyone present that the twenty-one gun salute and a simple prayer would be sufficient.

In the end, tucked away in the corner of Schriever Air Force base, the square patch of dirt with sweeping vistas proved to be a fitting final resting place for the larger than life operator. Mike 'Cowboy' Desantos, consummate professional, doting dad, and loving husband would be missed by all in attendance.

***

Cade stopped the Cushman outside of the mess hall. "Are you sure you want to walk to Annie's from here?"

Patting her carbine Brook answered, "We'll be alright."

"C'mon Mom I'm starved," said Raven, pulling her mom towards the door.

Aren't we all, Brook thought. Over the last two days the slop the cooks were trying to pass off as food had been barely edible.

"Can I bring you back something Dad?"

"No sweetie. I've got it covered," Cade replied. "And I won't be in until after lights out... so don't wait up."

"Do we ever?" Brook intoned.

Noting the tension, Raven cast her eyes downward and kicked at a chip in the concrete walkway.

Cade massaged his forehead, trying to decide if he should further the conversation. Then his competitive genes kicked in, settling the matter. "What are you implying?" he said, eyebrows arched, his gaze unwavering.

Brook silently returned the stare.

"So we're having one of these... right here... right now? Can't it wait until I get back?"

"I might not be here when you get back," Brook spat.

Clearly the last twenty-four hours had taken a toll on Brook. Cade decided to leave it at that and take the high road. "Raven sweetie... I'll give you a kiss when I come in. Brook, if you want to talk..."

"Don't bother," Brook countered. And before Cade had a chance to finish the thought she said, "We *will* talk when you get back from your mission... some things are going to have to change."

Cade took it all in stride. This wasn't the first time Brook had gotten heated before one of his missions—and he was damn sure that it wouldn't be the last. *Damned if you do and damned if you don't,* he thought as he wheeled the golf cart into the drive and then stole one last glance at his wife and daughter entering the mess hall.

Chapter 5
Outbreak - Day 10
Schriever AFB
Colorado Springs, Colorado

Civilian Quarters
Honk! Honk!

"Keep your shirt on," Elvis muttered. Then, after remembering who his driver had been the day before, he instantly changed his mind. *On second thought, take your shirt off,* he mused as a Cheshire Cat-like grin swept his face.

Leaving the canvas Quonset-style tent which was one of many set up to house civilian refugees at Schriever AFB, he snagged his black nylon day pack, a long sleeved work shirt and clicked a bulging black fanny pack around his waist. Then as an afterthought he grabbed his well-worn Nebraska Cornhuskers ball cap and jammed a red sweat stained bandanna into his back pocket.

The harsh high plains sun stormed the room the second he opened the door. *Not another one of these days,* he thought. Thankful for the carrion free fresh air, he drew in several deep lungfuls. After the run of danger filled days, he had learned to savor every second he wasn't at *work*.

The same dust-coated green and brown camouflaged GMC pickup that had taken him to the job site the day before was parked in front of his wooden steps, a camo-clad soldier waiting behind the wheel.

Flip flops slapping his heels, Elvis went around the side of his tent and repossessed his detritus-covered work boots from the buzzing mass of black flies. The foul smelling boots went into the truck bed and Elvis climbed up front with the driver who immediately thrust a sweaty hand in his face. "Private Mark Farnsworth... you can call me Mark or just *Farns* if you like, pleased to meet you."

Not wanting to conjure up the image of an aging, leather jacket-wearing greaser from the fifties every time he talked to the soldier—who come to think of it looked eerily like Richie Cunningham from the same television show—Elvis settled on calling the soldier Mark. After returning the handshake he introduced himself to the Opie looking fella—"Name's Elvis Pratt and I'm damn glad to meet you Mark," he said in a southern drawl tinged with hints of the street. The fact that the first female he had been within sniffing distance in more than a week had apparently been replaced by *this* soldier sitting to his left was a monumental buzz kill and a rotten start to his day.

"Forgive me but it's killing me. I've gotta know. How'd you get the name Elvis?" Farnsworth asked without a trace of shame.

"I was born August 16th, 1977, the very day *the* Elvis died on the toilet face down and ass up. My parents... they happened to be dyed in the wool fans of his."

"So you inherited the name."

"Yep... they hoped I'd be the next King. Can't play a lick on the guitar and my singin' voice *does not* leave the shower," Elvis stated wryly.

"Any other family?"

"That's a sore subject."

"I'm sorry..."

"No it's OK," Elvis said. "Shit, I don't think I'm going to find a confessional anywhere near here—I might as well unload on you."

"My wife always said I was a good listener," Farns proffered.

"So I'm in Minot, basically in the middle of nowhere on that first day... when the strange news... you know the conflicting reports and all the stuff our government denied at first started to come out. I check my phone and I've got a voicemail from my folks in Oakland."

"What happened to them?"

"Dad... he left the message... he said things were *real* bad and they were going to load up the car and get on the I-80 and get the hell out of the city... get to a temporary military shelter in San Francisco."

"I heard the Omega outbreak got real bad, real quick in Oakland. Infected on every street, National Guard shooting civilians, and civilians shooting civilians," Farnsworth noted.

"Apparently things got so bad that in order to *protect* their precious *San Francisco* the Army dropped the Oakland Bay Bridge into the drink. The second and final voicemail I got was my sister Steph telling me they were stuck in traffic on the bridge. Said they were nearly on the west side and as soon as things started moving again they would be safe... said she would call me right back." Elvis looked out the window and discreetly dried a tear.

"They were on the bridge when it was demoed?"

Seething inside Elvis nodded and said, "Upper deck... and I hold the government fully responsible for not telling the truth about the virus *right away*... and secondly, for the murders of my family."

"I don't know what to say except I'm sorry for your loss..."

Elvis chuckled and looked coldly at Farnsworth. "*Sorry* is not going to bring them back. So I'm just gonna put my nose to the grindstone and get to work buryin' the dead. And later... later I'm gonna drink myself numb."

Farnsworth shifted uncomfortably in his seat, put the truck in drive, and drove slowly across the base. After a few minutes of uneasy silence he rekindled the conversation, taking it in another direction entirely. "You said you were in Minot before Z day. What the heck were you doing up there?"

"Working for a drilling outfit."

"You drive a tractor there too?" Farnsworth asked as the truck skittered and bounced along the rutted track paralleling the twelve foot concertina topped fence, a thick plume of dust roiling in its turbulent wake.

"If it was made outta steel, painted a bright ass gay color and just so happened to have an engine... I was operatin' it." Elvis paused for a tick, his brow furrowed as he squared his shoulders towards Farnsworth. "If they sent you to *interrogate* me... then y'alls paperwork is fouled up. I sat down with a sour faced MoFo for an hour this morning... and I'm gonna tell you *exactly* what I told them, I came to Colorado Springs cause there was nothing left for me in Minot."

Farnsworth glanced sideways at his passenger. The big man looked like he should be playing tight end for the Cornhuskers, not just sporting their hat. Behind the yellow-lensed safety glasses, Elvis's ruddy sun-touched face wore a pinched expression—almost as if he was carrying the weight of the world on his shoulders. *Hell, aren't we all these days*, Farnsworth thought to himself as he slowed the truck near the edge of the base proper. "All I know is that Colonel Shrill put each and every one of us on high alert. *Stay vigilant* is what we were told," he said responding to the civilian's accusation. "No I wasn't prying. I was just being friendly... that's all."

Farnsworth brought the truck to a full stop in front of a padlocked double gate in the far northeast corner of the base, and he quickly rolled up his window in order to ward off the stench of death and decay and to keep the encroaching tail of dirt from invading the truck's interior.

As the dust vortex subsided, three walkers materialized ambling towards the gate.

"No disrespect," Elvis said, "but what happened to the cute lady soldier who picked me up yesterday?"

"I've got no idea. We're all spread so thin. And it's only gonna get worse before things turn around... if they do."

Elvis adjusted his hat, keeping a watchful eye on the advancing corpses. "I heard downtown Springs was nearly cleared out."

"Getting close. The power outside of Schriever might be back on within a week," Farnsworth said, shaking his head slowly side to side. "And I thought I'd never see that day. You've seen all of the zombies—shit—you're the man burying them. It's different now. Not only are we fighting the dead...but there is a group... there is a group of very connected people that want the old United States to disappear."

"I can kinda sympathize," Elvis said with a shrug.

"But Elvis... there are so few of us left now," Farnsworth said solemnly. "Humans fighting humans... I fail to understand the rationale behind that shit."

"It's gotta end sometime," Elvis added, a sly grin visiting his face.

"Give me a second, I'll be right back," said Farnsworth matter-of-factly. He let the engine idle, exited the truck, and unlocked the interior gate. Then he approached the padlocked outer fence with his Beretta drawn.

From Elvis's vantage point in the truck, the first zombie to reach the fence looked pretty fresh—a brand new turn. Major portions of flesh had been rent from her torso, exposing glossy muscle and half eaten internal organs. Inexplicably her gait remained smooth—almost natural.

The other two zombies, badly decomposed first turns, lurched after—forming a macabre slow motion procession.

Farnsworth couldn't decide which was harder to ignore, the moaning and raspy hisses coming from their dry pie holes or their milky dead eyes trying to stare the flesh from his bones.

He waited patiently until all three noisy creatures stood shoulder to shoulder, their pale bodies pressing the fence inward. Then he walked from left to right efficiently dropping each ghoul with a single gunshot to the eye socket.

Farnsworth clambered into the truck and wheeled the bucking quarter-ton vehicle over the three prostrate zombies and onward through the gates. "You know Elvis... I don't think I'm ever gonna get used to that squishy crackling sound," he proffered as a sudden wave of nausea churned his guts.

When the truck cleared the threshold, the fair haired private jumped from the GMC, his head and eyes constantly scanning for walkers, and loped the dozen feet to the gate. Doing his best not to look at the pulped mess, he quickly closed the gate and snapped the lock. An involuntarily shudder wracked his body as he padded back to the truck with his gun drawn. He hated the oppressive feeling of total vulnerability he shouldered when venturing outside of the wire. And that feeling increased exponentially whenever he had to exit the false security of the unarmored GMC pickup.

Silence occupied the sweltering cab as vestiges of the old world—the world of the living—slid by on the passenger side. Foreboding and dark, a fence-ringed sporting goods store sat adjacent to a partially boarded up strip mall. Inexplicably the shrines to instant gratification and retail excess had somehow escaped the widespread looting rampant in the days following the declaration of martial law.

Finally, after passing a half dozen empty, Olympic swimming pool sized pits carved into the sunbaked earth, Farnsworth ground the truck to a halt. He surveyed the expanse of cleared acreage a mile and a half from the safety of the base and said cheerily, "Here we are. Your chariot waits."

The fifty ton D9 armored dozer Elvis would be calling home for the next few hours sat baking in the sun, heat waves shimmering from its desert tan skin.

"Is it too late to resign?" Elvis deadpanned. "Just joking, I don't know why I volunteered... but I'm going to see this one to the end. Someone's gotta be a worker among workers."

"You are appreciated, Elvis. In fact by volunteering to do this nasty little detail you're freeing up one of the soldiers to go out and kick doors and kill Zs."

"Lucky guy... or gal... I *suppose*," Elvis replied.

"This zone has already been cleared door to door," Farnsworth stated with a sweeping motion of his hand. "But you should never ever let your guard down... stragglers and swarms are common and can happen anytime and anywhere in Springs. One day someone's going to erect a statue honoring the efforts of the door kickers *and* the Civilian Corps."

"I'm holding my breath," Elvis muttered. Somehow the smart ass comment was lost on Farnsworth as he droned on.

"Here's your two-way, it's got fresh batteries and it's tuned to the same frequency as mine. Range on these—"

Cutting in Elvis said, "Heard the speech already. The pretty lady ran it by me yesterday and much as I'd love to hear it again—you just ain't holding my attention like she did." He exited the truck, grabbed his hard hat, ear protection and work boots from the bed and then slapped the truck's roof. "Thanks for the *up*-lift *Farns*," he added with his thumb upturned Fonzielike.

"Wait one!" Farnsworth hollered.

Elvis glanced over each shoulder checking for Zs, then poked his head into the passenger compartment and arched a brow. He knew more of the spiel was about to be delivered. *Where's my girl?*

"First rule: Stay in the cage. Do not leave your cocoon... under any circumstances. Second rule: Keep your radio on. I'll be back and forth between the front gate and the flight line all day. Call immediately if you attract a crowd and I will be here ASAP," Farnsworth said.

"Just you?" Elvis blurted, feigning a startled look. Then for a heartbeat he tried to appear that he was seriously contemplating getting back into the truck and saying *"Home James."* But instead he said, "The lady *loaned* me a .45 yesterday... just in case..." He pointed at the glove box before continuing. "She put it right back in there... before she dropped me off last night. Any chance it's still in there?"

Farnsworth leaned across the seat, punched the glove box open, and extracted the .45 semi-automatic pistol. "Take it," he said, thrusting the weapon butt first in Elvis's direction.

Before the Husker fan could voice his gratitude, Farnsworth's Motorola beeped announcing an incoming call which he promptly fielded. "Copy that," he replied to the person on the other end. Then he glanced at Elvis and said, "Trucks are on the way. I'll be back in about two hours or so with water and MREs."

Silence.

While Farnsworth had been blabbing on, Elvis had been thinking about his parents sitting on the I-80 Bridge, full of hopes that were so quickly and literally crushed when their car along with untold tons of concrete and rebar plunged into the frigid bay.

Still ignoring the soldier, Elvis perused the sign declaring the tract of land was to be the future site of *Freedom Hills Estates*. He surveyed the comatose subdivision which sprawled several hundred yards beyond. The dozens of one- and two-story homes fronted by overgrown lawns sat darkened, lonely, and uninhabited. Little did he know every house in the zone had already been cleared of Zs thanks to General Ronnie "Ghost" Gaines and the door-to-door grid searches performed by the combat hardened soldiers of the 10th Special Forces Group.

One specific word on the developer's sign jumped out at him. *Future*, the six-letter word caused a morbidly funny thought to cross his mind. He wondered if the developers had had the foresight to pull a permit allowing thousands of zombies to be interred on the site. Oh how the environmentalists would have had a field day with that one. Employment would have surged among the picketing crowds. And the fines the local government could have levied. Hell, scrap the fines, the greedy sons of bitches could have written a whole new tax code. Elvis shook his head. He didn't know which was worse: the shambling, flesh eating living dead or the old guard: politicians and fat cats who had lived only to strip every last monetary morsel from the average Joe's bones.

Steering clear of the gut-encrusted tanklike treads he climbed atop the bulldozer. The hulking Caterpillar remained as silent as the Motorola radio. The Husker fan waited patiently, sipping a water to pass the time.

Soon a house-sized cloud of boiling earth loomed on the horizon followed by the bass heavy rumble of a mustard yellow monster-dump truck.

Elvis's radio crackled, "Incoming dead sled. Don't move your machine."

Mimicking military speak Elvis answered the unknown man on the other end, "Copy that."

Backup alarm blaring and belching a dense black plume of diesel exhaust which did little to mask the stench wafting from its cargo, the dump truck, which loomed taller than most houses, reversed to the edge of the tawny gash.

Elvis watched the enormous dump box slowly hinge back. As soon as the dual gleaming thirty-five foot long hydraulic pistons reached half extension, putrid corpses began to spill forth, a dizzying dance of flailing arms and legs ensuing as the lifeless shells cartwheeled and tumbled like so many dead whirling dervishes into the pit. The mosh continued until the hundreds of waxen bodies settled into the massive grave.

Elvis thumbed the call button on the two-way and craned his neck in order to see the driver perched three stories in the air. "You workin' alone today?"

"Just me," came the driver's tinny reply over the radio. He waved a gloved hand and honked a couple of short cheery sounding toots as he goosed the big diesel and drove away.

Maybe dude likes his new job, Elvis thought as he shot the big driver a salute. *Oh well, to each his own.*

Gears gnashing the dump truck pulled away, its box trailing a viscous mess; as the dust cloud cloaked the retreating vehicle, hundreds of ravens descended on the carrion pile in a blast of black feathers and rushing wind, squawking in raptor pleasure.

"Gotta fight the birds today," Elvis muttered under his breath as he made sure the Kimber was loaded. *One in the pipe.* He removed the magazine and counted the rounds through the milled slots in the stamped steel. *Seven in the grip.* He jammed the pistol home near the small of his back and leaped from the five hundred horsepower steed. Then he pulled the red bandanna from his pocket and cinched it tightly so that it tracked across the tip of his nose, squashing it flat. Now a card carrying member of the mouth breather's club, he yelled at the flying rats. "Move it fuckers. I've got a job to do." His nasal twanged rebuke had no apparent effect and the birds kept up their feeding frenzy even as he stepped into their midst.

Chapter 6
Outbreak - Day 10
Schriever AFB
Colorado Springs, Colorado

Mess Hall

"Eww... *what* is that?" Raven squeaked. Her nose crinkled in disgust as she recoiled from the scoop of brown substance clinging to the cook's industrial-sized spoon.

"These are grits m'lady," the airman replied. He looked exhausted, and judging by the bags under his eyes and the days' old bristle on his face, sleep and hygiene had taken a back seat to more important things. "I usually whip up Eggs Benedict when royalty is present but I'm short a few ingredients... do you want the *grits* or not?"

Still pissed from her verbal spar with Cade, Brook unloaded on the man behind the glass sneeze shield. "Listen *a-hole*... my daughter is eleven. You wasted that smart ass Eggs Benedict crack; it went way over her head, but not mine. And considering the circumstances I might have let that slide if you were addressing me... but you weren't and you *cannot* talk to *my* kid like that."

Suddenly at a loss for words—especially snide remarks—the man gaped, still clutching in his ham-sized hand a spoonful of paste hovering over Raven's tray.

The airman had unwittingly set off a mini Vesuvius. Neck and face flushing to red, Brook slapped her empty tray down and

39

clenched her fists. "Apologize to her or I *will* come back there and make you."

"*I'm sorry* young lady... and ma'am. It's been a long stretch," the cook replied awkwardly as he carefully spooned the food onto Raven's tray. And as an amends for his rudeness he added, "The color is just the brown sugar we added. We ran out of the white granulated days ago."

While Brook's skin tone crept back to normal, she willed her right hand open and examined her palm. Blood seeped from four half-moon shaped puncture wounds, the culmination of a week's worth of stress and a few seconds of release. Unbeknownst to the cook, his smart ass comment had set in motion a chain of events that could not be recalled, because in those few short seconds Brook had realized what she needed to do. She had finally made up her mind that protecting her girl was the first priority and had been since that surreal day in Myrtle Beach when Raven accidently witnessed her mom shotgun Grandma. Brook had come to the conclusion that protecting wasn't the same as hovering and babying. She wasn't a "helicopter parent" —in fact she loathed them in the old world and she wasn't about to become one in the plague-infected new world. She would be doing Raven a disservice. Furthermore she had come to the conclusion that providing for Raven was the same as protecting her with a weapon. And with Cade's absence she was going to have to go outside the wire and help out wherever she was needed. With winter around the corner and the dead beginning to migrate, the only thing that she was certain of was her family's need for food and medical supplies.

Forcing a half smile Brook said to the cook, "Apology accepted."

Looking somewhat relieved the cook nodded and went about doing his job.

Brook steered Raven to a nearby table and they sat down to eat.

"Mom's going to see the Colonel when we're finished here."

Raven looked up from her food, "Are we shooting again?"

"No sweetie... Mom's going to be doing some volunteer work. There might be shooting involved, but just for me. You will be with Annie's family... OK?" Brook cocked her head to look Raven in the eye. "OK?"

A tight smile flashed across Raven's face. "I'm used to Dad being gone... I guess it won't hurt if you go for a while. But you are tucking me in tonight... right?"

Somewhere, outside of the wire a diesel engine coughed to life and roared to a crescendo. *Burying the dead*, Brook thought, a job she wouldn't wish on anyone. But if that's where Shrill ultimately said she was needed, then that's where she would gladly report.

With more urgency, Raven repeated her question. "*Mom... are... you... tucking ...me... in tonight?*"

"Of course I am honey."

"Are you gonna get mad at Dad again tonight?" pressed Raven.

Obviously Raven was a little worried over the family conflict, so Brook chose her words carefully. "Raven... what is the most important thing?"

"*Family*," she replied forcefully and without hesitation.

Brook beamed inwardly. Since the day Raven could grasp the concept of family, she and Cade had drilled this simple tenet into her. Brook was also proud of the fact that she answered a question with a question, thus avoiding having to think about what she was going to say to Cade until the time came. Although she thought she had enough conviction and intestinal fortitude to really confront him, in the back of her mind she knew one rare smile from the big bad Delta boy had been known to derail even her best laid plans.

A long drawn out fusillade of small arms fire resounded from the burial detail's general direction. *Anything but that*, Brook thought as more shots rang out.

Brook had learned early on that as a parent you didn't always *have* to answer every question submitted to you by your kids. "Come on sweetie, time to go," Brook said, one hand gripping Raven's, the other cradling the ever-present M4 carbine at low ready. Staying alert, her head constantly moving, "on a swivel" is how Cade described it, she scanned every shadow they passed, wondering how many more like Pug were on the base and waiting for the opportunity to create more mayhem. And though she didn't know how the damage wrought by one lone man could be eclipsed—she was keenly aware, as the old saying went—*where there is a will, there is a way.*

Traversing the parade ground, Brook let her guard down a bit to reminisce about her home in Portland and the perfect fifteen-month sliver of bliss sandwiched between two life altering events: Cade walking away from Delta, followed by the Omega virus, which spread like wildfire, changing everything in a matter of days.

Fifteen months prior Cade had finally returned from the *sandbox* for good—or so Brook thought. He was whole in mind and body, and in just a few short weeks she saw signs that he was reverting back to the *old* Cade. With his mind no longer *down range*, his demeanor was slowly making the transition from alpha warrior to family man.

Those good times now seemed a million miles away and a million years in the past. Those fond memories now returned yellowed and fuzzy, like an ancient newsreel film chattering in her brain. Cade had shaken the rust off and was back to doing what he loved. Part of her—the selfish, self-centered part that she rarely listened to—wished that the people who were inadvertently driving a wedge between her and Cade would get eaten by the dead.

They stopped abruptly in front of the vacant Family Resource Center, a two-story brick and glass building which no longer served a purpose. Since the base had become an island in the midst of the dead, the number of intact families at Schriever could be counted on one hand, and the resources needed to sustain everyone else were running dangerously low.

Brook dropped to one knee and looked her eleven-year-old in the eye.

"What, Mom?" Raven said pensively.

"Your birthday is in two days. Do you remember the deal I made with you before the bad things started happening?"

Raven twirled a pigtail between her thumb and forefinger, lost in thought for a second.

Brook helped her out. "Your Dad and I decided you could start babysitting without supervision when you turned twelve... do you remember?"

"What are you getting at Mom?"

"I was hoping you would help Aunt Annie babysit for a couple of days. She's going to have a difficult time with Uncle Mike gone. You and I both know that the twins can be quite the handful. What do you think... It will be good practice for when you have a baby brother or sister?"

A dreamy look crossed Raven's face.

Brook capitalized on the advantage. "So that's a yes?"

"Sure Mom. What will *you* be doing?"

"Helping out in any way I can. You saw what the cooks are serving, we're going to need food—seeds to grow food and fuel."

Raven had shown incredible moxie during their harrowing trip from Myrtle Beach, South Carolina to Fort Bragg in North Carolina. The diminutive girl's resilience was tempered further by their flight from the Special Operations base as it fell to the living dead. But Brook had noticed a change in Raven's demeanor. The attack that took place the night before had shaken her confidence. Her affect seemed flat and her sense of humor had disappeared.

"Sweetie."

"Yes Mom."

"I'm taking you over to the Desantos' quarters. And then I have to go see the nice Colonel."

Clapping her hands Raven shouted, "Yeahhh, I get to see little Mike!"

Chapter 7
Outbreak - Day 10
Schriever AFB
Colorado Springs, Colorado

Elvis stood at the edge of the mass grave. He stared at the tangled bodies which were engaged in a morbid game of post mortem Twister, then let his gaze shift to the tons of infill that would hide them forever.

Not too surprisingly the ancient Anglican burial prose *Ashes to ashes, dust to dust* had woven its way into his thinking. For his sake he certainly hoped the finality the phrase signified held sway over this mass of twice-dead zombies.

A cloud of fine talc swirled around his head as he snapped on a pair of latex gloves.

The drop from the hardscrabble edge of the pit to the surface layer of putrefying humanity was barely five feet. He picked one of the larger specimens for his landing spot and then gingerly lowered himself onto the stinking biohazard.

Hope I don't have any open blisters on my feet, crossed his mind, as he let go of terra firma and entrusted the cadaver to support his entire body weight. *So far so good*, he thought. It held for a heartbeat, and then with an unexpected pop his right boot disappeared entirely inside of the creature's ample beer belly. The displaced matter looked like regurgitated lasagna, and the smell was a million times worse as adipose tissue and greasy yellowed fat erupted around his ankle. And to add insult to injury, before he yanked the boot free, the fluid had already invaded his sock. *Fuck*, he thought, *the flies are going to be dry humping this pair of boots for days.*

Once he found firm footing, he gophered up to survey the road which ran east to west paralleling Schriever's northern perimeter. He saw none of the telltale dust columns indicating an approaching vehicle and there were no stray walkers in the vicinity. *Time to make the doughnuts.* He had already decided that all extracurricular activities would be performed near the edge. Setting foot anywhere near the center of the pit which had been slowly settling since the dump truck driver had deposited his latest load would be suicide.

Gurgles, hisses and invisible geysers of rank escaping gasses coupled with the muffled moans and groans emanating from the area directly underneath his feet kept him on edge.

When picking his victims he didn't pay too much attention to the age, sex, or decomposition of the specimen—what mattered most to Elvis was how close they were to the edge. The last thing he needed to do was root around among the dead for any length of time and take the risk of getting bit or being caught with his hand in the cookie jar—so to speak. He noted the time. *You've got ten minutes Elvis.* Get in and get out—was the mantra running through his head. Therefore, since he was already shin deep in the guy's guts, Fatty would get first honors. Then the badly decomposed female that Bob's Big Boy was currently pressing his flesh against would be sloppy seconds. Lastly, he would take advantage of the nearby fresh kill. The brunette had been a looker when alive and wasn't so bad in death. The slender zombie had tumbled into the pit, limbs askew, exposing her goods for the entire world to see. Elvis made a concerted effort to avert his eyes but found he couldn't help himself. Something about the arch of the dead woman's back combined with her total lack of clothing tripped the hardwired evolutionary urge which kept him from looking away. It was decided—she would be his last before lunch.

Elvis fished a scalpel from his fanny pack then planted his right knee on Fatty's sternum. Up close and personal he noticed that the man's facial Feng Shui had been permanently altered by a large caliber bullet. The impact hadn't damaged the lower mandible or neck area, but had blown the upper portion of the Z's skull, away exposing the intricate chambers and channels that had once supported a brain.

Using the rounded tip on the razor sharp scalpel, with one fluid stroke he opened up the cadaver's neck. The ease with which the alabaster dermis parted, like gutting a trout, momentarily reminded Elvis of a trip he had taken with his little boy years ago. He remembered how Billy had been squeamish and unwilling to make the first cut. That was how he felt two days ago after receiving his orders. It hadn't been easy then, but he had somehow made that first cut. Now, two days later, he could perform the procedure with his eyes closed and after this final harvest he would be finished with his inexplicable task.

As he made his next pass, cutting deeper with the surgical blade, brackish liquid began to dribble from the severed carotid artery which had long ago ceased delivering oxygenated blood to Big Man's brain. By the time he had finished his final cut, the incision traced from the cadaver's left ear, tracked just above his frigid triple chin and finished its journey beneath the right ear where earlobe meets neck. Without hesitation he jammed both latex-covered hands two knuckles deep between the upper half of the incision and the lower jawbone. Then with an upward yank, accompanied by a sound akin to shucking an ear of corn, he peeled the lower half of Big Man's face—skin, blubber and all of the attached muscles—up and away from the cranial bone. Next he folded the flabby mess over Big Man's gunshot-stunted dome, leaving unimpeded access to the prizes within.

The rail thin first turn yielded her treasure much quicker. It took a minuscule amount of scalpel work for Elvis to peel away her face. *Two down one to go*, he thought.

Before delving into the fresh beauty at his feet Elvis held statue still and listened for any engine noises. The only sound, save for the occasional gust of dry air pushing tumbleweeds, originated from within the grave. He hadn't even decided how he was going to explain his foray into the mass of dead if he were caught in the act. He supposed he'd just drop trou and pretend he was a sick and twisted Dahmer disciple. No—fuck that. He'd rather die in a shootout than even pretend for one second he was a corpse fucker. Necrophilia and cannibalism—without definition the words alone seemed morbid and evil. He momentarily contemplated which was worse—fucking the dead or eating them. It didn't matter, he finally decided—either way there was a special place in hell for Jeffrey Dahmer and monsters like him.

Fighting the tug of gravity and a pair of thoroughly soaked boots, Elvis hauled himself out of the ground, bellied up to the desert floor and rolled over onto his back. With the .45 biting into his back he stared up at an azure sky streaked with wispy horse tail clouds, then, without sitting up, he unzipped the fanny pack and by feel stuffed the yield from all three cadavers inside.

He was still enjoying the clouds when the moaning commenced. The chilling sound sent his neck and arm hairs standing on end. Hinging upright, he reached behind his back and had the pistol in hand before he had eyes on the walkers.

An invisible hand clenched his heart when he spotted the shambling crowd of zombies. A half dozen angled from the west while at least a dozen were closer and steadily advancing from the other direction. In all, nearly twenty walkers had gotten the jump on him and he had only seconds to save his own ass.

The .45 barked twice sending the nearest creature to the sandy ground—down but still moving. *Shit!* He could feel his heart rate returning to normal as he made a mental note to self, *six rounds left.*

Scrambling to his feet he peered over his shoulder at the dozer sitting twenty feet behind him, and then stole a glance at the larger cluster of walkers that were about to cut him off from the Z-proof metal island. Holding the .45 in a two-handed grip, he crabwalked sideways, keeping the moaning rotters somewhat on his right flank.

"You sneaky bastards almost got me!" he shouted.

The intruders snarled and hissed in response and their pace quickened, as if hearing the fresh piece of meat talk had an effect.

Ignoring the smaller knot of walkers, which were still on the far side of the mass grave and posed little threat, he focused on the leaders of the other pack. With the initial shock from the ambush wearing off and the effects of the resulting adrenaline spike having plateaued, his shaky hands steadied and he began to act solely on muscle memory and training.

Still moving backwards and away from the grave, Elvis put the nearest zombie in his sights.

Swishing hypnotically with each clumsy foot fall, the first turn's bloody, pus-stained skirt hung from her gaunt frame like a butcher's soiled apron. The hissing walker had closed to within an arm's length by the time Elvis brought the Kimber to bear. The gun roared, and at point blank range the .45 caliber bullet found flesh and bone. The energy from the lead missile plucked her off her feet for a split second before gravity unceremoniously smacked her back to terra firma where she lay stilled, a smoking powder-burned hole where her eyes and nose had been. The second .45 caliber flesh shredder blasted her wingman through his open mouth. The middle-aged zombie did a whirling pirouette before landing on his side in the ochre dust with a gaping grapefruit-sized exit wound leaking brains from the back of his bald head. Undeterred by the fate of their two fallen compadres, the remaining eight abominations closed in.

Four shots left, Elvis reminded himself. *Not good.*

A cold hand brushed his arm, then gnarled fingers flexed tightly around his wrist, dead weight tugging. He whipped his head about only to see, inching closer to his exposed forearm, the clutching rotter's colorless lips bared tight over a yellowed picket of teeth. He put the pistol to the thing's head and squeezed off one round. *Three left*, his inner voice warned. The walker hinged over, an explosion of bone fleck and vaporized brain sprayed the trailing zombies. Inexplicably the skeletal hand held fast. Ducking low, boots churning dirt, the former Husker put his shoulder down and bulled through the right side of the group still dragging the corpse in his wake. *I knew the P90X was gonna do more than just get me girls*, he mused as he tried to shake the corpse from his left wrist. The headshot creature jerked along the chalky orange topsoil raining brains with each jounce. As Elvis neared the side of the D9 the dead hand released and in a puff of fine silt he left the headless corpse in the dust—literally.

Newly unencumbered, Elvis felt like Superman, like he could leap tall buildings. Cold talonlike fingers swiped at his gore-covered boots as he leaped onto the tanklike treads, shredding both knees in the process. Luck was on his side. His forward momentum had saved his life and he pulled his lower extremities from the hungry mob and scrambled up—ascending the tractor's frying pan hot armor plate. The badly shaken civilian volunteer sat with his back against the cab letting his breath come back. "Close but no cigar... *bitches*," he said as he opened the door and climbed into the driver's seat. The dozer started up with a high pitched whine followed by a belch of black diesel soot. "You can run but you can't hide."

The statement came to fruition for the dozer driver as the zombies, eyes locked on the meat driving the tractor, walked right into the path of the four foot tall blade. After three passes, all fourteen of the former humans were reduced to a dirt coated gray pulp.

Elvis let the D9 idle as he looked at his handiwork, amazed that the only evidence of the zombie swarm that had nearly killed him were scraps of flesh and bone embedded in the tractor's treads.

***

One hour and forty-five minutes later

The dirt-ensconced GMC crunched to a halt, and after the pursuing dust tail swirled into nothing Farnsworth slid out. "Bet you're about ready for these," he said, holding up a liter of bottled water in each hand.

"Just what the doctor ordered," replied Elvis, who was sitting with his back against the driver door scarfing down an MRE, while taking full advantage of the minimal shade cast from the small cube shaped roof of the upper cab. "Worked me up quite a thirst," he added between bites.

Farns paced to where the edge of the pit had been and planted his hands on his hips. He surveyed the darker patch of packed earth and the cross hatch patterns left by the dozer's crushing tracks. "You weren't shitting me when you said you knew how to operate a tractor... man you work quickly!" he said as he tossed the bottled waters up one at a time.

"Ain't getting an hourly," Elvis said, a grin cracking his features. "I would have stretched the job out a little if I was on the clock. As it is I had some visitors that slowed me down a bit... but I took care of them," Elvis intoned, shooing the flies from his detritus-caked boots.

"Another load is inbound from downtown Springs."

With a slight cant of his head Elvis asked, "Is the situation improving?"

"You wouldn't believe me if I told you what downtown is like."

"Try me," Elvis challenged.

"Give me a second. I have to get something from the truck and then I'll give you the Cliffs Notes version."

Farnsworth returned from the GMC carrying a small yellow device in one hand and clutching his Beretta with the other. He punched a button and the device powered on with a shrill beep, then began emitting a constant symphony of static, chirps, and clicks.

"Is that what I think it is? Elvis asked.

"It's an RDS-80A Contamination Survey Meter—in military talk. Or in layman's terms—a Geiger counter."

"You are checking me for *radiation*?" Elvis said slowly.

"Sorry. New orders from Colonel Shrill," Farns proffered as he passed the noisy plastic device over the civilian's entire body.

Elvis's eyes widened as if he had just correctly answered the Final Jeopardy question and won an all-expenses paid trip to Hawaii, "The other night... air raid sirens, then those two *really loud* blasts to north—*nuclear*?"

Farnsworth grabbed the civilian by the shoulder and turned him around avoiding eye contact. "No comment," he stated firmly as he finished checking the man for excess radiation.

Nuclear, Elvis thought grimly. *And I was knee deep in the fuckers.*

"All done, you've got trace amounts... we all do. Like I was saying—you gotta be careful. Some of the walkers have been showing up burnt to hell and very hot with radiation. At least you didn't get a dose from the stiffs you just buried."

Relief replaced concern as Elvis continued mining the Private for information. "So tell me about downtown. When are we going to be free from the dead? When are they going to fall apart and not be able to stalk us?"

"Well... the shooters have all of the ammo they need to finish the job. Thanks to the depot mission they now have half a million rounds of 5.56 NATO and half that much in various other calibers. The ammunition was earmarked for our guys in the sandbox... they won't be requiring it now. It is stunning how few came home after this shit started," said Farnsworth, "and as far as the creatures deteriorating... The doctor who was killed two nights ago concluded that the decay process is slowed down in the living dead's flesh."

Elvis took a long draw off of his water then pressed, "How do they get the staggering number of kills without getting wiped out themselves?"

"Listen... you're a civilian. I shouldn't be divulging this much to you. This is between you and I... make sure everything you hear stays here—agreed?"

"Mums the word," said Elvis, pantomiming locking his mouth and then throwing away an imaginary key.

A distant drone sounded from the far side of Schriever.

"Hercules going out on a foraging mission," Farns said looking skyward.

The engine sounds rose in volume becoming a deafening roar as the dappled gray turboprop skimmed overhead, climbing swiftly away from the base.

Farns tracked the four-engine plane with his eyes then resumed talking when the refueling tanker was out of earshot. "The echoing gunfire keeps the dead interested during the day. After dark the SF boys fire up the searchlights... that keeps them coming in all night. Snipers change long guns every thirty or forty rounds so the barrels don't get too hot. The bodies pile up fifteen feet or so then the Little Birds and Chinooks come in and airlift the whole operation to another high rise a few blocks away. While the action is drawing the dead to the new spot, cleanup crews—mostly civilians like you—come in and load the dead sleds." Farnsworth suddenly went silent and gazed towards Pikes Peak. "I wouldn't wish that job on anyone... we lose one or two a day. All those dead aren't really *dead*. The fuckers have started playing possum."

51

"No way!" Elvis said incredulously.

Farnsworth said nothing.

Elvis continued shaking his head, eyes closed, thinking about the ramifications. "So why bury them here and not closer to the city?"

"Eventually everyone is going to move back downtown and the surrounding suburbs. This is a better place than most I guess."

The Motorola squawked, breaking the silence. Farnsworth conferred with the voice on the other end then said to Elvis, "The sled is inbound—*be careful*."

No shit, Elvis thought as a chill traced his spine. "I'm getting back inside right now." He banged on the armor to get Farnsworth to look up. Then he asked in a low voice, arched eyebrows conveying his concern. "*Playing possum?*"

The thunderlike noise of the dump truck rolled over the horizon.

"*Be careful*," stressed Farnsworth once more.

With a latex-covered thumbs up Elvis answered, "Roger that," and after double checking the door lock he fired up the dozer. The comforting throaty rumble masked the sound of the approaching yellow meat wagon. *Time to make the doughnuts*, Elvis thought to himself.

Chapter 8
Outbreak - Day 10
Schriever AFB
Colorado Springs, Colorado

Brook stood before Colonel Cornelius Shrill's private office, wrestling with her emotions while at the same time trying to summon enough courage to rap on the door.

As if somehow sensing her presence the Colonel hauled the door inward and boomed a warm welcome. "Well, well missus Grayson. Please come inside. To what do I owe this pleasure?" he asked, ushering her in with a sweeping motion of his winglike arm.

Brook swept her gaze around the base commander's office as she stepped inside. Plaques and framed decorations earned during the man's long lived Air Force career covered the office's four walls.

Before the Colonel could offer her a chair Brook blurted, "I want to cut to the chase, Sir."

"What do you need?" he asked in his low baritone voice. "Anything you need... considering all that your husband has done—"

"This has nothing to do with Cade. This is all about me," Brook said, letting the statement hang for a tick. "I need to do something useful—to feel like a part of this struggle. Cade's gone—or he will be soon. I want a *mission*."

"What about Raven?"

"I'm getting her ready," said Brook, a look of intensity burning in her eyes. "For the day that will come when she is alone...

when she will be *forced* to fend for herself. You know as well as I do... *nothing* is guaranteed these days."

"I think I worded that wrong," said Shrill as he paced to the wall and gazed at a photo positioned prominently on the wall at his eye level. In the picture the Colonel, in full dress uniform, ribbons, medals and all, had his arm around the shoulder of a much younger African American man.

Brook stole a closer look. Shrill and the other man, who was wearing a flight suit and holding a helmet in the crook of his arm, were standing in front of a U.S. Navy fighter jet. Broad smiles creased both of the men's faces. Brook guessed the photo commemorated a very special moment in both Shrill's and the pilot's life. "Is that your son?"

"Affirmative."

"When was that taken?"

"Seconds after I had informed him he was going to Miramar on his own merit."

"Miramar..." Brook had heard of the Naval Air Station which was in San Diego. "Top Gun school—very *impressive*."

Silence.

"You would have *never* left him would you?" Brook asked.

The Colonel's face softened when he answered. "What I meant when I said—*What about Raven*... I was just being nosy... wanted to know who you are leaving her with while you are gone? *Not—why in the hell are you abandoning your little one?*"

"Sorry I took it that way. Raven is with Annie Desantos right now—so technically Annie will be the responsible party."

"And she's OK with that?"

Brook's eyes narrowed. "Who, Raven or Annie?"

"The new mom who also happens to be a newly widowed mom, that's who."

Brook took a deep breath. "They are both willing parties. Annie's a hell of a fighter, but she's no superwoman. She could benefit from the presence of an overachieving eleven-year-old and Raven needs to learn some self-sufficiency."

"I concur," Shrill proffered.

"Where do you need me?" Brook asked.

"They always need help with Z disposal outside of the wire. Burial detail—"

Brook testily interrupted, "What else?"

"Not enough adrenaline in that one?"

"Too much stink," Brook said, holding her nose.

"Get down to the motor pool," said Shrill. He looked at his watch and then shot a disappointed look Brook's way. "The foraging convoy left an hour ago, and the grave diggers are already outside of the perimeter."

"Tomorrow?" Brook asked with a pleading look.

"If you insist," he said in a funereal voice. "Make it to the motor pool tomorrow before noon."

"Once again... Thank you Colonel."

Shrill said nothing as he strode to his desk.

Confused, Brook looked on.

On a sheet of legal pad the Colonel scrawled a few illegible words, then added at the foot of the page what Brook assumed was his John Hancock. "Take this to Staff Sergeant Lafayette. He's 10th Special Forces Group—you know the patch. Besides there is no way you could possibly miss him. The man is *solid* in my book. Good as they come, and I'm certain he knows Cade from before."

"Before?"

"Prior to Z day," Shrill offered. He caught himself staring at the army wife, trying to determine why he suddenly felt so indebted to the petite woman. Then like a bolt from the heavens it suddenly dawned on him where the sudden feeling of kinship stemmed from.

"What?" Brook asked.

"I see a lot of similarities between my son and you. His burning desire to succeed and be the best... at everything he tackled. Collin's bravery and tenacity had been evident before he took his first step. As an adult he just wanted to be accepted as an aviator—no different than any other Hornet driver in a very competitive environment vastly underrepresented by young men who looked like him. Nevertheless I have to be honest with you. I owe you and Cade that much. The real reason I feel compelled to furnish you with a mission outside the wire..."

Looking up, past the dark bags and into Shrill's red rimmed eyes Brook cut in, "Why, then?"

"We already have a contingency in place for anyone who gets bit in the field. It's pretty cut and dried—a *permanent* fix," Shrill said soberly. "You, little lady, are a *nurse*. Your skills are in high demand— and there aren't a whole lot of people left who have worked in *any* capacity in the field of medicine. Besides I already know you can shoot—seen it myself. But if anyone gets a non-life threatening injury—I expect you to help them out." Shrill's disarming smile left his face and he said sternly, "Nurse first... shooter second—after all of the bandaging is done... OK?"

The perceived sentiment, and the tone in which he had delivered it bothered Brook for a fleeting second. Then just as quickly as the emotion swelled in her she let it ebb and nodded— accepting his offer.

"That *tardy* note I gave you didn't have any specifics... it just said to give you a *shooter's* job. He's going to probe... bust your balls a bit." At that Shrill winced and cast his eyes at the well-worn carpeting. "Sorry 'bout my choice of words... I figured I'd leave it up to you to divulge to the sergeant whatever information you feel is pertinent." And after a moment of contemplation the Colonel added, "He won't know about you and Captain Grayson's relationship—at least not from what *I* scrawled on the note."

Brook felt a tingle of fear manifest in the pit of her stomach. She received the folded note, promptly stuffing it in her jeans pocket.

"Make sure you go to the armorer. Have him clean and inspect that M4 of yours. Then go get some Multicam ACUs, a rucksack, and MOLLE gear," Shrill said as he paced over to the photo of himself and the young pilot. "And hoard as many extra mags as you can talk Lafayette into parting with."

"I know what the ACUs are but you lost me on the *Molly*... gear?" Brook said awkwardly. *If I'm going to play Cade I had better learn the lingo,"* she thought.

"Stands for Modular, Light-weight, Load bearing, Equipment, that's military speak for the canvas webbing on which you attach pouches to carry spare magazines and other gear. There are other acronyms... but I'll spare you," Shrill intoned as he traced a finger over the glass covering his son's photo while ostensibly wiping a nonexistent layer of dust away.

"Thanks again Colonel," Brook said as she approached the tall bald black man, her arms outstretched. "I'm so sorry about your son." Then standing on tip toes, she wrapped her arms around his ribcage and gave him a baby bear hug.

"Yes... I am too," the base commander proffered as he covertly wiped a rare tear. "Now get along before I change my mind... and don't forget your rifle," he added in a soft but bass heavy voice.

Startled, Brook jumped an inch yet held the embrace for another second as she took in the smiling face of the fighter jock that had obviously made his dad proud.

***

Grayson quarters

Instead of the dreaded talk she was going to have with her daughter, Brook settled into the bunk beside Raven and began reading aloud a chapter from the *Lucy Rose* book she had scooped up from the lobby of the base commons.

Before delving ten pages into the precocious fourth grader's adventures and misadventures both mom and daughter were sound asleep—the victims of a harrowing sleepless night and a long sorrow filled day.

***

By the time Cade had finished getting his lead-out in order it was nearly midnight. He had fully broken down, cleaned, and oiled all of his weapons. His Gerber—the very blade that had ended Mike Desantos' life—received a thorough sharpening. He clipped a pair of the newest generation NVDs to his tactical helmet. Two M84 flash bangs and two M67 fragmentation grenades found a home attached to his MOLLE rig. He checked and rechecked his kit. Finally satisfied he was fully prepared for the upcoming mission into the belly of the beast, he left the other operators and flight crew to finish with their individual pre-mission preparations.

Since there was no way of knowing who had come onto the base during those first hectic days—good or bad—he ratcheted his situational awareness meter up several notches. With a Glock in one fist, he left the Cushman behind and traversed Schriever's darkened pathways on foot—alert and prepared.

***

Just hours after Mike's passing, Cade had started his own impromptu investigation; after his initial interrogation of the killer who called himself Pug he would have bet the naming rights to his yet-to-be-born child that he had not acted alone. He was certain the killer had received help from somebody else from within the base. Pug didn't strike Cade as being the sharpest tool in the shed. The man had proven to be crafty and cunning but he was no Rhodes Scholar.

Cade had quickly ruled out the soldiers in charge of processing and placing new arrivals in quarantine. Every one of them had passed the sniff test. That they followed the wet footsteps and took Francis into custody all but absolved them of any guilt anyway. Cade scrutinized the newer arrivals first. He interviewed the people who had entered Schriever with Francis and quickly ruled them out. Next he focused on the survivors who had entered Schriever during the initial days of the outbreak.

With Colonel Shrill's help Cade had narrowed down the number of civilians currently on base, excluding those with military connections, to roughly two hundred.

"The refugees," Shrill had said, "trickled in at first. And then we experienced a huge surge coming between days five and six of the Omega outbreak. Then there was a total dry spell with less than ten of them trickling into Schriever between days seven and the day our murderer arrived."

Most of the survivors, having escaped the violence in and around Colorado Springs twenty miles to the west of Schriever, had shown up outside of the base with nothing but the clothes on their backs. Unfortunately many of them were already infected from bite wounds received during their flight to safety, and sadly, those people were now buried in one of the many mass graves outside of the wire.

With help from the base security personnel, Shrill had started vetting the roughly two hundred civilians on base, and since the government's databases were no longer accessible the work had been tedious.

Colonel Shrill then indicated it was all that he could do just to organize the foraging parties alone. "People have got to eat," he'd said. His hands were more than full trying to utilize the civilian volunteers based on their skills and abilities, let alone determining who was trying to conceal their real identity.

Cade returned to his billet as a new twenty-four, complete with a whole new clean slate, started counting down. That it was after midnight all but assured that his family would be sleeping. He just hoped that when he got up to go to the flight line for the pre-mission briefing Brook would also be awake.

He inserted his key and then quietly opened the outside door, taking every precaution *not* to wake the slumbering duo inside. After the covert entry he tossed his beret atop the metal table adjacent to the door, unknowingly sending the handwritten note that Brook had left for him floating to the floor.

Chapter 9
Outbreak - Day 11
Schriever AFB
Colorado Springs, Colorado

One hour before sunup and once again sleep had proven elusive. Cade kept rehashing the Castle Rock mission in his head. Was there any way he could have saved Mike? The simple answer— no. Fate had intervened. *"When it's your time, it's your time. The only thing you can do is prepare for the worst and hope for the best."* Those were Mike Desantos' words, and Cade would never forget them.

He ceased waiting for the Sandman and quietly slipped out of bed. Except for the one good night of sleep since leaving Portland, this current stretch of insomnia numbered in double digits. He didn't need a theoretical physicist like Stephen Hawking to help him put two and two together to come to the conclusion that this current stretch of sleep deprivation was directly related to the walking dead. Hell, he had been able to shut down immediately and power sleep for hours at a stretch in the stifling heat of Iraq where bottled water nearly boiled. Or in the bone numbing cold of the Hindu Kush Mountains in Afghanistan while surrounded by fanatical killers who would cut off his head without a second thought—no problem.

Yes, the common denominator was painfully obvious. They were seemingly everywhere and there was nothing that he could do about it.

So with his family still sound asleep in the adjacent bunk, Cade took a seat on a wobbly Government Issue folding chair, covered his bearded face with his hands and sat in silence, jaw clenched, eyes closed. Then he began his pre-mission ritual of stuffing the distractions of family and the state of the world in which they were all struggling to survive, deep down inside himself. For Cade, this mission was about righting a wrong. Not just one wrong. Mike Desantos wasn't the only casualty as a direct result of Pug's actions. The small percentage of the population, not yet infected, might have eventually been saved when Doctor Fuentes finally perfected his antidote. All that hope was now forever lost. The doctor and all of his sticky notes, computer files, thumb drives—everything lost in flames—thanks to Pug's orgy of murder and sabotage. Cade made no effort to lock away his feelings concerning Mike's murder. He wanted those emotions as close to the surface as possible—accessible, fresh and crackling through every nerve in his body—to be extinguished only when Mike's death was finally avenged.

Unfortunately, killing Pug would have to wait. First and foremost on the agenda was finding the man responsible for launching the human missile on his pointless mission of death and destruction. One way or another, Cade thought, Robert Christian was going to pay.

Shrugging away murderous thoughts, he took one final glimpse at Brook and Raven. Asleep, Brook's face was bereft of the new granite set of her jaw. The old Brook stared at him—the mommy Brook. Yes, Cade thought, with or without him she would weather Omega just fine.

Raven, fully eclipsed behind her mom's blanket-clad form with her face buried between her mom's shoulder blades, still needed to be protected from Omega's reality. Cade supposed his daughter didn't fully have a grasp of the odds that were stacked against her. He shuddered at the thought of what the future might look like for his Raven when she was grown. He closed his mind to the staggering numbers the dead had on their side, and the lopsided uphill battle humanity certainly faced. For now he had a job to do.

Cade departed the Grayson quarters quietly and took in a lungful of the crisp high plains air. Then he glanced to the east, where the sky, as if ablaze, glowed like the inside of an ironsmith's forge.

Finally he looked west where Pikes Peak and the surrounding Rockies still huddled in black, not yet caressed by the rising sun. He found it hard to believe surrounded by so much beauty that just two nights ago nuclear devices had been detonated less than fifty miles away.

Although the initial mushroom clouds hadn't been visible immediately following the two simultaneous explosions, the debris thrown into the air lingered, and had been clearly visible for hours. As it retreated eastward depositing radioactive isotopes for tens of miles, it began to look like an aerial lava flow.

Cade looked north and uttered a silent prayer for any survivors caught downwind who had not only the walking dead to worry about but also the slow painful death radiation poisoning promised.

***

After a quick meal of sweet grits and four cups of Schriever's finest hot brown water, Cade used his captain's bars to requisition transportation. He then set out to collect the operators that would be accompanying him to Jackson Hole.

Maddox and Lopez were up and ready when Cade's Cushman came to a halt outside their billet. Somehow their internal clocks intuitively knew they were going down range.

Tice, on the other hand, took a little bit of rousing to get up to speed.

Cade nixed the CIA man's usual tropical attire and ball cap. "Tactical chic is not good to go today," he told the spook before leaving him alone in the billet to get squared away.

A few moments later Tice emerged, squinting in the morning sun, tactical bag in one hand, M4 grasped in the other. The sometimes impatient—often times surly—yet always talkative CIA nuke specialist wasted no time before addressing Cade. "Where are we going young Captain?"

"Best that we not discuss it in the open. I'll brief you when we get in the air." Cade reached between his feet and retrieved a padded black nylon bag big enough to accommodate a seventeen pound bowling ball, then handed it over as the CIA man took a seat.

"Don't tell me... let me guess. We're gonna make some more big radioactive holes in terra firma... right?"

The Cushman started rolling. Cade was no Desantos when it came to speed and cornering but he wasn't Morgan Freeman driving Miss Daisy either. He took his eyes off of the path long enough to put everyone in peril and hollered to be heard over the whirring rubber tires. "Just look in the bag and tell me you know how to use the thing."

Tice eyed the five thousand dollar digital camera complete with Nikkor 200-400 mm telephoto zoom lens then replied, "Nash briefed me. This was supposed to be used as a last resort."

"What's your concern?" asked Cade.

Tice swallowed before answering. "I truly hoped it wouldn't come to this... because we're *all* going to take some major *rads*." And as the word *rads* slipped from his lips a ball of ice formed in his gut.

Cade stabbed the brake stopping short of the flight line and jumped from the Cushman. He gripped his SCAR, then handed Lopez, Maddox, and Tice their black kit bags before retrieving his own. "Are you gentlemen good to go?" Cade asked.

Both Lopez and Maddox emitted a "*Hooah*" as they stepped to the waiting Ghost Hawk.

"Are you sure you need me?" Tice countered. "Because if you don't... I can stay *right here* and up my rad levels a little slower than you guys." A crooked grin crossed the CIA nuke specialist's clean-shaven face.

"How about we drop you right on top of ground zero? You can give us an up close assessment. Maybe even provide an accurate body count. Or a *pieces of bodies* count," Lopez offered over his shoulder. Pushing the CIA man's buttons was becoming an equal opportunity, everyday occurrence for the dwindling Delta unit.

Ignoring the ribbing, Tice replied, "I got my Depends cinched tight and my Desert Eagle cocked and locked... *I'm good to go*."

Cade approached the flight line still in awe of the technological marvels sitting on the apron. After years of riding around in the UH-60 Black Hawk, he wasn't used to the Ghost Hawk's silhouette, let alone its capabilities, and was still taken aback every time he saw one. The angular Jedi Rides crouched menacingly on the tarmac, their matte black skin devouring the light. Even static and powered down the GEN-3 helos looked like they were moving along at Mach-one.

Cade recognized Ari Silver from a distance. The SOAR pilot, immersed in his pre-flight walk around, appeared totally oblivious of the approaching operators.

"Night Stalker—" said Cade, using the official nickname of the aviators and aircrew that served in TF-160, "is she loaded and bloated?"

Ari glanced up, his piercing hazel eyes flashed recognition as he threw Cade a quick salute. "She was empty on ammo when we came home last. Hicksy musta poured three thousand rounds into the Zs when we pulled you and..." The loss of Desantos, fresh on the aviator's mind, momentarily caused him to choke up. "Hicks made it *rain* on those putrid fuckers. Whipper only had enough ammunition for half a load-out and that's the good news," Ari added.

Cade's eyes narrowed as he gripped Ari's shoulder. "And the bad news is..."

"First Sergeant Whipper indicated he was bingo on JP-8 for the time being. He has the remainder of his tanker fleet on forage patrol, and if all goes as planned full tankers should be wheels down tonight or tomorrow."

"Ari... that *is* bad news... how much fuel does she have aboard?"

"Bird's at nearly sixty percent, but I figure we can refuel somewhere on the ground. I'll find a muni airport for us along the flight plan and a few alternates in case we encounter too many *ambulatory deceased* at the first option." Ari smirked at his own play on words. "I bet if the *paper pilots* were still flying the Pentagon that jargon would stick." Changing his voice to a deep baritone mimicking his idea of how a rear echelon desk weenie would sound, Ari added theatrically, "*Ambulatory Deceased*, that has a nice ring to it don't you think General? Why yes General. It rolls off the tongue. I like it... *make it so.*"

The newly promoted captain shook his head. "Ari...you ever consider moonlighting as a stand-up comedian?"

"Before Pandora's Box opened and the dead started walking that *had* been my retirement plan. Free beer and fried food. Up late and sleeping in. What am I gonna do now?" Ari quipped as he resumed checking the flight surfaces and wiggling moving parts. Thoroughly satisfied the Ghost was airworthy, he patted the helo's composite skin. "Now boarding rows AA through DD. Anyone needing help with a wheelchair or walker please see a flight attendant, and a friendly reminder—*no* drinking in row AA."

"That means you Langley boy," Lopez said, suppressing a laugh.

Cade threw his bulging kit bag into the helo's open door and slipped the suppressed SCAR-L SOPMOD carbine in after, then hauled his weary frame into a seat. He donned a flight helmet and plugged its coiled wire into the onboard comms jack.

After having given the helicopter a thorough looking over, Ari and Durant loitered on the tarmac; they hadn't yet begun their usual preflight banter and jovial ribbing. To Cade the quiet inside the helo was deafening. He closed his eyes and used the temporary lack of sensory bombardment to run the upcoming mission by his mind's eye. This particular operation had been thrown together on the fly, and considering the possibility of a spy inside of the base, only essential personnel were allowed to attend the secret pre-op briefing. Tice had been conspicuously absent but the Delta boys and flight crew, along with Major Nash and the newly promoted General Ronnie "Ghost" Gaines, had huddled in a remote corner of the Satellite operations room and hashed out a course of action. In a normal real world operation the team would have had weeks if not months to prepare. Any buildings that were to be assaulted would have been mocked up in full scale so Cade and his men could learn the layout and run the mission over and over until they could execute it blindfolded. Normally, in an urban operation such as this, the Delta team would fast rope directly on top of their target and take immediate control through speed, surprise, and overwhelming violence of action. But for this op, the presence of Patriot surface-to-air missiles, their powerful radars guarding the sky, dictated otherwise.

Like a couple of ninjas, Ari and Durant had silently boarded the helo, gone through their pre-flight routines and had lit the fire—all without uttering a single word.

Mike's death is on a lot of people's minds, Cade thought. The pilot's usual chitchat would have been preferable to being reminded once again of the fallen warrior.

The familiar smell of kerosene filled the air as the Ghost Hawk's dual jet turbines spooled up.

In the pilot's seat Chief Warrant Officer Ari Silver's fingers danced over the glass touchscreen. He keyed in the GPS coordinates to the insertion point south of Jackson Hole and then inputted the multiple waypoints needed to fly NOE (nap of the earth) using the landscape's natural contours to mask them from enemy radar.

At the briefing Ari had been informed that Major Nash's satellite operations officers had not been able to get a satellite parked in a geo-synchronous orbit over the mountainous city, so he would be flying without benefit of the usual real-time satellite imagery. Since he had to deliver the four-man team as close to Jackson Hole as possible he would be careful to steer clear of roads and towns the closer they got to the NA stronghold.

To sum it up, Cade and his team would be doing exactly what they were trained to do: operate covertly and unimpeded behind enemy lines without the luxury of air cover or a quick reaction force of Army Rangers as a backstop. The four men would be left to operate down range with full autonomy.

"We're off," Ari said.

And with that the black Ghost Hawk leapt into the air—onboard a payload of rough men eager to deliver a little payback.

Chapter 10
Outbreak - Day 11
Grand Junction, Colorado

Dickless wavered in front of the window, a permanent sneer frozen on his decomposing face.

Taryn's former boss, Richard Lesst, who inexplicably had preferred that he be called Dick instead of his given first name, was molesting the door again. The quarter-inch thick safety glass had taken on a gray sheen due to his constant feeble attempts to get to the meat within the office still bearing his name.

The airport scuttlebutt was that Richard Lesst had probably earned his nickname the first time he announced himself *"present"* during roll call and correcting his teacher by pointing out that he preferred to be called Dick.

Though the power had been out for more than a week, Richard Lesst's top floor office which Taryn had been forced to take refuge in was far from dark. Ambient light streamed steadily through the wall of windows that faced the jet taxiway and the two runways beyond.

The air inside the main terminal was rife with humidity, and riding on it was the all-encompassing stench of death. Taryn guessed that it had to be well over one hundred degrees inside, and probably a good one hundred twenty on the shimmery blacktop outside. *Definitely not a dry heat*, she thought. She hated hearing, *"It sure is hot in Colorado"* or *"At least it's a dry heat,"* or any other variation of that same worn out saying nearly every Tom, Dick, and Harriett that crushed her stand for their *foo foo* coffee drinks thought mandatory to bleat.

Hotter than a motherfucker outside, was more to Taryn's liking, and if blurted ad-nauseum from the mouths of her usual clientele—she supposed she could get used to it. Hell, she thought, some frumpy schoolmarm declaring, *"It sure is hotter than a motherfucker today... but at least it's a dry heat,"* in a matronly warble while ordering her *skinny, half-caf, almond latte* would be one to spout off about on Facebook.

Facebook—that reminded her. It was about time to reposition the solar charger into the direct sunlight.

If there was one thing Taryn was most proud of when discussing her personality, it was her never-ending supply of hope. For she was sure that any moment her iPhone, which was currently tethered to the glossy black panel positioned in the rectangle of sun blasting through the skylight, would come alive and start spewing sounds akin to AOL's old tagline *You've Got Mail.* Beeps that meant she had a voice message from her family saying they were still alive and busy looking for her. Or the hollow tone alerting her that she had just received an instant message from one of her many friends who had already left Grand Junction and gone ahead to Denver hoping to get the apartment closest to campus—or as her best friend Miley had declared she was going to do two weeks ago—*"Bribe someone and get us the best corner dorm room."*

Though she could fantasize about such things, the oppressive heat and the ever-present smell of rotting flesh served as a constant reminder of where she was and that the prospect of ever getting to Denver was probably just a ton of wishful thinking. And as hopeful as she was, the brief messages she had received that were still stored on her iPhone spoke volumes. Chilling texts from friends who were trapped and freaking out about how many of the dead things were walking around their streets. YouTube footage sent to her showing civil unrest, and worst of all the horrible zombie attacks that she could barely watch let alone fully comprehend. Then, just days after the dead began to walk and *all* of her friends and acquaintances had gone totally silent she received an even more ominous message—her own intuition telling her she was on her own.

Taryn tore her eyes from the useless smart phone and sniffed a pit—*ugghhh*. Unfortunately the four inches of water left in the five gallon water cooler wasn't earmarked for sanitation nor improving her olfactory experience. She was resigned to the fact that a simple luxury such as washing her pits would have to wait until she made it out of this scrape alive. Besides, she mused, compared to the dead, her pits smelled like a dozen long stemmed roses.

Ignoring her former boss and his hungry eyes, Taryn low crawled across the office floor in order to get a better look through the terminal windows below. Painted white and splashed with Tar Heel blue, Allegiant Flight 6651 was still nestled next to the gate where it had been since arriving from Las Vegas the Sunday before last, and alongside it, docked to the other gate, sat the red, yellow, and white twin engine from Salt Lake City. The two planes, with a combined manifest of two hundred and eighty-nine people aboard, including crew members, had efficiently delivered infection and death to Grand Junction Regional.

Landing only minutes apart, the jet liners disgorged hundreds of terrified people, a host of them already infected but not yet turned.

Two passengers onboard Flight 6651 from Vegas who had turned while the plane was still airborne succeeded in infecting ten other passengers before finally being subdued.

"The two men were insane or something, biting and clawing at those heroes," was how a stunned flight attendant had described the incident, hands trembling, as she waited for the Venti Americano that Taryn was sure would only add to her shakes.

Adding to the horrific events that had already unfolded while Allegiant 6651 was still in the air, three of the plane's passengers, having had succumbed to their horrific bite wounds, expired on the paisley carpet in front of Jet Way A. Within minutes—or seconds— Taryn couldn't remember, the two men and the blonde girl with pig tails, who couldn't have been a day over six, had reanimated and were stalking people across the gatehouse floor.

As Taryn watched, with one hand clamped over her mouth holding in a scream and the other frozen in a death grip to the espresso machine's still gushing steam nozzle, an air marshal who had

69

been on the Las Vegas flight drew his pistol, identified himself, and then issued a few ludicrous orders to the pale monsters.

The marshal, whose permanently dead body still lay where it had fallen amongst his own scattered organs, had failed to discharge his weapon at the newly turned. He had seemingly been frozen by the incomprehensible scene he had just witnessed and his split second hesitation allowed the dead passengers to get their hands on him and drag him to the ground.

Taryn watched on as a man in skinny jeans wearing a painfully trendy felt Pork Pie hat scooped up the air marshal's black pistol and scampered away holding it with two fingers as if he was supremely terrified of the prospect of protecting his own life with the hated boom stick.

She couldn't tear her eyes away as the monsters gorged themselves on the marshal's neck, tearing large hunks away and swallowing them whole.

That the marshal still had a second gun strapped to the outside of his argyle sock next to his right ankle hadn't been lost on the young barista. In fact she had been eyeing it since that fateful day and it figured prominently into her escape plan—whatever that entailed.

The airport security, EMTs and firefighters who had been stationed inside of the airport around the clock, though thoroughly trained to handle death and chaos, fared no better than Flight 6651's passengers against the reanimated dead. A few of the former first responders now shambled the concourse downstairs and the jet way and tarmac outside.

As Taryn concentrated on braiding her long jet-black tresses, a fat sweat bead traced the ridge of her nose, stopped against the gold hoop that had been there since her thirteenth birthday, and then took the path of least resistance plummeting onto her knee-length black shorts. The tats on her well defined biceps moved as she worked, the demons and skulls seemingly alive. As she stared at the heat mirages performing their ethereal dance outside on the tarmac an inane thought crossed her mind. *Trapped at work during a zombie outbreak and in the middle of the worst heat wave in fifteen years — good going Taryn.*

Braided hair now coiled in a bun—so Dickless or Karen or one of the many nameless creatures lurking below would have one less thing to grab onto—Taryn cracked the door and craned her neck to assess the situation below.

Either gunned down by airport security or torn apart and consumed by the lifeless mob, the bullet-riddled bodies and piles of bloody remnants which were formerly human posed a gory minefield Taryn would be forced to navigate.

The yellow Subway sign beckoned from the far end of the terminal. The only food option in the airport, save for the gift store, had been positioned where the building took a slight bend so that passengers waiting to board and people meeting arrivals would have equal access without having to overwork the security personnel by going to and fro. With over two hundred flights daily, ninety percent of them private planes and helicopters, GJT, the moniker given the airport by the Federal Aviation Administration, had been a hopping little place.

A thin trail of saliva escaped the corner of the teen's parched lips. All she could think about was a veggie foot long on wheat. *Earthy tasting bean sprouts, cool ripe tomatoes, crisp green bell peppers, and red onions. No cheese for this vegan please, oil and vinegar... what's the point? Hell I'll take three white chocolate and macadamia nut cookies. Better yet six and a forty-four ounce pop.*

Taryn, a little voice informed, *you don't drink pop.*

"The hell I don't." Startled by her own voice, she returned to reality just a little freaked out by the vivid food fantasy. Boys—certainly, she daydreamed about the boys of Denver State often in between making iced Americanos, blended Frappuccino's and Caramel Macchiatos, all the while feigning amusement in the random musings of the annoying travelers passing through her line.

Slumping, back to the wall, she let her body slide down until she sat on her haunches. "*I'm on my way honey. Be ready. I'll pick you up outside of Chester's post.*" Those were the last words her dad had uttered. She looked at her phone wondering if anything had changed. Was the ringer on? Taryn came to the realization that she was slowly losing it and that her overexuberant wellspring of hope was quickly running dry.

71

Chapter 11
Outbreak - Day 11
Schriever AFB
Colorado Springs, Colorado

Waking up and realizing the handwritten note was missing from the table and that Cade was already gone had been the straw that broke the proverbial camel's back.

The paragraph of no more than fifty words had simply asked him to wake her before he deployed. The fact that he hadn't honored her one tiny request triggered something inside of her, and like a Jack-in-the Box whose jester had been replaced by something demonic, she snapped.

Still shocked and confused, a crestfallen Brook escorted Raven in total silence to Annie's quarters. As Brook trudged on, embarrassed beyond belief by her actions, she performed a sort of mental inventory—searching for an answer to her outburst.

Instead of acting out in front of her very impressionable soon-to-be twelve-year-old she wished she would have harnessed all of the pent up negative emotion to wield against the dead.

She wondered whether the anger and blind rage she had exhibited had actually stemmed from stuffing the emotions brought on by Carl's murder, or if it was from the creeping feelings of abandonment that grew stronger each time her man went on one of his missions. In her heart she hoped it was the former and not the latter. The former would be sorted out when she started her mourning process for Carl. Dealing with Cade was going to be interesting. Hell, she thought, one look from his brown eyes and she might forget all about the perceived sleight. However, the one thing she did know with an absolute certainty—the person who had smashed up the Grayson quarters was *not* really her. And she vowed silently to herself that she would *never* let it happen again.

Brook's stomach knotted as she recalled the baffled look on Raven's face after witnessing her usually calm and collected mom topple one of the unused bunks, which, in domino fashion took another, and then yet another with it. Then, with the covers pulled above her nose and wide-eyed like she had seen the dead, Raven had uttered the question that caused Brook to ask at that terrifying moment, who, or what she had become.

"Mom..." she had whimpered, "is it a mountain or a mole hill?"

***

Motor Pool Mission Staging Area

As was her penchant for punctuality, Brook was at the motor pool half an hour early. She killed the time standing in the middle of the dusty staging area, sweltering in her newly issued ACUs as her brain baked under the Kevlar helmet.

She amused herself by watching Colonel Shrill dart about issuing orders to the thirty or so civilians dressed in colorful shirts, blue jeans and tennis shoes, who were milling around and talking about anything and everything in loud boisterous voices.

To Brook it almost looked like he was herding feral cats; calling the scene in front of her controlled chaos would be way too kind.

Distancing herself from the cacophony, she gravitated towards the half dozen rough looking men clad in the newest multi-cam fatigues. Judging by their tactical helmets which bristled with night vision goggles, and high-tech streamlined comms gear complete with boom mikes—the men had to be Special Forces operators. As she got closer she noticed that although their weapons were M4 carbines similar to hers, theirs had obviously been highly modified to suit each of their personal tastes. All of their rifles were outfitted with scopes and silencers for stealthy longer range engagements as well as vertical fore grips and collapsible stocks making them effective for close quarter battle as well. These were multi-purpose weapons—that much Brook knew. She also knew she wanted one.

Shouldering her plain Jane vanilla M4 she tried to blend in— as well as a five foot tall female amongst a forest of men could.

"You... little lady," Shrill said singling Brook out. How he knew it was her underneath the bulky helmet and the military garb was a mystery. Surely there were short men on the base. "Find the..." he paused to consult his clipboard, "I'm designating you gunner in the Dakota truck. You're riding with... a civilian by the name of Wilson."

Designated gunner, Brook thought, sounds better than *burial detail*. She envisioned herself, wrapped safely in a plate metal turret with a .50 caliber Ma Deuce blazing away. She wasn't sure, but she thought the Dakota was one of those exotic gun trucks from the Stan that Cade had once mentioned.

As Shrill's booming voice continued pairing people and assigning vehicles Brook headed to where the desert tan military vehicles sat cooking in the sun. She didn't want to waste any time finding her "Dakota" gun truck and the fella named Wilson.

"Brook," Shrill bellowed.

She stopped and aboutfaced.

The base commander jabbed his finger in the opposite direction.

Confused and slightly embarrassed at being called out by her first name by the baritone voiced colonel, Brook avoided all eye contact, especially with the men dressed much like her, and padded off towards the cluster of liberated U-Haul trucks.

She set course for the nearest truck and the shaded soil next to it. Before she had tromped twenty paces rivulets of sweat had soaked into her fatigues up and down her back, under her arms and worst of all the fabric in direct contact with the tender flesh of her inner thighs and crotch.

"Fuck me..." Brook said at the sight of the U-Haul truck. Looking down on her as if passing silent judgment for her earlier outburst were the likenesses of four former presidents. Originally carved in stone on Mount Rushmore but now just a silk screened image adorning the moving truck's slab side, the stern faces of

George Washington, Thomas Jefferson, Teddy Roosevelt and Abraham Lincoln hovered above the words, *Visit South Dakota, Great Faces—Great Places.*

Sadly her mental image of the sexy Dakota truck and its manly gun turret disappeared like a desert heat mirage and the revelation that she *was* standing in the shade of her real ride dawned on her. *Now if I could just find this Wilson guy,* she thought.

"You must be Brooklyn Grayson," said the pup of a kid who had snuck up on her blind side. The twenty-something wore an olive green tee shirt which clung to his lanky frame, its short sleeves from the pits to the cuff stained white with dried sweat. His knee-length tan cargo shorts barely held up by a thick leather belt swished when he moved, and with the unruly mop of flame red hair bursting from under his desert tan boonie hat Brook thought the kid looked like a younger version of Carrot Top. And as she sized up her new traveling partner, she surmised that the niggling sensation that she was experiencing was a portent of things to come and the heat was the least of her worries. In the back of her mind she feared that the day was probably going to get much worse before it got any better.

Chapter 12
Outbreak - Day 11
Castle Rock, Colorado

As Jedi One-One closed the distance to Castle Rock, the two radioactive craters, which resembled twin asteroid strikes on some distant desolate moonscape, crept into view. Ari nudged the stick, feeding the Ghost Hawk incremental course corrections in order to give the hot zone a wide berth. Several hundred thousand Zs had been destroyed by the two strategically placed five kiloton nuclear warheads. The destruction below was incomprehensible; starting at ground zero, nothing was left standing for miles in every direction. And nearly a full day after the Z horde that had surged from Denver was destroyed, fires still raged on the periphery, leaping from house to house, voraciously consuming the fuel rich suburbs and everything standing in its way.

Ari had a hard time trying to fathom the full scope of the destruction. He wondered how many survivors had been holed up, hiding from the dead, when the devices went off. Collateral damage was to be expected in war, *but on a scale such as this? Was it all worth it?* he asked himself. Ari knew it wasn't his place to second guess the President, but still he wanted to know why other measures hadn't been undertaken before they went with the nuclear option. Resigned to the fact that he would never be privy to the Intel that shaped Clay's final decision, Ari shelved it and focused on flying.

"Desperate times called for desperate measures," Cade said matter-of-factly and to no one in particular over the onboard comms as he took in the blackened landscape. "Pretty wild that the bombs didn't even leave a scratch on Castle Rock."

Ari shook his head. It was as if the Delta operative had read his thoughts. "Cade, my man, that pile of red rock is going to be standing a thousand years after we're dead and gone."

Tice shifted in his seat, pointing the camera at Castle Rock and the devastated infrastructure passing below the starboard side. His Nikon stuttered, capturing dozens of images during the low speed flyby. "Just think what it would have looked like down there if we would have used the 150 kiloton yield. We wouldn't be able to get close enough to see the craters without all of us glowing like fireflies afterward," the CIA operative and nuclear weapons specialist opined. He had proven himself with the Desantos-led Delta team on both of their previous missions. That he was knowledgeable when it came to all types of nuclear weapons and power plants made him a very valuable asset to the team, and the fact that he was a counter terrorism expert who had headed the JTTF (Joint Terrorism Task Force) while serving under former President Odero only sweetened the deal.

Directing his question at Tice, Sergeant First Class Lopez asked, "Spooky man... why are you taking all those pictures?"

"I have orders," Tice stated, keeping his eye glued to the viewfinder as the camera whirred.

"General Gaines?" Lopez asked, furrowing his brow.

"No. Not that high up the chain," Tice retorted. He knew Ronnie Gaines from running joint ops in the field with the operator, but calling the man General was going to take some getting used to. Gaines was one hell of a SF officer and fully capable of running Delta as well as leading the diminished Spec Ops cadre garrisoned at Fort Kit Carson. Battlefield promotions were to be expected, but rising from Captain to General in one fell swoop was extraordinary. That Mike Desantos had enjoyed the same rapid promotion from President Valerie Clay spoke volumes to the attrition rate suffered by all branches of the United States military since Z day. Cade's words, uttered only moments ago, recycled through Tice's mind. *Desperate times call for desperate measures. Yes indeed,* he thought to himself before answering Lopez's question. "The President ordered Nash to re-task all available KH-12 satellites to fully recon the CONUS (Continental United States)."

Never taking his eyes from the ground below, Sergeant Maddox queried, "Why aren't they deploying drones for this TMZ overflight? If they did, then we wouldn't be hovering over Chernobyl getting unwarranted x-rays."

Ari interrupted. "You bozos think I would fry my balls so you all can get some digital shots?"

"Misery loves company," Cade replied grimly.

"The pilot is correct," Tice said reassuringly, patting his portable rad meter. "If this baby was humming I assure you I would have barged up there and taken the stick myself."

"Over my dead body... tough guy!" Ari jokingly spat back.

"Calm down Night Stalker," Tice said, suppressing a grin. "I wouldn't want to get between an aviator and his stick."

The Ghost Hawk's comms crackled with laughter, and that was the best medicine for men going into harm's way against an unknown foe.

Ari spurred the bird on. Taking the airspeed beyond 100 knots, he pointed her on a westward heading towards the towering Rocky Mountains and the New American enclave that lay beyond.

Tice lowered the Nikon lens, silently hoping the topic of drone aircraft wouldn't be revisited any time soon. If it did, he was certain his input would not be well received.

Chapter 13
Outbreak - Day 11
Jackson Hole, Wyoming

Jackson Firehouse

Daymon awoke to a new day of the apocalypse. His knees still ached from running several miles in heavy thick soled boots and his body felt like a side of beef worked over by Rocky Balboa.

Though he didn't know what day of the week it was, somehow in the back of his mind he remembered that he was back in Jackson Hole, and in a near state of panic, with the nagging feeling that he had overslept hovering on the periphery of conscious thought, he bolted from the bed. He knew that in order to escape Chief Kyle's wrath, and possibly a week's worth of kitchen duty, he had to be dressed and down the pole before the transgression could be logged and duly noted. As he rifled through his closet for a fresh uniform, he shrugged off the shroud of sleep. In the next instant the realization that he was alone in the firehouse, and Chief Kyle and the guys were gone and probably never coming back, struck him full force.

Daymon quelled the impulse to scratch the four vertical gashes. Instead he gently plucked at the cotton tee shirt which had fused to the discharge during the night. The wounds he had suffered going over the wire at Schriever two days prior were starting to knit and itched like hell and his abdomen, still viciously red and hot to the touch, needed attention. First Aid was the furthest thing from his mind as he trotted off towards the bathroom to relieve his full bladder.

After a three minute piss he washed his hands thoroughly then opened the medicine cabinet perched above the sink looking for something with which to clean and dress his wounds. He spotted just what the doctor ordered tucked away behind a couple of canisters of Barbasol shaving cream. *Perfect.* The unmistakable brown plastic bottle with the white cap sat right next door to a full tube of Neosporin antibiotic ointment.

As he studied his wounds in the mirror, he asked himself, *Are you sure you want to go through with this?* Then, after a moment's hesitation, he doused the infected gashes running from his navel to just below his sternum with half of the bottle's contents.

"*Motherfucker...*" he gasped between pursed lips. "*That shit stings.*" He gritted his teeth, letting the invasive foaming napalm do its thing for a couple of minutes. The pain was so intense he envisioned the piranha-toothed creature from *Alien* about to burst from his gut.

After allowing the hydrogen peroxide to bubble in the wounds for as long as he could stand, he wiped away the foamy yellow pus and slathered on a liberal amount of the antibiotic ointment. Then, grimacing through more pain, he labored to pull a clean black tee shirt on over his dreadlocks.

Walking gingerly he made his way to the brass pole where for a New York second he lingered, entertaining the crazy notion of taking the fast way down. *Pole or stairs?* he asked himself. Since he didn't feel comfortable with the idea of the pole contacting his chest all the way to the first floor, he picked the latter; then, after trudging down thirty-four stairs, he paused at ground level, light headed and winded.

Never before had a handful of simple tasks caused him to expend so much energy. Hell, he thought, that was the first time he had ever gone down the stairs empty handed. Only a couple of instances came to mind: once after he tweaked a knee jumping from a perfectly good airplane and the other time after he sprained his ankle tripping over a root while fighting a back country wildfire.

While Daymon wolfed down a cold can of Chef Boyardee raviolis, he allowed his mind to drift back to the fateful sundrenched

Saturday when he left Jackson Hole. The day had started off on a bad note with Chief Kyle hunting him down, then rousing him out of bed and going ballistic on him (which was at least a once a day occurrence in the firehouse) over a formal 'Request for Leave' chit that Daymon had sneaked into his in-box the day before.

A rash of shit over a leave request was to be expected—especially in the middle of summer—but his tirade had been one for the books—until the Chief paused, face flushed, and said "Yes."

Daymon remembered scraping his jaw from the floor and the Chief's next action — which still baffled him to this day.

The Chief tossed him the keys to the mint green BLM Forest Service Suburban that had been recently retired and was destined for public auction. "Just fucking with you, take the old Suburban. She's parked out back," Kyle had said with a sly smile. "Shit, the color might even trick you into thinking you're driving your Lu Lu."

"I doubt that Chief... but thanks for the wheels," Daymon had replied. He was taken aback to say the least, to the point that he had contemplated pinching himself to make sure he wasn't still asleep. Though the fire season up to then had been an unusually slow one, he still hadn't expected to hear the one word that up until that morning rarely came out of the Chief's mouth. But before the last consonant rolled from Chief Kyle's tongue he was up and halfway dressed.

"And Daymon..."

"Yeah Chief." *Here it comes,* Daymon thought. *This other shoe that's about to drop oughta fit Shaquille O'Neal.*

"Keep your phone on. In case the big one happens... I want to be able to get ahold of you and reel you back in," Chief Kyle said prophetically.

Daymon shouldered his pack before saying, "You got it Chief... thanks again."

As the iron door sealed off the last few inches of daylight he remembered hearing Chief Kyle yell at his back, "Give your Moms a hug for me."

He left without acknowledging Kyle's last order. He didn't want to hang around lest the mental sadist was playing some cruel joke and planned on revoking the liberty pass. He left Jackson Hole with a sense of serenity (a rare occurrence for him.) He had been known to say, "My mind is like a bad neighborhood, I go to visit, but I try to keep my visits short." Leaving with the knowledge that the Chief hadn't really been angry made it easier to reconcile the survivor's guilt that had been festering within him since he first heard about the entire crew's one way journey to Idaho Falls. The fact that there had been no further communication from them didn't bode well. Little did Daymon know at the time, but his growing the cajones to actually ask for the leave to see his mom in Utah, coinciding with Chief Kyle having a rare good day, were the two things that saved his life.

That Saturday had been the world's final normal day.

Chapter 14
Outbreak - Day 11
Winter's Compound
Eden, Utah

Camera 6 tripped first, its electronic alarm warbled loudly and grabbing the attention of anyone within earshot of the compound's security center. Seth reached across the desk and lowered the volume, spilling his bottled water in the process.

"Motherf..." he reined in the eff bomb just in time.

"What do you have?" Logan cried, ducking his head as he burst into the low ceilinged room.

"I was just getting there and this—"

Logan cut him off. "Forget about the water... what do you see on the monitor?"

"There's not a cloud in the sky, so the capture is pretty washed out from the sunlight.... Let me try something..." Seth fiddled with the contrast until the grainy image on the flat panel resembled two people walking side by side in the direction of the concealed airstrip. "Oh no! How in the *fuck* did they get inside the fence line?"

Lev burst through the door, went to a knee, and peered over Seth's shoulder as the room filled with the sounds of clomping boots and excited voices all chattering in tense, clipped syntax.

Though the image on the monitor was less than perfect it was evident one of the bipeds captured by the digital game camera was missing an arm.

"*We've got rotters!*" Lev bellowed.

Seth snatched up his radio. "Come in Gus. Camera 6 just picked up movement. Be careful... looks like we have rotters inside the perimeter." He released the transmit button and waited for a response.

Nothing.

He tried again. "Gus... this is Seth, if you cannot talk click your mic."

Click. Click.

Lev and Logan exchanged knowing looks.

***

Gus smelled carrion riding the air just moments before Seth's frantic voice came through his earpiece. Not wanting to give himself away he ignored the call and remained silent. His first thought was that a lone straggler, a crawler or maybe a child zombie had somehow wormed its way through or under the barbed wire and tripped the nearby trail camera.

Once again, but with more urgency, Seth's voice invaded his earpiece confirming there were rotters inside the fence.

Gus acknowledged what he already knew by clicking the transmit button on the two-way radio twice then continued scanning the forest floor twelve feet below for the source of the stench.

The well concealed two-person tree stand was in a copse of trees overlooking both the gravel road that connected with State Route-39 roughly two miles to the north, and the primitive airstrip bisecting the lush green meadow in front of him. For a brief moment he entertained the idea of climbing down and scouting on foot, then, remembering the wandering packs of rotters he witnessed tearing people alive in Salt Lake City he wisely decided to stay put.

Gus pressed the Bushnells to his eyes and glassed the clearing in the foreground. Then he panned along the tree line beyond where the compound's entrance was hidden and continued on to the right scrutinizing the single engine Cessnas and the two helicopters secreted under the canopy at the forests edge. With no walkers in sight he set the binoculars aside and fetched his LaRue Tactical M4. Chambered for the 5.56 NATO round and outfitted with an Eotech close quarter battle holographic sight with a flip down 3x magnifier, it was a perfect all-purpose weapon.

Ironically, Gus had liberated the rifle from its last owner a few miles south of Arsenal, Utah, moments after Dispatch in Salt Lake City had gone eerily quiet. He had just fled the National Guard's temporary triage center and the hastily erected FEMA shelters, both of which were overwhelmed with dead and dying, and had driven a few miles down I-15 when he made his final traffic stop.

***

The thirty-eight-year-old Salt Lake Sheriff pulled his cruiser alongside the parked Ford F-350 to perform a welfare check.

The truck was the same type of gun rack-equipped obscenely lifted 4x4 nearly every male in rural Utah owned or aspired to own one day.

Unfortunately the driver had already been infected and was beyond help, so with Glock drawn Gus opened the driver door, being careful to stay out of the male zombie's reach. Being a full thirty pounds lighter and a head shorter than the infected creature, he didn't want to get anywhere near its grabby hands and snapping teeth.

As the zombie fought and struggled to get to the *meat*, Gus went around and leaned in the passenger side and with the pointed end of his telescoping baton unlatched the good ol' boy's seatbelt. Before that day, he never thought he'd use the baton for anything other than ruining knees or elbows or skulls—anything he had to do in order to gain submission from unruly bad guys.

As soon as the belt popped the two-hundred-and-fifty pound monster slid off of the slick leather seat and hit the blacktop face first with a resonant snap. By the time Gus had closed the passenger door, the lurching, beer bellied cadaver was already up and stalking him around the truck.

Gus steadied his Glock on the truck's side mirror and methodically put two rounds into the center of the creature's already cratered face. Then, instead of returning to his patrol car, he took the dead man's Ford and his customized rifle and continued north to SR-39 then East to Eden, Utah.

That day it seemed like someone or something was directing his actions. Like he was a marionette and fate was pulling the strings.

Some called it divine intervention—others called it desertion.

***

Heavy footsteps combined with the firecracker like reports of snapping branches brought Gus back from his ten second journey to the past. He flicked up the 3x magnifier, tucked the rifle into his shoulder, and sighted on the spot where he guessed the culprit or culprits would emerge.

The one armed walker bulled its way into the clearing beneath the tree stand. The flesh on its remaining arm and legs bore deep lacerations from its one-sided battle with the thorn studded undergrowth. As Gus watched from above, the creature abruptly stopped and cocked its head like a dog. Then after swaying in place for a few seconds, apparently hearing something that Gus didn't, the one armed walker altered course and staggered off into the forest, moaning as it went.

***

In an identical tree stand near the far eastern edge of the property close to SR-39, Glenn Sampson, a forty-year-old former ski instructor from Park City, Utah, stood watch, listening to a pair of crows cawing overhead bickering like an old married couple.

Seth's voice, sounding stressed and nervous, crackled from the two way radio. "Rotters *are* coming your way and there are too many to count... better stay in the stand."

No shit. "Roger that," Sampson said. "Can we get some help out here?"

"They're two minutes out."

"Well tell them to *fuckin'* hurry—I can already smell the rotters."

The noisy birds went silent.

Sampson poked his head through the square cutout serving as a window.

Gasping for air, two men, one obviously helping the other along, wormed their way through the shadow filled underbrush.

Sampson shouldered his AR-15 and tracked them briefly before they melted back into the forest. *Holy shit... those weren't rotters,* Sampson thought to himself.

Just then, the smaller trees near the road began to quiver and sway. The moans and groans began, followed by what sounded to

Sampson like a herd of blind elephants making their way up the slight rise from the fence line bordering the road below.

Then he detected engine sounds in the distance—like one or more vehicles were on the move, heading south on SR-39.

The moans and breaking twigs and rustling leaves rose to a crescendo as the rotters emerged from the forest all at once. Clearly the uphill battle with Mother Nature had taken a toll. Weeping purple fissures covered every exposed inch on their bodies. Still they continued on, trudging lockstep in unfaltering pursuit of their quarry with only one thing on their collective minds—fresh meat.

***

"Alert *everyone* and make sure you break out weapons for *all* of the adults,"Logan barked as he absentmindedly twirled his black handlebar mustache, something he did when he was under a great deal of stress.

As soon as the order left Logan's mouth a symphony of electronic alarms sounded as the remaining game cameras concealed around the perimeter tripped in rapid succession.

Seth darted his eyes over the eight separate camera feeds displayed on the monitor, and after a few seconds said frantically, "We have rotters infiltrating from the northeast corner, the east perimeter near thirty-nine, and from the south. The cameras west and north near the entrance are still quiet." *And I hope they stay that way*, he thought. The idea of rotters and possibly bad guys with guns fully encircling the compound stood the hairs on his neck at attention.

"Just walkers?" Logan queried.

Seth pressed his face closer to the flat panel scrutinizing each individual pane. "As far as I can tell, but it's hard to tell from these images... at least none of them appear to be armed."

"Especially not this guy," Lev cracked, tapping the feed from camera six.

"The rotter's still got one arm, *smartass*," Seth shot back.

"Come on Lev... not now," Logan added as he snatched half a dozen Motorola radios off of the shelf near Seth's head. "Who's on security?"

Seth answered, "Sampson and Gus are in the stands. Jamie and Jordan are on the ground."

As he passed the handful of two-way radios to Lev, Logan said, "Here... distribute these and grab me a rifle." Then twirling his 'stache like a propeller, he added, "Who said it was OK for Jamie to take Jordan out there with her—considering the dirtbags we just killed? And Jordan is as green as they come."

"Jamie's a big girl. She knows the score. Don't worry Logan... Chief and the rest of his quick reaction force should be topside in a moment," said Lev, trying to reassure his friend who had done a poor job of keeping his crush on Jamie under the radar. "Besides, if it's just a few rotters Jamie can handle them with one of her foliage-covered arms tied behind her back."

The mere thought of his favorite woman dressed head to toe in her ghillie suit brought a brief smile to Logan's face.

"Seth... go get my brother. I don't care *what* he says, or how much he argues with you... and he will argue. Just make sure he comes back here with you," Logan said as he took the taller man's post.

Three men sidestepped their way through the security center heading towards the armory.

As an afterthought Logan yelled at the retreating men, "Make sure *everyone* vests up. There are bound to be bad guys with guns out there—rotters don't use wire cutters." *This has to be directly related to those fellas we killed the other day*, he thought to himself. Then he remembered the bullet-riddled zombies they had left in the middle of State Route 39. *Just like a trail of bread crumbs showing the way.* He cursed his stupidity soundly, hoping it wouldn't cost them their lives.

Chapter 15
Outbreak - Day 11
Schriever AFB
Colorado Springs, Colorado

Fully a day removed, Freda Nash couldn't stop reliving the solemn service.

General Desantos' funeral was not the first she had attended during her twenty year career.

A career spent working behind the scenes in one capacity or another with the 160th SOAR and the covert operators the Special Operations Aviation Regiment ferried to and from battle the world over.

Desantos' casket wouldn't be the last to resonate with the impact of dirt and rock. In her mind's eye she could see Cade, Lopez and the other shooters grieving over Mike's final resting place in the Colorado Desert. She kept seeing the tense expression paining Annie Desantos' face as the first volley from the twenty-one gun salute honoring her husband's ultimate sacrifice rang out. She remembered Annie holding her newborn, Mike Junior, while her twin daughters crushed in from both sides each with a tiny arm encircling Mom's waist. *The family circling the wagons,* Nash thought. What she would have given to experience that one more time.

She removed her cover with slow deliberate movements and placed the rigid navy blue hat on its wooden perch, wedged between a C-130 model airplane and a framed photo of her and a much younger—nearly carbon copy version of herself. Frozen in a loving embrace, the two women in the picture were standing in front of an enormous white house adorned with vertical box columns, dental molding, and multi-colored stained glass.

The petite woman unpinned the gray streaked brunette bob, releasing her shoulder length hair. Her gaze lingered on the photo which had been taken on orientation day in front of the Widney Alumni house on the USC campus—one of the best days of Freda Nash's life save for the day the young girl in the photo had been born. It seemed like she had escorted her daughter from Colorado to the West Coast only yesterday. Yesterday in Colorado, she thought, was nothing like that warm So Cal day in late August three years ago. In fact, she wanted to forget yesterday entirely.

Nash strode to the gray filing cabinet nestled in the corner partially obscured by an American flag. As she pulled on the top drawer, the tracks, which were in dire need of a shot of WD-40, screeched an ominous warning that seemingly implored her not to venture inside. Then a little voice in her head said, *It's after five somewhere.* After a second on tiptoes, armpit deep in the top drawer, she extracted the unopened bottle of premium tequila given to her by Mike Desantos *after* the famous Bin Laden raid in Abbottabad Pakistan. An olive branch no doubt—since the Major had been left out of the loop on that one. Only the President, his high level cabinet officials, two drone drivers and the SEAL and Delta commandos who were conducting the raid had known who Geronimo really was.

With an anticipatory grimace Freda slammed the drawer shut; the resulting rusty squeal warned, *You'll be sorry.* In no mood to heed her own common sense she pulled three shot glasses from deep within her desk, placing them in a neat line parallel with the name plate parked atop her desktop. The smell of pure agave tickled her nose when she cracked the seal, and after filling the three shots to the brim she took a long pull from the bottle.

While the flat screen monitor flickered to life, Nash retrieved the remote from underneath a pile of weeks' old paperwork that would never see the inside of a filing cabinet. She thumbed play, starting the recorded feed from the Global Hawk. Since she had already watched the mission unfold live she saw no reason to revisit the entire mission from start to finish. Nash bumped the DVR to 10x speed and watched the Delta teams in their three fast attack vehicles skitter along the screen looking like cockroaches fleeing the light. "There," she said aloud as the child zombies swarmed the FAV and proceeded to attack Mike Desantos. Trying to ignore the fateful moment, she let the DVR blaze ahead. *Out of sight, out of mind,* she told herself. *Yeah right.* She picked up the first shot glass downing the tequila without pause. "For you Cowboy," she said, choking from emotion more than the unaccustomed sting from the 80 proof alcohol.

She watched the special operations buggies dart along the freeway, like Speedy Gonzalez on amphetamines, before stopping abruptly atop an overpass. The operators hopped out and scurried around, machine guns blazing, while the second group armed the final nuclear device, all in an attempt to save Colorado Springs from the undead juggernaut.

Nash bumped the DVR speed to 30x, squinted her eyes, and waited for the inevitable flash. A few seconds later the screen went white. The major's finger hovered over the pause button, hitting it only when the feed returned to normal and after the camera zoomed in on the remnants of the walking dead. The horde, several hundred thousand strong, had been obliterated, their ashes darkening the two roiling mushroom clouds.

"Mission accomplished," she whispered, hoisting and quickly downing the second shot.

Once more Nash fingered the fast forward button, sending the hard drive into a fit of clicking and chirping. The rapidly advancing color feed changed to black and white and without looking at the transposed coordinates ticking by she knew it was the days old Keyhole satellite footage. She had risked career suicide by having the satellite retasked in order to confirm what her gut had already told her.

Parked in a geosynchronous orbit directly over Southern California, the military satellite recorded the very disturbing week old images. Nash felt her stomach free-fall as the white, concrete and glass Webb Tower, bracketed by Lyon Center and Fluor Hall, came into view. Blue-black smoke billowed from the fourteen-story student housing building. The career Air Force officer looked over her shoulder to make doubly sure that she was alone, then let the hot tears flow while staring at the carnage that had taken place in and around the USC campus. Scattered about the pristine grounds, bodies of victims and walking dead filled the screen. An emergency vehicle tore down the street in front of Fluor Hall, its destination a mystery. The sense Nash had harbored in her gut since Z Day plus three had just been confirmed. Nadia's personal safety never made it high enough on the Major's triage list. The country, in its final death throes, had inexplicably sucked up all of her time, attention, and resources. Therefore she had totally abandoned her only daughter to a fate unknown, and for that she would forever hold herself responsible.

"For you, Nadia," Nash expelled the words between body wracking sobs, and then finished the final shot of tequila. "I miss you honey..."

As the night wore on, frightening footage of Los Angeles falling to the dead churned across the flat screen, and the level of Patron Anejo in the hand blown glass bottle gradually closed the distance to the desk top. "Gotta be careful," Nash slurred to herself. "One too many and I might be tempted to put a bullet in Pug's brain myself."

***

Nash opened one eye. The 50th Space Wing logo caromed around the LCD flat panel. Leave it to the U.S. Air Force brass to squander the taxpayer's money on a vanity screensaver, she mused. Was there any other reason a flying toy like the Global Hawk could cost a hundred million dollars? The pork-loaded bills that had passed so easily through the Senate and the House of Representatives in the years before the Omega outbreak only added to the ballooning national debt which had been running away from its masters for more than a decade. She smirked, then tilted her head back and closed both eyes.

***

From her vantage point, the rectangular screen seemed to have been stood on end. She opened the other eye, and then became aware of her head's relation to the metal desk top and the pool of saliva lapping at her cheek.

92

What have you done Nash? she asked herself. It wasn't like her to let personal matters infiltrate her professional life. Being a career officer didn't mean you couldn't be human. It meant you had to be human on *your own* time. With the events of the last twenty-four hours and the possibility of more saboteurs roaming the base she should have never opened the bottle. And furthermore, she reasoned, if Colonel Shrill had come by, her ass would have been grass, and he would have been mowing it.

As she swiftly disposed of the three shot glasses and the damning bottle of *to-kill-ya* a very large transport flew at tree-top-level over her office. That it had come in from the east meant it had to be one of the Hercules that set out foraging for fuel hours earlier. As if on cue the second turboprop blazed overhead, also on approach to the westernmost runway.

The cacophony, though hard on her pounding head, was music to her ears.

Chapter 16
Outbreak - Day 11
Schriever AFB
Colorado Springs, Colorado

Motor Pool

Formalities out of the way, Brook climbed up into the cab and took her 'gunners' seat on the passenger's side. She placed her M4 between her legs, barrel pointing downwards with the butt stock fully collapsed.

Wilson emerged from behind the truck.

Brook watched him in the side mirror as he checked the tires on his side. *Kid's got a head on his shoulders,* she reasoned. *I hope he can drive this thing.*

The door creaked open and the spry young man hopped in. "So you're my gunner... better you than me," he opined.

"What makes you say that?"

"My track record with firearms hasn't been stellar," he said as he patted the handle of his prized Todd Helton-autographed Louisville Slugger, which had obviously seen better days and smacked more than just baseballs. "Let's just say I know how to wield this much better."

"You mean to tell me you don't have a gun."

Wilson nodded towards Brook's black rifle, his eyes tracking to the three magazines on the seat and the two easily accessible extra magazines secured by Velcro in the front pouches of her MOLLE rig and said, "No but it looks like you've got us both covered... and then some."

Without acknowledging the very astute observation she asked, "Have you been outside of the wire yet?"

"Today will be the first time since I got here from Denver."

"When was that?"

"Two days ago. My sister and I... along with two others were stranded on 25 north of here. This fella named Pug saved all of us... we came here in his truck."

Brook's face turned ashen as she absentmindedly fiddled with her carbine. "What was the guy's name—the one who saved you?" she asked.

"*Pug*... strange name. He's a strange guy—how he came upon us and where he disappeared to after quarantine is still an effin' mystery to me. I didn't even get to thank him."

"Tell me all about your trip from Denver," Brook said through gritted teeth.

"It's going to take a while. I'll tell you all about it as soon as we get underway. Right now... I've gotta go to the bathroom. I'll be right back," he said as he jumped out of the truck.

Five long minutes later Wilson returned.

Brook squirmed, barely able to contain her rising angst.

"Better now than when we're... *outside the wire*... that sounds like something John Wayne probably said in that one Vietnam war movie..."

"*The Green Berets*," Brook muttered as she rolled her window down and craned her head to see what was happening. Up near the front of the convoy, which was made up of ten large moving trucks and three military vehicles lined up bumper to bumper, she noticed the lead Humvee start up with a puff of black exhaust. Then she continued, "We're going to be on the move shortly... and the second you take your foot off of the brake you had better start spilling your guts."

Brook had the redhead's full attention. Wilson sat speechless, mind trying to reconcile why the lockjawed lady was holding him in such contempt.

A sudden knock on the driver's door caused Wilson to jump, freeing him from Brook's Medusalike glare.

Colonel Shrill, who had been walking down the line of U-Hauls giving one-on-one briefings to the civilian drivers, made a circular motion with his hand implying that he wanted Wilson to roll down his window.

"Yes sir," Wilson said nervously, his stomach in knots. He had a feeling the looming soldier had somehow found out his secret. Sasha's scathing diatribe replayed in his head—"What makes you think they will let you drive one of their trucks? You *had better* evaluate your last statement *Wilson*," the teen had said, spitting out his name, "you *are not* a good driver. You *totaled* Angela and Saul's Suburban in Castle Rock for eff's sake. What makes you think you can drive something bigger... with different results?"

Without responding to his sister's venomous attack he had left their tent in a huff with the recruitment flyer he had torn from the mess hall corkboard in hand, and went straight to the staging area. Two hours had elapsed since then and if he knew his sister—who when scorned would do anything to ruin the offending parties' day, week, or month—he was certain she somehow had a hand in this. Therefore he had no doubt in his mind that he was about to be yanked from the truck and sent packing.

"Brooklyn Grayson..." Shrill intoned, completely ignoring Wilson. "Your wish is apparently my command. You keep an eye on this kid," he said with a wink and tapped a thick finger on top of Wilson's boonie hat. "He says he's a pretty good driver."

"Will do Sir... and thanks for this opportunity," blurted Brook.

"Ear muffs, kid."

Wilson made a face but complied by cupping his hands over his ears.

Shrill smiled at the sight and said, "Believe me Brook, I know how you feel. I've been imprisoned on this base since Z day minus a week, give or take. Sure I've been busy... Lord knows that. But I'm going stir crazy. Get some, will you? The sooner we mop up these walking biohazards the sooner the rest of us can start searching for our loved ones."

Sensing movement reflected in the passenger mirror, Brook momentarily broke eye contact with the Colonel. A burly gun truck bristling with weapons had formed up on the *Dakota's* bumper.

Shrill handed a laminated map and a pair of radios across to Brook. He went over their basic functions and went on, "The freqs are set. Your call sign is Dakota"—Brook rolled her eyes—"don't stop unless the lead vehicle stops. Anyone else stops... breaks down, etcetera, keep moving. The soldiers on your six will check on 'em. Red... if you break down, or get a flat, hit a walker and can't continue... *anything—do not exit the vehicle.* The same holds for you Brook. Wait for the guys in the MRAP to come to your aid... any questions?"

Continuing to sit stock still with his eyes boring into the roll down door of the truck in front, Wilson inquired, "What exactly is an MRAP?"

"Stands for, Mine Resistant, Ambush Protected vehicle. That's the truck Staff Sergeant Lawson and the boys are riding in behind you. I don't think mines will come into play today, but the ambush part—it's a noisy rig so the Zs are going to come a running... or staggering at least. There are still a lot of them in and around Springs and the farther out you go the worse it gets. Gaines and his boys are good... but they aren't God. By the way... you all are honored to roll with the general today. Gaines is riding point in the lead gun truck," Shrill said, arching his eyebrows an inch.

Oh great, Brook thought to herself, wondering if the man who had recently been promoted to replace Mike Desantos still held a grudge against her. Although she wasn't proud of the sneaky stowaway move she had pulled in order to go along on the hospital foraging mission, she didn't regret her actions. The byproduct of the mission alone made her act of subterfuge worthwhile—because the antibiotics she brought back had saved her ailing brother's life. Then she winced in pain as she remembered, one more time, that Carl was gone forever.

"Carry on," Shrill said stone-faced.

Wilson watched the tall Colonel scrutinize the dead Presidents of Mount Rushmore as he strode by the U-Haul heading towards the hulking MRAP. "Intense," he exclaimed wide eyed.

Brook remained silent, her thoughts focused inward.

Chapter 17
Outbreak - Day 11
Logan Winter's Compound
Eden, Utah

Strident banging, like a jackhammer on a construction site, nudged Duncan from his stupor. He came to feeling like a dump truck had driven over his brain, and then, making matters worse, promptly reversed, depositing a full load of sand in his mouth. Just to make sure it wasn't actually swelling to beanbag size and then imploding in on itself— black hole-like, he gripped his throbbing head with both hands. Every action, word, and memory after the last beer from the six pack was a blur—choppy like some artsy Tarantino flick.

"*Arrgghh*," was all he could muster. *I sounds kinda like a zombie*, he mused. His mission: *to do a little forgettin'*, as he had stated so eloquently the night before, and the night before that, had been accomplished in spades. If he wasn't careful, he told himself between crushing throbs, he might have to answer the dreaded Twenty Questions. Hello, my name is Duncan...

Begging God to ease the pressure pounding in his head, he focused on the ceiling which was cut up by evenly spaced steel cross members that ran the length of the rectangular-shaped subterranean dwelling. His first impression of the room was that it had the feel of an old Fleetwood single wide: thin pile carpet covered the cold floor, and pale wood paneling mostly hid the rust colored steel walls. Institutional plastic chairs and tables, sturdy and functional, furnished each working and living space. The two dozen people sharing the good sized bunker slept on bunk beds yet still had enough elbow room to keep them from wanting to strangle each other. Duncan had to admit—Logan did a stellar job of acquiring the steel shipping containers for the right price, and with the help of friends and a rented Caterpillar excavator, had arranged and buried all ten in a semi H shape. The rigid boxes measuring twenty feet long, eight feet wide, and eight feet tall were outfitted as a bug out shelter where Logan and his closest friends could retreat in the event of a societal collapse.

Duncan was certain of the fact that *never* in his baby bro's wildest dreams did the kid envision the fall of civilized society caused by the worldwide spread of a deadly virus capable of making the newly dead reanimate.

Baby bro spent his inheritance wisely, Duncan thought to himself between nauseating pulses of pain and cold sweats. *If only I had done the same.*

A succession of clangs echoed somewhere in the distance followed by another series of sharp raps on the door.

"Duncan... you up?" a muffled voice inquired from the other side.

"Am now... come on in, I'm decent," Duncan drawled. "Just *do not* slam that door."

The Vietnam-era aviator recognized the tall, rail thin fellow the moment the door cracked.

"To what do I owe the *pleasure* Mr. Seth?"

"Get dressed, take this, and follow me."

Pushy runt, Duncan thought. Then he took the offered weapon, checked the safety, removed then checked the magazine and gently laid the AR style rifle next to him on the bunk. As he laced his boots he quipped in his southern drawl, "What... I don't deserve a good morning?"

"Morning happened hours ago," Seth said with a wan smile.

Grabbing his head with one hand and the weapon with the other, Duncan rushed out the door close on Seth's heels.

When they arrived at the security room it was jam packed with people focusing their attention on the monitors.

"Hey brother... hell of a wakeup call. Most of our security cameras have been tripped. I need you to take these three men with you and go secure the aircraft and keep eyes on the western edge of the compound," Logan said as he tossed a Motorola to his older brother. "Freq is already set—just push to talk."

"Copy that... got any aspirins?"

"Can it wait?" Logan asked.

"In for a dime, in for a dollar," Duncan replied sardonically then mumbled a few expletives; turning around he smiled and greeted the men, all three of whom were armed with AR-15 style rifles and in their late forties or early fifties he guessed. "We're all equals here... why don't ya show me the way boys," he said.

"Be careful old man," Logan said to Duncan as he exited the room.

Suddenly the Motorola base station crackled to life. "Sampson here, be advised you have thirty plus rotters coming your way... and I can't be sure but looks like they are hunting two men."

"Copy that. Stay put—Lev, Chief, and Seth are headed your way... Logan out," he said.

"Roger that," Sampson answered.

"You still OK out there Gus?" Logan queried.

"Gus here... I spotted only one rotter moving from the northeast to the east."

"Did it have only one arm?"

"Yes sir."

"Hold tight for now, you've got four men coming your way, Ed, Carter, Phillip and my brother Duncan. They're securing the aircraft."

"Roger that," Gus replied.

***

Lev, Chief and Seth struck out on a course that would have them flanking Sampson's hide.

Duncan watched Ed and Phillip exit ahead of him. Ed, who was heavyset and balding, took ten steps to the left and went to one knee. Phillip, rail thin and with a swarthy complexion, took a knee on the right. Both men looked alert, keeping their heads on a swivel with rifles at the ready.

101

Good job, Logan, Duncan thought to himself. *Someone's taking security seriously.* He sniffed the air—no carrion—*yet.* The door closed behind him with a soft thud. Carter secured the locks then replaced the camouflage netting.

"This way," Carter said as he trotted towards the green meadow which was barely visible through the trees.

The sun's rays infiltrating the branches overhead were like miniature branding irons to Duncan's optic nerves. At that moment, sorely missing his sunglasses, he cursed the God of hangovers—if there even was such a being.

He searched for his shades in the pockets of his ACUs which seemed to him like the cup holders in a minivan—plentiful and poorly placed. He came up empty. Resenting the brutal orb above, he followed behind Phillip as the four of them crossed the clearing towards the far tree line.

***

Jamie stopped quickly, brought a closed fist to head level, and glanced over her shoulder to evaluate her newest student.

Standing stock still and nearly invisible in her ghillie suit, Jordan had read the hand signal correctly.

Flashing thumbs up Jamie melted back into the forest, picking her way north while trying to demonstrate proper stealthy movement.

Watching her own boots a little too closely, Jordan nearly collided with Jamie who held a closed fist in the air. Jordan stopped at once; then she heard the soft exhaust notes and the thrumming tires passing on the road to their right.

"Let's get back," Jamie whispered. She pulled out her radio and called the compound. "This is Jamie... I just heard multiple vehicles pass by our position heading south on SR-39."

Logan answered and said, "Where are you?"

"We're south of the compound. A few hundred yards from the hunting cabin," she said, alluding to the scene of a violent shootout she had been involved in a few days ago.

"Is Jordan with you?"

"Yes," Jamie replied.

Silence.

"*Why*... is that a problem?"

"We've got at least two dozen rotters inside the fence. I don't want you to get bit or shot by one of our own so it's probably best if you two find a place to hole up for a while... OK?"

"Sure. Then we'll circle around and I'll show Jordan the emergency hatch," Jamie said in a low voice.

"Please be careful out there," Logan said softly.

"That's sweet, Logan. See you soon."

Jordan tugged on one of the burlap strands on Jamie's ghillie. "I think he likes you," she whispered.

Jamie smiled. "I know. He thinks he's in stealth mode." She turned the volume down and stowed the radio. "I've known since we ran from the cities."

"And..."

"Now is not the time, but *maybe* when this Omega stuff is sorted." Jamie slung her rifle and drew her semi-auto pistol, checked the chamber and pushed ahead, picking her way through the ankle grabbing creepers.

***

Chief sniffed the air then motioned the three-man patrol forward—Seth in the middle—Lev watching their six.

Seth had only taken a few steps forward, trying to keep an eye on Chief's hand signals, when the hundred and twenty-some-odd-pounds of stinking flesh caught him blind side.

Grunting something unintelligible, the emaciated man picked himself up from the ground, naked and shivering—seemingly pleading for help with his eyes.

Seth jumped to his feet, training his rifle on the pathetic sight whose arms were zip cuffed behind him with a generous portion of silver duct tape stretching from ear to ear.

"Seth... what the hell are you waiting for? Rip it off already," Lev chided the younger man.

"What if he has a mustache?"

"That's the least of his worries," said Chief. "He has many bites on his back."

The man's eyes bulged and he struggled to stand.

"Seth. Do it."

"OK. OK," Seth answered and gripped a corner of the tape.

Sweating profusely, violent tremors wracking his body, the man's eyes clenched shut.

With a quick tug Seth removed the tape.

"Aaaaghh," cried the man.

"He *had* a 'stache—" Chief observed.

Lev pulled his Beretta, took a step back, and started peppering the man rapid-fire with questions. "Who were you running from?"

The man stammered then answered meekly, "Them... the monsters."

"Are you alone?"

"No..." the man sagged to his knees. "They got my friend Alan back there a ways," he added, gesturing towards the woods with his head.

"And that's when you got bit?" Lev asked.

"Yes... " The man started to cry.

Seth, dancing from foot to foot, asked nervously. "Want me to cut him loose?"

"Can't chance it." Then gesturing with his pistol Lev asked, "You didn't say who did this to you?"

"I have no idea... we were ambushed outside of Logan last night. They took our van... *oh man*. Our food and our gun. *Everything* we had was inside that van."

Chief interjected. "You didn't see *anything?*"

The man shook his head vigorously. "No, they pointed flashlights in our eyes and then put a hood over my head."

"How far back is your friend?" Lev asked.

"A hundred feet... I don't know."

"Get up," Lev said.

The man struggled but finally got to his feet. As the other two men watched Lev led the man into the woods.

Thirty seconds later, a grim look on his face, Lev returned.

"This way," Chief said, "Watch your spacing... the rotters are close."

***

Sampson had been ready for a shift change even before his started. Growing weary of the tree stand, he decided he'd take a quick recon of the road. See if he could find the breach in the fence. Maybe repair it and feel a little more useful.

He descended to the forest floor, pistol in hand, and slid into the dense undergrowth. The going was as tough as it had sounded when the rotters were ascending the hill. He noticed that every branch that slapped him left traces of blood and fluids on his fatigues. After much more work than it was worth he was standing beside the road at the bottom of the hill. He inspected the ruined barbed wire fence. All three strands had been neatly clipped near the gnarled wooden post, leaving Logan's property open to man and rotter alike.

Pressed firmly into the road's soft shoulder, the pair of tire tracks suggested a vehicle had stopped here recently.

He holstered his pistol and stood with his hands resting on his hips, scanning the stretch of blacktop in either direction.

Nothing.

"Someone set us up," he said aloud. "*And* they want us dead."

The two-way radio warbled, and then Logan's voice emanated from his pocket. "We need everyone back to the clearing *now*. There are rotters everywhere."

He popped the radio in his pocket then pivoted about to leap across the culvert.

Staggering down the hill, a barely perceptible hiss escaping its parted jaws, the one-armed *first turn* had built up a head of steam.

The zombie lurched between the fence posts; its forehead clipped Sampson on the temple, knocking him to the blacktop where he lay on his back in a daze, watching black tracers dart about the cerulean sky.

After falling into the ditch the zombie rolled onto its distended stomach and immediately began a one-armed breast stroke, clawing its way towards the meat.

Chapter 18
Outbreak - Day 11
Schriever AFB
Colorado Springs, Colorado

Motor Pool

Hurry up and wait had finally taken on a real meaning for Brook. She hadn't fully grasped what Cade had meant when he used the term to voice his displeasure at the Army's lack of expediency in just about everything it did. Then, finally, after what seemed like an eternity sitting and sweltering inside the truck in full battle rattle, Brook heard the words she had been anticipating. The Motorola crackled and a voice informed the convoy they would all be "Oscar Mike in five."

On the move, she thought. "Five minutes Wilson. Better start warming up your vocal chords."

Then as soon as the U-Haul started creeping forward, in an ominous tone Brook said one word, *"Pug,"* then glared at Wilson.

As Wilson recounted his flight from Denver (leaving out *all* of the driving mishaps as well as *Operation Arm Removal*) Brook listened minimally, dividing her attention between the Zs pressing in on the fence and the eleven-vehicle convoy spooling out ahead of them. Wilson had Brook's undivided attention only when he came to the part of his story when he and the other survivors first crossed paths with Pug.

The second that Wilson finished his story Brook began the inquisition. "What is Ted's last name?"

"I couldn't tell you. Sasha and I only met Ted and his partner William after the dead started eating *peeps*."

"Did your psychiatrist neighbor Ted interact with Pug?"

Wilson mulled over the question before answering. "Some words went back and forth between those two—most of the interactions *were not* positive."

Seemingly on the verge of an epiphany, Brook pumped Wilson for more information. "Did Pug seem *threatening* or *homicidal* to Ted and William—or to you and your sis?"

"The dude was creepy and forward—but not *threatening* or *homicidal*—not to us. The way I see it he singlehandedly saved our collective butts," Wilson proffered. He hadn't wanted to give Pug *any* extra accolades but if the facts were what the lady wanted—then that's what she was going to get.

"If I heard you correctly, you said that when Pug came on the scene he seemed totally coherent. He was in control of all of his faculties, engaged multiple Zs unflinchingly, and then he *introduced* himself as *Francis* before he told you all that he wanted to be called *Pug*."

With a bewildered look Wilson asked, "Why do you want to know so much about the dude?"

"My husband told me that Pug had something to do with the fire." She paused for a beat and took a deep breath. "The fire in which William and numerous others perished. I'm sorry... but I can't tell you anymore," Brook replied forcefully.

Wilson tried to pry further but his words were snuffed by Brook's icy glare.

The convoy began to slow as they neared the front gates. But Wilson's eyes were not on the road; he continued staring at Brook while trying to fully comprehend how a person of her stature—a woman no less—could intimidate him so. Sensing the Dakota truck about to hit the U-Haul in front of them, Brook reached for the grab handle and shouted, "*Hit your brakes!*"

"*Shit!*" exclaimed Wilson as his Louisville Slugger, half a dozen bottles of water and their lunch, which happened to be MREs, shot off the bench seat and landed on the floorboards near their feet.

Brook glanced disdainfully at the poor excuse for a driver, then directed her gaze forward at the orange and silver rollup staring her straight in the face. "Almost ate their lunch, Wilson. Are you sure you weren't *misrepresenting* your behind-the-wheel prowess to Colonel Shrill?"

"*Positive*," Wilson lied. Then he asked, "Why are we stopped?"

"The dead gather at the gates. Most of the walkers stay in downtown Springs but a good number of them straggle in either from the city, the suburbs, or the surrounding countryside. Just a few days ago there were hundreds... if not thousands out there," Brook said as she unknowingly rubbed her shoulder, fondly reminiscing on her time in the guard tower behind the sniper rifle. "We have to wait for the guards to put down the walkers before they open the gates for us."

"Gotcha," Wilson said.

Listening to the sporadic bursts of automatic rifle fire, Brook sat in the truck and stewed. Ever since the outbreak and those first unforgettable days when she had been forced to put down her parents she had been a different person. Now she hated being left out of the fight. *Don't worry Brooklyn,* she reassured herself, *you'll get your turn soon enough.* While the guards cleared out the walkers she used the time to process the key points of Wilson's story and revisit his first impressions of Pug. She adjusted her helmet so the straps would stop biting into her chin. "Are you sure Pug was *grounded?* That he wasn't talking to himself... or speaking to a figment of his imagination?" she asked, breaking the silence.

"His *name* seemed retarded but he wasn't. He wasn't crazy either. Trust me... I worked *fast food* in South Denver. I know *retarded.* And I know *crazy.*"

Wilson's final statement changed Brook's hunch into a solidly handicapped certainty. She snatched up the Motorola. "This is Brook Grayson in the Dakota truck. I need to speak to General Gaines— *now!*"

"Wait one," the monotone male voice on the other end instructed.

Brook said nothing.

Who in the heck is this lady, Wilson thought as Brook's stature grew to giant size in the impressionable twenty-year-old's mind.

The Motorola spewed an irritated voice. *"Brook Grayson... how in the heck did you weasel your way along for the ride this time?"*

"That's not important right now *General,*" replied Brook firmly, her tone with the general making Wilson flinch.

In the lead vehicle Gaines massaged his temples as he watched his men drag the leaking zombie bodies from the roadway. "You sure are a burr under my blanket, Brook. You should feel blessed that Captain Grayson holds you in such high regard," he said, tongue in cheek. "What can I do for you ma'am? And make it quick because we are about to leave the Green Zone and enter Indian Country."

"I need you to get ahold of Shrill or Nash. Have one of them locate the civilian psychiatrist named Ted who entered the base and served his quarantine at the same time as Pug. If this guy Ted has the credentials, he needs to do an evaluation of Pug... provide you with a clear *before* and *after* report. I have a hunch the murderer was sent here with a role to play and then for some reason or another he went off of his meds somewhere along the way—"

Gaines cut her short. "Brook, Brook—take a deep breath."

At once Brook became cognizant that Wilson, who had been able to hear the entire conversation, was looking at her with one arched brow and his head cocked aside. Then he mouthed the words *"murderer"* and *"sent here"* and a look of bewilderment parked on his face. Still locking eyes with the redhead, Brook took Gaines' advice and refilled her lungs.

"I don't give a rip if that man's mommy didn't breast feed him long enough. That crazy *son of a gun* is still a *murderer* no matter how you spin it... so what *in the hell* is a second look into his mind going to divulge, Missus Grayson?" Gaines asked in a tired sounding voice.

The two-way radio stayed silent for half a minute as the U-Haul's tires hummed along the blacktop.

To Brook it sounded like Gaines wanted her to butt out and keep her hypothesis to herself. After all, who could blame him? Though it hadn't, the stunt Brook had pulled sneaking onto the CH-

47 amongst the chalk of Rangers could have ended badly. She became his problem then—and she was his problem now. But Brook had a stake in the game—she had lost her big brother and she owed it to Carl to call the general's hand on the issue. "Cade told me Pug is not the only personality inhabiting that man's mind. If Ted what's-his-name notices a drastic change in Pug's demeanor... or picks up on what Cade mentioned to me, then he might know a way to get him to talk. Maybe—if you pump the right pills into the man, you just might be rewarded with a *lucid* prisoner—one that you can properly interrogate."

"You are going to owe me one Brooklyn Grayson. I will do this for you... I'll do this because I know you aren't crazy... *are you?*"

That's two favors I owe the brass, she thought. Then as the Motorola went silent she glanced sideways at Wilson who had been hanging on every word, and exclaimed, "I can't believe it. The general is on board..."

Shaking his head Wilson said, "I'd be excited but I'm lost... now I think it's *your* turn to tell *me* the *whole* story."

Brook recounted to Wilson everything that had happened between Pug's release from quarantine until the soldiers in bunny suits found him bawling like a baby alone in his tent.

She omitted only two facts: that her brother Carl had been among the victims and that both the stocks of antiserum and the data used in its manufacture had been lost in the conflagration.

Shuddering with revulsion and trying to come to grips with the fact that he had been rubbing elbows with the psychopath, Wilson stated in a low voice, "Wow... he killed all those people *and* William in cold blood. That is *so* hard for me to believe... he didn't seem like a deranged murderer."

Brook tilted her head back until her helmet touched the seatback and stared at the stained headliner. After a mile or two of silence she said, "It's a lot to process... but *all* of it *was* his doing. However, there may be more like him on the base. That's why my husband and the others need to interrogate him further."

Wilson, who was still paying more attention to Brook than the road, replied, "You know... I assumed both of the fires were accidental. Now I'm effin pissed that I didn't notice the coincidence. I guess I was still tired and in shock from our run from Denver."

"Pug and the fires that he set took us all by surprise... " Brook said in a voice tinged with sadness.

Suddenly remembering that Ted probably hadn't seen his partner since they all had been put in quarantine, Wilson blurted, "Oh man. When Ted finds out Pug killed William he's going to tear him limb from limb. Ted's a *big* bear of a guy..."

Trying to sound reassuring Brook added, "Don't worry. Shrill and Nash will treat Ted with kid gloves... they will tell him *everything* he needs to know..."

"You mean *after* they *use* him—*right?*" Wilson stated, narrowing his eyes.

"Probably," Brook conceded, looking away.

Chapter 19
Outbreak - Day 11
Grand Junction, Colorado

In the grand scheme of things, the city of Grand Junction, Colorado didn't fully live up to its name. Established alongside the Colorado River, which received the smaller Gunnison River from the south, Grand Junction had been a crossroads for commerce between Utah and Colorado and a place to stop and resupply for wide-eyed expansionists heading to Nevada and beyond.

Compared to Denver and Colorado Springs, the city of sixty thousand people failed to peg the *grand* meter anywhere near the top of the scale. Although not Grand Canyon *grand*, or Grand Central Station *grand*, the city still spread out across a sizable plot of western Colorado.

To the north, Book Cliffs stood sentinel, while backstopping the western edge of Grand Junction, Colorado National Monument loomed. Painted red and orange by the mid-morning sun, the series of cliffs, canyons, and red rock mesas looked like they were transplanted from the surface of Mars; like arthritic fingers, huddles of gnarled Joshua trees probed skyward. Ari jinked the black helo around the taller specimens while diving in and out of the many weather-scoured arroyos. The SOAR (Special Operations Aviation Regiment) pilot was in total control of the helicopter, and seemed to have formed a symbiotic relationship with the Ghost Hawk dubbed Jedi One-One.

Ari halved his airspeed on approach to the city, and, in a gut wrenching maneuver, popped the helo to five hundred feet AGL (Above Ground Level) in order to survey the rapidly advancing sprawl through his smoked visor. After a drawn out whistle, he said, "That's a *bigger* city than I was expecting. I sure as hell hope the Zs aren't congregating anywhere near Grand Junction Regional."

Craning his neck to see the ground through the port side glass, Tice added, "I've been in and out of most of the airports in the CONUS when I was assigned to the Joint Terrorism Task Force... took the grand tour just after the 9-11 attacks. Since then *all* of the airports have added pretty formidable fencing. The Department of Homeland Security and the FAA mandated the extra security measures to keep unwanted folk from sneaking in with *deadly* stuff."

Ari couldn't resist. "Yeah... like the *genius* underwear bomber. How's that working out for you, Mister Sits to Pee?"

After hearing about the fall of Fort Bragg first-hand from Brook and the fall of Camp Williams similarly from Duncan, Cade had a hard time putting any faith in fencing. A few feet of chain-link topped with razor wire keeping out a small cadre of terrorists or drug smugglers *maybe*, but a thousand hungry, determined, and mindless ghouls, *no fucking way*. "Where is your secondary forage location if this one is no go?" he asked.

Durant consulted the flight computer, which was still being fed GPS (Global Positioning System) and other necessary navigation information from the series of GPS satellites controlled by the 50th Space Wing back at Schriever AFB. "Well sir," Durant replied, "we'd have to probe further into Utah. Moab has a smaller airport *and*, more importantly, a much smaller population—about five thousand, give or take..."

"Moab... been there. The place has awesome slickrock tracks and *microbeers*... anyone bring a mountain bike?" Ari quipped.

"We aren't on vacation, Night Stalker. We're on safari," Lopez said darkly.

For the interruption, Cade shot both men an annoyed look.

After the peanut gallery piped down, Durant continued. "The downside of the Moab facility is that it caters to general aviation only.

The chance of us getting a full load of JP-8 at Canyonlands is a crap shoot at best."

"Besides, from where we are now..." Ari did some calculations in his head and continued, "that's about a two hundred and twenty mile round trip, and it looks like we would be backtracking to the south to boot. Even for this numb ass aviator *that* is a lot of flying for a whole lot of maybes."

Cade chimed in. "I'm not comfortable with *maybes*. Since we don't have eyes on Grand Junction Regional yet... why all the hypothesizing?"

"It's what we do, Sir. Cover all the bases," Durant replied.

"How bad can it be down there?" Tice asked.

Ari finessed the controls, making course corrections as a hot thermal updraft bounced the helo like a ship at sea. "*Jesus Christ...*" Ari cried. "Did the *spook* just say what I think he said? You *never, ever,* say jinxin' words like that in my presence."

Tice greeted the comment with a casual shrug of his shoulders.

As the Ghost Hawk rapidly cut the distance to the city, Cade tilted his neck in order to see through the cockpit glass between Ari and Durant. Wisps of smoke curled into the air. The entire southernmost part of the city was obliterated; the conflagration, having already burned itself out, had left standing only the scorched shells of a handful of concrete structures. The metal streetlight standards and the few scattered trees that had somehow escaped the cleansing fire cast shadows over the soot-covered thoroughfares. Like alabaster soldiers trudging through a blackened battlefield, scattered groupings of zombies moved about on the ground.

"We are approaching the airport. It'll be on the port side. I'm going to orbit once and set down quickly when we find what we need," Ari said via the shipboard comms. "All eyes need to be on the lookout for a fueling station or a mobile fuel bowser."

"We're going to have to do a hot refueling. Meaning the pilot *will not* cut power. Since a fire would be very *baaad* I'm going to have to egress with the shooters," Hicks added. "If we see *any* Zs roaming the grounds, one of you will have to stay on the mini-gun and the other three are going to have to watch my back while I work."

Durant's voice invaded the comms. "Don't look now, but I think... the airfield is full of Zs."

"OK, heads up gentlemen," said Ari. "Make sure you watch yourselves around the tail rotor. *Very important*, at all costs keep the Zs away from our ride... the last thing I need is for one of those things to martyr itself into my tail rotor. Be advised—if that happens—*we will all be walking home.*"

Cade stole a look. The scene below started a dull ache in the pit of his stomach. It was the small dose of fear that always came along for the ride whenever he went into harm's way.

"Hey Lucy, you've got some esplainin' to do," Ari deadpanned over the comms. "Looks like someone crashed the gate and left it wide open... *literally.*"

In order to let the operators come up with their game plan, Ari kept the bird close to the deck and moving at a crawl. As soon as the black helo crossed over the southwest corner of the airport, the walkers' point of entry became evident.

Tice spotted the deep furrow in the black earth first. He cut in, "Wow... she came up *waaay* short. Must have been moving at a helluva clip too, judging by the dirt she plowed after the initial impact."

The debris field started roughly one hundred yards before the crushed cyclone fence, where a piece of the plane's landing gear, seemingly intact and with the wheels still attached, had become embedded in the churned up sod. The jetliner's nearly unscathed tail section, emblazoned with the glossy scarlet and royal blue Delta Airlines logo, lay canted to one side, directly on the center line of the rubber-streaked runway. The majority of the jetliner's burned out skeleton rested some four hundred yards farther and off to the right of Runway 11/29. Littering the distance between the site of impact and the scorched earth marking Delta 1221's final resting place were jagged pieces of fuselage, greasy hunks of scorched human flesh, and fluttering in the oppressively hot desert air—hundreds of colorful fabric scraps and the ruptured pieces of luggage that once contained them.

"Shouldn't they have at least foamed the runway?" asked Maddox, his visor partially obscuring his bewildered look.

"I'd be willing to bet the airport was closed and the emergency personnel had already vamoosed. There was nobody left *to* foam the runway when the *heavy* came in," said Durant, pointing out the dayglow yellow emergency vehicles still parked next to an oversized aviation hangar directly adjacent to the rambling airport terminal.

"I concur," Ari said solemnly as he circled a hundred feet above the blackened wreckage. "Poor bastard probably had no one in the tower to talk to, no one on the ground, and probably no glideslope to follow. As for the fire guys... if I were in their boots I would have gone home too. *I woulda been looking for my family.*" Ari spoke the last sentence in a small voice. Then, with a tear caressing his cheek, he thought how grateful he was for the flight helmet's smoked visor.

"Eleven o'clock port side," Durant intoned.

"I see them," Ari grunted as he pulled heavy g's nosing the near silent Jedi Ride around in a tight circle.

Cade also saw the two white tanker trucks, the words *West Slope Aviation* plastered in big red letters on their sides. The vehicles sat on the tarmac positioned in a manner that told Cade someone had recently refueled from them, and he silently prayed that they hadn't already been sucked dry.

He made out dozens of unmoving zombies carpeting the ground in a rough semi-circle which extended from the near side of the tankers. He also noted the staggering walkers, which numbered no less than fifty, loitering dangerously close to the spot where Ari needed to set the Ghost Hawk down.

"It's going to be tight," Ari cautioned. "Hold on to your hats, ladies."

"Switch me places," Tice said to Hicks.

"Are you familiar...?"

Tice cut off Hicks before he could finish the interrogation. "I'm proficient with the Dillon mini. Shot the shit out of them in training... never got a chance to in combat though."

Hicks relinquished the gun. "They're pretty much idiot proofed," he said while he unlatched the cabin door. "Use it *only* as a last resort. And remember... *short bursts*, short as in a fraction of a second short."

"Copy that," Tice said as he clicked on the safety strap, plugged his helmet into the nearest receptacle, and started reacquainting himself with the complex weapon system. *Idiot proofed my ass. What the hell do I have to do to earn these guys' respect?*

Cade, Lopez and Maddox swapped their flight helmets for their smaller and much lighter tactical ballistic helmets.

In order to communicate with the Delta operators and act as another set of eyes while they were on the ground, Durant switched the onboard comms to match their frequency. "Mic check. How copy?" he said.

Cade flashed the co-pilot a thumbs up; Lopez and Maddox also followed suit.

Ari, who could now be heard in everyone's helmets, said, "We're good to go... wheels down in three mikes."

As he unplugged from the bulkhead, and donned Tice's tactical helmet, Hicks's thumb hinged up indicating he was good to go.

Ari engaged the Ghost Hawk's landing gear which locked into place with a solid clunk.

Hicks hauled open the starboard side door and immediately a superheated blast of gut churning stench invaded the helo. Riding the turbulent air, the sickly sweet smell of dead meat co-mingled with the chopper's kerosene-tinged exhaust instantly triggered Tice's gag reflex which in turn started an unstoppable chain reaction inside of him. As he fought to hold down the rising bile, his overactive salivary glands went to work only hastening the process.

Again the helo shimmied, buffeted by an invisible pillar of superheated desert air.

Sensing his stomach about to let go and acting purely on reflex, Tice made the mistake of poking his head into the slipstream where it was nearly ripped off due to the added weight of his flight helmet.

"What are you doing?" Hicks yelled. "We've got bags for that—"

Tice heard nothing but the throaty roar of rushing wind mixed with the subliminal hum of the main rotor before he vomited. The puke spewed from the CIA man's mouth and entered the air vortex surrounding Jedi One-One. Instantly, bits of undigested spaghetti and meatball MRE, which now resembled an Orange Julius, were blasted right back into the cabin.

A look of disgust evident, Hicks methodically wiped the white bits of noodle and reddish-gray meat splatter from his face, and then dabbed at the particles clinging to the interior of the Ghost Hawk. "For fuck's sake Spook, we've still got a long way to go... and now I'm wearing half the contents of your stomach."

"Sorry," Tice sheepishly announced to everyone aboard as he transferred oily spittle from the corner of his mouth to the back of his gloved hand.

As the runway unspooled below the helicopter, Cade shot a stern look, and then took a rare swipe at the CIA man. "Your shooting better impress me, Tice. In fact, if you want to live this one down—then you're really going to have to shine during this *entire* mission. Once a puker... always a puker," he bellowed.

"I'll second that," Ari chimed in. "And if you don't rise to the occasion, when we get back to Schriever we'll get you a commemorative *"Puker"* patch that you can Velcro to your ACUs."

More grunt than words, Tice said, "I'll pass, but I will accept my *'I saved Schriever by jury-rigging a few nukes,'* patch when we get back to base. Who knows... maybe you ballbreakers might still be in need of my expertise." He shot a smart ass grin at Ari who was eyeballing him in the curved mirror atop the flight instruments. Then, looking ground ward, he powered up the electric mini-gun and tested its range of motion by panning it back and forth. Once he had a general idea of its coverage and blind spots, he flashed thumbs up to Hicks and said, "Good to go."

Durant checked in with the communications shack back at Schriever, informing the officer monitoring the mission that Jedi One-One was going wheels down for a refuel. Then a nagging question struck him, *Why hadn't Major Nash responded to the situation report personally?*

"Wheels down in one mike," Ari said, alerting everyone aboard Jedi One-One. "Stay frosty. I'm taking two slow passes. Clear as many walkers from the tarmac as you can—and Tice—make sure you *do not* hit either one of those fuel trucks."

No shit, Sherlock, Tice thought, wondering who hung the plank labeling him their personal whipping boy around his neck.

On the initial pass Cade succeeded in felling a dozen walkers and taking chunks out of several others. Give him a M249 SAW, he thought, and the numbers would be vastly different. Unfortunately, like the onboard mini-gun, a light machine gun with a cyclic rate of eight hundred rounds per minute, such as the SAW, wouldn't be the weapon to use effectively around a few thousand gallons of JP-8—especially not from a platform in flight.

When the Ghost Hawk finished the final approach, Cade and Hicks emptied their mags into the walkers and prepared for egress.

As the ground rushed up, Cade crouched low and steadied his breathing. He changed mags and charged his silenced SCAR, then, following Lopez's lead, performed a hasty signing of the cross.

Before the wheels kissed the tarmac, Hicks's boots hit the ground running. He took a few long strides aft, brought his M4 to bear, and engaged three walkers, one female and two male, who were dangerously close to the spinning tail rotor. The nearest Z, an elven-featured female clad in a summery ensemble consisting of a watermelon hued halter top complete with spaghetti straps and a pair of white, hip hugging short-shorts, caught his first salvo. Three rounds of 5.56 hardball walked from her pointed chin to the hairline above her right eye. The petite creature's pale emaciated body rocketed from the ground following the same trajectory as the scrambled contents of her cranium. While airborne, her corpse completed a half twist compliments of the triple mule kick delivered by the bullets' kinetic energy, and then, arms outstretched performed a perfect face first Pete Rose slide in her own moist gray matter.

Safe, Hicks thought as he swept the black rifle to the right. And with very little room for error sent a three round burst into each of the flanking male walkers, pulping their pallid faces in the process. "Ari, your six is clear," he said as the monsters' putrid bodies fell dangerously close to the whirring tail rotor.

Hicks looked over his shoulder. Satisfied his backups had exited the black helo, he put the M4 to his shoulder, and then set off for the nearest tanker truck, engaging targets on the run as he threaded through the zombie throng.

Durant watched awestruck as Hicks dropped four walkers in quick succession, dinging the last creature on the forehead point blank and relocating shards of skull and brain onto the broiling tarmac. "Didn't know Hicksy could shoot like that."

"Neither did I, Night Stalker, *neither did I*," Ari admitted.

Hicks couldn't see the other two operators but he knew they were there. He could hear the pings of brass hitting blacktop, and the rapid-fire clanking coming from the piston driven bolts on the silenced rifles as the spent shell casings spit out and live rounds chambered.

Hicks let his rifle dangle from its center point sling as he navigated the sea of leaking bodies, his boots sending spent shell casings skittering in all directions. *Lots of brass,* he thought, *someone fought hard for their fuel.*

Three left. He had purposefully left the creatures nearest the tanker alone. They were going to have to be killed up close and personal. The last thing he needed was an errant round igniting the tanker and roasting him, the Ghost Hawk, her crew, and the dismounts.

"Your six is clear Hicks... just those three that I can see," said Durant, starting his play-by-play as Hicks slowed to a walk and drew his combat knife. Durant remained radio silent, and watched as the stout SOAR operator covered the last ten feet in a combat crouch, clutching his Cold Steel blade right handed.

***

Taryn listened as Dickless clomped down the steps. Silently, she hoped the monster who used to be her boss would take a tumble and break a leg. For a heartbeat she contemplated opening the office door and kicking the pusbag between the shoulder blades. Anything, she thought, to keep the rancid thing downstairs permanently.

At least the decomposing asshole would never again say, "*Another new tattoo Taryn? Better cover that up Taryn.*"

Nor would he ever again condescendingly talk down to her, *"What are you going to do for a real job when you grow up Taryn? Stock the cups Taryn. They're not going to stock themselves Taryn."*

She had never before wished anyone dead let alone Richard, but judging how things ended up it was obvious someone had. For Christ's sake, the asshat wouldn't even let her plug her battery challenged iPhone into the kiosk's extra electrical outlet while she worked. *"You don't pay the electric bill,"* he had said at the time. So she brought her little solar panel phone charger to work with her just to spite the fucker.

Taryn waited until Dickless was out of ear shot, then, curiosity getting the better of her, she arose from the floor and padded across the carpet to the wall of windows that wrapped around the elevated office.

Dickless lurched over to the floor-to-ceiling windows where the creature Taryn called Subway Karen (due to her soiled, garish colored uniform with nametag still attached) stood with her distended stomach pressed tightly to the glass. As soon as Dickless formed up next to the former *sandwich artist* a steady low pitched moan escaped her unmoving lips. And while Taryn watched from on high, a half dozen other nameless creatures trudged to the windows and jostled for a spot.

That leaves four of those things unaccounted for, thought Taryn. Three passengers from one of the doomed planes still stalked the concourse, all three of which she hadn't seen in a few days. Then there was Chester the baggage porter. The fifty-something had been a little on the slow side. Taryn had heard people like Chester described as *touched*. Although far from politically correct, she preferred saying: *The wheel is spinning, but the hamster is missing.*

During her grueling three year stint at the "Bucks," a day hadn't gone by when she didn't serve Chester at least one black Pikes. He seemed to be at the airport night and day. *Well*, Taryn mused, *Chester's had his last Pikes, and he isn't leaving for home anytime soon.*

Olivia, one of Taryn's co-workers, had once pointed out that Chester lived for the tips—though strangely enough he never ponied up one as appreciation for his piping hot Pikes. After hearing that little tidbit Taryn supposed the man was probably afraid that if he went home he might miss the big one. *Well Chester,* Taryn surmised, *if that gigantic tip hasn't hit your palm during your twenty year stint, chances are it never will.* She had wanted to break it to him earlier but hadn't had the heart. And now that he was one of them, she was glad that she hadn't. After all, who was she to put the damper on someone else's hopes and dreams?

Shoulda gone home when you had the chance Chester... I wish I would have.

Taryn was pretty sure there were only twelve walking corpses on this side of the concourse. *Only,* she thought. Even one of the walking corpses made escaping from the airport seem impossible. At first, a mere glance at one of the dead caused her to immediately seize up. Little by little she was getting used to looking at them. Their stench—not so much.

As for the south side census, she knew the zombies were there. She had heard them moaning from time to time, but because of the bend in the building she hadn't been able to see them or get an accurate head count.

"What the hell are you two gawking at?" Taryn said softly as she low crawled to a better vantage point and peered along their sight lines. *Shit,* was the first thing that came to mind when she spotted the wasp-looking aircraft sitting adjacent to the runway with its slow spinning rotors throwing blinding daggers of sunlight her way.

Looks like the black helicopters that refueled here the day before yesterday... only silent and sleek, she thought to herself. She hadn't liked the looks of the men in black who had jumped out of those first two noisy helicopters, and she didn't quite know what to make of these guys in tan and their whisper quiet, spaceship-looking helicopter.

While she watched, a lone man wearing a short half helmet and carrying a black rifle sprinted to the refueling trucks, shooting as he went. Three other men wearing the same tan uniforms fanned out and seemed to be watching out for the first man.

Even though Taryn couldn't hear the soldiers' black guns, her intuition told her what the recurring winks of orange meant. The men were shooting at the creatures, and in response the creatures were falling left and right.

Good guys or bad guys? She didn't know what to do. The sobs came in waves and her body convulsed. She expelled a long drawn out sigh, took a deep breath, and then emitted a guttural soul shuddering sound into her clenched fists.

Fearing that her outburst had summoned Richard and the gang but too afraid to look, she remained out of sight and scrutinized the chipped black polish on her nails. The fact that Dickless hadn't hassled her over *them* was a mystery that died with him. Beads of sweat rolled from her face forming a tiny pool on the carpet an inch from her nose. Finally she summoned the courage, raised her head, and stole another look. The lone man had made his way to the fuel trucks and it appeared that he was being attacked by three of the monsters.

Taryn sighed as she came to the realization she wasn't wired for this, and now having lost the distraction provided by the soldiers it was too late to bolt for the revolving doors and try to get home.

She heard the footfalls of the dead once again climbing the stairway to her own personal hell on earth. She had exiled herself in her dead boss's office, was down to her last Luna Bar, and nearly out of water. *What a way to die,* she thought.

Chapter 20
Outbreak - Day 11
Jackson Hole, Wyoming

Except for beginning his search at the bar where Heidi worked, Daymon had no clear idea how he was going to find his girl. Filled more with fear than hope, he stepped out of the quiet old building and into the mid-morning sun. And since he had already poked around the Firehouse the day before, checking every crack and crevice and finding it completely empty, he locked the thick iron door on the way out, hoping to keep it that way.

Lu Lu was out front right where he had left her, blocking the immense roll up doors and the relic of a fire engine contained within. *What the hell*, Daymon thought. Someone, Police Chief Jenkins he presumed, had spray painted a large letter E on the Scouts' driver's side door. The amateur job, complete with rivulets of black paint that had run down and dripped on the concrete before drying, made Lu Lu look like an entrant in some rural demolition derby. In disbelief, he skirted the truck noting that the passenger door had also been tagged with the same hastily applied markings.

Daymon shook his head. *What's next? Tattoos on the inner forearm?* The bad vibe he was feeling in Jackson Hole was so strong that he almost wished he would have stayed aboard the Black Hawk piloted by the crazy flyboy Duncan and gone ahead to Eden instead of being dropped off in Driggs. Furthermore, he couldn't shake the nagging feeling that he might have traded one type of prison for another. Though he never told Duncan, the need to leave Schriever and find Heidi easily overrode every other impulse. Besides, he could never see himself acclimating to the structured nature of life on the Air Force Base, nor getting used to the cramped quarters and razor wire topped fencing which only heightened his claustrophobia.

Jackson Hole, on the other hand, had seemed like a no brainer. That was all before Chief Jenkins filled him in on this New America nonsense.

I hope this thing heals before I have to leave this place in the rearview, he thought to himself, wincing with each twist of his torso as he folded his lanky body into the truck.

As he backed Lu Lu into the street, two tadpole-looking helicopters tore up the air overhead. He watched as they gained altitude, climbing steeply, and then continued on a northwest heading towards the Teton Pass roadblock thousands of feet above the valley floor. He could have sworn the all black aircraft bore the same red and white flag as he had seen on the black Humvees in Driggs and the lone Hummer at the Teton Pass the day before. A sense of foreboding fell over him as he processed how many obstacles stood in the way of him *ever* reuniting with Heidi.

To keep his rubbernecking to a minimum and remain as inconspicuous as possible he practiced moving only his eyes as he drove the streets of Jackson. Except for the lack of tourists who usually wandered the streets at this hour in search of a morning cup of Joe, everything about downtown remained virtually the same.

He turned right and wheeled down Main Street which was deserted save for a couple of tanned men busy preening and watering the colorful wildflowers bursting from their planter boxes. One of the men looked up from his chore, furrowed his brow, and shot him an angry contempt filled glare.

What the fuck did I do to you hombre, Daymon thought as the glitzy Silver Dollar sign redirected his attention from the budding resentment. His longtime girlfriend had been lead bartender there year round since cracking the rotation a number of years ago. The money was so good that nobody left willingly. Usually when a position opened up at the hot downtown night spot—someone had either died or screwed up and gotten fired. Old Earl, who had helmed the Dollar from behind the bar for more than three decades, died the victim of a massive coronary at the age of sixty-nine doing what he loved. Earl's unfortunate demise opened up the much sought after full time position for Heidi and she had been there since.

Steeling himself against the disappointment he was certain to experience, Daymon set his jaw and nosed Lu Lu into the curb.

Ignoring the blinking *time expired* warning on the solar powered parking meter he set a course for the cowhide-swathed door. Using only his body weight and not his core muscles, he pushed on the steer horn door handle and discovered the Silver Dollar Cowboy Bar unlocked. *Strange*, he thought. The bar thrived on late night business and wasn't usually open this early. "Hello, anyone in here?"

Golden dust motes hovered in the air, which Daymon noticed lacked the usual stale beer, bleach tinged, mop water odor usually prevalent after a *wham bam* night at the Silver Dollar Cowboy Bar. The rowdy honkytonk, which was located conveniently within staggering distance of the handful of hotels and motels peppering downtown Jackson Hole, was the place to see and be seen in the tourist town. Why it was open during the zombie apocalypse baffled him.

Daymon ran his hand over the richly lacquered bar top admiring the embedded silver coins before giving it a couple of sharp raps. *"Hellooo, anyone in here?"* he yelled.

A hollow thump sounded from underneath the counter. Then a man hinged up, massaging the back of his head. He fumbled in his pockets, produced a pair of bifocals, and donned them as he spoke. "Just me... *the owner...* doing a little refrigeration work. I woulda called someone in to fix it, but seeing as how the phones don't work and all of my employees are gone..." The sixty-something, barrel chested man stopped mid-sentence and paused for a beat, "Daymon! Well, well... what a sight for sore eyes. I had a feeling I'd served you your last beer. What'll you be havin'?"

"Whatever you're pouring, Gerald," Daymon answered as he put his boot in the stirrup and carefully bellied up to the bar. Festooned with too many Morgan silver dollars to count, the bar top ran the length of the building, finally wrapping around like a corral encircling the well-worn mechanical bull. It was rumored among the locals that a million of the antique silver dollars were used to decorate the saloon and restaurant. Although a little small to accommodate a man of his length for any duration, he still got a kick out of the real leather saddles that served as bar seating.

Emanating from the airspace above the Silver Dollar, Daymon recognized the unmistakable sound of the little black helicopters as they buzzed the city center low and fast. He looked at the hewn timber ceiling and listened to the rotor noise pass from left to right.

Gerald hitched up his pants and cleared his throat. "Since you're an *Essential*—how about a few fingers of Knob Creek?" he said with a nod and a conspiratorial wink.

Daymon noted that the word '*Essential*' didn't come easy to Gerald. Then a light bulb popped inside of his head. *The stenciled E on Lu Lu stands for Essential.* He felt like a dumbass and a little foolish for not realizing earlier the reason he was on the receiving end of so many dirty looks. Hell, the only two vehicles he encountered had given Lu Lu the right of way on the road and that hadn't registered either. Still he remained extremely pissed off that Lu Lu had been desecrated during the night. *How did I not put two and two together?* Then after a couple of heartbeats he answered, "Knob Creek is *better* than perfect."

"Now son—two fingers is *neat*...not *perfect*," Gerald said emitting a wheeze tinged laugh.

Daymon tented his fingers and put his elbows on the bar top. "As long as it's wet and it helps me forget." Then he smiled— probably for the first time since the smart ass Duncan dropped him off in Driggs.

Daymon watched the owner-cum-repairman, cum-bartender stretch on his tip toes to retrieve the square bottle from the top shelf.

"I presume you are looking for Heidi," Gerald said as he poured four fingers of the tawny amber bourbon into a tumbler. "And I have a feeling that what I'm about to tell you isn't going to sit well," he added as he slid the glass to Daymon.

Over drinks in the dimly lit bar Gerald recounted how one of Robert Christian's *recruiters* came to the bar at closing the Monday after the outbreak. "So this little guy — along with a couple of rough looking fellas... all armed of course..." Gerald raised his bushy eyebrows an inch. "They weren't soldiers yet they openly carried automatic weapons... you've seen 'em... the kind with all of the doo dads attached. Like in the movies you know. Then Flat face... that's the little one—he puts his pistol on the bar top like he's Billy the Kid in an old western saloon. Then the little roach"—holding his hand near his chin—"he looks up at me and says he's *borrowing* all of my lady servers for a party at the *House*. You know the place on the—"

Not wanting Gerald to waste more words than necessary Daymon interrupted, "Yeah... I know the place. That movie star's *palace* on the hill—whatever happened to Mr. *Action Flick* anyway?"

"I hope the joker ended up a meal for one of his former fans. What a sight that woulda been," Gerald wheezed. "But I digress. That party wasn't thrown by the Tinsel Town Turd. A fella named Robert Christian—real big money guy from Atlanta. He took over Jackson a couple days after the outbreak."

"Was Heidi one of the girls they *kidnapped?*" Daymon asked.

Avoiding direct eye contact, Gerald looked past Daymon towards the front door. "I'm sorry Daymon," he said running his fingers, thick and calloused from years of honest work, through his hair.

"Why didn't anyone try to stand up to him?" spat Daymon.

"He had more men and a helluva lot more firepower than Chief Jenkins—and all of the other officers combined," Gerald said in a near whisper. "Some of the boys down at the VFW hall... they talked about starting an organized resistance but Bishop got wind of it and had them all beaten within an inch of their lives. Freddy Joe, you know him. He *was* the bomber pilot from the big one—he died from the beatin' they gave him."

Seething Daymon said, *"That's fucked!* Freddy beats the odds. He survives thirty over Hitler's Germany without buying it and then some opportunist pricks murder him?"

"Chief Jenkins could do nothing about it either. And then after Fred Joe died... that broke their back. The rest of the guys— they lost the spirit to even *discuss* the NA in public."

The building shook once again from the bass heavy sound of rotors thrashing the air as another low flying helicopter transited the airspace over the city's center. This one sounded different—*larger*—Daymon noted.

After a minute the noisy chopper faded into the distance and Daymon finished his thought. "The veterans meant well—but *really* what did they think they were going to be able to do against men armed with weapons like you describe? Now that's just one country boy's opinion. I have a gut feeling it's going to take some real badasses to get rid of the dudes."

"What's the number for SEAL Team Six?" Gerald said only half joking. "I know it's not in *my* Rolodex."

I know a few badasses, Daymon thought to himself. *Unfortunately their number isn't in my Rolodex either.* "If you ask me, I think the city is as dead as the walkers. A fuckin' shame too. You know... once I find Heidi... I'm getting the fuck out. Pardon the cursing sir—"

"Heard it before, Daymon," Gerald proffered as he downed his Knob Creek.

Thinking the walls might have ears, Daymon waited a tick before speaking. Then he cast his eyes towards the rafters trying to decide how much he wanted to say. "If the Police Chief and his men couldn't stop the bad guys... then I don't know how this place is ever going to get out from under their thumb. And when I spoke to Jenkins yesterday he seemed *overwhelmed*—to say the least. Those storm troopers sure have him spooked."

Gerald wore an intense look as he said, "Those men in black are *evil*." The old man spoke slowly, and then drew out the word *evil* his voice gravelly. "At first Bishop's fellas were only pushy and demanding. But that all changed when Chief Jenkins stood up to him... called him out in front of his men. Bishop took it as an insult. But instead of hurting Jenkins—he made examples out of Darby, Palmer, and Doreen. Doreen—God rest her soul. She suffered *extra*." Gerald pushed his bi-focals up, pinched the bridge of his nose and exhaled forcefully before continuing. "The mongrels had a party with her before they fed her to those creatures."

The visual turned Daymon's stomach upside down. "Where did the flat-faced guy take Heidi and the other girls?" he asked staring intensely across the bar.

"To the mansion... I'm sure of it," Gerald proffered.

"Will you do me a favor?" Daymon said over the top of his glass, savoring the nose of roasted nuts and honey wafting from the room temperature bourbon.

"Depends on what you're asking of me," replied Gerald softly and slowly.

The singsong cadence of the old man's voice brought goose bumps to Daymon's skin.

"I came from Driggs with one thing on my mind..." Daymon intoned. "Find Heidi if it kills me." He pinned his dreads behind his ears and hardened his expression as he planned his next words. "It appears this Robert Christian and his muscle Bishop and Flat Face have opened up a whole new can of worms for me."

Gerald leaned in close enough to make Daymon think he was about to be on the receiving end of a head-butt.

"Anything else you want to tell me?" Daymon asked as his claustrophobia kicked in, causing him to lean back thus widening his bubble of personal space.

"The one place that I *know* of where you can have an audience with Robert Christian..."

To hell with phobias. Daymon leaned back in. "Go on," he said.

Gerald resumed where he had left off. "One of the other Essentials let it slip after one too many imbibed right here in my bar that this Christian fella takes a daily meal in the elk refuge, usually before noon, but sometimes after. It's second hand info—so take it with a grain. If you need to vamoose in a hurry... a word of caution... the monsters seem to be coming up 189 from the southwest so the NA boys have the bridge by Hoback ready to blow. *Do not* go that way. If you leave, take the pass or go north past the airport. But be careful, there are NA baddies on both roads. *Young man...* promise me you will think before doing anything *stupid* where Christian or Bishop is concerned."

"Doing *nothing* is stupid. I ain't got a thing to lose—and *everything* to gain," Daymon said, his voice trailing off. "Thanks for the heads up about the Snake crossing." He downed the bourbon in one shot while the niggling voice he chalked up to conscience warned him about drinking and driving. *Who's going to give an Essential a DUI anyway*, crossed his mind as he shook Gerald's hand. Then, a little tipsy and armed with his new knowledge, he took a lingering look around the empty honkytonk and tried to detect a little bit of Heidi's presence before venturing out into the sunlight.

The last thing he wanted to do now was draw attention to himself. If he was going to find out what had happened to Heidi he knew that he was going to have to start asking around, either that, or set up surveillance on the house. Daymon shook his head and racked his brain. Neither of those options were acceptable since most people in Jackson knew him—and to those that didn't—he would stand out to like a sore thumb. He was one of those people who if you had met him even once—however briefly—the chance that you'd remember how to describe him easily topped one hundred and ten percent.

Daymon was left with only one clear place to start, and to rule out whether or not his girl was among the crucified, he was going to have to return to the place he had privately dubbed '*The valley of the crosses.*' And to get there he would have to take the Teton pass highway which he'd decided to call the highway to hell. With that thought, the old AC/DC song of the same name began looping through his mind.

Chapter 21
Outbreak - Day 11
Logan Winter's Compound
Eden, Utah

"The radio has been awfully quiet. You think we ought to check in?" Phillip asked.

His question was answered by several staccato bursts of gunfire coming from the east side of the property.

"Let's stay put lest we get ourselves shot up," drawled Duncan. "Let's just watch our backs and not get trigger happy."

"I second that," Carter proffered.

Three minutes later Lev's voice came over the radio. "We're coming into the clearing. Do-not-shoot."

"Copy that," Duncan replied into the two-way then he watched the tree line for signs of movement. Finally, backpedaling, Lev, Chief, and Seth burst into the clearing.

"Where the hell are Gus and Sampson?" Ed, the balding heavy set fellow asked.

Duncan looked at him and said, "Think good thoughts."

The three men sprinted across the clearing with two dozen rotters in pursuit. Chief slowed to a walk, turned, and dropped four of the advancing crowd.

By the time the trio reached Duncan's position they were all winded from fighting through the underbrush while trying to avoid being surrounded.

"There are more of them in there but they're busy eating some bastard," Seth blurted.

"Calm down," Duncan said to the young man. "I say we let 'em get a little closer and then POW, we finish 'em right here."

"Gus and Sampson are still out there somewhere," Lev said. "They're between us and the road."

"Don't worry about the other two," Chief said soberly. "They were in their tree stands and should be safe."

"Lock and load," Duncan said, taking charge of the situation. "Carter, Ed, Phillip... fan out towards the bunker entrance. You three spread left... we'll get the Zs in a crossfire." He waited until the rotters were right in the middle of the clearing before yelling "Fire!"

After a fifteen second lead storm all of the creatures were down.

"Reload," Duncan bellowed. He felt like he was taking place in a Civil War re-enactment. "Let's see if the gunfire tears the others from the feedbag."

"Let's make some noise," Lev said. "Should get their attention."

Duncan started hollering.

The others followed suit.

Shortly after, the brush parted on the other side and rotters started staggering through the shin high grass.

"Wait." Duncan paused.

"Now!" he said as he fired his borrowed shotgun into the decaying clutch. Though not very effective at this range, the scattergun still took some pieces off of the shamblers.

As soon as the gunfire died out, Lev noticed his Motorola begging to be answered. Relieved to hear Gus's voice leap from the speaker, he inquired about Sampson.

"Not good," said Gus. "They got to him. I need help with the fence... bring tools. And there are some more walkers down here but I think I can hold them off for a minute. Hurry though."

A call from the compound came over the two-way. "This is Logan. Has anyone seen the girls?"

"Negative," replied Lev. "We're going to the road to help Gus. We have some fence to repair so Seth is coming to the compound to get some tools."

"Copy that. All right!" Logan shouted, unable to hide his glee.

"What's happening?" Lev asked

"The girls just snuck in the back door."

"I'll pass the word," Lev added. *Lucky you.*

***

Cordite haze hung in the still air as Lev walked among the fallen rotters finishing off anything that moved. Sampson's body was wrapped in a blue tarp and he would receive a proper burial later.

Sitting with his back to a fence post, Gus was still trying to come to grips with the fact that he had been forced to put down a friend. Sampson was already turned when Gus found him wandering on the road. It hadn't been easy but he pulled the trigger, an action that no doubt he would never forget.

Seth and Carter tackled the fence repair while Duncan paced the fence line, saddled with the subtle feeling that someone was watching him. "Lev... Gus... can I get your ears?"

Duncan held court with the two men that he suspected were the most capable of the group. "I have a feeling we're being probed. I don't think this has much to do with the good old boys you all offed the other day. However, we have just tipped our hand as far as personnel is concerned."

"What do you propose?" Gus asked.

"I think we should lay low for a couple of days and then take the chopper up and go on a scavenger hunt. If we're going to hold this compound we *will* need more arms and stuff that goes *boom*."

Lev perked up. "We could find a National Guard Armory. Good stuff there."

"Would seem like a good a place to start but the Guard was deployed early and suffered from it. Poor bastards didn't know what they were up against until it was too late." Duncan shook his head slowly. "Just an idea, we'll have to kick it around with the others. From what I understand that's how things get handled around here."

"We can kick it over later," Chief said. "Right now I need help burying Sampson."

Chapter 22
Outbreak - Day 11
Grand Junction, Colorado

Hicks crabwalked slowly to the right. The knife, perfectly balanced, felt like a natural extension of his hand. This would be no normal knife fight—if there even was such a thing. There would be no incapacitating attacks to the torso—wouldn't work on the dead, he reasoned. He figured he would only have one chance: go for the head once the lumbering monster got close enough.

The creature to his right wore a heavy two piece uniform with the words GROUND MAINTENANCE stenciled front and back in an easy to read black font. An impossible to miss gaping chasm had been chewed into the heavy set man's neck, the obvious cause of his first death. The ghoul had nothing beneath his chin save for bits of dried yellow trachea and streamers of glossy flesh. Hicks could easily make out vertebra and burnished cords of muscle rippling as the Z's head bobbled with each ungainly stride. The thing's blood had sluiced out and dried in a crazy tie-dyed pattern staining the bright yellow uniform; it almost looked like it should be at a Phish concert scoring a joint instead of lurching around hungering for human flesh.

In addition to Tie-Dye who emitted raspy groans as he approached, two more zombies angled silently in from Hicks's left.

The first creature, a middle-aged woman who in her human life had obviously been a tanning bed addict, had wisely dressed for a hot summer day: plaid Bermuda shorts, a tight black tee shirt with garish golden lettering that said Viva Las Vegas stretched taut across her fake boobs, and a pair of scuffed and bloody high backed sandals wrapping her dainty feet. Mister ultra-violet spectrum, fake or not, hadn't been kind to her in life and he hadn't given her any slack in death.

Bites marked her leathered hands and arms. The deep craters, ringed with purpled ridges, proved she had tried in vain to ward off a ferocious attack before finally succumbing to the virus and joining the ranks of the dead.

Trailing ten feet behind and to the left of the female version of Wayne Newton staggered the hairiest Z Hicks had ever seen. Wearing nothing but a blue Speedo banana hammock, the groaning creature angled for an attack, its bare feet slapping out a steady cadence on the super-heated tarmac.

Hicks, taken aback by the out of place oddity, nearly dropped his blade. He presumed the nearly naked walker had left his last pool party, enticed by the plane crash and ensuing inferno, then come in through the shattered fence along with the rest of the Zs. *A fiery spectacle the mindless fuckers couldn't resist*, Hicks thought as he crouched, bouncing lightly on the balls of his feet, prepared to engage Tie-Dye first.

***

Sweeping his SCAR carbine to the left, Lopez delivered final peace to one badly burnt walker, its partially melted flesh sagging in places revealing pink fissures and contrasting white bone underneath. Through his scope he witnessed his three round burst cleave the Z's head in two. Gray brains blossomed in the air, and as the blackened monster became one with the scorched tarmac it appeared the demon was being welcomed back into hell.

He dropped the spent mag and back-pedaled, jamming a fresh one in the well as a phalanx of similarly burnt creatures vectored his way. "Get a move on Hicks!" he bellowed into his mic before letting loose with half a dozen three round bursts, most of which found their mark, dropping four more of the advancing crowd. His final salvo, however, went wide and found one of the massive plate glass panes fronting Grand Junction's north concourse several hundred yards distant. The quarter inch thick glass which had been tempered to deaden the high decibel shriek of a jet engine would normally have been able to withstand a single errant 5.56x45 mm NATO round without shattering completely. Against three simultaneous bullet strikes, each hitting only a fist width apart, it stood no chance.

***

Inside Grand Junction Airport

Taryn's full attention had been locked on the soldiers and their strange helicopter when the wall of windows directly below and opposite the office exploded inward. The ensuing implosion of glass shrapnel peppered the opposite walls, sending minute kernels bouncing across the carpeted floor like so many shiny spotless dice.

With the window that had been supporting Subway Karen now scattered about the concourse in a thousand pea-sized bits, the decaying corpse tumbled into the void face first.

As Dickless and the other creatures teetered on the edge, Taryn silently chanted *Go, go, go,* urging them to follow Karen's lead. With the newly created opening she had expected the high pitched whine and popping rotor sounds to invade the concourse. Instead she heard only a strange harmonic whirring emitted by the helicopter. She thought about yelling out for help but quickly shelved the idea. The men were far too distant; furthermore, the only attention that her screams would garner would be from the dead.

***

Meanwhile, near the fuel trucks, Hicks, knife firmly gripped in his right hand, waited for the creatures to close the gap.

Tie-Dye lunged first, leaving his destroyed throat vulnerable. Hicks dipped his hips and exploded off of his right heel. The well-muscled sergeant's body uncoiled as he followed through with a Cold Steel uppercut. The triple hardened blade easily pierced the soft flesh under the big zombie's chin, and continued on through the upper palate scrambling the monster's brain.

"Hicks—ten o'clock," Tice called out as his finger hovered longingly near the mini-gun trigger.

Hicks shuddered at the sight of the skewered creature—a pre-puke dry heave caught in his throat. He let the dead walker slide from his knife, and then squared his shoulders, feet spread slightly, ready to accept the next threat.

As Speedo lurched closer, a trio of 5.56 hardball crackled by Hicks's right ear and hammered the nearly naked walker to the ground. With its jaw pulverized and shredded left arm hanging limp and of no use, the Z struggled to stand.

"You trying to kill us all *Captain?*" Hicks hollered without taking his eyes from the struggling corpse.

"It was nearly on top of you... I had the angle," answered Cade calmly. "I didn't seal the deal though—finish him for me, will ya."

Taking a calculated risk Hicks drew his Beretta with his off hand, took a stride forward, and, risking conflagration, delivered the kill shot point blank to the rear of the Z's head.

While he estimated the spacing between the female zombie and the two fuel trucks, Hicks quickly mulled over which weapon he should use: gun or knife.

A second wave of nausea wracked his body. He was used to the stench from the air—not up close and personal. *Gun it is,* he thought as he sheathed his gore slickened blade.

Truth be told, Hicks didn't want to earn his "Puker" patch. He had avoided that *Scarlet Letter* for more than a decade—while engaged in combat aboard a jinking, jiggering helicopter—pulling high-g maneuvers while hanging into the slipstream secured by only a wire that seemed as thin as a piece of dental floss. Even a couple of autorotations followed by very hard landings hadn't taken his cookies.

While the Z in the Vegas shirt closed the distance, Hicks crabwalked to the right, and when the walker got between the Ghost Hawk and the two refueling trucks—which he hoped held thousands of gallons of JP-8 aviation fuel—he double tapped her in the forehead.

Then he then went to all fours to look for rotten feet shuffling around on the opposite side of the parked vehicles. *Good to go.* The coast was clear.

Cade and Lopez loped ahead, separated by a dozen feet, stopping only after they were a few more yards removed from the spinning rotor. Each man then went to one knee as their silenced rifles started dealing final death to the walkers.

"Wyatt, your six is clear," said Maddox, who also was on one knee alternating between watching the port side of the helo and keeping an eye on Cade and Lopez's backs.

"Copy that Maddox," Cade answered back. Then he looked toward Hicks, who was now striking the tanker with the synthetic butt stock of his M4 starting near the top and tapping every six inches or so while walking it down.

Then Hicks, his breathing labored, said into his mic, "Left tanker is half full. Rough estimate—fifteen hundred gallons—more than enough to top the bird off... and then some. I was worried that the fueling nozzle might not be compatible—but gentlemen it looks to be our *lucky day*. I like being wrong—*sometimes*."

"Anyone spots a 7/11 en route... be sure and remind me to land so we can buy a few bucks worth of Mega Millions tickets," Ari deadpanned, clapping his gloved hands and stretching in his seat to try and get the blood moving again in his extremities.

"Your six is still clear... you're good to go," Cade proffered as he continued dinging Zs.

After a moment's hesitation Hicks answered, "Copy that." Though he trusted his life to the Delta operators explicitly, and relying on others to watch his back had been drilled into him over the years of training and then practiced successfully in combat—still he felt compelled to check his own ass. Then, after peeking over each shoulder, he holstered his pistol and spun around and began trudging towards the helo with the nickel plated fueling nozzle clutched in his gloved hands, and the large diameter hose steadily unspooling behind him.

***

Inside Grand Junction Airport

As Taryn looked on, one of the men ran towards the helicopter and plugged a hose into its side. In the years she had worked at the airport she had witnessed a refueling or two, but never while the helicopter's blades where still spinning.

The other soldiers had retreated closer to the black aircraft and Taryn could make out their orange muzzle flashes as they held off the monsters during the ongoing refueling process.

The entire surreal event, from the moment she had started watching and the soldiers initially fanned out on the tarmac until they finished their task and the black helicopter bolted from the ground, took less than eight minutes.

That's about how long it would take me to make two lattes, a cappuccino extra foam, take the money, and pocket the tips, she mused. *Whoever those freaking badasses were—I hope they're the good guys.*

Chapter 23
Outbreak - Day 11
Jackson Hole, Wyoming

Southwest Jackson Hole, I - 189 Crossing

Ian Bishop hated a fair fight, and during his days in the teams he rarely got caught on the wrong side of that equation. He and the SEALs he went down range with had always been blessed with the best intelligence: human and electronic—giving them the edge in almost any situation. Through superior training, overwhelming firepower, and sheer determination they oftentimes tackled a far larger force, and ninety-nine times out of a hundred they emerged victorious.

This was an entirely different scenario. On the south side of the bridge, the horde of walking dead numbering several thousand strong were being held at bay by a steel wall of city busses.

Overnight the zombies had successfully breached Bishop's first line of defense. Man-sized gaps had appeared between two of the busses allowing two or three hundred of the persistent creatures to squeeze through every hour.

This enemy was like no other, Bishop thought, as he watched the line of vehicles across the way shimmy and shake behind the crushing dead. Truth be told, he was deathly afraid of the abominations and had been fighting the urge to cut and run the entire twenty-four hours he and his skeleton crew of defenders had been hammering away at the steady stream shambling across the bridge towards him.

Moving his combat boot side to side with a sweeping motion, he cleared a spot in the midst of the growing pile of spent brass. The sturdy scaffolding, pilfered from a commercial painting outfit, had been erected along the back side of the city busses serving as a second line of defense across the north side of 189. The scaffolding, while sturdy enough to support several men on each section, was not tall enough to allow the shooters the proper angle to cull the zombies that made it across the span. In order to do so a defender had to crawl along the semi-sloped roofs of the city busses, dangerously close to the edge, in order to fire down on the creatures.

Keeping his eye to the scope and a steady rhythm to his fire, Bishop asked the well-muscled shooter to his right, "How many rounds do you have left?

"Two hundred loose rounds and four full mags Sir!" Daly said, shouting to be heard over the moans of the dead and the staccato fusillades of gunfire echoing up and down the battle line.

Bishop raised the binoculars, and through the gray veil of cordite haze surveyed up and down the line of Teton County busses. The cobalt blue Southern Teton Area Rapid Transit or START busses were low slung Gillig models parked end to nose, stretching from the woods on the west side of the choke point across the four lane highway and finally abutting the strip mall to the east. If the first line failed then these ten people movers were the only thing standing between the living dead that had been arriving in large numbers during the last three days, and the few people still living in the city of Jackson Hole. He scanned the shooters to the left and the men positioned every few feet to his right. After confirming that indeed his orders were being followed and all of his men were wearing their makeshift harnesses tethering them to the tops of the vehicles they were shooting from, he let the binoculars hang around his neck and ran both hands through his dark hair.

He fished the Vicks Vapor Rub from his thigh pocket, slathered a liberal amount under his nose, and then chucked the empty blue jar at the moaning dead. His gaze followed the jar as it bounced then landed in a pool of blood next to someone he knew.

Bishop grimaced at the sight. Jacob's corpse was splayed out as if afloat in the crimson pool of his own drying blood. With tangles of the man's glistening entrails still clutched in their pallid hands, a half dozen unmoving zombies lay scattered around the black fatigue-clad body. As Bishop stared at the gory sight he relived the younger man's death. In his mind's eye, he watched Jacob's arms flail and his face contort as he realized he had just lost his footing and there was no recovering from his inevitable fate. Jacob dropped his rifle and fell hard to the roof, then rode its slick curvature face first into the waiting arms of the dead. He screamed and pleaded to the other shooters for help, then his mom became his savior of choice; as he chanted her name, the dead pulled him down.

Bishop had reacted quickly but before he could draw a bead on the closest Z the creatures were already into his friend's chest cavity, their greedy white hands stuffing steaming entrails into their mouths. Bishop shuddered at the recollection.

One bite, he thought, and there is no such thing as help. The dead had an effect on the former Navy SEAL that no man had been able to accomplish.

Violence of action had been SEAL Team 10's calling card. The dead weren't affected by violence or intimidation. All of the tools of modern warfare that Ian had been taught in BUDs and had since refined on the battlefield weren't applicable to the dead. And just as Bishop was about to revisit his single mercy shot to Jacob's forehead, Daly's words saved him from reliving that dreadful moment.

Daly looked at Bishop, who was seemingly zoned out gazing at the dead SEAL's body, and gave him a quick inventory of his remaining ammunition.

Bishop didn't respond.

Thinking his words had been drowned out by the cacophony of the one-sided gun battle, Daly repeated his update, "I'm down to four mags." Then he punched an empty to the ground and inserted a fresh thirty rounds of 5.56. "Down to three mags now Sir!"

Bishop snapped back to the present and said, "Here, take these." He placed five full magazines near the younger man's feet. "I've got to talk to the boss man." *And this may be the last time if all goes according to plan.*

A POUND OF FLESH: SURVIVING THE ZOMBIE APOCALYPSE

Since that frigid gunmetal gray day in Coronado when he had finally earned the coveted Budweiser pin, which featured a golden eagle clutching a U.S. Navy anchor, trident, and flintlock style pistol, which acknowledged his completion of BUD/S or Basic Underwater Demolition/SEAL training, he had been unflinching in battle and confident under duress—in one word, Ian Bishop was unshakable. He had been the best of the best that the U.S. Navy had to offer. He was a predator of men and had never before faced such a driven, emotionless force, one that was not deterred by injury and was merely slowed by missing limbs. Unlike the living, this adversary didn't bleed to death and never stopped in its relentless drive for human flesh. Worst of all, Ian thought, this enemy could only be felled by a bullet to the brain, and supplies of those were dwindling fast. He supposed this feeling of vulnerability, which was foreign to him, was precisely what every one of his previous adversaries on the field of battle had felt like going up against him and his former Navy SEAL brethren.

Ian Bishop knew he had a difficult decision to make. It wasn't in his nature to cut and run—never had been—he finished what he started, always seeing things through to the end no matter how hard the task. That drive and work ethic came from somewhere else in the family tree—it definitely hadn't been passed down nor instilled in him by his father, who had disappeared when he was nine. The man, Ian had been told, had been a first class fuck up of the royal order and for all Ian knew was rotting in some prison somewhere.

Staring at the hungry eyes coming across the bridge had made up his mind for him, and when he talked to Robert Christian next he was going to hold nothing back. He hadn't signed on for this and neither had his most trusted brothers in arms—most of whom were still disgruntled at the previous two Presidential administrations and the stuffed shirt politicians for meddling in the two wars in the sandbox. No, this time things were going to change, Ian told himself. Nothing would be gained by staying around and continuing to do Robert Christian's bidding. *Yes my Liege. No my Liege.* He felt he was compromising what little he still stood for by sticking around against such insurmountable undead odds. Hell, he thought, this whole

Extinction Level Event wasn't what he and his dwindling group of men were hired to guard against—nor prepared to deal with.

Bishop cursed the minty smell of death invading his lungs as he hauled his tired carcass into the brand new Range Rover. He cranked the A/C, hoping the new car smell recirculating through the vehicle's Hepa filter would somehow overpower the odor of the dead.

He thumbed on the Iridium 9555 satellite phone and pushed the number two key which was preprogrammed to connect directly to Carson, a former Army Ranger and Navy SEAL hopeful, who had washed out very early during his BUD/S training in Coronado. He didn't inform his number two man of the reason he was being flown to rendezvous with the second convoy aboard one of the NA's Little Bird helicopters, and after years of fighting alongside Bishop, Carson apparently knew better than to ask. By now, Bishop thought, the convoy should be nearing the predetermined spot he had chosen to stash the nuclear warheads that his men stole from Minot Air Force Base, and now that he had solidified his position he would bring Carson into the loop. Bishop waited patiently for his call to vault into space and route through one of the Iridium Corporation's still functioning cross-linked Low Earth Orbit satellites. Then after a couple of seconds and two rings, a man answered at the other end.

"Carson here."

"This is Ian, what is your position."

"We are at the first set of GPS coordinates that you sent with me."

"Punch the second coordinates in and order the driver and the rest of the convoy to proceed directly to that location. Do not deviate. Do not stop. And do not let anyone or anything slow you down. Wait for my call," Bishop said briskly.

"Copy that," Carson replied to an already dead connection.

***

Bishop watched the strip malls with their dead signage and pitch black interiors creep by. The Golden Arches and Wendy's, half a block apart, were both darkened and uninhabited. He blew through intersections, ignoring the dormant traffic signals as he wheeled the Range Rover through the four block long cluster of new and used car lots, which usually had an army of white shirts and ties waiting to descend like vultures on anyone who looked halfway in the market for a new set of wheels. The colorful plastic pennants strung from corner to corner dominating the airspace above the dusty cars and trucks popped in the wind like semaphores on a ghost ship.

As quiet as the streets and sidewalks had become, it seemed like he was driving through Jackson Hole on a holiday. It didn't break his heart so much as it served as a reminder of how upside down normal had become.

He slowed the SUV at the Teton Pass split and took a slight left on East Butte Drive. After climbing the hill and following a series of switchbacks that cut through dense woods, the two lane blacktop ended at an oversized cul-de-sac in front of the mansion on the hill, which the locals not so lovingly called *The House.*

Inside the mansion, a man who had been monitoring the hidden security cameras moved a joystick and zoomed tight on Bishop's face.

"Wait one sir," a male voice said over the intercom.

"Thanks Cliff," Bishop replied blandly.

Then after a few seconds, the gate swung inward; much to Bishop's chagrin no one approached or challenged him once he was inside the compound.

He watched the gate in the rearview and waited for it to close before stepping from the truck. The circular drive, which was usually choked with SUVs and the occasional NA Humvee, was unoccupied except for his ride. With the hairs on the back of his neck standing at attention, he padded to the large ornately carved double doors, M4 held at low ready.

He paused for a moment, listening to the humming generators around the side of the mansion, and then punched his six digit code into the lighted keypad. He pulled open the heavy door, waited a tick, then cautiously entered the mansion. Except for the single beep of the alarm rearming itself, the house was quiet. Much too quiet for the former SEAL's liking. Slinging his rifle, he drew his Sig Sauer. Leaving the grand foyer with its travertine, exotic plants and floor to ceiling Tuscan paintings behind, he went up the right side stairs, taking them slowly one at a time with his 9mm semi-auto pistol held in a two handed grip. His soft soled Blackhawk boots performing as advertised allowed him to sneak up on the security room unannounced.

He tried the handle.

Unlocked.

On well-oiled hinges, the door opened noiselessly, revealing a man sitting behind a bank of flat screens. It was the same man Bishop had just talked to via the main gate intercom.

"Cliff."

The security guard fumbled a nearly full bag of Cheetos as his rear jumped from the seat. "You scared the shit outta me man," he said, policing up his spilled snacks. With an open palm he wiped the greasy orange seasonings from the control panel. "Why did you have to do that?"

Ignoring the portly guard's question, Bishop shot back, "Where in the *hell* is everyone?"

"The brothers went on a run to Driggs. Hutsell and Ed are here somewhere."

"What about R.C.?"

"He's not here," Cliff said, wiping orange fingers on his black pants.

Bishop keyed in on the guard's shaking hands.

"Look me in the eye *Clifford*. Where - did - they - all - go?" he asked slowly.

"R.C. waved them off."

Bishop slapped the black ball cap from the seated man's head. "What the *fuck* do you mean *Christian waved them off?*"

"He and Tran took a truck..."

"Where were they going... *all alone?*"

"The elk refuge," Cliff said as he smoothed his mussed locks into place.

"Did they take all of the house vehicles?"

"Like I said—Tran and the boss took the black Cadillac. I didn't watch the brothers leave."

"When the brothers get back here I want you to call me ASAP. My phone better be buzzing before they pull in the gate—got it?" Bishop holstered his pistol then turned and faced the window, lacing his fingers behind his neck. "Watch those monitors like a fucking hawk... *you hear?*"

Cliff mumbled an apology.

Bishop left the man alone to collect his hat and a little dignity. He slammed the door behind him and retrieved the sat phone from his cargo pocket. He stalked down the hall, thumbing a number into the Iridium. After several rings without an answer, a string of expletives erupted from the former SEAL's mouth. He thumbed in another set of numbers from memory.

"Joshua here."

"This is Bishop. When did the brothers go through the pass?"

"About an hour ago."

Bishop felt his temples flush hot. "How many vehicles and personnel?"

Joshua answered tentatively, "Just the brothers in the Escalade."

"And you thought that was normal? Did they say where they were going?" he said as he pushed through the set of French doors which fronted the top of the landing where the circular stairways from the foyer joined.

"Ammo run or something like that," Joshua answered cautiously.

Standing on the outdoor veranda which stretched around in front of the master suite, Bishop gazed at the Tetons. "Joshua... you're not as dumb as the others. Did you really ask or did you just let them pass without thinking?"

"I didn't ask. I assumed you knew... that they had already cleared it with you."

"What was the protocol?" Bishop asked, struggling to keep from saying something he might regret. Joshua wasn't officer material as evidenced by this latest slip, but he was trustworthy. He had covered up all evidence from the massacre of the 4th Infantry Division soldiers without screwing that up. And sooner or later Bishop knew that he was really going to need former combat veterans like the swarthy New Englander. Probably much sooner, he surmised.

After a few beats the pass sentry replied, "I am to call you immediately if anyone comes or goes through the pass."

"X gets a square—good answer sir. I'm relieving you of pass duty. I want you to leave a couple of the newer guys there," said Bishop.

"Copy that," Joshua said forcefully, his mind turning over the unusual orders.

As an afterthought Bishop added, "Pull the snipers. Tell them to take as much ammo as they can scrounge up and get to the bridge."

Wondering why Bishop would leave the Teton pass so poorly manned and against his better judgment Joshua asked, "Are we retreating?"

"Keep your phone on," the former SEAL said cryptically.

Bishop thought back to his multiple deployments in the Sandbox. He had spent more time there with his SEAL team riding on the skids of a little bird killing insurgents and conducting midnight snatch and grabs than he had stateside with his wife and little boy.

In a moment of weakness he thought about Samuel, his boy, now ten, who was with his mom back in Little Creek, Virginia. Much to her credit, Naomi had agreed to stay near Ian's stateside post even after the divorce had been finalized. He had only had a chance to visit Samuel a handful of times in between deployments. Those meetings had been strange and surreal. His own son pushing him away was the precursor to his free-fall from the teams.

Shoving those thoughts back into the black hole he called a heart, he pulled out his phone and dialed Robert Christian. Two rings later the President of New America—who was more so in title than in reality—picked up. "What do you want Bishop?" the slowly unraveling man slurred.

"Where are you *sir*?" Bishop queried as he realized his continuing deference to the ambitious man had diminished to next to nothing.

"The question, sir, is have you taken out my garbage yet?"

"Negative."

"What are you waiting for *boy*?" Click. The phone went dead.

Bishop lashed out, landing a solid kick on Christian's teak chaise lounge and sending the broken piece of furniture pancaking flat to the veranda floor. Being called boy and the slap in the face the dead phone line represented pushed him over the edge. He could only hope to calm down enough during his little errand so he wouldn't snap the old man's neck at first sight.

At that he thumbed the phone off and headed for the master suite; without knocking he barged in, setting his sights on the small shrouded form swallowed up by the California king.

Heidi felt her body rising from the luxuriant bedding. *This is it*, she thought. *I'm going home*. Bruises covered her formerly alabaster skin from head to toe and her front teeth had been loose since she tried to eighty-six the crooked nosed smartass who had worn out his welcome at the Silver Dollar where she tended bar.

She had been drugged and then sexually assaulted multiple times by the silver haired man and who knows who else. Each time the dosing of drugs was more powerful and the attacks more vicious. Those demeaning violations and the utter helplessness of her situation had had her wanting to die now for two days. That her soul was seemingly leaving her body filled her with a hopeful feeling. Maybe she would get to see all of the loved ones that she knew were dead, and Daymon, certainly he was gone. After hearing the stories coming from Salt Lake City and the towns along the Wasatch front, all hope for his survival had faded even before she had been put through this latest trial.

She was ready.

Take me home, she pleaded silently.

What little wind remained in her lungs expelled as someone or something heaved her limp body into the air and brought her back down rather harshly on an unyielding surface.

The drugs which the old man had been forcing her to eat were still affecting her to the point where her autonomous systems were on the verge of shutting down. She didn't possess the strength to regain her lost breath let alone mount a struggle against the rough treatment at the hands of the stranger.

Well if the Devil wants me that bad then he can have me, she thought before blacking out.

Chapter 24
Outbreak - Day 11
Grand Junction, Colorado

Onboard Jedi One-One

The north end of Grand Junction blurred under the Ghost Hawk, and ahead loomed the Book Cliffs which rose in red-orange splendor two thousand feet above the Grand Valley floor.

"Someone give the spook a bag," Ari intoned as he pulled stick and skimmed the helo just feet from the nearly vertical cliff face.

The G-forces pressed Cade firmly against the seat and bulkhead as he stared forward between the two pilots at nothing but blue sky. Then as the helo leveled off he finally cut in, "Great job team... Lopez, way to go, and Tice, thanks for getting our six with the mini. And Hicks... *that* has got to be some kind of a record... topping this *thing* off in under three minutes... makes those Indy pit boys playing with their little toy cars look slow."

"Don't hold me to the same lofty standards if we are forced to come back this way," said Hicks. "Our ride is going to be on fumes and filling her up is going to take at least ten mikes. And taking into account the number of Zs we left behind—shit could get hairy."

"Hey, Spooky might even have a chance to fire Betsy and get his mini-gun merit badge," Lopez ribbed.

"It took every ounce of restraint in my trigger finger not to save your butts back there," Tice said with a wide grin. Then he added, "Just joking fellas. That melee couldn't have been choreographed any better. With Wyatt and Low-Rider gunning away and Hicksy here with the Bowie knife moves... shit... Cirque De Soleil has nothing on you guys."

Even though the fact that he had saved the helicopter's tail rotor assembly from chopping up a couple of stiffs didn't get a mention in Tice's glowing review, the always quiet Maddox let it slide. Though he was of the new generation in the teams, he was still old school, eschewing the war stories while letting his actions speak for themselves.

"Cirque duh what," Cade interjected.

"Never mind," Tice answered sheepishly.

"Don't worry ladies," Ari said as he leveled the helo and sped over the ochre mesas, keeping the sun over his left shoulder. "By tomorrow, if his foraging parties hit paydirt, Whipper should have a fuel-laden Herc for this bird to drink from."

"You're assuming, Ari, that Spooky here didn't jinx us," Lopez stated, poking a thumb towards Tice.

"Durant set the waypoints," Ari added, ignoring the quip. "We're going north via the Flaming Gorge route... anyone been there?"

Ari was greeted by a chorus of "*Negative.*"

"It's a ninety-mile long reservoir stopped up by a pretty good sized dam."

Ari tapped the glass touchscreen to his right, bringing up a colorful high definition topo map of the ground they would be overflying. "I'm going to take us through the canyon, staying close to the reservoir. When the Flaming Gorge spits us out we will be very close to the insertion point handpicked by your captain."

Granted there were very few threats to the Ghost Hawk during the day now that the United States was in its final death throes, but dropping the Delta team off in broad daylight in the forest only a couple of miles from the bad guys was still going to prove risky.

Ari had lobbied hard to execute the insertion at night when he, the aircrew, and the Stealth Hawk would be in their element.

Cade pushed to leave as soon as possible. He made it no secret that he wanted to strike back swiftly and brutally at the people who had sent Mike's killer.

In the end, even though Ari was the one with thousands of hours on the stick and hundreds of insertions and exfils already under his belt—executed mostly in the dark—the choice hadn't been his to make. Major Nash had made the final decision, which was no doubt influenced by the anxious Delta operator whose two cents often times held more purchasing power than most with the woman.

Cade looked away from the window and let his gaze linger on the men going into Jackson Hole; he wondered to himself how many of them would be coming home alive.

Chapter 25
Outbreak - Day 11
Jackson Hole, Wyoming

The drive from downtown Jackson Hole to the *Valley of the Crosses* was much too short. The wide open field, lush and green, where Ian Bishop's *"examples"* were crucified alive and then left alone to die in the worst manner imaginable came into view as the International Scout rounded the corner.

Daymon got to the end of the line of crosses and pulled Lu Lu onto the shoulder. There he cursed God and pummeled the steering wheel until his palms ached and the inflamed gashes on his torso resumed their steady throbbing.

Since his solemn drive into Jackson the previous day, three additional crosses had been erected, and three more of Jackson's unbendable residents had joined the *examples*. Framed in the Scout's flat windshield, two thirty-something males and a woman who looked to be of Heidi's age hung limp, each crucified with three railroad spikes, one impaling each wrist with the third skewering the tops of their feet.

The woman stood out in contrast to the men. Like royalty in an Edwardian painting, her skin had a muted pink hue suggesting she might not be dead. On the other hand, both men had been dead for some time, their pallid bodies hanging slack—unmoving. Daymon guessed the men had succumbed to shock, exposure, or a combination thereof. The ravenous blackbirds and crafty ravens wasted little time, beating the turkey vultures to the warm meat. The corpses were left with gaping black voids where their eyes should have been. Apparently the soft white morsels were the most coveted, Daymon noted, bile rising in his throat.

Jackson Hole was the kind of town where nearly everyone that worked and lived there year round knew one another. During the summer, the apex of the fire season, Daymon lived for weeks at a time in the firehouse, rarely crossing the Teton Pass to go home. To his chagrin he found Jackson to be a very difficult place to remain anonymous, let alone retain a modicum of privacy, and given his exotic appearance—light mocha skin, green eyes, and dreadlocks—everyone knew Jackson's BLM firefighter-in-residence. It was also common knowledge that he and Heidi were together.

Daymon stared at the lipless grinning corpses. He was certain he had never seen either of the men before. The woman was a different story. His stomach clenched as he realized that although her face was swollen and bloody, she bore a striking resemblance to Heidi. There was only one way to be positive. His mind screamed *jump over the fence and save her.* His muscles wouldn't respond. He stood rooted, paralyzed by fear, gut freezing, sphincter clinching fear. It was a sensation unlike anything he had ever experienced.

Daymon placed his hands on his face and arched his back, letting out a guttural cry. As he did so his wounds reopened, adding an agonizing punctuation mark to his anguish. When he finished his outpouring of emotion, he gripped the gray weathered fencepost, using it to pull himself up. As he swiped the dreads from his face he sensed a glimmer of movement in his peripheral vision. He turned towards the woman he feared *might* be Heidi in time to see the fingers on her right hand waggle. It seemed like the kind of wave two girlfriends might exchange on a packed dance floor in a noisy nightclub where gestures ruled and words conveyed nothing.

Was she trying to communicate?

Daymon remained static, swaying on his feet, wracked by pain and stricken with remorse. Remorse from letting down his Moms. Remorse from not fully reconciling past transgressions with his dad before the monsters started to walk. Remorse from not having enough sack to scale the barbed wire fence, climb up the cross and then try to figure out how to pull *her* down. It wasn't that he was still gun shy from tangling with the scalpel-sharp twelve footer that surrounded Schriever. His trepidation stemmed from not really wanting to know if it was Heidi hanging in front of him or if it was her badly beaten body double. Either way he was going to have to confront some hard truths. If it was her—how the hell was he supposed to save her? Hippocratic oath or not, there wasn't a doctor in a hundred mile radius willing to risk the wrath of the NA storm troopers in order to help a defector. Assuming he got her help, how was he going to explain the obvious piercings to her wrists and feet? On the other hand, if it wasn't Heidi, then he was right back to square one: his Moms and Pops and now Heidi would all be in the same back-of-the-milk-carton limbo. Not dead, and not alive, just perpetually missing.

But first he had to be sure that she had moved and he wasn't just seeing things. So statue like, he waited and watched.

Before long the crows had each reclaimed a man, and after feasting on the gray matter that had been hidden behind the windows to the soul, they began earnestly ripping away the other fleshy bits while cawing back and forth, apparently very proud of their conquests.

"Get the fuck out of here!" Daymon bellowed as he shouldered the crossbow and drew a bead on the nearest scavenger.

The crows voiced their displeasure, and then in an explosion of black feathers reluctantly took flight.

"Go find some road kill motherfuckers," he muttered under his breath.

As he turned his attention back to the woman, she lifted her head and moved it incrementally first left and then right. The gesture reminded Daymon of how survivors acted after being involved in a fatal car wreck. Trudging around the scene, heads wagging in disbelief—seemingly saying, *Why the fuck me?* Then her eyelids began to flutter and she looked directly at him.

Daymon braced himself with one hand on the gnarled fence post as a wave of relief, which began deep in his gut, raced with dizzying speed to his head.

Though the woman's face bore an uncanny resemblance to Heidi, when she opened her slate gray eyes he realized he had been mistaken. Then, when she mouthed the words *kill me*, he released the deep breath he had been holding and steeled himself for what was to come. *You pass up one mercy kill and guilt decides to rear its ugly head.* Daymon mused grimly. *Then, the next thing you know, you're Jack-fucking-Kevorkian compelled to make things right.* He lamented the fact that he hadn't blown Hosford Preston away when he had had the chance. For if he had, then maybe, just maybe, the big lawyer would stay out of his nightmares. Furthermore, he hoped that by putting this young woman out of *her* misery he would right his wrong while at the same time possibly keep her from making nightly cameos alongside the pasty lawyer.

He loaded the crossbow with a scalpel sharp arrow. There was no reason to finish the woman with a shot to the brain. She wasn't a zombie. She hadn't been bitten—or at least, not anywhere that he could see. He leveled the crossbow, making sure to avoid any eye contact with the poor woman, and then aimed at a spot just below her sternum. From where he was standing, and taking into account the elevation of the cross, he figured one perfectly placed shot should pierce her heart and end her suffering.

The arrow left the bow with a *snik* and found its mark. The woman slumped. Daymon prayed she would find peace.

He gazed at the seemingly unending row of crosses; no less than a hundred dotted the landscape. Far from the perfect symmetry of the head stones in Colleville-sur-Mer Cemetery in Normandy or the arrow straight rows of grave markers at Arlington National in Washington D.C., these crude wooden devices of torture were canted, each one leaning at a different angle, like drunken monuments to misery and suffering.

The lanky firefighter left Lu Lu and marched back towards town following the long ribbon of blacktop, eyeing every cross along the way, all the while hoping and praying that he wouldn't find Heidi nailed to one of them.

By the time he returned to Lu Lu, two hours later, he had been forced to finish off two more *examples,* a teenaged boy and a twenty-something man; both had been beaten severely about the head and neck and he would take their faces to the grave with him. How they had survived the crucifixion process and then endured who knows how many days hanging in the Valley of the Crosses wearing only tattered shirts and shorts would never be answered. That they had somehow survived for so long, while exposed to the elements, only meant their suffering had been of epic proportions.

He threw the bow on the passenger seat, slid in and started the engine. Happy he hadn't found Heidi, yet angry at the monsters and the atrocities that they had committed, he spun the tires and wrenched the wheel over. Gravel pinged underneath Lu Lu as he conducted a hasty three point turn and then with a head full of morose thoughts, guided his ride back into town.

Along the way he passed another vehicle, a green SUV. It slowed but didn't stop.

Daymon nodded at the driver and raised his hand in acknowledgement.

***

Bishop slowed as the speeding SUV passed, and considered turning around and seeing what the dreadlocked man was up to. Then, upon seeing the E which marked it as an Essential's vehicle, he dismissed the idea and continued ahead.

A mile down the road he pulled over and killed the engine. He went around back, opened the hatch and easily removed the woman's limp body and placed it on the roadside. After closing the hatch he paused and considered the pale form at his feet. He had to admit, except for the goose egg on her head and the vivid purple bruising which encircled her neck, she was damn easy on the eyes. Why Christian offed his conquests when he was finished baffled the hell out of him. Under no circumstances would he kick this one from his bed. Especially now—because the last time he checked most of the females left were of the zombified variety. *Fuckin lunatic*, he thought, *what a waste*. But orders were orders; still, Bishop didn't feel like taking the time or effort necessary to nail this woman to the cross. He picked her up and heaved her small body into the knee high grass on the other side of the barbed wire fence, then watched with grim satisfaction as her body bounced and then rolled, finally stopping at the base of the cross that was supposed to have been hers. He didn't know if she was dead, seemed so, but the truth was he didn't give a shit. If she wasn't already dead, she soon would be.

Bishop never acknowledged his part in dealing with the *examples* as anything but normal. They were no different in his mind than Iraqis or Afghans, he was just following orders in a manner that suited him—one that would ensure there would be a few less zombies traipsing the earth.

Chapter 26
Outbreak - Day 11
Nineteen miles Southwest of Schriever AFB
Fountain Valley, Colorado

The gunner atop the lead Humvee called out the walkers as he saw them. Mostly solo or clustered in small groups of twos and threes, the pathetic creatures standing in the road and those milling about the side streets posed no threat to the convoy as it snaked along Squirrel Creek Road, heading for the sleepy subdivisions and strip malls dominating the landscape southwest of Schriever.

Beyond the sprawling communities which had housed mostly military personnel lay their objective.

The Pershing business park consisted of blocks and blocks of two hundred thousand square foot warehouses and its location, east of I-25, had been chosen due to the close proximity to Colorado Springs to the north and I-25 connecting to Pueblo to the south. The sprawling complex, erected on six square miles of desert, received goods from all points on the compass and served as a distribution hub for the entire eastern side of the Rocky Mountain range.

The foraging caravan wove between the increasing amount of stalls and multi-car wrecks as they neared the interchange that would eventually take them south towards Fountain Valley.

The lead gun truck, a Humvee GMV (Ground Mobility Vehicle designed specifically for the Special Forces) stopped short of the entrance to the gated upscale community.

Next to the secure entrance, a vinyl banner sporting a crude hand painted warning flapped in the breeze. The kindergarten style lettering read: *Go away. We are armed and will shoot looters on sight.*

We shoot back, thought General Gaines as he cracked his first and probably last smile of the day. "Rogers, pop the gate."

A man in full battle rattle leapt from the rear of the GMV and deftly placed breaching charges on the hinges and in the center between the wrought iron where the gates met. He unspooled a few feet of cord and ducked down near the wall, his back to the gate.

"*Fire in the hole!*" he said clearly, depressing the hand detonator. With a soft '*karumph*' all three charges went off simultaneously. When the smoke cleared seconds later, the gate was still standing.

"Double the charges," Gaines said to the dismount.

"Roger that," came the reply.

Two minutes later the gate and portions of the wall it had been attached to were reduced to rubble.

After clearing a path through the wreckage, the military vehicles and moving trucks turned into the neighborhood dominated by earth-toned cookie cutter McMansions fronted with like-colored grass.

The first contact came barely three blocks into Fountain Valley Estates. A large group of walking corpses, mostly first turns and likely drawn to the explosions, crowded the thoroughfare ahead.

"Looks like we underestimated the amount of Z infestation, Sergeant Hill," Gaines said casually to his new driver.

Compared to the zombie-infested streets in downtown Springs during the first days of the cleanup, this pusbag parade was nothing. Sergeant Howard Hill had been in the thick of that battle downtown. The twenty-nine-year-old Midwesterner was a trained SF sniper and loved being behind the gun, and most of all, above the reach of the dead. But as he had quickly learned about sniping Zs, he couldn't have it both ways. As the saying went in Springs—you drill 'em, you fill 'em—referring to the oversized low-slung mining dump trucks the soldiers had taken to calling *Dead Sleds*.

At Fort Benning he had been taught to sit still for hours at a time behind the gun waiting for a target—he hated sitting behind the controls of an armored bulldozer for even a minute. So in order to escape the sights and smells that went along with loading the mangled draining bodies into one of those *Sleds,* he instead volunteered to drive General Gaines's Humvee.

Deftly wheeling the gun truck around the hungry walkers, Hill answered matter-of-factly, "Yes sir. Looks like a good number of the residents tried to shelter in place. But after we get through this subdivision there's a good two or three mile buffer south that is totally devoid of residential. The dead *should* thin out the closer we get to the warehouse district... I think as long as they haven't been migrating north from Pueblo we'll be alright, Sir."

"I concur. Thank you for the assessment Sergeant Hill." *Will they ever stop walking... stop hungering?* Gaines asked himself. Then after a drawn out sigh, he went on, "If they are *migrating* or whatever you want to call it... when we get back to Schriever let's start working on a viable cleanup strategy for the southern corridor from here down to Pueblo and implement it ASAP. We may need to build a temporary blockade out of shipping containers and Jersey Barriers like we did on I-25 north of downtown. A permanent barrier may be our *only* option if the Zs are moving this way in large numbers."

"Roger that General," said Hill.

The convoy wound up a long twisting hill, ending up in a part of the subdivision where the mansions were situated such that they all had panoramic views of the Rockies; as Gaines' team neared the south entrance to the gated community, they encountered dozens of walking corpses.

"Stay frosty, Ick," Gaines said into the comms, addressing his team leader who was riding shotgun in the MRAP bringing up the rear. "We have multiple contacts. *Hold fire* and *do not stop*—we're going to push on through to the gate."

"Copy that," said Zack 'Ick' Lawson. The lanky, newly promoted, 10th Special Forces captain resembled Ichabod Crane and was a veteran of the Springs clean-up campaign. He grabbed the Motorola with one oversized hand, thumbing the talk button to address the civilians whom he had the undesirable task of running sheepdog over. And after he warned the civilian convoy of the walker situation, he reiterated the rules of engagement. He wanted to be thorough. The volunteers were all he had for this mission and he knew full well that it would only take one of them losing his or her shit to ruin his day.

***

In the Dakota truck at the rear of the convoy, Brook also noted the increasing numbers of zombies. She switched the M4 selector from safe to single shot, then, thinking to herself that the Kevlar heat trap would only slow her down, she undid the chinstrap and flung the sweat drenched brain bucket on the bench where it bounced around between her and Wilson. "Fuck it's hot in here," she bitched. Supposedly the truck's air conditioning was running, but with only tepid air smelling of death blowing through the vents she finally relented and cracked her window an inch.

Wilson had found the going easy for the first fifteen blocks or so. It was the same as every so called *pony ride* his mom had taken him on as a kid—all he had to do was concentrate on following the ass end of the truck in front of him, purge the other realities of his situation from his mind, and everything *should* be OK.

The first creature Wilson mowed down with the Dakota truck was a female first turn. He couldn't avoid her. The ferocity of the impact and the sound her body made as it was slowly ground into hamburger trapped underneath the truck took him back to Castle Rock and Sam the butcher—the gigantic zombie that nearly ruined everyone's day. Anticipating a geyser of water from the ruined radiator, his pulse quickened and he began to perspire profusely. Then his stomach clenched as his fight or flight instinct was aroused. *PTSD,* he thought to himself, *Post Traumatic Stress Disorder... they're only letters Wilson... relax.*

The soldier's warning that had just blared through the two-way set Brook's nerves afire; she sat squared-up with her finger braced against the trigger guard, head constantly on the move as she tracked the rotting first turns futilely reaching and swatting at the lumbering U-Haul. "*Watch your spacing kid!*" she barked. "*We cannot afford to stop here... no matter what.*"

As if in response to her admonition, the brake lights on the U-Haul in front of them flared solid red as the ungainly truck swerved left and its dually rear wheels spit forth chunks of rancid

163

flesh and stuff her stomach didn't appreciate her looking at. And then as if driven by a drunk, the truck inexplicably wheeled right, reversing course as it slewed to a stop blocking both lanes.

"Good God," Wilson gasped. "What just happened?"

Brook had no answer. She peered into the side mirror so she could ascertain what action the armored MRAP was going to take. Suddenly out of nowhere, a gray palm slapped her window followed by the sneering creature's peeled lips and rheumy milk-colored eyes. The vile image caused her to instantly flash back to her escape from the Ford dealership in Lumberton with Raven snug in the middle and her crazy brother behind the steering wheel trying to kill them. Running the gauntlet of living dead on foot and then in the souped-up orange truck en route to Fort Bragg had left indelible images in her brain that she wouldn't soon forget.

"Back up," Brook implored the novice driver. "Give 'em some room."

Duh, lady, I was about to do exactly that. "Then what? Sit here looking like an oversized Happy Meal to those things?" Wilson quipped as he threw the truck into reverse and backed away, bouncing over a fleshy speed bump in the process.

Once again forcing herself to ignore the whining she barked an order, "If the MRAP continues through... *follow them!*"

No sooner had the prophetic words left Brook's lips than the motorized behemoth pushed around the stationary Dakota truck on the right side, and with springs protesting, jounced over the curb, its deep channel tires churning up mocha-colored sod.

To Brook's amazement, the decaying nightmare next to her window disappeared under the MRAPs left front tire—its leering mug replaced by the driver's distorted profile as he flashed by.

The MRAP stopped and the driver eased the monstrous bumper against the stranded U-Haul; then with a burst of power from the rig's 9.3 liter power plant and a screech of crumpling sheet metal, the fourteen-ton armored vehicle spun the twenty-six foot moving truck like a toy.

The maneuver left the road temporarily impassable and both vehicles side by side.

Unable to go around or move forward, Wilson and Brook could do nothing but sit in the cab and wait.

Happy Meal, Wilson thought morbidly.

In a matter of seconds no less than twenty zombies approached from the right-hand side, jerkily lumbering across the brown lawns like some hellish welcoming party.

In no time, panicked voices started to filter through the civilian comms, each overriding the other—an unintelligible morass of terror.

"*Drivers...* I want you to push through. Do not slow. Do not stop for anything. Civilian gunners, *safeties on... hold your fire,*" Gaines ordered, bellowing to be heard over the frantic chatter on the civilian comms.

Easier said than done, Wilson mused as he tried to tune out the people and their foxhole prayers. He wanted desperately to get moving again—especially after seeing what the horde did to his neighbors and their friends in front of the Viscount Arms back in Denver—shredding them like barbecued pulled pork. He *did not* want to be left behind surrounded by the dead. He put on his mental blinders, pretending the monsters weren't there, and struggled to purge the bloody images from his mind.

"Oh no," Brook said in a low voice.

As if anything could be worse than the situation they were in. Wilson pried his eyes open and asked, "What now?"

"House on the right, there's a little girl poking her head out of the door," she said, directing Wilson's gaze. "*No honey, go back inside!*" she implored the young girl who appeared to be no older than Raven. "*Don't let them see you sweetie. Go back, go back, go back!*"

Wilson stated the obvious. "She can't hear you."

By now the Dakota truck was pressed with zombies and the two trucks to the fore still blocked the road.

Brook cranked her window down and leaned back in order to escape the reaching hands. "What the hell are you doing?" Wilson blurted.

She brought her rifle up and engaged the nearest walkers point blank. Ear-piercing reports bounced around in the cab as she fired controlled single shots into the pack. Then as she changed mags

165

she noticed one of the abominations stalking up the pavestone walk towards the blonde girl, who had left the relative safety of the open front door and was now standing in plain sight in the center of the wide front porch like some kind of sacrificial offering.

"Go back into the house!" Brook screamed through the open window.

In reaction to Brook's voice the girl whipped her head around and locked eyes with her.

"Go honey!" Brook yelled, making a shooing motion with her hand.

Inexplicably the girl stayed in place as the lone zombie trudged up the steps towards her.

Brook slammed the fresh magazine home and chambered a round. Then she kicked her door open, knocking the nearest walker to the ground. From her seated position in the cab she put a bullet in its brain, then tracked the short barreled carbine up and around firing rapidly. Hot shell casings pinged around inside the cab as brains exploded from the walkers outside.

"Close the effing door!" Wilson wailed, his voice nearly drowned out by the gunfire and moaning ghouls.

"I have to save the girl!" Brook cried. Dropping another spent magazine from the smoking carbine, she pulled a fresh one from her MOLLE rig.

"We are supposed to stay inside of the truck," Wilson argued.

She was already crunching up the sloped dried out lawn, firing as she went; his words never reached her ears.

∗∗∗

"Reverse now," Icky ordered his driver. The impact had opened the U-Haul's right side like a tuna can, entangling the MRAP's armored window covers and side mirror in the torn sheet metal.

In the Dakota, Wilson scanned the windows and doors of the darkened houses as he listened to the action on the two-way radio.

Out of the blue someone in one of the other vehicles began praying on an open channel—a civilian no doubt. The muffled gunfire picked up in the background by the two-way sounded far away and of no consequence—Wilson knew different.

"Get off the radio... unless you need... help... emergencies only," a soldier's garbled voice ordered.

The praying ceased.

From somewhere up front a series of heavy concussions rolled like thunder over the convoy, causing the picture windows of the McMansions on his left to flex and vibrate as if made from cellophane.

The steadfast birds that hadn't already taken flight when the noisy procession invaded their sanctuary filled the air at once.

Hurry up lady, Wilson thought as he felt his chest tighten, the first sign of a looming anxiety attack.

The radio crackled again. "Stay in your *vehicles* and stay off of our *comms*. We will be on the move soon!" General Gaines bellowed.

This pushed Wilson over the edge into a full blown panic attack. To him it seemed like the imposing figure was sitting on his chest and screaming directly into his face. Stars danced before his eyes as he labored to draw a breath.

***

To Brook the world seemingly slowed down around her as she sprinted up the walk. The explosions, gunfire, and moans of the dead dissipated and her vision sharpened—side effects of the adrenaline surging through her body.

"Hey monster, here I am," she cried out, trying to get the zombie's attention, but before she had gotten halfway up the stairs a shrill scream pierced the air.

Fear constricting her throat, she stopped short of the landing and shouldered the M4. Her finger tensed on the trigger as the ghoul came up with a bloody hunk of flesh in its maw.

The girl's screaming ceased.

The rifle pummeled Brook's shoulder as she fired round after round into the monster until it slumped atop the child. Hot gun oil assailed her nose. She adjusted her aim and put her last two rounds into the twitching kid's head, then froze momentarily, her eyes straining to detect any movement from the entangled bodies.

Nothing.

She scaled the stairs and stepped around the corpses and made her way to the open front door. *"Anyone inside!"* she shouted.

Silence.

She patted her body armor searching for a fresh magazine. Nothing.

A cold chill arced up her spine when she realized the M4 was empty and her remaining spare mags were fifteen yards away in the U-Haul truck. *A lot of good they'll do you there, rookie*, she scolded herself.

A horn blared.

She turned and counted the dead. *Eight.* "Fuck."

The horn again.

Brook jumped from the stairs, swinging her rifle like a club. The creature blocking her way crumpled hard to the walk, gray matter spilling from its split temple. She swept the barrel up, poking another zombie out of her way, then ran full tilt across the brittle lawn dodging the remaining walkers. Carefully she picked her way through the bullet-riddled corpses splayed out in the street, and exhausted and short of breath, slid in next to the ashen-faced Wilson.

Disgusted with herself, she grabbed a magazine from the bench seat and fed the M4.

Wilson remained quiet. He tilted his head back looking wild eyed and tapped himself on the chest.

"*What*," she said breathlessly. "I'm too old to play charades."

The psychologically imposed dam finally broke and Wilson drew a lungful of carrion-scented oxygen.

"Bad news..." he took a few deep breaths before saying, "the general... I think he knows you left the truck... or maybe he heard your gunshots. Anyway he was just on the radio... and he sounded really *effin* pissed off."

Brook said nothing.

Wilson's heavy panting was the only sound in the cab.

"You look like *you* just finished the marathon," Brook said glancing sideways at the redhead. "*I* was the one doing the dirty work. *Pull it together kid.*"

"While you were *out* I had a panic attack."

Brook put on her nurse's hat. "How often do you suffer from them?"

"Used to happen *only* when I had to deal with an irate Fast Burger customer," he answered through clenched teeth. "The general sounded like one of them... times a million... I *do not* want to be on his bad side."

"That *excursion...me* leaving the truck, that is to be kept between *you* and *me*," Brook said icily as she swapped out the empty mag. Then she took a quick inventory; she still had four fully loaded magazines plus the one in the rifle.

Kneading the steering wheel Wilson asked, "Why did you do that?"

"I didn't think—I just *acted*—that girl could have just as easily been my *daughter*. She was in danger Wilson..."

"Next time you decide on your own to *act*... ask me first. I had nothing but the baseball bat for protection. You left me high and dry. Even *Pug* wouldn't have done that—"

Brook shot an angry glare his way.

Wilson sensed something in his peripheral vision, then slowly panned his head to the right. The unpleasant smell of cordite hit his nose first. Then the realization he was staring down the barrel of the crazy bitch's assault rifle made his heart misfire.

"Take it back..."

Wilson pursed his lips in defiance, staring down the business end of the rifle.

Brook kept the M4 tucked tightly against her shoulder, Wilson in her sights.

The sounds of grinding gears and revving engines filtered in as the two vehicles in front continued their tug-of-war.

General Gaines' voice emanated from the two-way radio, ending the tense moment. "Dakota truck... we *do not* have a visual on you. Come in if you copy. Dakota—come in. Reply if you can hear me."

"Take it back," Brook hissed.

"You gonna answer the man—cause I'm not."

With her free hand she snatched up the blaring radio, threw it in the glove box, and slammed the door. *"Take it back..."* Then all of a sudden, as if a switch were flicked, the fight seemed to leave her body. Her shoulders slumped. She lowered the carbine and in a funereal voice whispered, "Pug killed my brother."

169

Wilson cast his eyes forward and tried to process the information.

That is why she is so interested in Ted. "Sorry to hear that," said Wilson. "I would have *never* implied what I did had I known about your brother."

Brook took a full breath and nearly retched. Though the air in the truck smelled of death and fear-laced sweat, it was the fact that she had just pointed a loaded weapon at an innocent person who was no different than her that made her stomach churn. "Sorry," she croaked between coughs.

"No problem. Promise me two things though."

A pained look settled on Brook's face. She couldn't believe that a few words had been enough to trigger that kind of response in her. "Sure... *anything*... and I am *so* sorry for what I just did... it won't happen again, I promise."

"That gets one of my requests out of the way. Number two... *you* get to deal with the *general.*"

"I'll take the heat," she proffered. "I saw my baby on that porch..." Though she didn't fully believe her words she added, "Gaines will understand."

Wilson sighed in relief.

The MRAP and U-Haul gassed forward at once and after a piercing screech finally separated.

"Go, go, go," said Brook as she rolled her window to the top.

"Thank God!" Wilson whooped. "We're moving again." He urged the accelerator, leaving the small clutch of hungry creatures grasping at thin air.

Brook kept her gaze on the crumpled unmoving bodies as Wilson accelerated and the gray mansion shrank from sight, then she said a prayer of thanks for not having to meet the girl's eyes when she delivered the mercy shots. One less face to add to her nightmares, she thought mournfully.

As quickly as the *fog of war* had descended on the convoy— throwing everything into chaos—it had dissipated and the comms once again went silent.

All thirteen vehicles were on the move; handprints and gore smears from the zombie throng traced their sides, yet all of the civilians had made it through alive.

"*Outstanding*, ladies and gentlemen!" said Gaines over the two-way radio in what Brook thought was *much* too cheerful of a voice for someone riding the tip of the spear.

Wilson pried one of his cramped hands from the wheel and removed his sweat-ringed hat. "That was *fucking* close."

Brook pulled wet strands of hair away from her face and tucked them behind her ears. "No shit," she said in a low voice, "they show up all at once... and their numbers." She shivered.

"You think they were residents?"

"Some of them, but I'd bet this place has more than two gates and one of the others must have been compromised."

"Where do you think they came from?" Wilson wondered aloud.

"They looked pretty beat up—road weary sort of—they could have come from anywhere... but my guess is Colorado Springs or Pueblo," Brook proffered.

"There's over a hundred thousand people in Pueblo if I remember correctly," Wilson said, arching an eyebrow. "Not as many as Denver by a long shot, but that would still be one hell of a horde."

Picking up speed, the trucks in front drove through the crumbling stucco archway and past the twisted and blackened gates of Fountain Valley Estates, and as the trudging dead disappeared in the rearview Wilson said a silent prayer. "What's next on the map?" he asked, apprehension apparent in his voice. "Hopefully there aren't any more *residential* areas."

"I'll check—you get to keep your eyes on the road," Brook said as she tried to figure out where they were on the laminated plastic map. Then as an afterthought she added sincerely, "Good driving back there Wilson."

Beaming on the inside from the accolades, Wilson took Brook's advice and as the white aspens flashed by focused solely on the winding road.

***

Civilians' Billets - Schriever Air Force Base

"Three, four, five," Ted muttered under his breath.

Ever since the immaculately dressed young airman had delivered the news of William's sudden death, he had spent nearly every waking moment equally divided between mourning his partner and formulating his final exit plan.

That he hadn't been able to see Will's body infuriated him. Pneumonia was the suspected cause of death he had been told. They were going to come find him so he could pay his respects... *but.* Why did there always have to be a *but,* Ted thought at the time. Oxygen fire, he had been told. The infirmary had burned hot with Will's body still inside. Too tired from all of the running and killing and death of the last few days, he took them at their word. Done fighting anything and everything, he had slipped into a deep depression.

Eleven, twelve, thirteen... that's how they do it, he thought to himself as he tightened the knot. Then he glanced up at the two-by-fours and covered his ears. "This is getting old," he shouted, barely able to hear his own raised voice. The tent shook slightly. The thin canvas ceiling did little to insulate the droning roar approaching from the east as yet another noisy airplane skimmed the base on approach to the nearby runway.

He had dropped three obvious hints that he wanted to be left alone. Finally, after a blatant lie that involved Yoga and his impending nudity, Sasha and her constantly running mouth vacated his tent.

Finally alone and able to think clearly, Ted mulled over his options, and in between bouts of uncontrollable crying and inconsolable rage he made up his mind.

He penned a brief note which stated in no uncertain terms that he wanted to be left alone and affixed it to the outside of the front door. *That should keep Sasha away,* he thought to himself. Then he picked up the worthless tangle of keys. He had been kidding himself when he stuffed these in his pocket, he mused. The faithful old blue Subaru, with only nine payments left, sat wrecked in the middle of I-25 near Castle Rock. And as far as his condominium at the Viscount Arms which he owned free and clear—without William—he was never, *ever* going to return to that tomb.

He removed the clear plastic photo fob from the wire key ring and discarded the rest on the adjacent bunk. Will's face, though sunburned, radiated the happiness they had shared on their 'honeymoon' trip to Puerto Vallarta, Mexico. He held the tiny faded picture in his palm and for the first time in more than a week felt something other than despair or loneliness touch his heart. That something was fleeting and ethereal—try as he might, no matter how hard he stared at the silver dollar-sized photo, he couldn't replicate the emotion.

You can't do this Ted, he silently chastised himself. *You're a shrink, Ted... you know better Ted...* his conscience went on. Trying to ignore the mental prattle, he scaled the folding chair and cinched one end of the rope to the tent's ceiling supports with a strong double knot. *With my rotten luck my fat ass is going to bring this whole place down on top of me*, he thought morbidly while he looped the noose over his head. A sudden notion rippled through the curtain of grief shrouding his rational thought. *What if there is no God and no Heaven? What if I never see Will again?*

With one foot hovering over the abyss, Ted steeled himself to follow through and hopefully have his questions answered.

Knock knock.

"Go away Sasha," Ted said, wiping his eyes with the back of his hand.

Knock knock.

Though she had tried to cheer him up during his two day self-imposed sequestration, even going so far as bringing him food, he had definitely had enough of her incessant advice-giving and chatter. *For Christ's sake*, he had asked himself. *Who was the shrink here?*

Knock knock.

"I couldn't give two shits about *Bella* and *Edward*," Ted bellowed at the door. "Furthermore, I hope whoever invented those characters got eaten by those things out there." He should have left it at that and stepped out of this fucked up dead world—instead he waited for Sasha's snotty response.

A muffled male voice said through the door, "I don't have a clue what you're talking about sir. My name is Davis and I *need* to talk to you... May I come in?"

As the metal creaked under his weight, inexplicably he heard Sasha's voice invade his head. *Do not invite him in. If a vampire doesn't have your blessing then he can't cross the threshold.* Followed by William's prophetic words resounding in his skull, *If you do it this way they will find you bug eyed and blue with the contents of your bowels in a puddle under your swinging corpse.* Then, *You are fucking going crazy, Ted,* his own voice informed him.

"Arrrggghh!—Give me a minute... I'm not decent!" Ted shouted. He removed the noose, stowing it over the flimsy two-by-four rafters. *Pussy, chickenshit, fucking failure—you can't do anything right.*

Ted kicked the chair, sending it screeching along the plywood floor. It hit the canvas wall with a hollow *thwop*, collapsed in on itself and hit the floor flat with a metallic bang.

Knock. Knock.

"Everything alright in there?"

Can't a guy even fucking kill himself already? Ted tore the door open and snapped, "What do you want?"

Standing at the threshold and looking up at Ted, Airman Davis methodically removed his camouflage patrol cap and waited a heartbeat to compose himself before he spoke.

Dressed in a dirty sweat stained tee shirt and checked pajama bottoms, standing half a foot taller and packing at least a hundred more pounds than Davis's five-foot-eight inch, one hundred sixty pound frame, the fully bearded man filling the doorway cast an intimidating first impression. The only thing that was missing, Davis thought, was a flannel shirt and a big blue ox. "Major Freda Nash sent me. She requests that you return with me to the security pod," said Airman Davis, seeing the worry creep onto Ted's face.

Crinkling his brows, Ted thought to himself, *Security pod... am I in trouble?* Then he said menacingly, "And if I don't?"

"We won't be taking you against your will if that's what you're thinking," Davis replied, nodding his head slightly and looking Ted in the eyes where instantly he noticed a change in the big man. The look of total defiance suddenly morphed into concern. Then Davis continued, "This is a matter of *national security*—your *expertise* is needed."

Ted shifted his weight nervously between feet. His curiosity piqued, he replied, "*Expertise—national security*... let me guess—the President needs her own personal head shrinker."

"No sir... but someone you know does."

"Who?"

Airman Davis stood his ground. "You will find out soon enough—you still coming?"

"Let's go," Ted said brusquely as he covertly tucked the poignant picture of him and Will into his pocket.

Chapter 27
Outbreak - Day 11
Jackson Hole, Wyoming

Daymon left Lu Lu parked at the end of a little used fire road behind a large stand of trees where her abnormal green hue would be hidden from view. Then, bent at the waist, he cautiously padded the twenty or so yards to the rusty barbed wire fence. Spying his target, he sank to his knees, then flattened to his belly and settled in to wait.

***

He had been laying stone still next to a gnarled fence post accompanied by only by the sound of brittle grass stalks rustling in the gentle afternoon breeze when he heard the familiar engine sound and then recognized the SUV as it came bouncing over the pasture, churning up divots of sod covered soil. It was the same vehicle that had passed him by earlier in the day in the valley—dark green, shiny, and new. The British made Range Rover looked as out of place in the middle of the elk refuge as did the small Asian man and his elderly white friend that Daymon had been monitoring for the past half hour. Daymon adjusted the focus ring. He was certain the fit looking, dark haired man who had stepped out of the vehicle was Ian Bishop, the man Gerald had told him about. Then the puzzle pieces locked in place. The old dude, as he had suspected, was in fact Robert Christian and the other man was an assistant or some sort of hired help. What he wouldn't have given for a high powered sniper rifle at the moment. The shotgun and crossbow were in his rig—they would both be useless at this range. So now that he had faces to pin on the names, the odds of finding Heidi had just improved drastically.

***

Bishop pulled his Range Rover up next to the boss's shiny black Cadillac Escalade. He scanned the surroundings. Satisfied there were none of the vile creatures in the vicinity, he emerged from the SUV's supple leather interior. The scene in front of him didn't seem at all unusual from half a dozen yards, after all, his boss had been taking at least one meal a day in *his* valley since Ian and the men of Spartan International had taken total control of Jackson Hole just days after the outbreak. Bishop distinctly remembered his boss explaining to him then how the early settlers of Jackson Hole enjoyed supping in the open, ringed by the Tetons—therefore the practice of dining al fresco among cow turds somehow seemed romantic to President Robert Christian.

The detail and preparation put into the lavish spread became more evident to Bishop as he walked forward.

In the center of the folding mahogany table, bright as a solar flare in the afternoon sun, sat a triple tiered oval serving tray festooned with dainty sandwiches, pastries, and scones. Arranged like sentries around the two foot high lazy Susan was an elaborate multi-piece sterling silver tea set which was also polished to a high luster.

You have got to be kidding me, Bishop thought to himself. *Afternoon Tea* in the fucking elk refuge. With a wan smile pasted on his face, he slung his M4 over a shoulder. Barely able to keep the thought of how absurd all of this was—with the walking dead amassing a few miles down the road—he bit his tongue and approached his boss.

"Did you get rid of the firecracker?"

"Yes sir."

"Real fighter, that one, it's a shame she didn't like the asphyxiation game."

"Well... she's no longer *your* problem."

"How goes the *stand* at the bridge," Christian inquired indifferently.

"For now it is what it is—a *stand*. Soon to be our last *stand* if we do nothing. And unlike the Sioux at Little Big Horn, these things are *not* going to be satisfied with only our scalps," Bishop proffered.

With a bite sized tuna sandwich poised near his lips, Christian looked up and said icily, "I didn't ask for your History Channel interpretation Ian. *I want facts.*"

"My men are very low on ammunition. We are losing more civilian conscripts each day... many of them just disappear into the woods when they're supposed to be taking a piss. Three defected in broad daylight yesterday..."

"Did you make *examples* out of them?"

Bishop looked around as if someone who might pass judgment at a later date were eavesdropping on their conversation. "I strung them up early this morning. We're not only running out of bullets... but we're running out of crosses also."

"Build some more—"

"The carpenter building them for me disappeared... can't really blame him if he left on his own accord though—hell, he couldn't even set foot outside of his front door after word got out about what he was making in his shop. Truth is, he probably got snatched up by the other Essentials and he's dead and buried in a backyard by now. Besides, Robert... we cannot afford to make *examples* of people any longer. We need living breathing bodies. The extent of the infestation is staggering. I-89 is a natural conduit from the south. The dead are coming. I'm not exaggerating. I sent out several helicopters to recon the roads this morning. The pilot who followed I89 was white as a sheet as he gave me his report. I think your vision for NA is going to have to take a back seat for a short time. The survivors are close to insurrection, I suppose."

"What is your expert opinion? What steps do we take to ensure my vision comes to fruition and move NA forward?"

"We need to slow down. My men are spread too thin. I recommend we pull back and regroup—our survival is at stake if we don't."

"*Tran,* more Dom Perignon... *now,*" the silver haired eccentric shouted, waving a champagne flute in the air. "Bishop—I need more details out of you."

He's fishing for the one positive nugget to cling to, Bishop surmised. "I trust my pilot's report. Besides... I've seen it with my own eyes. The tide of walkers isn't ebbing," he said, shaking his head slowly side to side, "fact is, more of them are showing up hourly. One of my guys has been going over the barrier and taking wallets off of the dead walkers."

"What the hell did he do a fool thing like that for? If he needed a new wallet there's a Gucci store on Main Street in town."

Ignoring the comment from his out of touch boss, Bishop went on. "We checked the identification and found that most of the dead are coming from Salt Lake City and the surrounding areas in Utah, but a good number are from as far south as Nevada. There were thousands of tourists in Jackson Hole when the virus surged. Gas stations went dry within hours. A good number of the dead— but not the majority I suspect—are those same tourists who choked the roads trying to leave and then took over the rest areas and campgrounds when their cars died and they realized getting home wasn't going to happen."

After a moment of uneasy silence, Robert Christian drained his Dom Perignon and bellowed for more.

Bishop raised his voice in order to get through the alcohol clouded shroud of denial that seemed to have left his boss unable to face reality, much less make a simple decision. "The walkers are moving in packs," he said, allowing a second for that to sink in. "Big fucking packs... *herds.*"

Christian continued to pick at his food, popping a mini croissant into his mouth. "Wonderful meal Tran..."

Tran merely nodded and kept his eyes locked on the ground.

"Continue," Christian implored, dabbing his lips with a stark white linen napkin.

"I have the bridge rigged with explosives," Bishop admitted.

"Who gave you permission? First the nukes and now this, I'm beginning to question your loyalty." Christian's voice was icy.

Bishop said nothing.

"How in the hell are we going to cross the river if we have no bridge? No... The bridge is off limits. That is final," Christian said, fixing bloodshot eyes on the man he was finding harder to trust with each passing second.

Bishop strode closer to the table and said slowly and confidently, "I'm finished asking permission."

Robert Christian froze mid bite and pivoted his head slowly. His watery eyes—burning with laserlike intensity—probed Bishop.

Matching Christian's glare, Bishop laid out his ultimatum— and for all he cared the loony fucker could take it or leave it. "I sent my men to the Air National Guard base near Boise to search for ammunition. They flew out an hour ago... if they come back empty the men holding back the dead will have no other choice than to drop the span into the Snake River and retreat into town. If it comes to that I'll come get you... but if you hear an explosion and you can't raise me on the radio or the Iridium... assume the worst has happened and you are on your own."

Bishop paced a few steps, giving thought to the ramifications of abandoning Jackson Hole. The Humvees, Bradleys and other assorted military hardware sitting near the airport would be lost, but seeing as how the vehicles were nearly out of fuel and had little ammo left, losing them wouldn't be a harsh blow. "Your G6 is fueled. I already alerted the pilots... give them a five minute heads up and they can have their preflight done and you will be wheels up. I cannot stress this enough—you *must* get to the airport as soon as possible."

"What happened to *our* army?"

"I'm losing men nightly at the barrier. I lost a good kid last night. I have sent half of my men over the Teton pass to recon west of here. We will need a safe place to retreat to when... I mean *if* Jackson falls." Bishop grimaced. Bad time for a Freudian slip, he thought to himself. Certainly Christian had noticed. "Following *your* orders—I sent the others out in smaller patrols. They were the troops who set up the garrisons that—once again—*you* ordered."

"And my *garrisons*... just call them back."

"Mack isn't answering. The men you sent south... haven't heard from them in forty-eight hours."

"*Get a handle on this Bishop!*" the self-appointed President of New America bellowed as he sprang from his chair red of face. Then, in a fit of rage he overturned the wooden table, spilling the sterling service and Tran's exquisitely prepared meal onto the ground.

***

From his hide in the tall grass Daymon picked up on some telling body language. *Oh-oh, trouble in paradise.* While the older man had remained seated, methodically working his way through the elaborate meal, the dark haired soldier paced the grass keeping his arms folded tightly across his chest in a defensive posture. The conversation was far from one sided by his estimation and when the man who he guessed was Robert Christian exploded and threw his tantrum and everything else he could get his hands on—Daymon knew something big was brewing.

***

"Face the facts, Robert. We are stuck here, and to make matters worse Francis kicked the hornet's nest but failed to kill the queen. Think about it—laying low won't be such a bad thing. Let this Omega virus peter out. Let the walking dead decay until they are no longer a viable threat. Wait the winter out someplace besides Jackson Hole and then we can reconstitute, rearm, and swell the ranks with the survivors hunkered down out there."

Finally calmed down a bit, Robert Christian ran his hands through his hair. "What about the gold—how are we going to transport all of it to wherever your contingency plan has us relocating? You've got that figured out... *yes?*"

Bishop shot him a look that said, *'weren't you fucking listening.'* "Sixteen tractor trailers are not going to make it no matter where we go. First off, the amount of fuel we'd need isn't available. Secondly, a convoy that big could be tracked by a third grader with pop bottle lenses. Valerie Clay's fleet of Keyhole Satellites are alive and well. There's no way we could move around the west without drawing the attention of every eye-in-the-sky orbiting this dead rock." He shook his head slowly side to side. "Face it sir... there's no use for the gold. There's no *demand* for the gold—and there will not be for a long, long time. It's ironic... man has always had a fixation with trying to turn lead into gold. Now... I wish we had a way to turn gold into lead."

"What do you mean by that Ian?"

"We need bullets sir. We can't cull the dead without them. Furthermore, if Clay comes banging on our door..."

"It's too late, Ian. Though Francis didn't 'kill the queen' as you so aptly put it, he did cause them significant pain. Not just in the near term because he didn't kill the principal, he went on a *tangent* to quote our man at Schriever. *Pug* made an appearance."

Bishop stopped pacing and with a bewildered look asked, "Who the hell is *Pug?*"

"All of these years Francis has taken care of my *problems*. The Senator who said he would swing a vote to my benefit and didn't follow through..."

"Shackleford... he died in a car wreck—right?"

Christian snorted. "That was Francis's doing. That bitch who said I *raped* her and then tried to extort me..."

"Francis?" Bishop said with a sly smile.

"She slipped in the tub and hit her head. Quite tragic don't you think?" Christian said with a wink.

"If he's so good at the *wet works* then what went wrong this time?"

"For some reason he snapped. Pug is a suppressed alter identity... super ego maybe. It's Greek to me. Pug has only shown up one other time which was fifteen years ago. *That* was a mess. Cost me two hundred thousand dollars and two bodies buried in the Nevada desert to make it go away."

Bishop pivoted and paced closer to Christian, saying, "So how bad did Pug step on his dick this time?"

Christian gazed at the Tetons and when he finally answered he sounded different—empowered. "Pug killed the government scientists who were working on a cure for Omega. In fact, he destroyed their research facility and the antiserum they had already perfected and used to cure at least one patient."

"You just made my case for me sir," the former SEAL said in a low voice. "They won't let that slide... they're coming. Time for you to make a decision."

Christian made a sound—part chuckle and part growl. To Bishop it was the sound a wounded and cornered animal might make. "It's too late," Christian muttered. "Any day now another blow will be dealt to those people. They didn't take Francis seriously when he wanted to serve them. And they persecuted you for doing the right thing... that was by all accounts a just cause in your eyes. They will pay—even if it kills me."

If I don't first, Bishop thought. He had a gut feeling he wasn't going to be able to sway the man's opinion but he had to fire one last shot across the bow. Maybe he could scare him into action. "Valerie Clay has already used nukes on Colorado soil. Not singular but plural—*nukes*— in case you didn't catch that little nuance."

"I know," the old man said in a tired little voice. Hunched over he looked withered, seemingly losing six inches in only two weeks' time. Finally he sat back down on the rickety chair in the midst of the broken china and dirt smudged tea service and burrowed his face into his hands.

A chink in his armor or a mental meltdown, Bishop didn't know and he could care less. He stayed on the offensive. "Why do you feel safe here? You know when the next attack is carried out she *will* be gunning for us with both barrels."

Silence.

"Why are you blinded to everything that is stacked against us?" Bishop continued, his voice rising. "We have no allies. Cranston—no way. The idiot father and son duo from Kennebunkport—forget it. Self-centered and self-serving, one and all. The other so called Guild members, the new money guys. Hell, they probably would have been adequate in any scenario—*except* for Omega."

"It didn't go as planned." The old man shook his fist skyward. "All of the pieces were in place and then Omega happened."

Silence.

"In the SEALs we have a saying, Robert..."

Christian watched Tran pick up shards of china, then humored the former SEAL. "How does that saying go Ian?"

"*The only easy day was yesterday.* Keep that in mind... answer my call and I'll come get you. It's the least I can do—after that consider us *equals.*" *My liege.*

183

With that Ian Bishop left his boss and marched to his luxury SUV. The same kind of rig the fucking Windsors favor, he mused. Or used to favor at any rate. He gunned the engine. The tires spewed mud on Tran who was in the act of policing the tangle of china and silver. Bishop watched in the rearview to see if Robert Christian had composed himself. Sadly he had not. He was still hinged at the waist, his hands covering his face—hiding from the truth he knew to be evident.

***

Click, Clack.

Daymon shuddered—a sort of Pavlovian response after hearing the unmistakable metallic sound. His breath seemed to have been sucked from his lungs. He lay perfectly still, listening to the overwhelming noise his heart made jack hammering in his chest while he waited for death or instructions. He hoped for the latter.

"Lucky I wasn't a *rotter* Mister Essential," the familiar voice intoned. "You could've gotten yourself bit—*whatcha doin'*?"

"Keep outta sight and I'll fill you in."

The Chief went to one knee, his shotgun unwavering.

Staring down the barrel of his shotgun Daymon replied, "I'm doing exactly what you told me not to do. I got some information from someone in town—"

Chief Jenkins clicked the safety on the stubby shotgun and laid it on the grass next to the prone firefighter. "I saw your green rig parked outside of Gerald's place this morning. You should think of getting a ride that is a little less conspicuous."

"The thought crossed my mind but I have a feeling there's a fine line between *liberating* and *stealing* these days... at least here in Jackson." Daymon pulled himself up from the ground, being careful to remain in the shadows, and retrieved the shotgun that Duncan had given him.

"I don't care if you go shopping. There are plenty of shiny new vehicles to go around. Hell, every one of the Hollywood crowd's mansions has got two or three parked in the garage. I'm pretty sure *they won't be back*," Jenkins said with an awful Schwarzenegger impersonation.

"I'm good with Lu Lu."

"You sure?" Jenkins asked, looking over the top of his mirrored aviators. "Cause something a little newer might be less likely to break down on you and get you stuck in the middle of a swarm."

Cryptic shit, Daymon thought to himself. *What does he know that he's not sharing?*

Jenkins removed his sunglasses and methodically polished the lenses one at a time as he watched Tran open the Escalade door so Robert Christian could take his place in the back seat. Then the little man climbed into the massive truck. He looked like a little kid as he swayed behind the steering wheel, maneuvering the bucking SUV through the muck towards the blacktop.

Once the Cadillac was out of sight Daymon said, "That little meeting didn't seem to go over very well."

"Very astute observation sir," Jenkins, replied hiking one brow. "I hope you've got your go-bag in order and that rig of yours is gassed up."

Daymon began the long walk back to where he had stashed Lu Lu. "Whose side are you on Chief?"

"These days... I'm on the side of Me, Myself, and I," Jenkins admitted as he tried matching Daymon's stride.

"I'm going to be frank with you Charlie. If I can't find Heidi—or if I find out something happened to her... I will find out who is responsible—and I will take my pound of flesh."

"Better hurry because there are thousands of rotters down the road just *dying* to beat you to it."

"Funny, Charlie."

Heading south in a hurry, a pair of Little Bird helicopters blazed overhead at treetop level.

"Son... I'm going to give you one last piece of advice. Better heed it—you may never see me again."

"You done working for the Storm troopers?" Daymon asked as he tossed the shotgun in the Scout's open window.

"Listen closely," Jenkins said. "Those monsters are walking the highways. The NA boys have the 189 barricaded north of Hoback... it's holding—but not for long."

"How long do you give it before the walkers breach?" Daymon asked. *Test coming up... what about the bridge?*

Chief Jenkins continued, "Bishop had them wire the bridge with explosives. C4 I presume. Even those *retards* can't foul that up. Eventually they are going to have to drop the bridge into the Snake."

"What did you mean when you said: I'm leaving as soon as possible?"

"You know as well as I do—with the shitty salaries Teton County paid us before the shit hit the fan—no way either one of us could to afford to live in this valley." Removing his hat Charlie ran a hand through his receding gray hair. "Sally got bit early on... she's gone and I have got no one to go home *to*. I don't know where I'm going... but it's not gonna be that house. It took everything in me to put her down. Shit... her body is still in the bathtub. I couldn't deal with it at the time. That thing I shot in the head *was not* my Sally."

"That's fucked up," was the only response Daymon could conjure up. "What about Pauline—she lived somewhere in Utah right?"

"Haven't heard from her," Jenkins said. He rubbed his eyes then replaced his glasses.

Daymon gazed at the Tetons.

"*My little girl Pauline*... she just got her divorce finalized, moved into a tiny one room studio in Salt Lake. I couldn't convince her to come back home and dammit it's all our fault. We taught her how to stand on her own two feet. She was always independent to a fault... a real strong woman like her mom."

Grimacing at that revelation Daymon cleared his throat. "Charlie... I'm sorry to hear about Sally, but you know Pauline sounds like a fighter. The kind that survives this shit... she's probably in her place riding it out."

"*Fuck off!*" Jenkins bellowed. "You already told me about Salt Lake, *remember?*"

"I do remember. I was just trying to remain hopeful for *you*," Daymon said awkwardly. "For me... hope is startin' to be a four letter word. As soon as I find out what happened to Heidi—no matter the outcome—I'm headin' someplace else, anyplace but here... too many memories here."

Silence reigned for a long moment.

"Maybe we can finally get the hell out of here... you and I," Daymon added, his voice filled with resignation.

"I'll chew on that for a while. Hell... the way you watch your own six... You're going to need someone to run with you."

Though Daymon was loathe to admit that since the shit hit the fan he hadn't had the best of luck going it alone, he nodded reluctantly.

Jenkins removed the radio from his belt and, handing it to Daymon, said, "In the event of an *emergency* we wouldn't want to have the Jackson Police Chief and the Jackson Fire Chief unable to communicate now would we?"

Daymon eyed the radio, looked up at Jenkins and said, "Good call." He tucked it in his pocket and climbed into Lu Lu.

"Be careful out there," Jenkins intoned, tapping a beat on the warm roof.

"I'll take that advice to heart," Daymon said, firing up Lu Lu. He glanced in the side mirror and watched Jenkins get in the Tahoe, initiate a three point turn on the gravel road—

then the truck disappeared in a cloud of dust.

Chapter 28
Outbreak - Day 11
Schriever AFB
Colorado Springs, Colorado

Security pod

Taking conservative strides, almost baby steps, Ted walked beside Airman Davis. "Why won't you tell me where you are taking me?" he asked, trying to anticipate which path the compact airman was going to lead him down next.

"We'll be there shortly. We have someone we would like you to..." Airman Davis stopped in his tracks, put his hands on his hips and stared groundward, searching his brain for the word.

"*Evaluate...*" Ted intoned.

"Correct... thank you Ted... I haven't been sleeping much lately. I once heard someone say *you can sleep when you're dead...* doesn't hold much water these days, does it?"

"I just lost my partner... apparently *he's* getting some shuteye," Ted spat.

"I'm so sorry Mr. Keller, bad time for gallows humor."

The two men walked in silence for a few minutes until Davis stopped them in front of the squat windowless building which housed Schriever's minimally staffed security facility. "This is our destination, sir," he said.

Ted shot him a suspicious glare. "Who am I evaluating?"

Saying nothing, Davis pushed through the plate glass door.

Feeling the blast of cool conditioned air shifted Ted's mood incrementally into the *good* column.

The waiting room was representative of any other government building, furnished sparsely with a handful of light blue plastic chairs and a single table filled to overflowing with old periodicals.

The walls in the lobby had been painted a battleship gray, the same gloomy hue as the exterior of the building. Apparently the Navy had given the Air Force some of their surplus paint, Ted thought to himself.

Airman Davis left Ted's side and approached the man sitting behind a sliding glass partition. The man, clean shaven with a high and tight haircut, looked up from the months' old issue of Popular Mechanic.

Davis flashed a quick salute as his superior stood and reciprocated.

"Come on in," the man said as he opened the metal door adjacent to the sliding glass divider. He quickly ushered the E-2 and the civilian inside then closed the door behind them.

Ted noticed the air temperature once again drop considerably. *Fucking government*— an interrogation technique straight out of Gitmo he guessed.

"Hi Ted—I'm Senior Airman Croswell... I'm babysitting Francis today."

Ted furrowed his brow. "You mean Pug?"

Croswell shook his head. "He *prefers* to be called Pug... but we like to call him Francis... it pisses him off."

Davis made a face at Croswell then interjected, "I haven't filled him in entirely."

Croswell shrugged his shoulders, as if implying it wasn't his problem, before he continued talking. "Let's just say he got out of line a bit... which led to some innocent people getting hurt."

Ted inched up to the one-way window. Inset into the wall, the four foot by eight foot piece of tempered glass allowed him to see Pug while still remaining anonymous. Except for two metal chairs, the only other furniture in the interview room was a compact table which appeared to be bolted to the floor.

Dressed head to toe in traffic cone orange, Pug rocked slowly in his chair, hands clasped in front of him as if in prayer, on his face a look of glazed detachment. Dried to black, blood caked his swollen ears. Suspended under each eye, puffed black bags bracketed his freshly broken nose.

Ted pressed closer to the viewing window and, noticing the manacles securing Pug's wrists and ankles said, "Pug's an asshole... I get that. Probably likes to fight judging by that fault line of a nose, but what did he do to warrant the beating and the four point lockdown?"

"He wasn't playing nice," Croswell reiterated, then handed Ted a leather-bound notebook and a silver pen. "You need a pipe... cardigan? Maybe a leather couch? I can save you the time... I have already diagnosed the..." The E-2 didn't finish his thought and wisely held his tongue.

The interior door opened suddenly as the diminutive Major Freda Nash strode in, followed closely by the base commander Colonel Cornelius Shrill who dwarfed everyone in the room.

Nash reached her hand out and said, "I want to thank you for accompanying Airman Davis especially without being allowed any of the details. I'm sure you're still mourning the loss of your partner. You have my condolences."

Ted shot her a skeptical look while he shook her hand.

Colonel Shrill, who stood a few inches taller, matched Ted's gaze and nodded in agreement.

For a full minute no one spoke, the only sound the steady thrumming of the air conditioner.

Ted withstood the uneasy silence by staring at Pug. He withdrew the picture of him and William from his pocket and handed it to the woman named Nash. "That's Will and me in Mexico." Then choking up he stated, "I didn't even get to visit him after he was taken away and I was thrown into quarantine. A lady soldier just wheeled him away the night we arrived... I just want to know how he spent his last hours. To know that he got the kind of care that I have been giving him these last few years."

"I'm not making excuses but I've been told he was very sick prior to quarantine. At first they suspected he was infected with Omega..."

"I *told* them he was HIV positive," Ted blurted.

"You have to appreciate the situation for what it looked like to our people. With that stuff going on out there they had to take every precaution to protect themselves," Shrill added. "We're in the business of protecting Americans."

"I know," Ted said weakly.

Nash added, "I'm sure he received the utmost of care before he passed. We planned on having an autopsy performed on your friend... it is standard protocol for anyone who dies while on the base. Our problem is finding someone to perform the autopsy. When we find a pathologist we will certainly know more. Then we can fill *you* in." Nash truly regretted that she was forced to lie by omission. But the need to know why Pug had done what he did was more important than any one man's feelings. Furthermore, the fact that he had obviously not acted alone made such expediency necessary.

"Do you need any special equipment to evaluate the prisoner?" asked Shrill. "If we have it here on base I'll send someone for it."

"How about a full size MRI machine... got one of them lying around?"

The Colonel made a face then coughed.

"Just kidding," Ted conceded.

Shrill's eyebrows relaxed.

"On the trip from Denver I looted... *wrong word*. I *liberated* medicine for Will from a drugstore in Castle Rock. I didn't know when we'd see another so I filled the bag with a myriad of other stuff... *just in case*. I wasn't stealing really. One of the soldiers at the quarantine facility took the medicine along with our weapons when we arrived."

"Everybody gets the same treatment when they come onto the base... merely precautions," Shrill interjected.

Ted smirked. He hated his time in quarantine, alone in his own head with nothing worthwhile to read—no Freud, no Wundt, no Watson. He continued, "I am going to need that bag of meds. If I remember right, the shelves I cleaned out had a host of different products. Also have the Airman find a large gauge syringe and a bottle of water—distilled if you can find it."

"Davis," Shrill barked. "Go down to the hangar and get Mister Keller's belongings."

"And the syringe?"

"*Ask around...*" Shrill barked.

"*Yes sir.*" The airman double-timed it out the front door.

Shrill addressed Ted. "Can you tell us about Pug? You came with him from Denver—right?"

After the door closed behind the retreating airman, Ted responded to Shrill's questions. "I spent a couple hours with the guy two... almost three days ago. I'm being honest when I say I *do not* like being in his presence. I mean... he treated me like a *dick* from the moment I met him." Ted looked through the mirrored glass at Pug. "Shit—from the looks of his face he got some of his own medicine."

Shrill glanced over at Nash—a knowing look exchanged.

Airman Croswell straightened a stack of loose papers, clacking them on the pass through receiving counter before handing them to Ted, who immediately noticed the forms for what they were: standard government medical boilerplate used in the battery of psychological testing which soldiers in basic training all the way up to higher level security clearance personnel were routinely subjected to. Paper waste—one of the few things the United States government had perfected—and it appeared the habit was proving to be a hard one to break. Before the world went to shit, Denver and Colorado Springs had a large number of active duty and retired military, and a large part of Ted's practice involved testifying in court, offering clinical evaluations and his professional medical opinion to help lawyers secure for their clients the largest service-related disability payments they were due. To say he had an intimate relationship with the type of paperwork he held in his hand would have been an understatement.

Pug lifted his head. He appeared to be looking at his reflection in the mirrored glass. His mouth began to move. Ted tried to make out what he was saying, but the fact that his lips were puffed and split made reading them, even minimally, virtually impossible.

"That room has got to be wired for sound. Is there some way I can hear what he's saying?" Ted asked, keeping his eyes on the subject.

"Turn on the microphone Airman Croswell," Shrill ordered.

"He's been repeating the same thing since he was brought in... hasn't changed much. Something about Mighty Mouse," Croswell proffered.

Pug's voice burst from the recessed speakers mounted in the low ceiling. "*Here I come to save the day. Here I come to save the day. Here I come...*" Then in a small voice he said, "*No I will not be quiet. You shut up Francis.*"

"I won't be needing these," Ted said, thrusting the blank forms back to the airman. "The lawyers are all dead anyway. Anyone have a pen light?"

"Will a mini Mag-Light do the trick?"

"It will have to do," Ted said, taking the small black aluminum flashlight from Davis.

"I can't in good conscience unshackle the prisoner for you," Croswell proffered.

"Nor would I let you," Shrill added gruffly.

"Someone gonna let me in to see public enemy number one?"

Freda Nash said, "Airman..."

Croswell hit the buzzer.

Concern evident in her voice, Nash said, "Be *careful,* Mister Keller."

Ted made a face, pushed the door open and stepped into the interview room. The smells hit him at once. Feces, sweat, and fear—thick on the circulated air.

Hearing the door open, Pug produced a wan smile. "Who are you?" he croaked.

"I'm Dr. Keller. I need to look at your eyes." Then, shivering, he yelled towards the one-way glass, "Someone kill the A/C please."

He went to a knee and with two fingers held open the lid on Pug's battered left eye. It looked like a broken red yolk, and blood had invaded the white. Holding the LED light a few inches away he panned it horizontally back and forth. Pug's pupil didn't react to the invading light like it should have. "Who did this to you?"

"Daddy did," Pug said in a gruff faraway voice.

Ted furrowed his brow and asked, "Who?"

"Daddy... he hurts us. Baaad."

"You're all right now, Pug," Ted said, suddenly struck with empathy for the smart ass road dog. "Your Dad isn't going to hurt you now."

"I know... *Mighty Mouse* won't let him."

"Who's Mighty Mouse?" Ted asked, as he checked the other eye.

"I am. And I can fly too," he said in a convincing little voice. Then, looking like a defeated bantam weight fighter, his head slumped forward.

"The nice man Davis is bringing you your medicine. Do you usually take pills or get a shot?"

"Yellow pills please." *Here I come to save the day.*

Ted knelt with his arms at his sides in a non-threatening manner and asked, "What happened to your pills?"

"Francis lost them."

"Where did you lose them Francis?"

"At the big black man's house. I killed him... then I stole his truck..."

"Do you feel remorseful about that?" Ted asked.

"I shot him."

"Did he hurt you?" Ted asked, his voice going soft.

"Dad *hurts* me. He hurts my *privates.*" Pug drew his stunted limbs in as far as the restraints permitted.

The intercom spared Ted from having to ask a follow up question. A female voice said, "Airman Davis is back with your medication Mr. Keller."

"Have him bring it in please."

Davis stepped in, shielding his eyes from the hundred watt bulb with one hand and with the other passed Ted the bag.

Ted rooted around in the large plastic sack and brought out a rectangular white cardboard box labeled Geodon (Ziprasidone Mesylate).

"Were you able to find a suitable syringe and the water?"

"Oh. Sorry Dr. Keller." Davis handed over the syringe which had been in his shirt pocket, then pulled the unopened bottle of water from a side cargo pocket.

With his back to the prisoner, Ted opened the box of medicine and retrieved one of the glass twenty-milligram vials and set it aside. Next he cracked the seal on the bottled water and set it on the floor between his knees. He then ripped the syringe from its sterile packaging and drew the proper amount of water which he injected into the Ziprasidone vial, then shook it vigorously in order to reconstitute the powdered medicine.

"I need a hand in here," Ted said in a low voice.

Pug shifted in his seat. Manacles rattled metal on metal. "What are you doing Dad?"

"It's OK son... I will *never* hurt you again," Ted said, playing along.

Davis and Croswell entered the room while Ted readied the injection; after withdrawing the proper dose he said, "This has to go into muscle... hold him tightly."

With the two men pressing Pug firmly into the chair Ted hiked down the man's pants and jabbed the thirty gauge needle into his right butt cheek.

Pug didn't have much fight left in him yet he still cried out.

"Thanks gentlemen... that went better than I thought," Ted said as he policed up the medicine, water and used syringe and tossed them back into the bag which he handed over to Croswell.

One at a time Ted, Croswell and Davis stepped from the room and formed up in front of the one-way glass.

"So one shot and he's just like new?" Shrill asked as he stared at the pathetic looking figure through the glass.

"Just like that?" Davis said incredulously.

"He's suffering from DID."

Nash tore her eyes from the prisoner and spoke up, "In layman's terms, Dr. Keller."

"DID... Dual Identity Disorder. This man is a survivor alright. He survived childhood horrors, probably sexual in nature, that caused him to make up an alter personality... kind of like an internal bad cop/good cop type of scenario. Sometimes the alter identity will go away after the trauma ceases. Other times new episodes of extreme violence or trauma—for instance the dead tearing someone limb from limb. Something like that can trigger an episode."

"When does the identity switch back?" Shrill asked.

"Since someone has recently beaten the hell out of him... I suspect it may not. I have a feeling he has been either off of his meds—probably some kind of an oral antipsychotic—or he has been under-medicating for quite some time. All very plausible because I know I haven't seen an open Rite Aid for a couple of weeks. At any rate his demons were let loose—so to speak. You'll have to give him the same dose after four hours," Ted said, shrugging his shoulders while making a face that said he had given it his best shot.

Shrill held open the exterior door. "Davis... Croswell... we need a moment alone with the doctor."

Nash turned from the glass and took a seat at the end of the long table, then cleared her throat and said in a soft voice, "Ted... I owe you an amends. I am *so* sorry for your loss. What I'm about to tell you is going to be very hard for you to accept—we had to make a snap decision."

"Who is *we*, and why are you apologizing?" Ted asked as a confused look crossed his face.

Nash went on, "William is dead... there's no changing that." She paused as Ted pulled a chair and sat down heavily. "Since there is no delicate way to say this, I'm going to lay it all out on the table. William was *murdered*, along with six other people."

After an audible gasp Ted slapped the table with both palms. "All I did was give William his drug cocktail and something to help him sleep—for two days you let me believe the sedatives I gave him caused his death. How-fucking-dare-you!"

Shrill maneuvered between Ted and the much smaller major, remained on his feet and said, "It had to be done—he had one or more people helping him—and they are still on the loose. We looked at the kid Wilson and his sister... hell, we even thought *you* were involved. We checked a Denver phone book and sure enough what you told the soldiers at intake checked out." The colonel took a deep cleansing breath then wagged a finger at Ted. "One... according to the Yellow Pages you all lived in the same building—except for Sasha—her name didn't show up but she's a minor so that didn't seem so unusual. And two... evidence led us from the crime scene right to Pug's doorstep—literally. He was shutdown... withdrawn. He gave up without a fight."

Ted emitted a drawn out chuckle and then said, "Wouldn't know it by looking at his broken nose."

"About all I can offer is a sincere apology. I am *deeply* sorry for your loss Ted. You know in a roundabout way that monster in there killed an American hero—a general, who just saved us from the horde that *you* saw firsthand. *Pug* or *Francis*... whatever person he really is... he also killed the two scientists who were working to cure Omega. So you see... you're not the only one who has lost someone."

"Doesn't bring William back," Ted said as he stood up and pushed his chair back forcefully, suppressing the urge to throw it through the one-way glass. He glared at the two Air Force officers and rushed from the room, slamming the metal door behind him.

Nash stood and made a move to follow. "Let him go," Shrill said. "That is an order."

***

After the long lonely walk fraught with more than one wrong turn, Ted found himself back at the *cave*. Scaling the two wooden steps seemed like summiting K2. The wood slat door banged behind him with a resonance seemingly signaling an end—only there was no director standing in the wings waiting to yell, *"That's a wrap."* The decision was his to make and came easier than he would have ever imagined.

The happiest chapter in his life had ended violently—cut short by a little bug and a little madman—sadly both manmade. Ted didn't have the energy to turn another page nor trudge through a fitting epilogue.

Right where he had left it when Airman Davis came a knocking, the folding chair beckoned. And no doubt Miss Nosy would also be knocking in due time. As if on autopilot he stepped up onto the chair and pulled the noose from its perch on the rafter. Standing on the chair left him very little head room and a smaller margin for error. He eyeballed the length of rope between the noose and the point where he had secured the other end, then guessed the distance of the chair seat to the floor. After a quick calculation he muttered to himself, "Six more inches." Then he looped the noose end twice more around the two-by-four support beams. *That oughta do it.*

Ted gazed at the small photo he held in his hand and said in a low voice, "Here I come William."

In order to drown out the rational head shrinker part of his brain chanting, *Don't do it, don't do it, don't do it,* he began singing his favorite Rolling Stones tune, and with *Sympathy For The Devil* echoing from the canvas walls he stepped off into the unknown.

SHAWN CHESSER

Chapter 29
Outbreak - Day 11
Utah/Wyoming Border

Flaming Gorge Recreation Area, Green River
The fuel-laden Ghost Hawk pushed along mere feet above
the deck at a conservative one hundred knots.

Red rock cliffs, with green firs clutching their flanks with
gnarled roots, rose from the desert floor.

Up ahead a snaking stripe of water blazed silver in the
afternoon sun.

"Flaming Gorge Dam," Ari said, indicating the cement
monolith rising above the trickle of a river. Dark streaks painted the
dam face from top to bottom where water continuously spilled
through the overflow sluice gates.

Continuing the impromptu geography lesson he added,
"That's what is left of the Green River. The rest is contained behind
that thing."

Slowing the helicopter considerably, Ari popped them over
the lip of the dam. "Durant... are you seeing what I'm seeing?" he
spouted over the shared shipboard comms.

Simultaneously, every operator in the back of the chopper
pressed a face against the nearest window to take in whatever sight
had gotten the usually unflappable aviator so worked up.

Durant slowly and deliberately panned his head towards Ari,
flashing him a look of disbelief from behind the impenetrable
smoked glass visor. *Ari had said some dumb things over the years but nothing*

199

came close to this, Durant thought to himself. He held his gaze steady and finally answered deadpan, "Seriously Ari. How could *anyone* miss that *thing?* It looks like Lake Havasu during Spring Break down there."

"Minus the college co-eds of course," Ari quipped, reining in airspeed and bringing the Ghost Hawk into a steady hover thirty feet above the blue-green wind whipped chop.

"Holy hell," Tice blurted over the comms.

"I second that emotion," Sergeant Lopez intoned as he performed a quick sign of the cross. "Only there ain't *nothing* holy down there."

Directly off the nose of the Ghost Hawk, in the center of the reservoir, floated no less than a hundred vessels clustered together. Open bowed runabouts, high performance ski boats, and aluminum party barges interspersed with multi-colored personal water craft rode the swells like an immense technicolor lily pad. Suddenly aware of their chance at salvation, several dozen people competed, all trying to win the chopper's attention. Arms aflutter and gesticulating wildly, the sunburned survivors appeared giddy at the prospect of escaping the fate that most of them had undoubtedly resigned themselves to.

"With that many boats down there, shouldn't we be seeing a lot more people?" Maddox asked.

Craning his head to get a better look Lopez added, "Where do you think the rest of them went?"

Tapping a finger on the window, Cade answered, "Most of them are on the beach on the port side."

Hundreds of weathered zombies dotted the water's edge. The largest concentration, a putrefying cluster of living dead, stood huddled on the algae mottled boat ramp nearest the fleet, patiently awaiting the next shore excursion of fresh meat.

Smaller packs of zombies staggered about the debris strewn campgrounds while others loitered near the general store/gas station—undead patrols in search of easier prey.

"*Madre...* it must have gotten too hot out there on the boats for some of them," Lopez supposed, indicating the numerous grounded boats and the bodies, splayed out in death poses, scattered around them.

"Yeah buddy. What a *motherfucker*... having to choose from dying of exposure... or facing that *shit* on shore. But you know what?"

"No Tice... but I have a strong feeling you're going to *enlighten* us," Cade said to the CIA spook/nuke specialist who had proven to be more than worth his weight in gold during the recent Castle Rock mission.

"Those dead bodies... the ones that are truly *dead* and gone, the ones baking in the sun down there... *they were the lucky ones.* If I ever fuck up and get caught by a swarm... and one of you doesn't off me...then *I hope and pray to God* those things eat enough of my ass so I can't come back as one of them," Tice said as he nervously adjusted his ballistic vest. The mere thought of being overcome by a swarm of zombies took him to a dark terrifying place he didn't want to visit. He closed his eyes and thought of puppies and other gentle harmless creatures—anything but the voracious living dead.

East of the main flotilla, Jedi One-One overflew about two dozen sailboats. The vessels, arranged side by side roughly a hundred yards from shore, formed a small floating white island—but strangely there wasn't a soul moving above deck on any of them.

Cade sensed the helicopter nose down and then begin a steady descent before Ari leveled off at about twenty-five feet above the water.

"God damn," Hicks said, training the mini-gun on the undead mass below. He silently longed for permission to light the fuckers up, but knowing full well the ammunition had to be conserved he shelved the urge.

"*God* didn't damn nothin," said Tice, pointing through the port side window behind the co-pilot's seat. "Lookie there... that's the rest of them."

Cade shook his head in disbelief. The series of sluices on the back side of the dam which could be opened or closed when excess rainwater runoff made it necessary was choked with hundreds of floating zombies. The monsters, most wearing life vests, beat the water to a white froth flailing their arms. "Fuckin' great, now I'm going to have the same kind of nightmares as Ed from *Deliverance*... only minus the Dueling Banjos soundtrack," Cade said. "And *that*, Lopez..." he added, pointing at the unsynchronized swimmers,

201

"explains why the majority of the boats are empty." Cade closed his eyes, imagining how the flotilla formed: first a few boats congregated to escape the dead, then more followed their lead, unwittingly bringing their infected loved ones along for the ride. It was a sure recipe for disaster that quickly turned into a floating microcosm of the reality on land that the survivors had been trying to escape.

Ari broke in on the comms, "I thought Ed was the one who had to squeal like a pig."

"*No way*," Durant chimed in. "That was Bobby... he was squealin'."

"Oooh, that's right. Ed was about to have to give the toothless hillbilly a hummer," intoned Ari. "That'd give me nightmares for sure."

"Sorry I mentioned it," Cade said as he opened his eyes and looked onto the reservoir, where he spotted one of the larger vessels which had apparently broken free from the main grouping. The vessel spun clockwise in a slow lazy circle.

Desperate faces turned upward as the nearly silent Ghost Hawk's shadow eclipsed the twin hull, aluminum and fiberglass party barge which was out of control and drifting steadily towards the dam's edge.

Loaded to the point of overflowing, the runabout had seen better days. The twenty or so survivors onboard huddled in a knot in the only respite from the unforgiving sun, a tiny patch of shade cast from the boat's flapping canvas roof.

"No gas. No oars. No hope. They're effed," the usually quiet Maddox added out of the blue.

"Yeah... they're hosed," Tice said matter-of-factly as his camera whirred, snapping images to take back to Schriever.

"Do you have to?" Lopez said. "You making a new *Many Faces of Death* movie or something? You guys lost your humanity?"

A man of few words, Maddox merely shrugged his shoulders.

"Just following orders *Lopez*," Tice spat. The CIA man had butted heads with a couple of the Delta operators since embarking on the mission to retrieve the stolen nukes. And Lopez's constant banter and good natured ribbing was doing little to win him over. If anything it was driving a wedge between Tice and the remaining members of the close knit team.

Lopez uncrossed his arms and held his palms up. "I'm just saying... that those people are deep in the *mierda* down there. You don't need to record it for our future generations. Besides Mr. Ansel Adams you are wasting your time... cause there probably won't be anyone left to gawk at your pictures anyways."

"There is a reason I'm attached with you D-Boys... and it's got nothing to do with my photo composition. And it certainly is not in direct proportion to how much I like and admire you cocky assholes. In case you all forgot there are still a number of nukes unaccounted for—"

"*Oh no, do not do that... sit back down,*" Ari said over the comms, cutting Tice off. "That party barge, starboard side at two o'clock... she is going over. I estimate thirty bodies are going in."

"Copy that," Durant replied from the left seat. "Looks like most of them are wearing flotation devices."

At the sight of their potential rescuers, every soul aboard the *Happy Hour* had stood at once. Then the entire throng foolishly rushed the port side of their floating sanctuary, eyes tracking the black helo, waving their arms in the air like they were in the Packer's end zone encouraging a 'Lambeau leap.' The vessel suddenly listed as the added bodyweight overwhelmed the pontoon directly underneath; the barge submarined, rolling over in slow motion, pitching all aboard into the tugging current.

Every man aboard Jedi One-One watched the horror unfold as the barge capsized and the people were sucked under.

"C'mon Ari... let me go hot," Hicks begged, finger on the mini-gun trigger. "They've got thirty seconds, *tops*, until they hit the Zs."

Owl-like, Ari twisted his neck, acquiring eye contact with Cade. "What do you think Captain?"

"There's not enough spacing to use the mini-gun without some collateral damage," proffered Cade.

Down below, one by one, the survivors broke the surface, their mouths silent O's sucking in air.

Cade quickly weighed his options as the *Happy Hours* passengers bobbed atop the water and drifted towards the water bound zombies. *Shit,* he thought. And then knowing full well that there wasn't any way to kill all of the hungry Zs before the helpless men, women and children were delivered into their midst, Cade made the toughest call of his life. "Come back around and put her in a tight hover," he bellowed as he moved to the sliding door and clicked the carabineer attached to the safety line onto his loadbearing gear. "I can't turn my back on them and I *will not* sit here and watch them get eaten alive." He quickly triaged the situation. He knew full well he didn't have enough time to remove the MSR sniper rifle, assemble it and bring it to bear on the dead. His only other choice was the SCAR, which he knew was a highly capable battle rifle for close in combat. Shooting long distance from a stationary position with the SCAR was doable—shooting accurately from the hovering helicopter was another thing.

"Ari, take me closer."

"Copy that."

Immediately the Ghost Hawk yawed sideways and a blast of hot air entered the open door buffeting Cade's face. Because of the engine whine and gusting wind, the inside of the helo had become a difficult place to communicate —even with the onboard comms.

"*Perfect, Ari!*" Cade yelled. He aimed towards the mass of Zs as the first of the floating survivors made contact. Bracketed in his cross hairs, a young boy's face, all terror and silent screams, filled the optics. Calming his breathing and clearing his thoughts he prepared to enter the shooter's zone. He had no time to calculate wind, elevation, or range—besides, doing so hastily in the hovering helo was almost a lost cause anyway. He was going to have to adjust fire after each miss. Cade knew that kind of thinking wasn't positive but it was the reality of the situation. He caressed the trigger. The silenced rifle bucked slightly as the round left the muzzle. A geyser of white erupted a foot to the left of the towheaded kid's orange life vest. *Shit!* Adjusting aim, he said, "Hicks, open fire on my command."

"Roger that," Hicks replied grimly.

Cade's second shot found its mark. The zombie nearest the boy stopped reaching and slumped forward, still wedged firmly in the spillway grating. Cade shifted aim and in moments a half dozen creatures on either side of the boy were stilled by his steady controlled shooting.

The young boy clambered from the bloody water, sprawling atop the wide walkway, his orange life vest rising and falling with each labored breath.

"Ok... I take it I'm shooting the Zs?" Hicks shouted.

"Mercy kill *only* if a civilian is being attacked," Cade ordered. Then he added—mainly for Hick's benefit—"You'd be doing them a favor... because they're as good as dead anyway."

Cade quick changed magazines and continued dinging the Zs, his accurate head shots widening the safe area.

"Eleven o'clock!" Durant called out over the onboard comms.

Half a dozen floaters who had been swept wide and to the left found themselves in harm's way. The living fought valiantly as they made contact with the dead, pushing off and stiff arming the monsters to avoid being bitten. But the current and their heavy clothing were too much to overcome.

Cade saw the writing on the wall when the water frothed red from the feeding frenzy. Though women and kids were among the dozen or so who were in the dead's clutches, he was left with no choice. "Do it, Hicks."

The starboard side mini-gun erupted with an ominous tearing sound as Hicks walked his fire through the roiling crimson chum.

Body parts floated to the surface and the water went still.

Cade briefly clamped his eyes shut and uttered a prayer for the fellow Americans he had just ordered euthanized.

More than half of the people thrown into the water followed the young boy's lead and crawled over the buoyant dead to safety.

The dead on shore, drawn by the black helicopter, copious amounts of gunfire, and the visceral screams of the dying, streamed to the cyclone fencing which had been placed there to keep people from accessing the narrow catwalk atop the dam.

All that for nothing, Cade said to himself, knowing the fence wouldn't stand for long.

Seeing the same thing, Ari replied casually, "Don't relax yet people... you're going to have some more running to do. Hell Durant, that fence might as well be made of wax paper... I give 'em five... maybe ten minutes *tops.*"

The apocalypse continued to amaze even Cade, always presenting newer and nastier visions for his subconscious to hold onto while he was awake, only to replay in nightmare form at a later date. He had already seen enough of the *floating dead* for a lifetime's worth of nocturnal horror features so he made the appropriate call. "Nothing more we can do for them. Ari, get us out of here," he said, impatience evident in his voice.

"Wyatt... haven't you heard the saying, *revenge is a dish best served cold?*" Ari countered, evidently implying they had plenty of time to get to Jackson Hole.

"That phrase has crossed my lips on more than one occasion Ari. But we are burning daylight... and JP-8. Let's get a move on, and that's an order."

"Copy that... point taken," Ari replied as he looked back into the cabin and nodded respectfully to the newly promoted captain.

Issuing orders still felt a little unnatural, and truth be told Cade had a strong suspicion leading this team on the mission to the NA capital in Jackson Hole wasn't going to be easy. With Mike Desantos' passing and General Ronnie Gaines opting to stay behind at Fort Carson to oversee the ongoing Z eradication and the daunting ongoing task of resupplying Schriever, the young captain found himself thrust into the leadership role. That this wasn't a ragtag band of apocalyptic survivors was a big relief. *Been there, done that,* Cade thought solemnly; these guys were seasoned Tier One operators. He had led a team of combat veterans before, both in Iraq and Afghanistan, and he had no doubt that it would all come rushing back to him the moment his boots hit the ground.

Ari coaxed the Ghost Hawk forward low and slow, passing only a dozen feet over the exhausted survivors, and then continued north, following the serpentine reservoir and keeping close to the slow moving water on the back side of the Flaming Gorge hydroelectric dam.

The shipboard comms crackled to life. "Starboard side, eight bodies. Appears to be...seven children and an adult female," Hicks said. "And they are currently hailing us."

Standing out in sharp contrast against the pristine white superstructure atop their single mast sailboat, the badly sunburnt survivors jumped up and down, gesturing wildly.

"Captain Grayson, permission to hail the crew?" Ari asked.

After a moment's thought Cade replied, "We can't pick them up so what do you propose we do?"

"Give them a little hope," Ari quietly answered. With pangs of guilt from leaving the passengers of the Happy Hour high and dry stabbing him in the gut, and the painful and not too distant memory of the mercy killings at the old folks home outside of Atlanta still fresh on his mind—helping these folks in any way—even indirectly—would go a long way towards reconciling his Karmic account balance.

"Go ahead Ari," Cade said, knowing full well the eight souls below were as good as dead already.

Ari tapped the glass touchscreen, switching the comms to the ship's outside speaker. "Survivors... we cannot take you onboard. We will try and send help. Stay put and await rescue."

Crestfallen, the children stopped waving and slowly lowered their arms, then the woman, displaying her obvious disappointment, fell to her knees on the boat's teakwood deck.

"That didn't have the effect I was looking for," Ari admitted. As far as the group still being alive if and when help arrived—that fell somewhere between slim and none—and if this was a hand of Texas Hold'em, Ari thought, *none* was holding a pair of pocket aces and had just pushed his chips *all in*.

As the dam disappeared behind them Ari addressed Cade. "You are one *lucky* man, Captain Grayson."

"How so?"

"Your family is safe and sound behind the wire. Mine... not so much. They went missing when Fort Campbell fell."

"I'm sorry to hear that Ari," Cade offered solemnly.

"I've come to grips...with a little help from Mark. Mr. Makers Mark."

Is this man ever serious? Cade asked himself. "As far as *me* being the beneficiary of good fortune, *luck* had nothing to do with my family making it out of Bragg. My wife willed herself to Schriever. She didn't give up... *no matter what got in her way she dealt with it in order to protect our daughter.*"

"You're shitting me Delta. You had *nothing* to do with it?"

Cade swallowed hard. "Not directly... I just told her where to find safety and who to trust. That's all," Cade admitted.

Durant entered the conversation. "Who helped her out then?"

"Desantos," Cade answered quietly.

Stabbing a gloved finger at the sky Maddox broke in, "Cowboy, you old warhorse, I'm gonna miss you."

Every head in the bird, including Ari's, tilted for a moment of silence and then, after an appropriately timed sign of the cross, Lopez spoke over the comms. "My madre...she was in Albuquerque. She didn't pick up the phone the last time I called her...before the *mierda* really hit the fan."

Cade looked over to notice that Lopez's entire body was shaking. Whether it was sorrow or rage, he had been there often since all of this bullshit started and he certainly wasn't one to judge Lopez because of his display of emotion. The stocky Hispanic operator had been nothing but professional since the moment they met, therefore Cade harbored no reservations that Lopez was good to go. Furthermore he held no reservations about trusting the man with his life.

Having composed himself, Lopez proffered confidently, "That was the day before all of the cellular circuits failed. I'm certain she went to Sacred Heart and she's safe with Father Brand. I feel it in my bones."

"She sounds like a strong, intelligent lady...a *survivor*," Cade said, co-signing the younger operator's hope.

"I'm just going to think good thoughts and trust that God will look after those unfortunate souls back there," Lopez declared, sounding a little more hopeful. "And I'm going to continue to do the same for my madre."

Cade had nothing more to add; Lopez had succeeded in beating him to it. He merely nodded, broke eye contact, and gazed out the window.

Like a modern day Hooverville—RVs, pop-up campers and tents of all shapes, sizes and colors dotted the shore and crowded every square inch of dusty ground inside of the tree line. If it weren't for the putrefying bodies and staggering dead, the scene that flashed by the helicopter might have been mistaken for any camp ground, anywhere in the United States on Labor Day weekend—overflowing to say the least. In reality, what Cade saw spilled a few more precious ounces from the imaginary glass in his mind—which was no longer half full—nor half empty—it was just about *bone dry*.

Despite having practiced his customary pre-mission ritual, Cade caught himself losing focus and zoning out, eyes locked on the glassy water gliding by mere feet below the helo's underside. Try as he might to concentrate on the task at hand, he kept obsessing over the prisoner back at Schriever and the well-earned punishment he was going to mete out. He also found it difficult to ignore his own bearded face reflected in the glass. The red-rimmed eyes staring back at him, witness to so much death in so short a time, gave him pause. He felt like he was at another convergence, and upon returning to Schriever, a long sit down with Brook was in order. It *might* be time to check his patriotism at the door and dig deep to find out where his real priorities lay.

Chapter 30
Outbreak - Day 11
South of Schriever

With the southbound lanes leaving Colorado Springs thoroughly obstructed with bumper to bumper cars and SUVs, the thirteen vehicle convoy navigated the northbound lanes zippering their way through the smaller number of stalls and pileups, oftentimes leaving the freeway altogether to circumvent major blockages.

Directing his question at the general, Sergeant Hill asked, "Where did all of these people go... it's like they just left their vehicles here and poof?"

"Some stayed put," Gaines said, indicating the many reachers and grabbers trapped in their glass and metal prisons. He swept his hand towards the countryside made up of scrub trees and red-brown hillocks. "The rest are out there somewhere, son. Waiting for us to slip up and become their dinner."

***

It chilled Wilson how the numbers of Zs began to increase exponentially the closer the slow moving convoy got to the interchange. Although nothing close to the hordes out of Denver, he couldn't help but notice the similarities between the two, and judging by their stained and ratty clothes most of the shamblers appeared to be first turns that had already logged lots of miles on foot migrating from somewhere.

"I have a question for you lady."

"Brook works for me," she said sharply. Still kind of heated from the earlier Pug comment, she sat coiled, waiting for the wrong words to spew from the kid.

"Where is your daughter?" he asked.

She swallowed hard and gazed at the modern day version of the Trail of Tears filing by on the other side of the divider, hundreds of vehicles manned by corpses—both moving and truly dead, cars packed with belongings of people whose fate she would never know. She noticed one truck in particular, its bed loaded with plastic yard toys, household furniture and all manner of worldly belongings—a poignant testament to that family's hope that they would find refuge somewhere.

Sensing her unease, he raised his palms from the wheel and said, "If you don't want to talk about it that's OK by me."

Brook turned away from the carnage outside to glare at Wilson. "Why do you care?"

"I heard the *hurt* in your voice back there... when you were trying to save the young girl."

"I do not want to go there so drop the personal stuff."

"My bad," he said quietly, returning his eyes to the road.

***

As soon as the lead gun truck reached the turn off that would take them towards the warehouse district, Gaines noticed the number of sun baked walkers trudging the interstate had inexplicably slowed to a trickle. For all he knew the stragglers at the tail end of the herd could have been victims of a house fire, hobbling along single file in ones and twos, blackened skin peeling and sloughing off.

"General Gaines," Hill pointed a little west of south, "there—you see the smoke?"

"Looks like we've got a forest fire in the distance."

"That's where the New Koreshians are coming from, eh?"

"Not funny, soldier. I lost a cousin in Guyana. Ever heard of Jim Jones?" Gaines said behind a withering stare.

Concentrating as he downshifted, Hill eased the Humvee around an overturned Suburban, and as they came up alongside the *turtled* Chevy a pale appendage reached from the blown out window.

He turned the wheel to the left ever so slightly and maneuvered the three ton Hummer's left front wheel over the groping hand.

Gaines shot a *why the hell did you have to go and do that* look at his driver as the sound of crunching bone made its way through the undercarriage and reached their ears.

"Sorry General," Hill said guiltily. Then, switching back to the first subject, he pulled the name from his memory. "Jim Jones... he was that guy who made people drink poisoned Kool-Aid... right?"

"You can call me Gaines. I'm still a door kicking shooter in here." He tapped his body armor over his heart. "And you are correct, the devil held a hell of a sway over more than a thousand people... enough to get them to line up and commit mass suicide. My aunt Laura and my cousin Lonna were among the nine hundred and nine followers he made drink cyanide. Lonna wasn't a follower—we were around ten at the time—tragic shit."

"I'm sorry I dredged that up sir," Hill said as he followed the onramp heading east. The roiling columns of brown-gray smoke now obscured the horizon off of their right shoulders to the south near Pueblo. "Two more miles," he said. Then he made a silent pact with himself to cut out the wisecracks and stick to the facts—yes sir, no sir—the last thing he needed was to get on the general's bad side. After all, driving the man around would come with perks that he could get used to.

***

Brook removed the magazine, noted the shiny brass, and then reseated it in the well. After running out of ammunition—which Cade would have pointed out as a dangerous rookie mistake—she vowed to always be more vigilant. She reluctantly filed that one in the '*need to know*' column. What had happened back there hadn't put their daughter in danger—therefore Cade didn't '*need to know*' about it.

She wriggled in her seat trying to rid the stiffness wrought from sitting in the truck for two hours wearing bulky ballistic armor under her fatigues. After the encounter with the zombies she contemplated removing the heavy piece of equipment until Cade's voice infiltrated her thoughts advising her otherwise. *Just a few more minutes*, she said to herself.

"That's got to be the place," Wilson said hopefully.

In the distance, at the bottom of the long gradually sloping four-lane highway they were currently on, sat a sprawling grid of gray metal structures. Consisting of acres and acres of identical two story square buildings—their tops bristling with antenna, refrigeration units and various HVAC apparatus—the business park resembled something the *Borg* might have cobbled together.

Wilson whistled. "That's a big piece of real estate down there, lots of nooks and crannies for a rotter to hide."

"I hope the general knows where to start. Because if he doesn't we may be staying the night."

"I didn't bring my pillow la... *Brook*." He almost said *lady* again but wisely corrected himself. There was no telling if the *lady* was over the Pug comment or not.

Brook shot Wilson a glare—held it for a second—then cracked a thin lipped smile.

"I want to get back and make sure Sasha is OK. Plus, the thought of staying overnight, in the dark, without a twelve foot fence to keep the rotters at bay is effing terrifying."

She stared at him. "What doesn't kill us only makes us stronger."

He stared back as long as he dared.

The facility was less than a football field away and the convoy was beginning to slow.

"Don't you want to get back to Raven?"

"More than you know."

The feelings Brook was experiencing *"outside of the wire"*—as she had heard Cade refer to the cities and streets and buildings beyond Schriever populated by walkers and death—was refreshing and like no other. The last time she remembered having felt this alive was at 11,240 feet above sea level on the summit of Mt. Hood back in Oregon. She had been chasing that high ever since and finally had found its replacement. To Brook, the adrenaline flow caused by combat had become like a drug and she wanted more.

***

Grand Junction, Colorado

Daylight was dwindling and so was Taryn's hope that she would ever see her family again. The smartphone's battery was officially dead. She was tired of rereading texts and tweets and looking at pictures of people she knew were probably dead anyway. She closed her eyes. *Time to go or you're dead,* her inner voice said forcefully. She stood and opened the door as quietly as possible. The smell blasted her in the face. Dickless's constant trips up and down the carpeted steps had left a discernible black slug track of bodily fluids down the center.

Get the gun.

She reached the main floor undetected and crept to the air marshal's rigid corpse. She stared at the lifeless eyes and the bullet hole in his forehead, and as her fingertips made contact with the gun, her wrist brushed against cold flesh, making her shiver. The cross hatched grip felt strange in her palm as she struggled to free the black revolver from the cop's ankle holster. *Unsnap the strap.*

Somewhere behind her one of the monsters began to moan.

She looked around frantically. Dickless was nowhere in sight; however, Porkpie was angling towards her from the right.

Taryn's fight or flight instinct kicked in. Flight won out. Hopscotching over bloated bodies, she made her way to the revolving door. She hit the handle running. The door moved six inches then seized up. Looking up the reason became clear—trapped between the partitions—Chester stared down at her with milky dead eyes. Taryn thought if she could get the door moving she could trade places with the undead porter and find herself on the outside. In a last ditch effort to escape the concourse and avoid the advancing hipster she threw all of her weight behind the effort. Still, the door wouldn't budge.

"Shit, shit...," she blurted.

With Chester blocking her way and more zombies bearing down, Taryn was beginning to panic.

With his mouth agape a hissing Dickless lunged for her.

Ducking the clumsy cadaver she scooted backwards on the gore slickened tiles, scrambled to her feet and ran for the upstairs office, her sanctuary, her prison.

After dodging the swipes of half a dozen other creatures she bounded up the stairs and slammed the door behind her.

Sitting there staring at the gun clutched in her hand brought little comfort. She didn't know whether she possessed enough courage to attempt another escape. And she was sure she didn't possess the nerve to turn the gun on herself—so here she was right back in the same goddamn purgatory she had been since the dead began to walk.

Three minutes later Dickless had trudged the stairs and was again rattling the door to *his* office.

Chapter 31
Outbreak - Day 11
Schriever AFB
Colorado Springs, Colorado

Civilian Billets

After a light rap the door slowly hinged open, allowing a slice of muted early evening light to wash across the floor. Footsteps, heavy on the wooden stairs, preceded the large form filling the doorway.

Looking up from her game of *hide from them*, the wide eyed girl retrieved a tattered cloth doll from under the covers and clutched it tightly to her chest. *He smells like one of them a little bit*, she thought, *but he isn't acting like one of them.* She decided quickly she wouldn't be scared.

"Hi little girl... what's your name?"

He's talking, that means he can't be one of them, thought the girl. "My name's Regina."

"Hi Regina, is your mommy here?"

Regina pointed a tiny finger vertically and whispered, "She's taking a nap."

A weary voice came from the top bunk. "I'm up here." Then a woman peered over the bunk's edge. "Why in the hell did you barge in here and what do you want?"

"I knocked."

"Not loud enough," the woman said as she lowered her medium sized frame to the wooden floor. She ran her hand through brunette hair; though dappled with gray she was still attractive (some would say a *catch*) and appeared much younger than her forty-one years. "You gonna answer my question?"

"Name's Elvis..."

"Like the *Hound Dog* singer guy," Regina blurted, cutting him short. She pushed a lock of golden hair from her eyes and said, "We danced to that in first grade."

"That's who *my* momma named me after," he answered in a soft drawl. "What's *your* name ma'am?"

"Theresa," she said nervously. "Listen... my sister in-law will be back soon if she's who you are you looking for?"

"No ma'am... I know it's a little late but I've got a day job here too."

"What's your *day job?*" Theresa asked.

"I just finished another long shift on BD."

"And what does that stand for?"

"I was trying to be discrete—it's short for burial detail," he said quietly. Though not quiet enough to escape Regina's ears.

"Ewwww," she squealed.

"That explains the smell," Theresa stated.

"Sorry," he said sheepishly. "I'll *git along* as soon as we get this out of the way. The base doctor has ordered everyone to get a flu shot," he said, laying the drawl on thick.

Regina crawled onto the bottom bunk, content to play with her doll.

Theresa made a face and said, "You are *positive* this is necessary?"

"All new incoming survivors have been inoculated... I'm just crossing T's and dotting I's," he said apologetically. "Don't worry; it's the kind of needle diabetics use... *real* small."

Elvis took the lid off of the Coleman six-pack cooler and removed two pre-filled syringes.

Regina's eyes widened. "What are *those* for?"

"Something to keep you from getting sick... it will only hurt a teeny tiny bit," he promised as he swabbed her arm with a funny smelling square of cloth. More as a distraction than to establish some kind of bedside manner, he asked her what her favorite color was.

"Pink... owww," Regina cried.

Elvis set the empty syringe aside and produced a cotton ball from his fanny pack. "Hold this," he said to the girl. Then he secured it over the tiny entry wound with a length of medical tape. "Next..."

As he readied the next booster he began chatting with Theresa. "You were in bed pretty early, are you feeling OK?"

"I'm just fine. I was sleeping because there is absolutely nothing to do here... I've read every single book I could get my hands on. It's monotonous as heck and I've found that sleeping helps pass the time. Are you sure *I* need this?"

He leaned over and whispered in her ear, "With all of the dead bodies lying around... even a little cold can kill. I highly recommend it."

He smells good up close, Theresa thought, *besides a little shot won't hurt*. "OK," she said as she looked away and hiked up her sleeve, offering her shoulder to the stranger.

He wasted no time. *This is too easy*, he told himself. Then he wondered if his comrade was having equal success on her assignment.

Theresa felt the sting then winced as the heat radiated down her arm.

"That wasn't bad, was it?" he said, taping a cotton ball in place. His gloved hands felt strong on her arm—reassuring and safe.

"I have felt worse pain."

"Any questions?" he asked as he gathered up his things and popped the lid on the cooler closed with a slap of his palm.

"What should we expect... will we get the flu or just feel a little puny?"

The younger man leaned forward a degree and smiled, a twinkle lighting his eyes. The gesture made Theresa want to pounce on him like a cougar—not the furry feline predator kind—but the forty-five year old Demi Moore jumping Ashton Kutcher's bones type of cougar. It was just enough to make a gal moisten a pair of knickers.

He suddenly got serious.

"The virus affects each person differently. I'd keep an eye on Regina. If she starts to show symptoms get her to bed and tuck her in." He smiled again.

Theresa stared at the cluster of brilliant diamonds on her ring finger, then cast her eyes away and offered a sincere platonic thank you.

"Bye," Regina said, adding a princess wave.

This one isn't going to get away, Theresa thought. *I can't have him... so maybe Nadine can work her magic. Hell, they are closer in age anyway.* "Hey Elvis."

"Yes," he answered, pausing at the door.

"My single... I mean my *sister* will be right back. Think you can wait for her?"

"I've inoculated nearly half of the civilian barracks—but I still have a lot of people to see—if I stand here yakking I won't get to 'em all. Not everyone has been as easy and accommodating as you and your daughter... I commend you both for that." He tipped his Huskers cap. "I better get going now. I'll come back tomorrow and stick anybody I missed today."

Theresa held the door open as he collected his things.

He smiled one last time.

She watched his backside as he walked away. *Nadine, where the hell are you?* A wet cough racked her body. Then another and she hawked a glob of phlegm in the dirt, then called after him, "She's a *catch.*"

***

The tall stranger had been gone less than five minutes when Nadine returned from the Porta-Potties.

Theresa accosted her sister at the door, begging her to run and find the man who she described as George Clooney's much younger doppelganger.

"I know, I just passed him. Black ball cap... big boned... tall and dark."

"Describes him to a T," Theresa said with a smile and a wink.

"He gave us a little baby flu shot," Regina added proudly as she made her doll do a little jig on the bottom bunk.

"Did he give your dolly a shot?" Auntie Nadine said playfully.

"It's for people, silly," Regina said.

Theresa looked at her hands then focused on the wedding band there. She couldn't help but worry about her husband who had been stranded thousands of miles away in New York City when the planes had been grounded. Would he ever make his way home to Colorado Springs to feel her loving embrace? Would daddy's little girl remember her father? Theresa felt a wave of sadness wash over her—sooner or later *she* was going to have to confront reality and find a way to move forward.

Noticing the faraway look, Regina asked innocently, "What are you thinking about Mom?"

Swiping at a single tear she said, "I was thinking about how you and I could go about setting your auntie up with the nice man who just left. And if *I* didn't know how afraid your Auntie Nadine was of needles, I'd go track him down right now."

"Forget the needle," Nadine said with a sly grin. "I wonder what else he's injecting..."

"Not around *Regina*," Theresa said, shooting her sis a stern look.

"Just kidding Tee."

"I bet you could catch him if you ran," Regina added.

"If you won't listen to me at least listen to your niece. *Elvis* told us that he only has a couple more *house calls* to make," Theresa said, bound and determined to live vicariously through her sister— Armageddon or no Armageddon.

Taking the advice to heart, Nadine rushed to the door and poked her head out, looked both ways; then she popped back in with a dejected look on her face. "Another one that got away."

"I noticed he wasn't wearing a wedding band... maybe you can find him tomorrow and schedule an *injection*," Theresa whispered.

"I could only be so fortunate. But I bet he's in an ongoing relationship. Heck, he's probably gay. That'd be *just* my luck."

The sisters broke out in laughter.

"Regina."

"Yes *Mom*."

"Time to brush your teeth and get ready for bed. Auntie and I are going to stay up and talk."

"Can I sleep with you tonight Auntie?"

"Certainly... crawl in my bunk. Sleep tight and don't let the bed bugs bite."

"*Ewww.*"

"That was just a figure of speech honey. So... when your Mom and I finish our grown up time I will snug with you."

"OK," Regina said as she crawled into the lower bunk clutching her doll firmly.

***

Eight down—two to go, Elvis thought to himself. The first eight had gone off without a hitch but he knew there was no room for error on his part. While keeping a wary eye out for the security patrols which had been recently doubled, he banged loudly on the temporary barracks door.

Nothing... but they could be sleeping.

His ball park calculations led him to believe that better than ninety percent of the people he had come into contact with during the last hour and a half had acquiesced, accepting the minor inconvenience of a little poke with little concern. His favorite line echoed in his head, *With all of the dead bodies lying around... even a little cold can kill. I highly recommend it.* The same line he had used to seal the deal with Theresa and every accommodating person thereafter. He smiled, picturing himself decked out in a tuxedo, soaking in the adulation as he held the svelte golden statue aloft. *I'd like to thank the Motion Picture Academy...blah, blah, blah.* "Yep... I shoulda went to Hollywood," he muttered. As he had made his way from tent to tent he noticed most of the civilians that he had *inoculated* seemed either deeply depressed or mired in a state of ongoing melancholy. He supposed it was what the early pioneers called Cabin Fever. Most had been in bed. A few had even been asleep well before the mandatory blackout hour—the hour right before dusk when power from the generators which had been keeping Schriever in the 21st century was shut off to the civilian areas. Only the mess hall and other vital military interests on base had the luxury of round the clock electricity. In addition, and as a precaution against attracting walkers during the night, other strict blackout measures had been put in place. All windows were to remain covered. Movement about the base was discouraged and air traffic was forbidden except in emergency situations.

Pushing the hows and whys from his mind Elvis scaled the steps. Ignoring the fluttering note he knocked loudly, and, after receiving no response, he pushed through the door. The humid air inside of the tent reeked of feces and death. "Son of a bitch," he said as the overwhelming stench hit him like a fist. The first thing he noticed after his eyes adjusted to the dimly lit interior was the folding chair lying sideways on the wood floor, and when he walked his gaze up, the source of the odors became evident. A pallid corpse hung slack, lifeless eyes bugged from their sockets like a surprised Loony Tunes character. This guy wasn't taking any chances, Elvis thought as he counted the requisite thirteen loops—it appeared the decedent had tied his hangman's knot by the book and taken great care to properly secure one end to the rafters. However, it didn't appear to have broken the man's neck, instead it appeared that he had died from asphyxiation. The man's face blazed red with broken capillaries. And to add insult to injury, an erection tented the front of his pajamas which were soiled when his bowels involuntarily released. The resulting lake of oily diarrhea pooled below the dead man's feet proved an irresistible attraction for the multitude of flies jinking and diving about the body.

The Huskers fan stepped from the dead man's quarters and looked down the long line of tents that he had already visited. Not far from where he was standing an Air Force security patrol crossed his path.

"Evening gentlemen," he said.

They nodded—scrutinized his *lunchbox*—but said nothing about the gloves.

Sweating profusely, Elvis waited a tick and observed the two men as they slowly prowled the civilians' living quarters.

Not bad for a couple hours work, he told himself, swinging the cooler like a pendulum—just a worker bee returning from another fine day spent burying the dead. He set off in the opposite direction as the patrol, walked a hundred yards then stopped next to a fifty-five gallon oil drum that been converted into a garbage can. The top layer of MRE wrappers and empty water bottles crinkled as he concealed the cooler underneath the refuse. Then he snapped the latex gloves from his hands one at a time and tossed them after. *Done making the doughnuts*, he thought, as he clapped his hands to rid them of talcum dust.

Chapter 32
Outbreak - Day 11
South of Schriever

With nervous civilian drivers behind the wheel, the ten idling moving trucks sat scattered haphazardly about the road like wayward sheep. And because there was only the lone MRAP for protection, Sergeant 'Icky' Lawson ordered the civilian gunners to remain extra vigilant.

As antsy and emotionally charged as Brook was, she had already decided there would be no more heroics unless one of their own got into trouble. Risking her life like she did in order to save someone who may have already been infected had been utter insanity on her part. Furthermore, she knew that she had risked Wilson's safety and that was at the least indefensible and at the worst a sign of dereliction she was not proud of.

Ten minutes later the two gun trucks wheeled around and took their places in front of the column.

General Gaines's voice crackled over the civilian comms. "Not a Z in sight on the surface roads. Still, you've got to remember to *stay frosty* and keep your guards up people."

As a military wife who had heard Cade utter it a thousand times, Brook mouthed the words '*Stay Frosty*,' a millisecond before Gaines offered the same sage advice.

***

Wilson maneuvered the U-Haul, keeping pace with the long line of trucks stretching out ahead of him. After a few minutes spent

224

driving through empty streets lined with juvenile dogwoods, the lead gun truck abruptly came to a stop behind one of the nondescript warehouses.

"Too many hiding spots," Wilson moaned.

"Lots of food," Brook countered.

"I just want to get this thing loaded and get back."

Being a nurse, Brook couldn't help but offer advice. "Better stretch—and lift with your knees—not with your back. You wrench something then you're done. I'll leave you for the dead before I carry you," she said facetiously.

Not fully aware she had been joking, Wilson smiled. In his mind he was flipping her the bird.

An annoying reverse alarm sounded as he backed the Dakota truck closer to the loading dock that stretched the length of the warehouse. Steel roll up doors painted white and numbered 1 thru 20 loomed above. He guessed the openings to be at least thirty feet tall and twenty wide, more than enough clearance for a fully loaded forklift to move in and out of efficiently.

Wilson looked on as the SF operators led by Gaines quickly gained entry. And after twenty minutes of '*staying frosty*,' whatever that meant, he noticed the doors begin to roll up. Ten in all. Once they were opened, one of the military men directed his U-Haul to door number 10 where the Dakota's rear bumper met the large rubber fenders attached below the lip of the loading dock with a bone jarring thud.

"Whoops," Wilson offered without looking at Brook.

She donned her helmet and smiled but said nothing.

***

Brook slid from the truck then scaled the loading dock. She stood a few feet in front of door number 10 and cast her gaze inside the shadowy building. Flashlight beams cut the dark as Gaines led a troop of civilians down the aisles, pointing out what he wanted to be loaded onto the trucks.

M4 held at low ready, Brook paced the loading dock. She wove her small frame between pallets stacked high with cans and boxes, marveling at the sheer enormity of the distribution center. Row upon row of floor to ceiling shelving containing everything from cleaning supplies and paper products to all manner of nonperishable foods covered every available square inch inside the building. Well before the old consumer driven world ground to a screeching halt this massive distribution warehouse had supplied restaurants and grocers all along the Rocky Mountain range. Now the food was going to allow the small slice of remaining humanity to survive for a few more weeks. She recognized most of the names on the delivery invoices—Olive Garden, Wendy's, Fast Burger and many more—their shipments sitting in front of her on a loading dock in Fountain Valley, Colorado, never to be delivered. No more drive thrus, no more pizza delivery, no more supermarkets—she pondered the austerity the future held for her family as she walked up the ramp away from the loading docks to take a look at the road.

During the hour plus that she had been on watch she hadn't seen a single walker, and with the forklifts' backup klaxons blaring and the soldiers barking orders, she had expected them to show up by now.

She looked down the roadway in both directions.

Clear.

The sound of chains rattling reached her ears as all ten doors began to roll down at once, followed by exhaust notes that echoed off of the building's ribbed steel walls as engines thrummed to life.

At a slow trot Brook made her way back to the Dakota truck and as soon as she slid into her seat Wilson looked at her and asked if the coast was clear.

Brook nodded. "There aren't any walkers on the road if that's what you mean."

Wilson breathed a sigh of relief.

"But don't get your hopes up... all of the walkers we passed back there will surely *still* be there waiting for us when we drive back through."

"Not good. Gaines reversed the driving order." *That's so he can keep an eye on you—Hair-Trigger,* Wilson thought. "That means we're going to be the *first* truck behind the Humvees... and the biggest *target* for the pusbags."

Just then a few sharp pings sounded on the steel roof above their heads. Then more patters on the hood and glass in front of them.

"Summer thunderstorm... that's good if it's heading towards Springs. Might just mask the noise this metal monster makes on the highway and we can slip past the majority of the Zs."

We can only hope, Wilson thought as he set the wipers in motion, smearing bugs and who knows what else into two greasy cataracts on the windshield.

Gaines' voice came over the Motorola two-way. "Move em out," he said brusquely.

Just then jagged fork lightning seared the sky. A half a second later a clap sounding like two trains colliding tore overhead. Then the confined loading area amplified the thunder and it rumbled on for several seconds.

"That hit pretty close to here."

"You want to know what my husband has to say about *close?*" Brook asked as Wilson nosed the U-Haul in behind the two Humvee gun trucks.

"I have a feeling you're going to tell me no matter what I say."

"*Correct,*" Brook stated forcefully. The rain was pounding the truck in earnest. The wipers cleaned the gore but could barely keep up with the cascading sheets of rainwater. Over the *whop-whop* of the wipers she said, "*Close* only counts in horseshoes and hand grenades."

"I get the horseshoes part..."

"The hand grenade part—you don't want to know the details. Cade told me all about it. Not pretty."

"Ohhh," said Wilson as he finally got the picture. "What does Cade do?"

"Sore subject right now—*drop it.*"

"Copy that..."

Wilson stared ahead glumly.

The two vehicles in the lead turned right onto the highway. Wilson scanned for walkers then arced the turn as well. He glanced in the side view, noting that the rest of the food laden trucks were falling in right behind.

Looking over Wilson's white knuckled grip Brook could see that the looming thunderheads had merged with the smoke and haze from the fire, creating a sullen pewter smudge stretching along the horizon as far as she could see.

Good, she thought to herself. *The storm's going our way.*

Chapter 33
Outbreak - Day 11
Fountain Valley, Colorado

Only a handful of zombies roamed the streets of Fountain Valley Estates when the thirteen vehicles started their *thunder run* through the gated community. As Gaines suspected would be the case, the dead had taken advantage of the wide open gates and struck out in search of fresh meat.

In the Dakota truck Brook had remained tight lipped since leaving the warehouse district, answering Wilson's never ending stream of questions with the occasional grunt or head nod. Then, as they neared the place where they had become trapped, Wilson noticed Brook start to squirm in her seat, hands opening and closing around the black rifle between her knees.

"That one looks a lot like the White House," Wilson said, trying to divert her attention from the opposite side of the street and the house with the dead girl still lying on the front porch. "See the columns... maybe it was the same architect."

"Good try kid. The architect of the White House has probably been dead for two hundred years." Brook noticed the Gray Tudor instantly—it had been burned into her memory. She was sure she would be revisiting it in her nightmares for years to come. As the U-Haul drew perpendicular to the McMansion, Brook saw the fuzzy pink robe and one pink slipper cocked at an odd angle. Then she caught a brief flash of blood and blonde hair and white bone. She buried her face in her hands, smelling the gun oil on them. Tears sluiced between her fingers, down her thin wrists and onto the brown vinyl floor mats.

"All clear," Wilson said as soon as the charnel house was out of sight.

Rubbing her eyes on her sleeve, Brook whispered, "That one was hard because she was still alive, *human*. She *was* someone's little girl."

Wilson nodded. "That thing took a bite out of her. She was already doomed." Then he remembered his neighbor's little girl Sarah who had turned and was probably still thrashing around inside of apartment 905 in the Viscount Arms back in Denver. He hadn't had it in him to finish her then, but if he had it to do over again he would brain the toddler in a heartbeat. At that moment his respect for the petite woman to his right shot up another notch.

The fifty caliber guns remained silent until the convoy reached the I-25 interchange, where the throngs of burnt walkers streaming from the south boggled everyone's mind. The way their skin washed away as the sheets of rain pummeled their naked bodies. The way their milk-colored eyes and ivory teeth stood out in sharp contrast to their coal black outer dermis.

Brook shuddered at the sight of the crispy diaspora.

"Shit... they're stopping," Wilson cried as brake lights flared and he narrowly avoided plowing into the Humvee he had been tailgating.

"Gotta clear the road," the general's driver said over the comms. Then General Gaines's voice came over the two-way radio as Brook watched the doors on both gun trucks hinge open. "Civilians must remain in their vehicle," he barked. Then he softened his tone and added, "That includes you, Brooklyn Grayson."

Sinking in her seat, she looked at Wilson, then shifted her gaze to the front.

"I knew you were trouble," he stated matter-of-factly.

They both watched as Gaines and his men fanned out across the road.

Brook estimated there were at least fifty walkers between them and the off-ramp to I-25.

A ripping high pitched whine reached her ears as one of the soldiers, armed with an M249 light machine gun, squeezed multiple short bursts of 5.56 bullets into the mass. Geysers of brain and charcoal coated skull rained down on the roadway as the soldier leaned forward, bracing against the recoil, and walked his fire head high across the front line of walkers; meanwhile, carbine pressed firmly to his shoulder, Gaines calmly advanced and worked his SCAR from left to right, felling a dozen walkers with near point-blank head shots. The encounter was over in a matter of minutes and Gaines and his men walked among the fallen Zs, delivering final death to the ones that still moved. The dismounts hurriedly cleared a path wide enough for the convoy, moving the corpses and body parts and stacking them up beside the road like some kind of blackened meat guardrail.

***

The remainder of the return trip was uneventful. The storm shadowed the convoy all the way back to Schriever, washing most of the evidence of their skirmishes with the dead from the vehicles. Aside from the occasional ten minute afternoon thunderstorms that rolled over the Rockies before descending upon Colorado Springs two or three times a week, this storm was the first substantial sustained precipitation the eastern side of the range had seen since the Omega virus blazed through the valley two weeks prior.

After the Zs at the gate were dealt with, the guards greeted the foraging convoy with smiling faces and cheers.

Chapter 34
Outbreak - Day 11
Near Hoback Junction, Wyoming

Ari flew the black helo just a few feet above the water through all ninety miles of the Flaming Gorge recreation area, changing altitude only to avoid clusters of boats and the occasional bridge or high tension wire. It was the type of flying that required him to not only have full faith in the aircraft, but also nerves of steel. The hardest part of that leg of the mission, he found, was trying to keep from gawking at the numerous scenes of carnage like those at the Flaming Gorge dam.

Scrutinizing the next waypoint on the glass display, Durant said, "We're coming up on Hoback Junction, so I inputted a new waypoint that will swing us around and to the right to avoid enemy contact."

"Copy that," said Ari. "Everyone keep your eyes on the ground. If we come across any NA patrols they must be dealt with before they get on the radio and give us up." He banked the helo hard right and, staying a few hundred yards away, followed the road for a quarter mile.

Cade had been staring at a small creek running parallel to the road when three things happened at once: Outside the turbines shrieked above and behind his head and he could hear warnings chiming from the cockpit. Then he felt his body weight double as he was pushed hard against the bulkhead, and as Ari dove the helicopter to the deck he found his butt and feet levitating as he experienced a split second of weightlessness.

An excited exchange of words passed between pilot and co-pilot. "Two rotor wing contacts, one thousand feet AGL, ten o'clock heading west by southwest," Durant said rapid-fire.

"Taking us to the deck," Ari fired back, his voice nearly overlapping his co-pilot.

"Are we going in?" Cade shouted over the comms as his stomach hit the floor when Ari leveled off.

"No, just hiding in the woodpile," Ari quipped.

By the port side window Tice, face like he had seen a ghost, was staring at the branches dancing thirty feet away.

Hicks shot Cade a look that seemingly said, 'no big deal, all in a day's work,' then flashed a big shit eating grin. Obviously his idea of an E-Ticket ride, Cade thought to himself. While sitting against the opposite bulkhead, Lopez and Maddox looked to have weathered the abrupt maneuver in stride.

"Did they make us?" Cade inquired.

"They didn't deviate," Durant interjected. "Points to no in my book."

"We'll give them a minute or two to create some distance between us," Ari stated. "In the meantime, anyone know any show tunes?"

Tice cackled and Lopez shot him a death glare. Meanwhile Cade continued to stare at the creek much closer than he had anticipated.

After hovering ten feet above the gurgling creek with boughs and leaves whipping from the turbulent rotor wash, the black Ghost Hawk arose slowly from the canopy, nosed down, and resumed the north by northeast heading.

"Just like that, gentlemen," Ari said with an air of cockiness. "And in broad daylight." An obvious jab at Cade's decision to nix the night infil. Thankfully another pre-marital spat ensued, taking the barb off of his mind.

"Goddamn, before Ari pulled that evasive move I saw a shitload of Zs on the road," Tice said.

"Watch your mouth *Spook*," Lopez said, glaring at Tice. "I don't need to hear the blasphemy... *pinche pendejo*."

"Sorry Lopez," Tice intoned. "Won't happen again." *Yeah right.*

Smiling, Cade shook his head and swapped helmets, preparing for the infil.

"Five mikes gentlemen," Ari said over the onboard comms.

After making sure all eyes were on him, Hicks held up an open hand to visually reaffirm Ari's message.

Cade checked his weapons for the umpteenth time. He made sure the SCAR rifle was strapped tightly to his chest and the Glock 17 snug in its holster on his thigh, locked and loaded. In his ruck were two fragmentation grenades and enough C4 plastic explosive to blow a Winnebago sized hole in the Grand Coulee Dam. For good measure he cinched his ballistic vest and MOLLE rig one notch short of tourniquet.

As he watched the other three operators making last minute preparations, he began to second guess himself. Was he putting too much faith in the Night Stalkers and the capabilities of their Jedi Ride? Would four operators be able to destroy the NA's ground defenses *and* pull off the snatch and grab? If they found their targets would he be able to resist the urge to put a bullet in Ian Bishop and Robert Christian at first sight?

Gotta take the first step and hit the ground running, he told himself, trying to shake the nagging doubts he thought he had squashed before leaving Schriever.

As the operators swapped their flight helmets for the low riding tactical helmets, Hicks began readying the fast ropes they would be using for the infiltration. He first checked the anchor points, then placed the thick plaited ropes coiled neatly near the doorway so they would be readily accessible. Once Ari had the bird in a hover over the insertion point, he would only need to throw the anchored ropes into the void and watch the commandos until they were safely on the ground.

In a perfect world, once the helo was on station, the time spent over target from hover to boots on the ground should be less than thirty seconds—Hicks was anticipating fifteen.

"Two minutes," Hicks said holding up a peace sign as he slid the door open.

Cade rolled with the bucking ride and watched the tall firs blur by. Their scent swirling around the cabin suddenly reminded him of Christmas, and made him long for the normalcy he had been enjoying in Portland before that Saturday in July.

Ari banked the craft hard to port, popped it up over a small hillock, and then nosed back down where the black helo would remain hidden from prying eyes—human or electronic.

He wasn't too worried because they were on the south side of Jackson Hole. The entire valley to the north was a different story, because it was being defended with American made hardware. The Ghost Hawk employed Frequency Hopping for its communications and radar as well as radar absorbing skin and ducted exhaust, all of which contributed to its ability to emit virtually zero electromagnetic radiation while maintaining a very low heat signature. In short, the bird was virtually undetectable as long as he kept it out of the valley and out of range of the stolen American made surface-to-air missiles.

Hicks extended a hand to Cade, helped him to his feet, and then checked his gear out. It was standard operating procedure. At the same time the other operators were doing the same for the man in front of him.

"One minute," Hicks bellowed.

Counting down in his head from sixty, Cade said a prayer and slapped his gloved hands together to get the blood flowing. At ten the helo nosed up, coming to an abrupt halt, then hovered thirty feet from the drastically sloping ground.

Ari held steady. The rotor blades had mere feet of clearance on each side. Through the cockpit Ari could see nothing but wildflowers and knee high grass bending in the rotor wash.

Gripping the thirty foot rope with both hands, Cade waited for Hicks' signal. Then once he received the go, he slid over the edge, the feeling of virtual free fall sending his stomach into his throat. Instantly his gloves went hot from friction and in two and a half seconds his boots hit the sloped hillside with a dull thud. Instantly he stepped aside to clear the landing spot and freed his rifle from the center point sling. He went to a knee, brought the SCAR up and had the tree line covered before Lopez hit the ground.

One at a time the other two slid down and formed up.

Hicks jettisoned the fast rope as the helo started to pull away from the hill. And by the time he closed the door, Ari had spun the Ghost in the other direction and they were off to the preplanned loiter spot.

Like a well-oiled machine, Hicks thought to himself as he looked down at his Suunto—*eighteen seconds*. He grimaced as he unhooked the safety cable because he knew the Delta boys could do better, then he took his place behind the starboard mini-gun and strapped in.

"Good job Hicks," Ari said.

"Over *fifteen*... not good enough sir."

"Look on the bright side—nobody was shooting at us."

"Roger that," Hicks replied coolly.

The cabin remained quiet as Ari slowed the helo and parked it in a hover inside a small clearing in the Bridger Teton National Forest, ten miles east of the insertion point.

As soon as Durant received Cade's all clear call he relayed the message, "Anvil Actual is good to go," referring to the call sign Major Nash had assigned the Delta captain.

Ari quickly forwarded a situation report to Schriever, then nosed the helo to the south as Durant searched the digital topo map for the butte they would be cooling their heels on while awaiting the Delta team's exfil request.

The abandoned logging camp where the SOAR aviators would be awaiting the exfil call had been located using old footage gleaned from an earlier flyover conducted by one of Major Nash's KH-11 Keyhole spy satellites. Their loiter LZ (Landing Zone), situated on a medium sized butte roughly five miles southeast of downtown Jackson, was far enough away and low enough on the horizon to keep them underneath the enemy radar.

With only one overgrown and nearly impassable road leading in and out, the Night Stalkers would be safe although a little bored.

It was understood by Cade and the other three men and reiterated by Ari in no uncertain terms that the team would be leaving the valley either on foot or some other type of ground transportation if they failed to disable—or more preferably destroy—the Patriot surface-to-air missiles deployed in the elk refuge.

Chapter 35
Outbreak - Day 11
Jackson Hole, Wyoming

Snow King Resort, Downtown Jackson

The team fanned out and took cover, each near the base of a mature fir tree; then, after a few minutes spent waiting and listening to make sure they hadn't been compromised, they trudged up a field of loose scree, their destination three hundred yards above.

Shadowing the team's uphill progress, flitting from tree to tree and sounding like a rusty pump handle, a Steller's Jay belted out a series of shrill calls.

Cade held up a clenched fist.

The other three men went still.

Looking directly at Tice and Maddox, Cade pointed to his left with two fingers.

The men nodded and moved in that direction, angling for the summit.

Cade motioned for Lopez to follow, and then he moved forward in order to create more spacing in case someone was waiting for them at the top. The last thing he wanted was for the mission to end on the side of the mountain, the entire team taken out by one hand grenade or a quick burst of machine gun fire.

"Clear. We're at the summit," Maddox said into his throat mic.

"Copy," Cade answered as he went to ground and low-crawled until he and Lopez met up with Maddox and Tice behind a termite infested snag.

Though the elevation was only 7,808 feet, the view from the top of Snow King Resort was breathtaking. The city of Jackson Hole started at the bottom of the ski runs where the massive hotel and convention facilities were, and rambled into the distance. Laid out in a grid pattern, the downtown core was dominated with bars, restaurants, art galleries, and T-shirt shops. The National Elk Refuge sprawled to the northeast and roughly ten miles beyond lay the Jackson Hole Airport. The Jackson Hole Mountain Resort was just twelve miles to the north and, in the middle of them all, rising to nearly fourteen thousand feet, the majestic Grand Tetons thrust skyward. Yellowstone with its geothermal pools and the Old Faithful geyser were a mere sixty miles to the east.

***

Six hours later

Cade was no stranger to the boredom and monotony a prolonged stretch of surveillance could bring on. He had spent days on end in the Stan and Iraq watching and waiting for an HVT (high value target) to show, only to paint the target with a laser and let someone else drop a two thousand pound JDAM (Joint Direct Attack Munition) or a couple of Hellfire missiles on their heads. This would be different; if they were lucky they would be rewarded with a HVT to take home with them.

Aside from the random vehicles and the occasional helicopter buzzing north towards the airport, the one constant during the team's six hour over watch had been the Humvee patrolling downtown Jackson Hole. Every twenty minutes, like clockwork, the flat black vehicle returned from the northwest, passed through downtown and then disappeared to the northeast.

Cade checked his Suunto—*one hour until full dark*. He addressed his men who were separated by only a few feet. "We'll lie dog a little while longer—we've got a sliver moon tonight," he said, looking at the clear darkening sky. "Then just after dark we'll work our way down and set up near those," he said, pointing at the alpine toboggan. The blue concrete run, its straightaways bookended by steeply banked turns, ran from the top of the lift to the bottom of the mountain. Cade figured the suspended part of the run near one of the corners where it banked sharply would provide them with the perfect cover until the patrol made its lap, allowing them to move into the city.

He brushed a termite from the Bushnells and continued glassing downtown and the valley beyond.

***

Silver Dollar Cowboy Bar, Jackson Hole

The mechanical bull was going full tilt, bucking in herky-jerky rhythms, as the rider's boots started to exit the stirrups.

Daymon knew without a doubt that the man was about to make an unintended dismount. *Three, two, one...* he counted down in his mind and when the count hit *one* the wiry kid with the blond crew cut was launched from the undulating fiberglass toro and with a hollow slap hit the considerable amount of padding covering the wooden floor.

Unable to control himself, Daymon laughed and peered over the wooden rail at the thrown rider.

The younger man stood slowly and grimaced in pain as he dusted himself off. He looked at Daymon, who was still laughing uncontrollably, and hissed, "What the *fuck* are you laughing at... *nigger?*"

At this point in a Western movie all of the boisterous talk and chatter would stop and the bar would suddenly go quiet; so great would be the vacuum of sound that you could hear a pin drop. This wasn't the case here. Daymon had to yell to get *his* point across. "*A sad fucking excuse for a bull rider, that's what I'm laughing at!*"

Crew Cut came out of the pit, and without taking his eyes off of Daymon defiantly got into his face.

"You sure you don't want to change your story, *nigger?*"

Daymon brought one leg around so that he was sitting sidesaddle on the bar stool facing Crew Cut, then he raised both hands from the bar, palms out in mock surrender.

Thinking he had bested the man with caustic words alone, Crew Cut smirked, hitched his thumbs into his front pants pockets and seemed to relax.

Trapping his dreads behind his head with both hands, Daymon tensed his abs then delivered a wicked head-butt to the bigot's face.

Without so much as a whimper Crew Cut dropped to the hardwood floor as blood poured from his destroyed nose; he lay motionless save for the occasional autonomous twitch.

Daymon massaged his forehead, checking it for blood. *Nothing.*

The bull resumed its steady *kachunk-kachunk* with a new rider in the stirrups as Daymon scanned the bar. Two men, both well north of six feet, played a game of pool on the other side of the bull pit. A handful of inebriated men dressed in all black slouched in a horseshoe-shaped booth swathed in sparkling red vinyl that looked like a transplant from Harrah's in Vegas. Since nobody seemed to be missing Crew Cut, Daymon reclaimed his space at the bar and waved to Gerald. When he at last made eye contact with the grizzled proprietor he raised the empty tumbler.

Oblivious to the one-sided melee that had just taken place, the bar owner shuffled over and poured the dreadlocked man another healthy dose of Knob Creek.

"What's the liquid courage for... you ain't thinking about tangling with the man are you?"

Daymon lifted the bourbon to his lips and met the barman's gaze. "You trying to talk me out of it?"

"No son... I'm concerned is all," Gerald said. He looked to see if anyone was interested in their conversation, then in a low voice added, "Rumors of people desertin'. Not just townies... hell, most of them are dead—been killed in the first outbreak or by the brothers after. I've also noticed fewer patrols around here lately."

"What about the helicopters that have been buzzing around all day?"

"Like I was saying... they are mobilizing. I think there ain't a soul in the NA that wants to go toe to toe with the dead *or* the U.S. army."

"And their crazy leader?" Daymon said under his breath.

Before Gerald could answer a fist fight broke out near the bull.

"Knock it off. Save that shit for the dead... or take it outside," Gerald growled.

Daymon slid off the bar stool and stepped over the man whose nose he had just broken, making sure to get one more lick in with his boot. Then he gestured towards the floor with his thumb and said with a smile, "Gerald... looks like someone's had one too many over here."

Gerald stopped mid pour, put a hand to his ear and said, "Huh?"

With a nonchalant wave that meant *'never mind'* Daymon made for the door while keeping one eye over his shoulder in case Crew Cut happened to have some friends in the bar.

Once outside he took in a lungful of fresh air, and being mindful of his healing wounds, stretched his entire body like a cat just waking from a nap. Feeling the wind nudge his back he commenced the four block walk back to the firehouse. Along the way he kicked over in his mind whether he would follow through with his plan and get some Charles Bronson *'Death Wish'* type of payback or whether he should just get in Lu Lu and drive over the Teton pass then continue past Driggs and onto Eden without stopping. More and more Eden was looking like the most attractive option of the two.

Over his right shoulder the sun was starting to glide behind the Teton Range, its reflection glowing orange in the massive mirrored windows fronting the main entrance to the deserted Snow King Resort. His eyes were drawn to the ground by the motion of his own dreadlocks bobbing at the end of his lengthening shadow. *Shit... Duncan was right—it kinda does look like a spider.* Even though he and the smartass comedian fly boy had gotten off on the wrong foot, he had to admit he kinda missed the old dude's gallows sense of humor. And more than that, he missed the unsolicited fatherly advice the man was prone to giving.

Chapter 36
Outbreak - Day 11
Jackson Hole, Wyoming

8:25 p.m.

Hearing the familiar sounding engine, Cade pressed the Bushnells to his face waiting for the patrol to come back around. As soon as the vehicle nosed around the corner he checked his watch and noted the time. The Humvee kept a slow steady pace as it moved southeast along the main drag, passing the town square and the raised beds of wildflowers and the archways made of stacked elk antlers before turning northeast.

Cade made another mental note. *Still spot on timewise every twenty to twenty-five minutes.* He could see that the passenger in the Hummer was armed with either an M-16 or an M4. The driver, he supposed, had a similar weapon and both occupants probably had some kind of sidearm. He shifted behind the log to get a better view on the retreating vehicle and watched until it disappeared from sight, then made yet another mental note of the time.

Shadows stretched long as the sun began to slip behind the Teton Range.

"One target at ten o'clock—moving our way," Maddox stated.

"I wonder why there aren't more people outside," Lopez said. "You would think with none of the *demonios* walking around they would be dancing in the streets... I know I would."

"That's because there aren't very many people left *anywhere... period*," Cade said as he swept the binoculars across the valley and settled them on the lone pedestrian. The lanky man appeared to be bobbing his head as he walked. For some reason Cade found his movements very familiar but couldn't put a finger to it, and because of the backlight he couldn't get a good look at the man's face.

The sun flared brilliantly as it dipped below the mountain, instantly cloaking the downtown area in shadow. Then as the man stopped in front of a two-story brick building, Cade realized who he was watching. And judging from the looks of the huge double overhead doors the building Daymon was about to enter had to be Jackson Hole's only firehouse.

"Change of plans men," Cade announced.

***

Snake River Crossing I-189

Sunset - 8:38 p.m.

Daly clenched his teeth then reluctantly caressed the trigger. The mule kick recoil of the Barrett .50 caliber sniper rifle rocked his tender shoulder, sending a supernova of pain racing up his stiffening neck muscles. With a detached coldness he watched the zombie's head explode in a halo of flesh and bone, then tracked the sniper rifle left a few degrees placing the crosshairs on the next lurching creature. A slow steady finger pull later he witnessed the frail creature, sans head, pirouette sideways over the smooth guardrail, free-fall limply and land atop the hundreds of other bodies piled up underneath the bridge on the far river bank.

Futile, he thought to himself as he turned and slid down with his back against the bus, the cool steel feeling good against his sunburned shoulders. The creatures were now pulsing through the bus barrier across the bridge. He patted his thigh pocket—a ritual he had performed countless times since dawn; feeling the rigid shape of the detonator momentarily put him at ease. He massaged the stubble on his face then banged his head against the bus, a steady resounding death knell. He had been at the bridge sending former human beings to the afterlife for more hours than he cared to count.

At dawn before his shift had started he had hunkered down in the very same spot he was now and watched the sunrise, hoping and praying that it wouldn't be his last. And as the black night sky softened to a dark shade of blue and the sun finally edged over the Gros Ventre, he'd had a frightening epiphany—or a psychotic moment. *What if I'm really dead and this is hell*, he had asked himself as he sat listening to the rasping wails of the dead behind him. He closed his eyes and took inventory of his various aches and pains. The throbbing in his feet and knees from standing hour after tedious hour on the swaying scaffolding served to remind him he was still alive. The ache in his right shoulder screamed in no uncertain terms that he was fucking still alive. No part of his body was off limits from the spirit-robbing pain, and at the moment he wanted nothing more than to find a bed and fall asleep.

Earlier in the afternoon before Bishop left him in charge he had said, "I'm going to get some sleep. If Holt doesn't drop you a load of ammunition or if you think you are close to running out, call me ASAP. If nothing changes call me anyway at midnight." Daly silently cursed his boss for the mere luxury of a few winks. After all, *he* hadn't slept for days and it was taking a toll on his mind and body. He also knew that without a bottle of whisky sleep wasn't going to happen. The whisky alone might take the edge off the pain but it wouldn't chase away the demons so he could sleep. *If only I had some real medicine*, he thought to himself. The NA was so poorly equipped he couldn't even get a few ibuprofen let alone a Valium or an Ambien. *So fuck you sleeping beauty Bishop. Fuck you Robert Christian— Mister President in title only. Fuck the NA, and fuck the dead*, he thought. Daly wanted it all to stop and had been fantasizing about desertion these last few hours—even going so far as planning where he would go and what guns and supplies he would take.

Not today though, he told himself—besides, going solo out there would be as good as signing his own death warrant. Figuring he had allowed the Barrett sniper rifle enough time to cool down, he finished his bottle of water, crinkled the empty, and tossed it on the pile with the others. He opened the olive drab .50 caliber ammo can. Looking inside he counted at most thirty rounds rattling around in the bottom. He pulled out ten and slowly clicked each massive bullet into the box magazine.

He was just inserting the magazine when he noticed the gunfire along the line increase in tempo then rise to a crescendo.

Not looking forward to the encore ass whipping his shoulder was about to receive, he stood and prepared to once again engage the enemy.

"Oh shit," Daly blurted. The bus barrier had been fully compromised and the bridge crossing the Snake River now swelled with moving bodies. Where before there had been a manageable amount of walking dead, now there seemed to be a never ending torrent.

Daly hefted the long gun and watched in abject terror as more creatures began to surge across the bridge. There were definitely more Zs than the amount of bullets possessed by the entire picket line of defenders. "*Retreat... fall back now!*" he screamed.

The noise of gunfire and moaning dead caused his words to fall on deaf ears.

He put the rifle to his shoulder. *I'm not taking this paperweight with me*, he thought, *might as well empty it*. Sighting the rifle on the zombies in the middle of the four lane span, he squeezed off all ten rounds rapid-fire; then he set the smoking Barrett aside as the first wave of decaying flesh slammed against the busses with a resounding crash. Their bodies quickly piled up, an eye watering mindless crush falling over each other, fingernails scratching steel and glass, reaching blindly for the meat they couldn't see yet their instinct told them was near.

With gunshotlike reports, the tires on the bus to Daly's immediate left exploded followed closely by the crackling of imploding windows. All along the barrier metal groaned and more windows shattered. A drawn out screech emanated from the steel undercarriage as the surging mass drove the low slung bus sideways. Snarling faces leered and pale arms probed the widening gaps.

To his right where the busses abutted the strip mall, men fell from the scaffolding screaming as the dead overran their positions. He looked left, noticing that the dead had broken through on that flank as well.

Time to drop the bridge, he thought to himself as he pulled the detonator from his cargo pocket and fumbled with the cap covering the firing toggle. Suddenly the scaffolding under his feet shimmied then tipped backwards. Worried that he was about to be crushed under several hundred pounds of falling pipe and lumber, he vaulted over the edge. The twelve foot free-fall went smoothly—his landing did not. Upon impacting the unforgiving blacktop his right foot hinged over at an unkind angle and the plastic detonator flew from his grasp and skittered across the roadway. Acutely aware of the prayers and pleas of the men who were dying all around him, he rolled to his stomach and clawed his way towards the detonator. If he was going to die today, he thought to himself, the least he could do was take two hundred tons of concrete and rebar and several thousand zombies into the Snake River with him.

Screech!

The undead mob moved the multi-ton city bus backwards another three feet.

Daly's body flushed cold as the zombies surged through the breach less than ten feet away. "*Fuck, fuck, fuck...*" he cried as the first one through the gap locked eyes with him.

A hoarse rasp escaped the creature's maw as it glared at him through milky, wanting eyes. It advanced on him dragging one mangled leg, its shattered arms swinging wildly. The glistening bones piercing its putrid flesh made the thing look like it had lost a fight with a speeding train.

"Looks like it doesn't pay to be at the *front* of the line," Daly said with a sneer as he shot the battered and broken corpse in the face.

Somewhere in the distance a revving engine resounded over the din of the dead.

Daly turned towards the sound and yelled and waved, frantically trying to get the driver's attention. His heart sank and with it all hope of escaping alive as he witnessed the out of control Durango careen into a light standard, spin sideways and roll multiple times, ejecting the driver in the process.

"Looks like it's every man for his fucking self," Daly said disgustedly as the realization that he had in fact seen his last sunrise hit him full on. He sat up in the middle of 189 and watched as the creatures poured between the fissure nearest him. He leveled his

Glock at the horde and squeezed off a dozen shots. Pale arms reached for him vinelike, and as a cold hand latched onto his shattered ankle he put the pistol under his chin and pulled the trigger.

***

The House - 8:45 p.m.

Gazing at *his* Tetons, Robert Christian's face reflected the sun's fiery orange glow. The wispy saffron clouds rode the twilight sky like zeppelins from one of the Beatle's acid-influenced films.

"Tran... bring more champagne and some of your fabulous toast points and a tin of beluga caviar."

On the bird's eye maple stand beside the California King bed, his Iridium phone began to bleat.

Christian corralled the phone answering with a curt, "Yes." He nodded his head in silence. Then he arose from the bed, strode thirty feet across the room, opened the French doors, and took the rest of the call on the expansive outside veranda. As he listened to the voice on the other end he nudged the broken teak chaise lounge with his toe. Finally he spoke into the phone, "Good job sir. When your work is done there I need you to return home. I have a certain someone who is getting a little too big for their britches. That someone needs to be dealt with." He went silent and listened for a moment before replying, "Yes, him. And I want you to terminate with extreme prejudice." Then after ending the call Robert Christian screamed, "*Who smashed my furniture?*"

Down the hall Clifford perked up. Eyes wide he contemplated spilling the beans. Then, deciding that he did not want to be involved, he swung the door to the security center shut leaving behind a trio of orange fingerprints.

Tran knocked politely before entering with the two bottles of Veuve Clicquot champagne and a sizable tray of finger food—toast points and caviar included.

"Set it there," Christian grunted.

Tran bowed and exited without saying a word.

Christian took one of the bottles to the veranda and with a *POP* sent the cork flying into the swimming pool. Then wrinkling his nose in disgust at the noisy generator he went back to the master bedroom, shutting the French doors behind him.

He looked at the empty bed and thought about having Bishop find him another girl. Then his gaze shifted to the two full bottles of bubbly and decided his libido could wait.

Chapter 37
Outbreak - Day 11
Schriever AFB
Colorado Springs, Colorado

Brook heard the peals of laughter from the sidewalk. And as she reached the door, raucous words devoid of anger and hurt and hate—kind words of kids playing and getting along and healing—reached her ears. For several minutes she loitered in front of Annie's door, basking in the sounds of life.

She knocked.

Raven squealed.

The door opened and fifty some odd pounds of Grayson vaulted the threshold and into Brook's arms.

***

While the kids played—Raven pretending to be Cinderella and the twins the Wicked Step Sisters—Annie and Brook held a quiet conversation.

"How are you doing hon?"

Putting her hand atop Brook's, Annie made a face and responded in a low voice, "I'm getting along... I had prepared myself for that day for the last twenty years. I just never believed it would happen. I knew that some cave dwelling terrorist wasn't going to get the best of my big bad Mike. And they didn't..."

Brook nodded.

Annie went on, "None of us saw this disease... virus... or act of God coming. I couldn't have ever fathomed something like this happening to as many people as it has afflicted. *You* know. You were just out there."

Silence.

"...and just when I think Mike still has his Teflon armor on. You know he talks to me... the mission to the White House. For God's sake, he had to cut off the President's hand to get the *football*," Annie said.

Mike Jr. rolled his tiny head side to side then went still, all swaddled and safe in his bassinet.

With a tilt of her head Brook asked, "What do you mean, *football?*"

"It's what the suitcase is called where they keep the nuclear codes."

Wide eyed, Brook nodded.

"He survived the mission to the CDC in Atlanta."

Brook just listened. In fact most of what Annie spoke of was news to her.

"And *my* Mike and *your* Cade survived the mission to retrieve some nuclear weapons that were stolen from Minot and then set off two of those nukes to save all of us from the Denver horde."

"He was a hell of a man," Brook stated.

Misty eyed, Annie went on, "And after surviving all of that... some fucker destroys the antiserum—kills your brother and ultimately signs *my* Mike's death warrant."

"I'm *soo* sorry Annie," Brook said as she wrapped her good friend in a loving embrace. "If you need *anything...*"

"I'll ask. I'm not shy," Annie said, wiping a fresh tear from the corner of her eye.

Instantly Brook feared for Cade. She had felt all of the emotions before but she hadn't actually acknowledged the fact that he would be gone for good someday, and for some reason or another it hit her harder than ever.

"Let's go Raven," she whispered.

Mike Jr. cooed, wormed his arms from the blanket and batted at his face

"You see. He's a fighter just like his namesake."

"I love you Annie," Brook said. "*Anything* that you need..."

***

After returning to the barracks, Brook went straight for the shower and as the water washed the smell of death from her body she tried to purge the specter of death from her mind. She stepped into the cool air and stared at her image in the mirror and then, trying to convince herself of something she had no control over quietly said, "Cade's coming home."

After toweling off she slipped into a pair of Cade's boxers and, completing the ensemble, pulled on an olive drab shirt with the word ARMY printed in gold.

"Mom."

"Yes sweetie."

Raven turned her big browns on her mom and asked, "What happened out there?"

"We got in the middle of a whole lot of *them*... but it's OK," she said, emotion seeping into her words. "Mom's here now and she isn't going to leave you alone again."

"I'm glad you're back..." Raven whispered, gripping her mom's toned bicep firmly.

"Me too sweetie... me too."

Brook stroked Raven's hair until the girl's breathing steadied and she had fallen asleep. Then she lay awake listening to the rain battering the barrack's roof. She couldn't help thinking about her brother and all that they had been through since the first days of the outbreak in Myrtle Beach. How he had miraculously escaped the blood bath at Grand Strand Regional Hospital only to come full circle and die in the infirmary at Schriever.

Falling asleep proved difficult. The Grayson family mantra ran on a loop through her head. For family truly is the most important thing.

Unable to calm her mind and uncertain whether she had latched the door when they returned from the Desantos billet, Brook swung her legs off of the bunk.

A flash of white caught her eye. Behind the table, trapped between the wall and the leg of the folding chair was the note that she had left for Cade to read before his mission to Jackson Hole.

She made sure the door was locked and then retrieved the piece of paper, placing it on the table where it had been originally.

She climbed back into bed free of resentment, and under the assumption that Cade had somehow missed seeing her note, she drifted off to sleep in her daughter's embrace.

***

Wilson drove the food laden moving truck to the mess hall after he dropped Brook off at the military personnel's barracks. He parked the Dakota truck behind the squat building and deposited the keys and Motorola radio in the glove box, then sat and listened to the rain ping against the roof.

A dull ache radiated from the base of his spine through his neck muscles on down his arms. Even his fingers were sore from strangling the steering wheel in a death grip over many hours. What he wouldn't give for a good massage. He thought through his options. Sasha—way too creepy. Ted—out of the question. Dejected, he pulled the boonie hat low on his head and grabbed his Louisville Slugger. Hungry but too tired to stop and get something to eat, he slid off the seat, slammed the door and trudged off through the forming mud puddles.

Chapter 38
Outbreak - Day 11
Jackson Hole, Wyoming

9:45 p.m.

The night sounds found their normal rhythm after the sun had fully set. The katabatic wind picked up and the temperature dropped to the lower fifties, forcing the men on the desolate ski hill to button up against the chill.

Scattered high clouds scudded across the slivered moon leaving the city below in full dark. Save for a few generators purring in the distance and the intermittently recurring engine growl of the patrol vehicle, Jackson Hole was deathly quiet.

After an hour had passed the four men powered up the Night Vision Goggles clipped to the front of their tactical helmets. Once flipped down, the NVGs turned night into a type of green-hued day in which the team had the capability to see without being seen.

Cade panned his head, surveying the glowing terrain as he picked his way down the steep Double Black Diamond run someone had named Belly Roll, while planted firmly in his mind the knowledge that should he slip the ride to the bottom would be anything but.

Their original plan of lying up on the ski hill until the early morning hours changed the moment Daymon was spotted entering the firehouse less than a mile away.

Cade thought with a little persuasion his old friend might be willing to help, and if he wasn't, well, then Cade had a zip tie with the man's name on it. At any rate, the building, two blocks removed from the main road through downtown, would be a perfect jumping off spot for the operation.

As the hill bottomed out, Cade went to a knee next to the Summit lift control booth and signaled for the rest of his team to follow suit. He trained his weapon on the half empty parking lot and motioned for the other operators to continue to the cluster of buildings to his right.

Lopez heel and toed it slowly towards the three-story resort hotel which loomed above and completely blocked out the ambient moonlight shining through the cloud strata. He viewed the luxury ski destination through the NVGs. It looked like it had been transplanted from downtown Beirut. Though still intact, from a distance the windows and doorways seemed to have been blown out, an illusion created by the goggles. As he neared the stone and timber lodge more details emerged. He could see the curved aluminum handles on the glass doors. Curtains, lamps and other minutiae stood out in the rows of darkened windows.

Grateful that he had yet to come face to face with any of the walking *demonios*, he silently pushed ahead, his silenced SCAR at low ready and his head on a swivel. He paced along the building followed by Maddox, then Tice who swept his M4 towards each new doorway, and then finally Cade bringing up the rear.

"Fifteen," Lopez said quietly. The whisper was picked up clearly by his throat mic. Brown grass crunched under his boots as he crept between the building and the sidewalk. He sprinted from cover and snaked his way between the dust covered parked cars in a combat crouch. He paused between a minivan and an older model compact to check his watch. "Twelve," he said, giving an update of the approximate time the patrol *should* reappear.

Cade paused beside the rear fender of the compact to survey their six which was clear—so far so good. Their infil was going as planned—no detection and no *demonios* as Lopez had taken to calling the Zs.

At a brisk jog, the team crossed East Snow King Avenue and melted into the two-story glass and brick canyon of the business district. They worked their way north following Cache Drive for five blocks, using shadowy doorways and alleys for concealment. Then with two blocks to go to target, Lopez signaled for them to hold up. The intense green numbers on his watch read *20:00*— "Five minutes," he called out.

"We are in the window Lopez... it's your call," Cade proffered.

That the captain had chosen him to take point puffed his ego a bit. He nodded and motioned a go with his hand. The team crossed the street in a noiseless push and one by one cleared the corner and disappeared behind the firehouse.

The men formed up in the shadows next to a pitted and dented steel door, their backs pressed to the brick wall.

Several cars and trucks were nosed in behind the firehouse. On one wall hung a basketball hoop, its tattered net twitching in the breeze.

"Maddox," Lopez whispered.

The other operator, already anticipating this task, came forward with his lock pick gun in hand.

Lopez, looking like a futuristic robot in the green glow, nodded as Maddox kneeled, propped his SCAR next to the door and went to work on the lock.

"Patrol," Lopez said into his throat mic as the low geared whine of the approaching Humvee reached his ears. Out of sight and two blocks away from their position, the vehicle moved slowly down Cache Drive, past the city square and the Silver Dollar Cowboy Bar, then turned away just as it had multiple times without fail over the last seven-plus hours.

A soft click sounded and Maddox flashed the team a green hued thumbs up.

Cade stepped in front of the door. "I'm entry, then Lopez... then Maddox. Tice, you've got our six."

After a trio of *"Copy that's"* Cade eased the door open.

***

Silver Dollar Cowboy Bar - 10:05 p.m.

Lucas Brother stared intensely at the conscript and shook his head. "What do you mean he blindsided you?"

"The black dude... I haven't seen him before. He sucker punched me... out of nowhere," the man replied with a nasal twang. "That's all."

"That's all? That's all that you've got to say for yourself? You had to have gotten *one* lick in," the six-foot-five giant said incredulously. "You're a *chicken shit pussy* Paul. Where the *fuck* was I when this happened?"

"You and Liam were playing pool..."

Lucas's tat covered biceps rippled as he cracked his knuckles. "You point the dude out the second you see him—you hear?"

Paul gave his big friend a look that said, *I don't need your help.*

"Let's go Liam. We got some drinking to do," Lucas said. Everyone in Jackson knew of the man's propensity for the drink. Though he and his brother possessed Scandinavian looks—blonde hair, blue eyes, and chiseled features—they told anyone who would listen they were part Irish and part Cherokee. That Liam also stood six-foot-five assured nobody ever called the brothers on their genealogical bullshit. Also the fact that the two men stayed in Robert Christian's guest house and provided security when Bishop wasn't available kept most at arms' length.

"Luke... where the hell are you," Liam bellowed as he tottered towards the exit, hand covering one eye, obviously three sheets to the wind.

Lucas shot his brother a pissed-off look. "You too shitty to drive?"

"*Have Pipsqueak drive!*" Liam shouted, though less than a yard separated the three of them.

The patrons of the Silver Dollar, who were mostly Essentials and rowdy as hell themselves, stopped what they were doing to gape at the sideshow.

"Drive safe fellas," Gerald said with an indifferent wave of his bar towel.

The first notes of a George Thorogood number emanated from the speakers as the two and a half man crew left the bar.

Flipping his collar up to ward off the chill, Lucas kept the song playing in his head. *Yeah, I am bad to the bone*, he thought as he tossed Paul the keys to the black Escalade. Hauling himself into the passenger seat, he looked at Paul and said casually, "Better not get any blood on the seats."

Paul removed the softball-sized wad of toilet paper from his nose and looked in the mirror to examine the crime scene. "The breeding stopped," he said to Lucas.

"Huh? I dishn't catch that," Liam slurred.

"Makesh two ob us," Paul answered as the Cadillac's parking lights flashed and the door locks popped with a pneumatic hiss.

Paul was doubly amazed Lucas had asked him to drive the Cadillac, seeing as how the man loved to drive drunk. "Drive fast and take chances," was one of the sot's favorite sayings. Holding the ass wipe tourniquet in place with one hand, Paul steered the luxury SUV south along 189 while keeping an eye out for wildlife on the road. It wasn't unusual to see elk, moose, coyote, and the occasional wolf in and around Jackson. But lately there had been more instances of bear, cougar, and other top of the food chain predators finding their way into the city. Some theorized the diminished human population served to embolden the animals. Others thought the walking dead were to blame for driving the woodland creatures to chance contact with the lesser of the two evils. Paul's vote was on the latter.

Lucas Brother gazed at the trees whipping by outside his window. The cognac had already begun to wear off. He felt cursed and blessed at once. He didn't suffer from hangovers and could function at a high level when he was on the sauce. As of late—though he had all of the alcohol he needed—his liquid lover seemed to have lost her luster. *It's the altitude*, he liked to tell himself—one of the many lies. "You're just a pussy," was usually Liam's stock piece of advice whenever Lucas broached the subject, but no matter how he dissected the problem he always came to the same conclusion: he needed to quit.

"Where are we going?" Paul asked.

"Any calls from the Barrier or his Highness... or Sir Bishop of Jackson?" Liam piped up. Then thinking the statement through, he added, "Do not repeath that kid."

Paul in fact hadn't even been listening. He shivered when he realized he couldn't remember where he had put the satellite phone. "Shit... " he gasped as he searched both sides of his seat. He yanked open the center console. *Empty.* Then he gave his pockets a thorough pat down.

"No you did not," Lucas said, slowly staring daggers at the smaller man. "Where in the *fuck* did you leave it?"

"Must've dropped it when the *nigger* smacked me."

"Wash your words kid," Liam slurred from the back seat. "Luke and me prolly got some 'Frican 'Merican somewhere in our family tree."

Arching an eyebrow Lucas barked, "Get us to the *House*." Then he closed his eyes, hoping that Bishop would be gone when they arrived. More pressing, he prayed that he wasn't going to give in to the compulsion and turn to the bottle in order to chase the soft glow rapidly leaving his body.

Chapter 39
Outbreak - Day 11
Schriever AFB
Colorado Springs, Colorado

10:15 p.m.

Regina jerked awake. Maybe it was the unusual sound of raindrops—or Mom's snoring. It didn't matter, she felt awful—like when she had the flu and stayed home from school.

Her mom had seemed sick earlier. *Maybe Mom got me sick*, she thought. She drew the doll in closer.

It started as a tickle. Like hair brushing her neck, then a low growl.

She tried to pry Auntie Nadine's arms from her shoulders. *Too tight... cold.*

"Auntie Nadine?"

"Regina... honey... I'm sorry, I know that I promised... but your mom pulled rank on me," Nadine whispered from the top bunk. "She wanted *snuggling* privileges."

More guttural sounds.

"Mom?"

The smell hit her in the face first—like Mom... and one of *them* combined. She covered her mouth, started to whimper softly.

Then the cold brush of something wet on her cheek.

The rain beat out a cadence on canvas.

Nadine resumed snoring.

Accompanying the first wave of agony white tracers flashed across her eyes, then a funny smell, like her prized penny collection, wet and running down her neck.

Mom's white teeth flashed in the dark.

Regina's screaming filled the air.

***

Screaming.

It came from somewhere across the base, a high decibel shriek. The kind Brook had been exposed to in the E.R.—from those who had been mortally wounded—the ones who had one foot in this world and the other in death's firm grasp. The shrill sound echoing outside meant that someone had just died—or was well on their way. The screaming lasted only a few seconds, then was replaced by more rain assaulting the roof over their heads.

"Shhh," Brook said, clamping a hand over Raven's thin lips.

As she drew the sheet up to her nose Raven asked in a near whisper, "What was that?"

"Mom's going to go and see."

"Please don't leave me Mom... *something* is out there."

A voice in Brook's head—real or imagined—begged her not to go.

Her feet slapping the cold floor, Brook retrieved her rifle and the compact Glock 19. She placed both on the top bunk, climbed up, and pulled Raven after.

"What are we going to do?" Raven asked.

"Hopefully nothing."

The moans and wails resumed. They went on for minutes before staccato bursts of gunfire answered.

Brook clutched her M4, held Raven tighter.

Somewhere from off in the distance came the sound of a Bradley's diesel chugging to life, the shifting of gears, hollow clunks echoing between the barracks and then the sound of a heavy machinegun firing. Then—only the patter of rain.

"Is it over?" Raven whispered.

"I think so, but we'll find out for sure in the morning." With those words began a long sleepless night in the Grayson billet.

***

Schriever Mess Hall

Though it was after ten o'clock and the rain had shown no sign of letting up, there were more people than usual in the Schriever mess hall.

The return of the foraging convoy had not gone unnoticed by the civilian shut-ins, the airmen, and the soldiers who called the sprawling base home. Word had spread quickly and the hall had been overrun and was at full capacity until an hour ago.

Wilson surveyed the rectangular room before taking a seat. "Good thing we waited," he said, thinking out loud. He shook the rain from his boonie hat and hung it on the back of his chair.

"Too bad Ted didn't answer when we knocked. He seemed pretty pissed off last time I saw him."

"Language Sash..." *Mom wouldn't let it slide and neither should I,* Wilson thought.

Sasha shot her brother a look that said, '*You're not the boss of me.*'

Wilson let it go and asked, "What did Ted say?"

"Something about nude yoga. If I didn't already know he was gay I would have been *more* creeped out. He wasn't *hitting* on me... *was he?*"

"Don't flatter yourself Sis. I suspect you were driving him crazy. Plus he's dealing with William's passing," Wilson said as a strange feeling washed over him. Knowing what he did and not being able to share it with his sibling wasn't at all easy.

Sasha picked at the icing, inspected the red and blue crystalline sprinkles, and popped the triangle shaped morsel into her mouth. She closed her eyes, let the pastry melt for a moment, and smiled wide, teeth showing.

"I told you they would have Pop-Tarts," Wilson said smugly.

"I thought you were talking about some Army ration kind of *Pop-Tart*... not the real thing." She took another nibble. "Have you tasted the crackers they try to pass off as *Ritz* in those nasty MRE things? Ugghhh."

Wilson massaged his lower lumbar then gripped the chair back and rotated his torso, forcibly cracking his spine. "I helped load ten cases of the things myself. I've got the knots in my shoulders and back to attest to it."

"If only Ted knew what he was missing. Maybe I'll sneak him some," Sasha said with arched brows as she stuffed a foil packet in her pocket.

"Good idea Sash."

She nodded and dove back into her Pop-Tart.

"How was it out there—did you see a lot of dead people?"

"Not as many as Denver. Not even clo..."

The sound of silverware skittering across the floor stopped Wilson mid-sentence.

A woman screaming and then a male's voice yelling, "He's infected!"

Serving trays slapped the floor followed by footsteps and raised voices.

Wilson arose just in time to see the zombie latching on to a soldier's neck. Crimson blood sprayed in a flat arc hitting the glass sneeze shields.

One of the cooks swung a pan lid, scythe-like, at the creature's head missing everything but the air.

Wilson's fight or flight instinct went into high gear. He grabbed Sasha by the wrist and led her to the exit. One of the most important lessons he had taken from his encounter with his zombie neighbors in the hallway of the Viscount: zombies were very dangerous in enclosed spaces. He had almost died that day and he was bound and determined to live this one out.

Chapter 40
Outbreak - Day 11
Jackson Hole, Wyoming

Jackson Firehouse - 10:30 p.m.

Cade eased the door open with his left hand and stepped across the threshold, SCAR leading the way. He hit the thumb switch on the carbine's fore grip toggling on the IR laser. The green beam, visible only to those with night vision goggles, lanced the air.

The other operators who had been stacked up behind him outside silently poured through the doorway, painting their assigned section of the room with a dancing laser beam.

Each of the operators had trained running the same room-clearing maneuvers hundreds of times over, guns hot, in a live fire environment either in Delta's Fort Bragg kill houses or in Tice's case, "The Farm" at Camp Peary in Williamsburg, Virginia. The four men didn't need to communicate as they slithered through the rooms clearing the lower level. They found themselves in a roughly thirty by twenty foot open floor plan kitchen rendered in glowing shades of green. Big enough to accommodate a crew of firefighters, a wooden plank table sat smack dab in the middle of the kitchen while an industrial size range and two side by side refrigerators dominated the wall to their left. Floor to ceiling open fronted cabinets filled with coffee mugs, dinnerware and various pots and pans covered the right wall.

Cade passed through the darkened kitchen and padded into the garage where an older model, almost antique, fire engine was parked. Nearby the ubiquitous firehouse brass pole pierced the floor and on the right side of the garage a staircase rose up to what he presumed was the living and sleeping areas.

Ascending the stairs, the Delta team covered each other and silently made their way to the second floor. Beyond the doorway at the top of the landing lay a wide open, loft style, communal living area furnished with a sectional couch and a handful of upholstered chairs encircling a flat screen television.

Cade skirted the living room and made his way down a darkened hallway which branched off to the left. Stopping near an open door, he craned his neck, working his NV goggles around the door frame.

Rendered in green a great room spread out before him. Three rows of low slung beds, twelve in all, occupied the room, each with its own side table, lamp, and metal storage locker at the foot.

"Contact," Cade said. His whisper picked up and amplified by his throat mic reached only the Delta team's ears.

The third bunk to the left was occupied and the sheet covering the green lump rose and fell in a steady rhythm. All at once a strange feeling of deja vu washed over Cade as he approached, crabwalking sideways to flank the person who could only be his old buddy Daymon.

With Lopez's laser hovering on the form, Cade pulled the sheet back revealing the sleeping man's placid face and wandering dreadlocks splayed out snake-like over the pillow.

Cade knelt down and ever so slowly retrieved a short combat shotgun from its hiding place underneath the bed, then passed it back to Maddox.

Using the stunted silencer affixed to his SCAR Cade nudged Daymon's thigh.

His lips moved as he murmured something unintelligible, then he rolled over onto his side coming dangerously close to falling off of the narrow twin bed.

"Daymon... wake up," Cade said in a stage whisper.

The man popped up, eyes wide open, reached to the floor, and fumbled around in the dark for the shotgun. "Shit," he said, eyes darting about the pitch black room trying to acquire a sliver of equilibrium.

"Daymon it's me... Cade Grayson."

"Sergeant Cade," Daymon said, relief evidenced in his voice.

"Close enough... is there anyone else in the firehouse."

"Nope... just me and I can't see a fuckin' thing. Can I turn on a light?" Daymon asked, already reaching for the lamp on the far side of the bed.

The sudden movement invited the cold steel kiss of Lopez's SCAR to his temple.

"Chill... I was just reaching for my lamp. Or if you would like I can go down to the basement and fire up the backup generator—noisy as hell—I haven't used it yet cause it's a big fucking pain in the ass. That and I'm trying to keep a low profile."

Cade flipped up his NVGs. "Lamp will be fine."

"What, are you planning on having a séance or something," Tice quipped as soon as Daymon flipped the switch. The lamp, as it turned out, was a battery powered model that barely threw enough light to read by.

Lopez aimed his rifle away from the dreadlocked man, asking him if he had anything brighter.

Looking like a baby foal, Daymon rolled out of bed and slowly unfolded his lanky frame. Then as he filed by the other operators on his way to the living area, he looked at Cade and quipped, "Looks like you brought the entire posse this time Sarge."

"A little different than when we first met," offered Cade.

Daymon chuckled. "Maybe so, but I still got the gun jammed in my face."

"Lopez doesn't cut corners."

Once they were all seated on the enormous sectional and a half a dozen candles were burning, Cade started the inquisition. "That shotgun you had in the dorm... it looked a lot like the one Duncan had when I met him outside of Portland."

"He made me take it when he dropped me off in Driggs."

"So he went on to Eden?"

"As far as I know," Daymon answered. Then he shifted forward on the sectional to look Cade in the eye. "I'm disappointed that after all we have been through together you haven't taken the time to introduce me to your entourage," he added, obviously alluding to their siege in the zombie-filled farmhouse in Hannah, their crash in the Black Hawk between Denver and Colorado Springs, and their subsequent mad dash to Schriever in the armored car.

"I'm sorry. Where did I put my manners...?" Cade intoned theatrically. "Daymon, I want you to meet Lopez... he hates the Zs more than anything on this earth. Maddox there is the tall handsome fellow with the big gun and you may call this other guy Tice. That's the only name I know him by... probably an alias anyway. He's our token Spook."

Bristling visibly, Daymon glared at Cade across the coffee table. "What did you call him?"

"He's CIA. *Spook* is an affectionate term given to those who work in the clandestine services."

Daymon shot Cade a withering look.

"I shouldn't have used those two words in conjunction... sorry..." Cade stopped mid-sentence and pushed a button on his watch starting the lap timer, then looked at Lopez, passing an unspoken message.

A few seconds later the unmistakable sound of the patrolling Humvee passed by a short distance from the firehouse.

"Do you have any bikes in the house?" Cade asked.

"Bikes?" Daymon said slowly as if he didn't understand the question.

"Mountain bikes preferably," added Cade.

"I'm pretty sure a couple of the guys kept theirs in the basement year round. Lots of single track to ride around here in the summer."

"Show me," Tice said.

Daymon pulled himself up from the couch and led the CIA man down the stairs.

Once Tice and Daymon had left the room, Cade motioned for Maddox and Lopez to follow him to the side window. He flipped his goggles down and pulled the curtain a few inches. In the distance, viewed through their NVGs, the opalescent yellow-green glow of the grass covered 25,000 acre National Elk Refuge looked like a landlocked algae covered sea.

"There and there," Cade said, pointing out the school bus-sized Patriot anti-missile launchers sitting in the open expanse. "And if Nash's imagery is correct—which it usually is—then the other two sites are on the opposite side near the fence lines. The whole round trip is maybe... four miles max."

"Good call on the bikes. They'll be easy to ditch if a patrol rolls around... and stealthy. And with our NVGs and the suppressed pistols we will definitely have the upper hand," Maddox proffered.

"We will be *very* exposed..." Lopez said as he made the sign of the cross. "I just hope there are no *demonios* in that big ass cow pasture."

Tice returned to the communal area. Daymon showed his face a moment later.

"Only two bikes downstairs," Tice said, shaking his head slowly, "and there are four of us."

Cade turned off his NVGs to conserve the batteries and flipped them up out of the way. He glanced at his Suunto and exclaimed, "Eighteen minutes until the patrol returns. Maddox... Lopez... you two will have to make it happen on the two bikes. Tice and I will be your eyes and ears from here and be your QRF (quick reaction force) if necessary."

Quietly observing from the doorway Daymon asked earnestly, "What are you up to Cade?"

"I can't go into detail except to say we're here to set some things right," Cade said, nodding his helmet.

"Picked the right time. Jackson is hemorrhaging people. Robert Christian's NA fools have been disappearing on a daily basis. And the civilians who are essentially slave labor prisoners slink away in the night and the ones who get caught deserting... you don't even want to know what happens to them."

"I can imagine," Cade said solemnly. "But I'm here with a sole purpose. We are going to need a reliable vehicle... SUV preferably." Cade paused in thought, and then shot a stony look at Daymon. "When Lopez and Maddox return I need *you* to drive us to Robert Christian's mansion."

A cold finger traced Daymon's spine as he rapidly thought through the possibilities. "I can take you there. No problem," he replied, instantly feeling the chill leave his body. He smiled inwardly and stared across the table at the heavily armed soldiers draped in body armor with their tactical helmets strapped on their heads, thinking to himself gleefully, *I'll do anything to get within striking distance of that Robert Christian motherfucker.*

***

Lopez and Maddox each put two detonators and four of the two pound C4 bricks into their individual packs. They travelled light taking only their silenced side arms, two extra mags, and their combat knives. Neither man wanted to leave behind their SCAR rifle, but, speed and stealth being necessary, it couldn't be helped.

The two operators waited twenty-two minutes in the shadows behind the firehouse until the patrol finished another lap.

Cade watched from the back door as the operators mounted their bikes, took a second to push their NVGs into place, and then pedaled off into the green-hued darkness.

***

While Tice took the first watch Cade and Daymon rehashed the events that had occurred over the last three days.

Cade covered everything that had happened at Schriever since Daymon and Duncan left, minus the parts about his brother in-law Carl and Doctor Fuentes and the antiserum.

Daymon described the trip from Schriever up until Duncan dropped him off near his home in Driggs. He didn't mention Heidi nor his surveillance of Robert Christian earlier in the day. He didn't think it would benefit him in any way.

Chapter 41
Outbreak - Day 12
Jackson Hole, Wyoming

Midnight

Bishop came to—disoriented and out of sorts. He rubbed the sleep from his eyes then looked at his watch— *zero hundred*. He had closed his eyes fully expecting to be roused from his catnap by Daly calling to say he was Winchester on ammo or by one of the Brothers checking in.

Things like this rarely happened to the former Navy SEAL. Though it was a minor mistake he was still pissed off at himself.

Bishop checked his phone and thought it strange that no one had called while he was asleep. He immediately dialed Daly. "Come on. Pick up... pick up. Answer your phone Goddamnit."

After half a dozen unanswered rings he thumbed off the Iridium. A chill feathered through him.

He left his west slope condo behind the wheel of the Rover, speeding towards the Snake River crossing while thinking the worst. Along the way he passed an NA security patrol manned by two of his newer conscripts. At the moment the black truck with the stenciled NA logo blurred by he realized he hated having to call his Spartan contractors New America soldiers. Furthermore, Christian's absurd notion that he was now a world leader thanks to Omega was growing increasingly irritating. That the man hadn't had the balls to run for the office of President before the outbreak spoke volumes to his character. It was probably because of all the bones in his closet,

Bishop guessed. Or most likely all of the bodies he had buried—figuratively of course. A shovel had never brushed the man's supple hands and one never would.

"Fucking dummy," Bishop shouted as he floored the accelerator. He would never admit it—such was his nature—but frankly he was more than a little embarrassed that he had romanticized the idea of leading and molding the NA military to his liking. In the original version of Christian's New World Order the possibility was most assured. Now he knew it was unattainable. For it had become evident the sheer numbers of dead were changing everything—except in Robert Christian's delusional thinking.

He covered the nine miles from downtown in less than five minutes, and as the darkened strip malls came into view he saw that both of the bus barriers were breached. Thankfully, he thought, most of the dead were still milling around the houses north of the bridge. The two strip malls on this side of the river were also teeming with the creatures.

The SUVs big tires chirped as he stabbed the brakes, bringing it to a sudden halt on the shoulder.

In the distance he could see a number of Zs huddled in the center of the road feeding on what he guessed was one of his men.

As the truck idled on the side of the road he tried Daly one more time. The phone trilled on. *No answer.* "Why didn't you blow the fucking bridge *genius*," Bishop bellowed as he tousled his short cropped hair with one hand and clouted the wheel with the other.

Some of the Zs arose from their roadway feast and in their usual arm swinging, head bobbing manner began to stagger in his direction, and in seconds the rest of the monsters, thousands he guessed, became interested and gave slow motion chase.

He gave up on Daly and called the Brothers one last time, thumbed the speaker on and shook his head disgustedly, waiting, hoping someone would answer. As the phone droned on Bishop came to the conclusion that the Brothers were either in trouble or had decided to cut and run. His sway over his two lieutenants lately had been stronger than ever—or so he thought. That they weren't answering his calls troubled him on many different levels.

He stared at the advancing horde and let loose a long string of expletives learned in the Navy.

He threw the annoying Sat phone onto the seat next to him and, seeing red, tromped the accelerator, steering the Rover into the nearest walker. The SUV clipped the female zombie on the hip sending her airborne, and like a lawn dart the pale creature plowed headfirst into the blacktop spraying brain matter on the yellow centerline.

"Take that bitch," Bishop said as a morbid smile creased his face. He wrenched the wheel over, performing a one-eighty and pointed the Rover towards Jackson.

Once the dead were behind him and out of sight he snatched up the Iridium and dialed another number from memory, and after two rings one of the pilots on standby picked up. "This is Bishop," he barked. "Pre-flight the Gulf."

"Why the Gulf? The Heavy gives us more range," the tired sounding voice on the other end replied.

"The Heavy severely limits our choice of airstrips. Most of the municipal airports are either overrun or the runways were blocked early on to keep the aircraft carrying infected from landing."

"Copy that," the pilot intoned. "The G6 will be ready when you arrive."

"One last thing... I need you to write these down and pass them on to all of the helo pilots." He pulled over, fished a scrap of paper from his pocket, and recited a string of GPS coordinates. "I want all of the operable birds fueled up and moved to that location."

Bishop powered down the sat phone and set his jaw as he passed East Butte Road, which he would have taken to get to the House had he still given a shit about his former boss. *You're on your own now R.C.*, he thought as he rushed north on the Wyoming Centennial Scenic Byway on his way to the Jackson Hole Airport.

***

12:34 a.m.

Daymon awoke with a start only to find Cade shaking his arm. That there wasn't a gun trained on him brought great relief. Maddox and Lopez had gone and returned and both appeared to be in one piece. And from where he lay sprawled on the sectional, he could see the candle nubs sitting in pools of melted wax, their flickering light still playing off of the kitchen walls.

"What time is it?" he asked blearily.

"Almost time to go," Cade answered cryptically.

While Daymon collected his things and stowed them in the back of Lu Lu, the operators used the down time to strategize, then spent the next thirty minutes paring down their loadout. The rucks stayed behind along with most of the C4. Maddox packed a few ounces in a cargo pocket just in case his lock gun failed him. They each took a silenced SCAR carbine as well as their personal sidearm—silenced also.

Daymon scaled the stairs, poked his head into the living room and said, "Your chariot waits."

Cade tried to restrain himself but failed miserably. "Gentlemen... let's get this goat rope on the road."

Chuckling to himself Lopez said, "Where have I heard that before?"

"We all learned from the best and I would like to think Cowboy is here with us in spirit."

Pointing towards the ceiling Lopez said, "I'm going to *get some* for you tonight *Vaquero*."

Daymon made a face and said, "Who is this *Cowboy* guy?"

"He was a *snake eater* of the old school variety... but he got bit on our last mission."

Cade's eyebrows raised an inch as he shot Lopez the look and said, "We don't need to revisit that here and now."

Mad at himself because of the slip, Lopez moved to the window. Seconds later the patrol Hummer reappeared down on Cache Street.

"There is our window. Lock and Load fellas," Cade said as he slid down the fire pole.

***

The House - 12:55 a.m.

Paul powered down the window and squared his face toward the black plastic dome housing the security camera so the guard could positively identify him.

"Hi Paul," Cliff said over the intercom.

Paul nodded. "It's really me Cliff," he said with a trace of sarcasm.

The gate opened inward allowing the black SUV entry to the compound. The Escalade's tires rumbled on the cobblestone drive which arced in front of the grand mansion. Lucas leapt from the Cadillac the moment it came to a stop, dashed through the unlocked double doors and scaled the stairs, his combat boots drumming the marble.

When he reached the second level landing he went straight to the security room.

"Cliff..." he said, shoving the door open.

The disheveled man pushed his chair away from the desk preparing to stand.

Lucas put a big hand on the guard's shoulder. "Where is Robert Christian?"

"He's sleeping."

Arching an eyebrow Lucas said, "Passed out?"

"More than likely," Cliff replied, reaching for a Cheeto.

"Did he raise a fuss about us being gone for so long?"

"No, but Bishop was pissed," Cliff added.

"Where is Ian?"

After a moment of silence Cliff wriggled nervously in his seat, took another second to adjust his ball cap and said, "I think he went to check on the guys at the barrier. That was a few hours ago though."

"Gimme that," Lucas said, motioning for the guard's sat phone.

He dialed Daly's number and looked to the ceiling as he waited for an answer. "Paul," he yelled downstairs. "Take the truck and check on Daly... he's not picking up."

Jumping at the chance to prove himself, Paul sprinted up the grand staircase and made his way to the security room; after making eye contact with Lucas he blurted enthusiastically, "I got this." Then he bounded down the marble treads three at a time, took a Mossberg from the coat closet, and rushed out the front door. Stopping for a beat on the circular drive he checked to make sure the short barreled shotgun was loaded then rounded the front of the black SUV and slid inside.

The luxury Escalade was nothing like the rattletrap Chevy Stepside he drove daily before the outbreak. The polished wood dash and plush leather coupled with the rig's smooth handling and soft springs gave him a deceptive sense of invulnerability. He really wanted to fiddle with the navigation computer, but seeing as how, for him, setting an alarm clock was a challenge, he opted not to touch. He slowly navigated the serpentine drive to the bottom of Butte Road, took a right, and bypassed the Teton Pass highway, continuing south on 189 towards the Snake River crossing seven miles ahead.

Amazed at the horsepower the truck held in reserve yet skeptical of the Cadillac's speedometer which indicated a top speed of one hundred and sixty, Paul had to see for himself. At least to a hundred, he thought as he pinned the accelerator to the floorboard. He had the SUV barreling down the tree-lined straightaway at well over ninety miles an hour when the headlights illuminated the first wave of walkers. He jammed on the brakes, praying they were as capable as the engine. The unloading g-forces instantly pushed him against the seatbelt as the rig slewed sideways, leaving two thick stripes of smoking rubber straddling the yellow center line. Then, still moving at more than fifty miles an hour, the fifty-eight- hundred pound Cadillac plowed through the moving wall of flesh and bone.

Simultaneously, all eight airbags deployed and every window on the passenger side erupted in a maelstrom of razor-sharp glass pebbles. As the vehicle lurched to a halt rocking on its suspension, the first moans of the dead reached his ears. Their stench quickly invaded his lungs and in seconds the creatures were pushing against the pliant side curtain airbags, thrusting their upper bodies into every available opening, trying to get at the meat.

He flicked open his pocketknife and lanced the airbag pressing against his face. As the bag deflated to reveal the view through the windshield, a chill cut him to the bone. Pale faces and reaching limbs, rendered ghostlike in the headlight beams, were all he could see.

Avoiding the clawlike fingers he threw himself to the floorboard, grasped the nylon sling, and drew the Mossberg to him.

The first living corpse through the passenger window wore the all black uniform of an NA soldier. Paul pressed his back to the driver door, thrust the barrel to the monster's chin, and squeezed the trigger. *So much for the interior,* he mused as he watched the Z's face melt away behind the hail of lead shot. His ears rang from the concussive blast.

Four left.

Moans sounded from the back of the SUV as the monsters wriggled their way through the rear quarter window.

The odds aren't looking good Paul, a little voice whispered. *Better save one for yourself.*

He popped up, aimed the shotgun over the seatback, and pumped two rounds into the encroaching undead duo.

"Take that fuckers."

Two left. Save one for a rainy day, the voice nagged.

He stilled one more snarling ghoul at point blank range then turned the smoking gun on himself.

Fucked up angle Paul.

He struggled to pull the trigger.

Do it, the voice chided.

The driver window spider webbed and a pair of gnarled hands thrust through, wrapping his neck in a frigid embrace. The Mossberg slipped from his fingers, and as he instinctively reached up more hands gripped him and effortlessly yanked his body through the window into eternal darkness.

Chapter 42
Outbreak - Day 12
Jackson Hole, Wyoming

Daymon hated how Lu Lu handled fully loaded down. Stopping on a dime wasn't going to happen and every anomaly in the road threatened to bottom out the neon green Scout. Hell, she usually handled like a moving van with only his buck-eighty aboard— filled to capacity with the four army men and all of their gear—what did he expect.

Cade rode in the passenger seat with Maddox behind him. In the center of the back seat, Lopez, the smallest of the team, got stuck riding "bitch" as Tice happily pointed out.

"Harder for the *demonios* to reach me here," Lopez said smugly.

Changing the narrative Cade said, "We should scoot by the patrol with plenty of time to spare."

"Maybe if someone feeds the squirrels," Tice quipped.

"Listen... she's due for a tune-up and brakes and... fuck it." Daymon glanced at Tice in the rearview. "I could go back to the firehouse and you all can ride to the mansion... two to a bike."

"Let's keep it professional men," Cade said brusquely.

Tice grumbled something from the back seat.

"Curious... what does the E on your door mean?" Cade asked.

"Stands for Essential and as the only firefighter to return to work after the rotten fuckers started walking... I've been elevated by default to Essential status."

"Copy that," Cade intoned as he gazed at the darkened storefronts.

"How far is the mansion?" Maddox inquired.

"Five minutes," Daymon answered. "The turnoff is just this side of 22 which goes through the Teton Pass. My house is on the other side in Driggs."

Cade popped the cover from the dome light and removed the bulb which he put in the empty ashtray. "Kill the headlights before you get to the turn off."

"There's lots of tree cover and it will be dark as hell. I might not be able to get us to the *House* without driving off the road. Please tell me you've got another pair of those goggles."

"No need. We're going in *quiet*... on foot," Cade said.

"What about me?" Daymon asked as he stopped Lu Lu at the end of Cache. Then out of habit he looked both ways and wheeled her left passed the Silver Dollar Cowboy bar—stole a long last look—and then accelerated down West Broadway.

Chapter 43
Outbreak - Day 12
Butte Road
Jackson Hole, Wyoming

Mansion Guest House - 1:30 a.m.

"What is taking that kid so long?" Lucas wondered aloud.

"He's been bugging me to drive thath beast since we got it from sha dealer," Liam slurred.

"You better take it easy on the scotch Liam."

"Why... we're all gonna die shoon anyway," Liam said. Then, ignoring his hypocrite brother's advice, he tilted the Dewars bottle in the air and took a long pull.

"Not in *my* plans bro. I'm leaving in the morning with or without you. Mom is not around to give me shit for not babying your ass."

Glaring at his brother, Liam struggled to rise from the leather pub chair and dropped the half full Dewars bottle on the cream colored carpet. Instantly a medicinal smell filled the air as the scotch glugged out, leaving behind a wet amber stain.

"Don't get up Liam... get some sleep why don'tcha," Lucas shook his head sadly. "I'm going to the mansion and check on R.C. and then walk the grounds for a second."

"Suit yourself."

Suit myself. That's exactly what is going to happen at dawn. Lucas mused. *And if you want to come along then you better sober up and get your shit together.*

Chapter 44
Outbreak - Day 12
Jackson Hole, Wyoming

Approaching Butte Road and I-189 Interchange - 1:35 a.m.

The old Scout's headlights fought a losing battle against the dark. Overhanging trees and a waning moon made sure the fight was anything but fair.

"This gutless wonder have another gear?" Tice asked from the backseat.

Looking over his shoulder Daymon fired back, "You're still more than welcome to walk." Then as he turned his head forward, he registered a gaunt face in his peripheral vision.

Cade's shouted warning came a split second too late as the Scout clipped the walker, sending it airborne towards the guardrail.

Instinctively Daymon worked the brakes.

"*No. Do not stop. Drive through and kill the lights,*" Cade bellowed as he flipped down his goggles and powered them on.

Daymon tromped the gas, and as he swerved Lu Lu around the throng, pale hands reached from the shadows, slapping the windshield and side glass leaving behind gory traces of blood and rancid dermis.

Suddenly, in a loud and excited voice, Cade inexplicably ordered Daymon to stop and pull over.

Daymon ground the SUV to a halt a safe distance from the pack of walkers they had just blown through. "Why in the hell are we stopping Sarge?" Daymon asked incredulously.

Rapid fire, Cade detailed what he was seeing through the NVGs. "There are more Zs on the road in front of us. Twenty plus bodies. Distance, seventy-five yards."

"*Fuck. Fuck. Fuck*...they're between us and the turnoff. This ain't no Hummer Sarge... I know she *will not* go over top of them," Daymon said as he reached for the stubby shotgun.

Shaking his head, Cade put his hand on the shotgun, "We do not want to announce our presence. We do them *all* quietly starting with the Zs we just passed." He looked at Daymon and patted the cylindrical suppressor affixed to the business end of the SCAR, flipped the 3x magnifier into place and folded the stock to full extension. He stepped from the Scout and sighted on the Zs on their six. Working the SCAR's trigger he delivered silent death as one by one the encroaching walkers crumpled to the blacktop.

Daymon hauled himself from Lu Lu, opened the rear hatch, and came back around wielding a wicked looking crossbow. "Quieter than yours," he whispered to Cade.

A different kind of crazy, Cade thought to himself as he turned his attention to the creatures farther down the road.

As Tice, Maddox, and Lopez fought to extricate themselves from Lu Lu's cramped backseat, Daymon took a knee near the front fender then brought the crossbow to bear on a twenty-something first turn. While the BYU sweatshirt-clad corpse limped closer, he aimed through the red dot scope placing the glowing pip on the zombie's bobbing head. "You're a long way from home Jack," he muttered as he let the arrow fly.

"Two door SUVs suck," Tice bitched to no one in particular as he squirmed through the open driver's side door. As soon as he was on the road he heard the unmistakable rasping sound of a first turn coming from the far shoulder near the ditch. He flipped his goggles down and scanned the glowing green foreground. Less than fifteen feet away he found the source of the sound. Hissing through a mouthful of broken teeth and trailing two broken legs, the female creature that Daymon had clipped a second ago clawed its way determinedly towards him. Without thinking about who the woman Z used to be, or whom it had loved, or been loved by, Tice double-tapped it in the forehead.

Standing by the open passenger door, Cade replaced the magazine and charged his weapon then braced the SCAR on the truck's A-pillar and engaged the crowd to their front. Starting with the closest Z, a freshly turned NA trooper, he walked his fire head high along their ranks, each good hit answered with a phosphorescent eruption of brain and bone.

A steady *thwap, thwap, thwap* reverberated from Daymon's crossbow as he scored head shots of his own.

Once free from the backseat, Maddox and Lopez brought their SCAR carbines to the fight.

The five men continued to shoot and reload until all of the zombies were down and they were no longer surrounded.

"Let's go," Cade said as he changed mags, then he collapsed the SCAR's stock and clambered into the rig.

Daymon went forward and removed his arrows from the dead Zs and hastily wiped them off on the tall grass lining the side of the road.

"Nice work with the bow," Maddox commented after Daymon had climbed back into Lu Lu. "You grow up hunting?"

"Yeah, I *used* to stalk bear and cougar in Idaho... I guess I need to add former humans to that list," Daymon said as he finessed the clutch and stick and with a clunk coaxed Lu Lu into first gear.

"That was strange... the *demonios* in front of us didn't make any noise," observed Lopez as Daymon steered his rig around the supine corpses.

"I figured they couldn't see us. It's pretty damn dark under the canopy," Cade proffered, "but no doubt there are more where they came from."

"How would you know Lopez? You were in here on the bitch bump the entire time," Tice needled.

"I warned you Spook... I'm tired of this."

"Save it for the Zs," Maddox said, glaring at the bickering duo.

In less than a minute they arrived at the interchange. Daymon downshifted and took a hard right onto Butte Road which wound uphill disappearing into the darkness. "I can't see shit," Daymon blurted.

"Keep going slow. We'll be getting out real soon," Cade said.

Easing up on the gas Daymon said incredulously, "And walk a mile uphill? The elevation gain is about fifteen hundred feet—that's an ass kicker."

"I noticed some ambient light up on the butte, and since the mansion is the only property up there, that tells me they have a couple of generators running. And if they have electricity, then odds are there are security cameras and motion sensors. Pull over... we'll go on foot from here," Cade said. He glanced at Daymon, and though rendered in shades of green, noticed the hangdog look on the man's face.

"I *have* to go with you," Daymon pressed, desperation evident in his voice.

"Listen, I'm indebted to you for getting us this far, but you need to leave before more Zs start showing up. Something happened at the river crossing, and from my experience where there are a few Zs there will soon be a lot more."

Now that Daymon had painted himself into a corner he finally decided to come clean and tell all about Heidi and the men who shanghaied her from the Silver Dollar. He made it clear that he hoped he would find her alive—and if he didn't—he would make Robert Christian pay in blood.

Cade looked at Daymon and paused for a beat, then said, "I'm very sorry to hear about Heidi but I promised President Clay I would bring Robert Christian back to Schriever so he can answer for his crimes. Eventually he will either be hanged or put in front of a firing squad. And from your description of the little bastard who took Heidi against her will, I'm confident that he is the man we have in custody at Schriever."

"Promise me you'll bring her out if she *is* still alive."

"Of course—can you quickly describe her?"

As they sat in the idling truck, Daymon pulled a photo from the glove box and handed it to Cade, who took a quick look then promptly put it in his breast pocket for safe keeping.

"The only reason I'm not kicking and screaming... and demanding I go along," Daymon went on, "is because Duncan spoke so highly of you. I can trust you... *right?*"

Cade nodded and slid out of the vehicle, then held the front seat forward until the three operators emerged from the backseat. He pulled Tice aside and held a brief conversation before returning to the Scout. He went around to the driver's side and passed a portable sat-phone in to Daymon and said, "I *will* call you either way. You will have closure... I promise. Now git..."

"How are you getting Christian back to Springs?"

Cade turned, looking robot-like with the NVG's four lenses protruding from his eyes. "Don't worry about us... just get *yourself* out of here."

With that the Delta team crossed the road and like four deadly apparitions melted into the pitch-black tree line.

***

1:55 a.m.

Daymon turned Lu Lu around then put the transmission in neutral and let gravity power her downhill to the junction.

At the bottom of the hill he turned right on the Teton Pass Highway and steeled himself for what he might encounter passing through the Valley of the Crosses.

Chapter 45
Outbreak - Day 12
Jackson Hole, Wyoming

Butte Road Mansion - 1:56 a.m.

Lucas drained the last few drops of gas into the noisy generator's tank, then made sure the idle backup generator was also fueled. *Good 'til daybreak*, he thought. With a run time of six hours and an output of 10,000 watts, one was more than enough to keep the lights on and in turn keep Robert Christian in his happy space. The second generator was merely insurance to keep him from getting killed.

He walked the mansion grounds checking the garage, pool house and the two swinging security gates. Lastly, before securing the mansion's interior he made sure the service door on the east wall was locked.

Satisfied the perimeter was locked down he climbed the stairs and tried the front door. *Locked... for once, a good job Cliff.*

He went in through the open garage, closing the overheads, and accessed the mansion through the mud room.

After checking in with Cliff, who had three crumpled Red Bull cans sitting on his desk, he passed the master suite to make sure Christian's door was locked and then completed his lap at the guest house where he found Liam passed out and German porn playing on the flat screen.

The thought that Paul might have gone back to the Cowboy Bar to retrieve the satellite phone crossed his mind, prompting him to try calling it once more.

After three rings a man answered.

"Paul," Lucas said.

"Gerald," a raspy voice replied.

"Who?" Lucas asked.

"It's Gerald... at the Silver Dollar Cowboy Bar and I'm guessing this is your phone."

"This is Lucas Brother. Is this the first time its rang since ten o'clock or so?"

"First time tonight," Gerald lied with a wide grin creasing his face.

"Good to hear," Lucas replied happily. "Hold on to it for me and I'll be by tomorrow."

Gerald continued wiping the bar top and replied, "You're here *every* day Mr. Brother. Why would tomorrow be any different?"

Pissed at being called out on his drinking habits, yet at the same time relieved he wasn't in Bishop's dog house, he thumbed off the phone without replying.

Lucas left Liam drooling on the leather couch and went to his room. The clock read 2:10 a.m. by the time he finally closed his eyes.

***

Valley of the Crosses - 2:45 a.m.

Daymon grudgingly repeated the same ritual as the day before. He parked Lu Lu in roughly the same spot and grabbed his Maglite and the shotgun and set off on foot. Taking his time and staying close to the barbed wire fence, he walked the bright beam along the rows of decaying bodies, illuminating every crucified person's final death mask.

At the end of the mile he found the last cross in the row, standing naked, silently awaiting company.

During the long walk back to Lu Lu, with the smell of death assaulting his nose, the faces of his Moms and Pop, Heidi and even Hosford Preston ran through his mind's eye like a chattering old Super 8 movie.

As he sat inside Lu Lu, in virtually the same depressed state mentally and spiritually that he had spiraled into the moment Cade broke it to him that he would have no shot at retribution—and an even smaller shot at finding Heidi alive—he made up his mind to leave Jackson.

Punching open the glove box he retrieved the small Thuraya sat-phone Cade had given him and placed it in the change tray between the seats. Then he grabbed the police radio Jenkins had given him and powered it on. He turned the volume up and depressed the talk button. "This is Daymon calling for Chief Jenkins."

Static.

"Fire Chief Bush calling Jenkins...over."

"Charlie here."

Informal. "I'm getting out of here and I thought I'd touch bases with you while I'm still in range with this thing."

"Well, I dropped in the Silver Dollar earlier and Gerald said I missed you by a couple of hours. Your rig wasn't at the firehouse and you didn't answer the radio so I figured I'd stop here and try you one last time."

"Where are you?" Daymon asked.

"I'm on 22 at the pass."

"Shit, I'm a few minutes from there. I'm in the valley and just spent the last hour looking for Heidi."

"Watch yourself down there... the dead breached the barrier a couple of hours ago... don't know exactly when they'll be here... but they *are* coming."

"Did you warn Gerald and the other prisoners—*Essentials*—whatever they're calling them these days?"

"I only gave a heads up to the good guys... the ones who deserved it. Pissed me off seeing Bishop and some of his mercenaries heading for the airport. Saving their own skin I guess. Now let's see if we can't save ourselves. So quit yappin' and get up here—*now.*"

"I'm on my way," Daymon said. He put the police radio aside and retrieved the mini sat-phone Cade had given him. He closed his eyes and slowly tumbled the phone in his hand, willing the thing to ring.

Chapter 46
Outbreak - Day 12
Grand Junction Airport

Grand Junction, Colorado - 2:45 a.m.

An artillery-like boom rattled the windows, waking Taryn from her deep sleep. While the thunderclap echoed off the surrounding red cliffs and liquid bullets battered the all glass terminal, she struggled to grasp reality.

In her dream she had been getting another tattoo—her seventh—this time across her taut stomach. And of all things, the Four Horsemen of the Apocalypse atop fire breathing steeds, with Death in the foreground, holding by the hair a human head strongly resembling hers.

Behind her, the door rattled in its frame.

She glanced hesitantly over her shoulder at the filmed over window, where Dickless stood, alabaster face pressed to the glass, reptile-like eyes following her every move. Shaking off sleep she lifted her shirt and glanced with relief at the still blank canvas that had seemed so realistically inked moments ago.

Just the momentary flash of skin caused her former boss to bang against the door fervently. In fact, Dick had been a leerer of the first degree *before* he received his comeuppance; therefore, Taryn wasn't at all surprised to see that his undead alter-ego also had a staring problem.

"Go away perv," she said, waving the revolver at the rotting corpse. *Tomorrow*, she thought darkly, *was going to be payback time.*

She rolled onto her side facing away and closed her eyes, pretending he wasn't there.

The banging intensified.

Taryn sat upright and felt around in the dark for the gun.

The hissing resumed.

Her fingers brushed the checkered wooded grips. She pulled the thingy so the cylinder would flip out and one more time counted the bullets. There were six. A machine gun it was not, so all six had to count if she was to have any chance of escaping the terminal.

***

The House - 2:45 a.m.

Though the four soldiers of the Delta team were in their early to mid-thirties and physically fit, the hump up the steep southwest face of the butte, weighed down with body armor, extra magazines, and the various other tools essential to modern war fighting, had been an ass kicker of the highest order.

Cade, who had been out of the teams for a number of months before the dead began to walk, was probably the least conditioned of the team. Still catching his breath from the arduous climb, he lay on his stomach in the tall grass and glassed the compound.

Ten-foot tall stucco walls ringed the entire landscaped property.

The mansion and outbuildings were illuminated brightly and a generator hummed away somewhere in the distance.

"I see three camera domes. One on the post adjacent to the gate and one on each corner," Maddox said, targeting them with the laser attached to his SCAR. "I have a feeling we are going to encounter the same setup in back."

"Motion sensors?" Cade inquired.

Herding a stray lock of sandy blonde hair back under his helmet Maddox answered, "With all of the wild game in this area, having sensors outside the wall wouldn't make sense."

Cade pulled the binoculars down to look at Maddox and said, "Inside?"

"A crib this size—most definitely," Maddox said, nodding his head. "Whether they have them activated is anyone's guess."

289

"Lopez... Tice... you two disable the generator and eliminate anyone who comes to investigate. As soon as the lights go out *we* go in the front door."

"Copy that," Tice and Lopez said in unison. Then the two operators backed away into the tree line and set off around the western wall in search of the thrumming engine.

With Maddox shadowing him, Cade faded into the woods and loped off to the east, the SCAR's green laser bobbing drunkenly with every footfall.

They crossed the asphalt road that wound uphill from the junction below, then continued another fifty meters around the perimeter, staying in the tree line until Cade halted and took a knee. "There," he said, painting the inset wooden door with his laser. "And there and there... cameras."

"Lopez, how copy?" Cade said into his throat mic.

"Good copy," Lopez replied.

Cade checked his watch. Three minutes had elapsed since the team split into two separate elements. "Situation report?"

"We've located the generator... one hundred meters to the north between the garage and the outer wall. Give us five mikes," Lopez answered.

"Copy that," was Cade's monotone response.

As the five minute mark neared Maddox stood poised with his lock gun at the ready.

Cade's laser dot skittered on the lens of the closest security camera.

***

"Go time," Lopez said as the timer hit five minutes.

The silenced M4 chugged twice as Tice put two rounds into the nearby security camera. A spritz of blue electricity arced from its shattered black cover. He targeted the second dome at his two o'clock, destroying it as well.

"Cameras down," Tice intoned.

Lopez bolted from the woods, crouched by the wall, and brought his SCAR up to cover the Spook's advance.

Tice shifted the M4 on its sling, securing it behind his back, and at a dead run crossed the open ground between the woods and the wall; then, squatting with his back pressed against the stucco and his fingers laced together stirruplike, Tice provided Lopez a leg-up, propelling the diminutive Delta operator atop the wall.

While laying lengthwise on his stomach, left arm and leg gripping the wall—a move learned by every soldier early on in basic training—Lopez reached down and with strength that belied his size helped Tice surmount the obstacle.

Both men dropped to the other side and scurried to a patch of shadow, rifles at the ready.

Lopez looked to the north. Two good sized generators sat roughly twenty feet in front of him, humming away, next to the biggest multi-car garage he had ever seen. Though not as tall, the building had a footprint the size of a small airplane hangar, and with eight ornately decorated roll up doors looked like it could accommodate a fleet of vehicles.

He padded down the ten foot wide breezeway between the outer wall and garage and knelt next to the generators, one running, and one silent.

Tice followed silently keeping an eye on their six, and anticipating the impending blackout lowered his NVGs.

"Killing the lights," Lopez said.

"Copy that," Cade replied from the other side of the property.

Lopez drew his Gerber Mark-II combat knife and deftly sliced the gas line on the running unit, plunging the mansion and its entire perimeter into full black. He flipped his goggles down, and then for good measure cut the other gas line and yanked the spark plug wires from both generators, pitching them onto the garage roof.

***

When the courtyard lights went out, Maddox attacked the lock. With only a pair of heavy duty Schlage deadbolts and no other surprises on the inside, the thick wooden door proved easy enough to penetrate. It brought him great relief that the security here was nothing like that at the CDC in Atlanta. Maybe the macho movie star really believed he was as capable of kicking ass as the persona he portrayed on the big screen. At any rate, the man couldn't hold a candle to Chuck Norris, Maddox mused.

"Blow the charges," Cade ordered.

Maddox pulled both detonators from his pocket, quickly armed them, and flicked the switches at once.

Deadly consequences stemmed from that simple act. Maddox thought briefly about the two men manning the Engagement Control Station, a school bus-sized trailer that had just been subjected to the explosive power of two pounds of C4. He had also rigged the generator, antenna mast and radar array set, all essential components of the air defense system, each with half as much of the malleable plastic explosive. He liked to see things go boom and was known to be thorough when it came to demolitions. That the Patriot systems operators were now incinerated was a certainty.

While Maddox had been secreting his explosives, Lopez had been on a covert bike tour of the Jackson Elk Refuge. He planted similar C4 charges on the four remote launching stations, each containing four—fifteen hundred pound— Patriot surface-to-air missiles whose solid rocket propellant and two-hundred pound warheads were now cooking off. The muted secondary explosions, sounding like train cars coupling at a rail yard, rolled over the butte.

***

Tapping the monitor with a knuckle, Cliff tried to get the display to refresh. He had seen the whole panel go black before but never patchwork style like this. In the time it took his tired mind to come to the realization that the closed circuit cameras had either been tampered with (which he deemed highly unlikely) or had suffered some kind of interference from the generator, the overhead light flickered off and the entire panel in front of him went dark.

"Oh damnit," he muttered as he fumbled around for a flashlight, but instead spilled his last treasured bag of Cheetos. The same *family size* bag he had been rationing for the better half of the day.

His left hand finally found the rubberized handle and he thumbed the switch, wincing at the intensity of the stark white beam. With the Glock in his right hand counterbalancing the hefty flashlight in his left, he waddled down the hall on soft soled shoes. Just as he made the top landing and brought the beam to bear on the marble staircase, a low distant rumble reached his ears.

Thunder, he guessed, as he double timed it down the nearest set of circular stairs. His breathing quickened—a combination of anxiety, stress and fear—primarily the latter. He needed to get the generator refueled before anyone realized he had let the tank go dry. "Fucking brothers," he muttered. If one of them would have taken care of this earlier he wouldn't be facing the prospect of upsetting Robert Christian and finding himself nailed to a cross feeding the birds. That poor houseboy Fredrick. He caught R.C. in the wrong frame of mind and under the wrong set of circumstances. The screams seemed to go on forever. It was something Cliff would take with him to the grave.

He froze in mid-step halfway down the stairs. In the distance, from somewhere near downtown, he heard a series of muffled explosions echoing across the valley.

Better wake the boss, he thought to himself as he fought the urge to go to the garage and steal one of the many toys parked inside. Who was he fooling, before being conscripted into NA service he had worked as an armored car driver, and if he had been at home in Chicago when the shit hit the fan instead of vacationing in Yellowstone there was no way he would still be alive. Furthermore, he was certain that if he left alone right now with only his Glock and a bag of Cheetos to see him through, he'd be zombie bait within the hour. Nope. Better to be safe than sorry, he thought to himself. Wake the boss first, and then his henchmen, was the strategy he decided would probably keep him breathing.

***

Cade followed Maddox through the doorway into the courtyard and paused to get his bearings.

The ski chalet-styled mansion rose in front of him, blotting out the stars; its circular drive and front entry was off to his left. Tinged green by the NVGs, moonlight played on a sliver of water visible between the rear of the mansion and what he guessed had to be a pool house.

"Going in the front," Cade said. "Team two... *sit-rep*."

"Clear so far," Lopez whispered.

"Give it two mikes then rendezvous at the front door."

"Copy that," replied Lopez.

Cade padded to the east side of the expansive porch. Sitting in the drive was a dark colored SUV. Crouched low, he dashed to its front fender and placed a palm on the hood.

Cold.

He crept back to the porch and up the stairs and slid next to Maddox, who was already hard at work on the intricate lockset on the wide wooden double doors.

***

Tran's eyes snapped open. The low distant rumble that had jerked him from a deep slumber sounded nothing like thunder. His worst fear had come to fruition. The man-demon Bishop must have blown the bridge, which Tran knew was the only thing keeping the walking monsters at bay.

He slowly climbed from bed, knelt on the cold wood floor, and began to pray.

***

The moment the flat screen flashed to blue and finally total black, Greta's moans and Hanz's Neanderthal grunting ceased. Liam stirred and opened one eye, wondering where in the hell he was. He barely remembered leaving the bar.

Did I drive?

Thankfully he didn't remember the awful German porn he had been watching before he passed out.

Suddenly he wanted a drink of water more than anything. He sat up, but his brain seemingly stayed on the couch for a second before slingshotting back into his skull throbbing painfully—a nauseating reminder of his overindulgence from the Gods of Scotch whisky.

He knew the explosions for what they were the second he heard the bass heavy report.

And so did Lucas, who barged from his room seconds later zipping up his black jacket.

"Let's go," he said, pistol in hand, "that was *not* the bridge."

"Wait one," Liam whined. "I'm still getting sorted."

"Hell of an understatement little bro," Lucas stated. And as the secondary explosions echoed outside, he visibly stiffened and shot Liam a look that screamed, *Hurry up.*

Laying an M4 on the couch next to Liam who was busily lacing his boots Lucas said, "Stay sharp—the dead don't blow shit up. We'll check the *jennies* first... I filled both tanks earlier so I think we probably have visitors." He opened the door and stepped from the darkened guest house, his big black Beretta leading the way into the inky blackness.

***

Maddox popped the lock open in under a minute. The two operators crouched low, awaiting the return of Lopez and Tice.

Cade heard Lopez's voice in his earpiece, "Approaching the front."

"Roger that," Cade answered.

Once the team had reunited, Maddox pushed the door inward and inched his way into the foyer.

The air inside was only a few degrees warmer than outside and an eerie silence seemed to permeate the mansion.

"Team two takes the right stairs," Cade ordered.

Silence.

Cade watched Tice peel away and shadow Lopez up the stairs, lasers sweeping the front as they cut the corner and crouched down, waiting for him and Maddox to summit the thirty-plus stairs on the other side of the foyer.

Cade ran point as the Delta team moved down the hall, the carpeted runner swallowing up the sound of their footfalls.

Putting a clenched fist in the air Cade took a knee.

The other operators followed suit. Lopez turned to keep an eye on their six.

Using hand signals Cade alerted the others that he detected movement around the corner.

As he inched his head around the corner, one degree at a time, the sound of rapid knocking filtered to his position.

"Mister Christian," a distant voice called out.

More knocking, louder.

Cade signaled that they were moving on the source of the noise. He crept around the corner and trotted swiftly down the hall; oil paintings rendered in washed out greens, portraits and landscapes, blurred by in his peripheral vision. The knocking continued and as he rounded the corner the source of the racket came into view. Holding a black pistol and dressed head to toe in dark clothing, a man of average height who was in dire need of a Gut-Be-Gone continued to bang on a door thirty feet down the hall.

"You have to wake up Robert!" the man bellowed.

Walking the green laser beam down the hall, Cade settled it on the man's temple then advanced swiftly to within ten feet of the guard and said in a low voice, "You move and you're dead."

The guard stopped beating on the door and pivoted incrementally on one foot, his right arm holding the Glock near his leg. "You fucking with me Ian?"

Finger tense on the SCAR's trigger, Cade barked. "Drop the pistol... now."

Cliff squinted at the blocky silhouette, and, forgetting to drop the pistol, raised his arms.

With a soft report two silenced rounds left Cade's SCAR. The first bullet entered the man's open mouth, struck his mandible bone, caromed slightly left and down severing his internal carotid artery, while the second 5.56x45 mm round hit squarely between his eyes. The resulting kinetic energy hinged him backward and spun his body to the carpeted floor, face down and dead.

Cade stepped over the bloody corpse to take stock of the door. He called Maddox forward where they conferred and agreed the door had a steel core, and since it was locked from the inside could not be breached quietly.

Builders of mansions typically used the best materials money could buy, Cade thought. And this door was no exception.

"Stand back," Maddox warned as he fired a tight pattern of slugs into the door and frame around the handle, then in one fluid motion kicked it inward.

Moving like mercury the team swarmed the room.

Each operator had taken down hundreds of rooms in this manner, both under fire and nice and quiet and serene like this one.

Lopez crossed the room, opened the French doors and checked out the veranda, calling "Clear," a second later.

Tice rushed through an open doorway which he guessed led to the master bathroom. And after probing the immense spa-like suite he yelled, "Clear."

The final "Clear," emanated from the cavernous walk-in closet a moment before Maddox stepped back into the master bedroom.

Cade stood at the foot of a four post bed that had to be a king plus if there was such a thing. A lone figure lay still underneath covers that through his NVGs looked like some kind of shimmering alien fabric. He clutched a corner of the bedspread and yanked hard. The satin sheets slithered to the floor exposing a frail looking man who Cade guessed had been playing possum to avoid detection.

Lopez removed a glove and checked for a pulse while Cade kept his SCAR aimed on the unmoving man.

"Is he alive?" Cade asked as he removed a handful of photos from his breast pocket and began comparing them with the man's face. Though the pictures that Nash had provided at the briefing were several years old, the likeness was unmistakable.

"He's alive... but it looks like he has self-medicated," Tice said, holding up a pill bottle. "Ambien... some kind of sleeping pill."

"That's not all," Lopez said, indicating the empty champagne bottles.

"Wake him up," Cade said impatiently. Then he went about the business of getting them a ride home. "Jedi One-One this is Anvil actual, how copy?"

After a second of silence Ari Silver's voice crackled in Cade's earpiece and said, "Copy that Anvil actual. We will be wheels up in one mike. How about those SAMs?"

"Benedict Arnold is in custody and all arrows are broken. I repeat arrows are broken," Cade said, speaking in code and letting Ari know that they had Robert Christian in custody and that the Patriot batteries had in fact been destroyed.

Chapter 47
Outbreak - Day 12
Jackson Hole, Wyoming

The House - 3:01 a.m.

Lucas swept the flashlight beam over the pair of generators. "The gas lines have been cut," he whispered.

"On both of them?"

"Yes. And some of the wires have been tampered with," Lucas added.

"Ian said that *bitch* Clay wasn't going to let Robert Christian get away with sending saboteurs and assassins into Colorado Springs. Like stirring up a hornet's nest." He cursed under his breath. "I bet there's a division of Marines in the valley."

"Get a grip Liam. Did you hear air transports or troop helicopters?"

"No."

"Then how in the hell does a Division of anything get into this valley?" Lucas asked.

Silence.

"No doubt we're dealing with a small group of Special Forces. What we need are the night vision goggles."

Liam wore a pained look. "Carson pulled rank and took every pair with him to Minot."

"That was days ago. He left nothing here?"

Liam shrugged.

"The M-60?" Lucas queried.

Liam replied, "It's in the garage in the back of the H2."

"Get it and fall back to the guest house. We'd be stupid to engage a team of shooters on their terms."

"What about Cliff and the guys in the mansion?"

"They're on their own," Lucas said, shaking his head slowly. "I'm saving my own skin."

"Amen brother," Liam said as he set out to get the big gun.

***

Miner's Butte SOAR Loiter - 3:01 a.m.

"Kick the tires and light the fires," Ari said as he tightened his harness and ignited the turbines. "We have a paying fare, gents—and they're bringing baggage."

The rotors spun slowly at first then spooled up, transferring minute vibrations through the airframe.

Ari pulled pitch and rocketed the Ghost Hawk into the crisp night air.

Durant, sitting in the left seat, input the GPS coordinates Cade had relayed to him and brought up the exfil point on the topo map. "The butte juts to the north fifteen hundred AGL. The mansion is on the north end of the finger."

"Copy that," Ari answered. Then tearing his eyes from the green glow of the burning SAM sites he looked aft and said, "Warm up the mini, Hicks."

***

The House - 3:01 a.m.

Cade snatched a crystal vase off of a side table which was flanked a couple of overstuffed chairs, and tossed the silk flowers on the carpet. "Flex-cuff Sleeping Beauty," he hissed as he went into the master bath.

A minute passed before he returned, carrying the vase filled with cold water.

The second the water hit the prone man he jerked awake, straining against his bonds, then rolled off of the bed hitting the ground with a hollow thump.

Cade put a boot on the man's boney ankle, then knelt down making sure that his knee was strategically placed on a softer more delicate area.

299

The man grunted and writhed, obviously in extreme pain.

Thrusting the picture Daymon had given him into the prone man's face he barked, "Where is this woman?"

A sly grin spread across Robert Christian's face.

Putting all of his weight behind the knee Cade asked slowly and forcefully, "Is she still here?"

Teeth clenched in agony the old man sneered and said, "You're too late Sir Galahad... she's gone."

"Tice... Maddox... take this photo. See if you can find her. I want all of the rooms in the upper floor searched," Cade said, thinking that the bedrooms were the most likely place for the dirt bag to keep his concubines.

Looking down at the prisoner, Lopez shook his head then turned his gaze towards Cade.

"I promised," Cade said in a low voice.

No, you compromised, Lopez thought.

"Give me a hand," Cade said as he pulled the prisoner to his feet.

Together the two operators hustled him through the French doors onto the veranda.

Cade roughly shoved Christian onto a teak chaise lounge chair. "Don't move."

"I'm declaring diplomatic immunity," Robert Christian blurted, "and as President of New America, a sovereign nation—"

Lopez removed a sweat stained bandanna from his cargo pocket and shoved it deep into the man's mouth. "Saddam Hussein tried that angle when they caught him in Tikrit... and look where it got him," he said, miming hanging himself with an imaginary noose.

"Nothing," Maddox stated as he walked in the door, having just returned from searching the rest of the upper level.

"We must have cleared fifteen rooms each with its own commode." Then closing the door behind him, Tice added. "How many shitters does one man need?"

As if in response to his question automatic rifle fire raked the door, pinging off of the steel core and sending shards of wood from the casing rocketing into the master suite.

"Taking fire from the hallway," Maddox calmly stated.

After another volley the firing stopped.

Stalking from the veranda into the suite, Cade leveled his
SCAR and fired a pair of full auto bursts into the drywall to the left
of the door. Screaming ensued from the hallway. Then pleading.
Cade emptied his SCAR into the wall near the floor.

The screams ceased.

"Maddox, you cover the door," Cade said as he made his way
out onto the veranda. Then, sensing the low timbre hum of Jedi One-
One, he activated an IR strobe and placed it on the roof's edge to
mark their location. The device, which flashed brightly in the infrared
spectrum, could only be seen with the aid of night vision goggles.

Durant's voice crackled in Cade's earpiece. "Jedi One-One to
Anvil actual, I have eyes on you. How copy?"

Craning his head to get a visual on the Ghost Hawk, Cade
answered, "Good copy. Are you ready for a tricky exfil?"

"I was born ready," Ari stated as he deployed the landing gear
and banked the helo gently while glancing over his right shoulder. In
the distance fires raged bright yellow and green in his NVGs as the
burning Patriot battery lit up a good portion of the elk refuge. "Good
job negating the air defenses," he added.

"Least we could do," Cade replied. "You're going to have to
perch one wheel on the deck rail."

"Just like the Hindu Kush," Ari said, referring to the desolate
high altitude mountain range in Afghanistan that he had regularly
ferried SF operators in and out of during his deployments there.
"Rock pinnacle... wood deck... what's the difference."

Cade watched the hulking chopper as it approached and soon
the thrumming Ghost Hawk's rotor wash was whipping the surface
of the infinity pool to a glowing froth.

The starboard wheel kissed the deck and the door slid back
revealing the Hawk's dimly illuminated interior.

Cade walked the prisoner ahead of him, and with a helping
hand from Lopez forcefully threw the billionaire President wannabe
into the open door head first. He glanced right and noticed the
reassuring silhouette of Sergeant Hicks manning the deadly mini-gun.
"*Go, go, go,*" he yelled over the comms.

Tice jumped in first and took a seat at the aft bulkhead.

Cade covered the French doors as Maddox climbed aboard.

Once everyone was onboard the helo Cade joined them, closed the door and strapped in on the port side.

Ari increased power, putting a couple of feet between the wheel and the deck, then retracted the gear. "No bad guys on the loose?" Ari asked Cade, immediately regretting his words.

Green tracers erupted from the large house a few hundred yards northeast of the swimming pool. The glowing bullets ripped through the night air barely missing the helo's belly.

Ari glanced right and slid Jedi One-One sideways and away from the mansion to give Hicks a clean angle on target.

"Engaging," Hicks said. The gun's electric whine filled the fuselage as he let loose with a three hundred round burst. The tracers chewed up the house leaving only tattered curtains where the upper story window used to be.

"Good shooting Hicks," Lopez said, high-fiving the usually reserved crew chief.

As the wheels seated into the fuselage with a dull clunk Ari pulled pitch and then skimmed the Ghost Hawk over the infinity pool before diving towards the valley floor below.

Cade glanced out the window and watched as tracer fire probed the night sky then disappeared when the mansion left his line of sight.

Ari's voice crackled over the comms. "Before you all start popping the party favors I have some bad news courtesy of First Sergeant Whipper."

"What now?" Cade interjected.

"His tanker pilots have foraged enough fuel to last a week or two... but..."

"Why is there always a but?" an exasperated Tice asked.

Continuing, Ari said, "Oilcan Five-Five took off a few minutes ago from Schriever and *was* going to rendezvous with us near the Utah border, but they had to RTB (return to base) because of a faulty fuel line."

Tice chimed in again. "Pretty ironic huh... big old Herc gets grounded because its engines can't get enough fuel."

Shaking his head at Mr. Murphy's poor sense of humor, Cade asked, "How soon until Whipper has another tanker fueled and wheels up?"

"That Hercules was the *only* bird left. The other tankers went back out to suck the tanks dry at Altus AFB in Oklahoma," Ari said. "I'm going to have words with Whipper when we get back. And odds are Nash knew nothing about it."

"Talk about putting all your eggs in one basket," Tice said bleakly.

"It's your fault Spooky," Lopez said. "You jinxed us Mister *What Could Go Wrong?*"

"Bottom line... we'll need to refuel at the Jackson Airport or chance Grand Junction again," Ari said, then returned his full attention to his beloved Ghost Hawk.

***

Teton Pass Highway 22 - 3:07 a.m.

Lu Lu labored to conquer the ten percent grade of the Teton pass highway. *Girl's way past due for a tune up,* Daymon told himself for the umpteenth time since the start of summer. *Fuckers probably ate my mechanic,* he mused.

Suddenly an overwhelming feeling of loss washed over him as the memories of the past—before the dead began to walk—came flooding back. Would he be able to find someone to take Heidi's place? No person on the planet could fill her size nines, of that he was certain. He thought about going into his wallet for her picture until he remembered that Cade had it.

There was always the probability that there might be one or two stray photos back at the house in Driggs. Or at the very least, he thought with a grin, one of the many disposable box cameras that he never got around to having developed. No more one hour photo guarantees—yet one more thing he used to take for granted that was forever altered by the apocalypse.

Shapes began to materialize from the dark, no thanks to the Scout's one remaining headlight. The collision with the errant zombie on 189 had broken the driver's side headlight and Lu Lu's coolant temperature had been in the red since midway up the pass which led him to believe the truck's radiator had been punctured.

The burned out school bus he remembered from his last trip over the Teton pass came into view, its twisted blackened hulk still blocking the highway.

He stopped in the center of the scorched highway and set the e-brake.

Where the hell are you Jenkins?

As if in response to his thought, a shrill buzzing emanated from between the front seats. He snatched up the police radio and then realized that he was hearing the satellite phone.

"Is that you Sergeant Cade?" he blurted into the handset.

"Daymon... I'm very sorry," Cade said, getting right to the point, "we searched the mansion and found no sign of Heidi."

Silence.

Cade went on, "We have Robert Christian. If it's any consolation he will pay for the atrocities committed by him and his men."

"The Bishop guy?" Daymon asked.

"He squirted like a rat on a sinking ship," Cade proffered, confirming what Daymon already knew.

"Thanks for following through—you didn't have to," said a morose sounding Daymon.

"I gave you my word."

"That you did," Daymon intoned. "That you did..."

Cade grabbed the bulkhead as Ari banked the helo hard to starboard. Once his stomach returned to its normal position he said, "We just overflew a massive herd of dead bearing down on downtown Jackson... where are you?"

"Teton pass... then home."

"After that?"

"Probably Eden. I miss that old coot Duncan."

"That makes two of us. Keep the phone near. Call if you need anything and I'll help if it's humanly possible."

"No doubt," Daymon said.

"Take care and thanks," were Cade's parting words.

Daymon thumbed off the phone and laid on Lu Lu's horn in frustrated dismay.

SHAWN CHESSER

The police radio rang—a more pleasant sound than the sat phone. Daymon hoped the news was going to be better. "Hello."

"Get your gear and leave your truck. Do it now and hurry up about it."

Daymon did as he was told. He was too tired to argue and too tired to question. Leaving his beloved Lu Lu in the road he trudged around the bus, lugging all of his gear: shotgun, crossbow, Kelty pack, and the sat phone. He noticed the two dead NA soldiers first, and as he stepped over their corpses the gunshot wounds to their faces were impossible to miss.

Chief Charlie Jenkins exited the Jackson PD Tahoe in his blue JPD uniform. Gone was the all black NA uniform he had been expected to wear. Coming forward he extended an arm to help Daymon with his gear. He took the bow and pack. "I'll put these in back, best to keep the shotgun close by."

Daymon nodded at the corpses and asked, "What happened to these two?"

"They chose the wrong side. Get in," Jenkins said as he went around the front of the Chevy.

Moving slowly, obviously in pain from old injuries, Daymon complied.

"Look who I found," Jenkins said, pointing a thumb towards the second row seats.

Daymon looked over his shoulder and noticed the shock of dirty blonde hair snaking from under a shiny foil space blanket. "*Heidi?*" he blurted, turning his gaze towards Charlie.

"I found her at the end of 22—by the crosses."

"*Alive?*"

"She was hypothermic when I found her draped over the barbed wire. She was smart to take clothes off of the dead. That and the fact that she made herself visible saved her life. She can't talk...or didn't want to... her neck looks awful... all black and blue—someone tried to strangle her."

Daymon crawled into the back seat, making the blanket crinkle as he edged close to her. "Take us home," he said. He alternated between gently stroking her hair and wiping his hot tears that seemed to be never ending.

Chapter 48
Outbreak - Day 12
Jackson Hole, Wyoming

Jackson Hole Airport - 3:10 a.m.

Cade stowed the sat phone and as he did so caught Lopez looking at him. He shifted his gaze to Tice, saying, "Get your counter out, Spook. Ari, we are going to need a standoff recon of the airport before we go in. See if there are any personnel or Zs we will have to contend with."

"Copy that Captain," Ari said as the elk refuge with the still burning hardware blazed by. He nosed the helo closer to the deck then leveled off and flashed the Delta team a thumbs up.

Two minutes later Ari parked Jedi One-One in a hover a mile off while Durant operated the FLIR (Forward Looking Infrared) camera. Contained in a dome mounted on a motorized rotating gimbal underneath the helo's chin, the camera transformed whatever it was trained on into a thermal image. Hot spots, such as engine blocks, exhaust pipes and even a human body glowed white while cold surfaces remained gradient shades of black. To Durant the luminescent scene displayed on the flat screen made the airport and support vehicles look like kids toys. Rendered monochrome and lacking true depth, a phalanx of tractor trailers parked side by side stretched the length of the runway. The Airport Authority's refueling bowsers, which were high on Ari's priority list, sat quietly near a grouping of hangars. Several fixed wing aircraft including what looked like a 757 commercial airliner sat idle, blocking the taxiway.

The single runway, labeled 19, ran northeast by southwest. Beside it the squat airport built primarily with exposed wood beams and girders sat empty and dark.

"No real hot spots to speak of except for the vehicles—I estimate forty or fifty in the parking lot east of the airport—and based on their low heat sig they have all been parked for some time," Durant commented.

"They didn't exactly park between the lines," Tice said with a chuckle.

"What you have there is a meter maid's wet dream," Ari quipped.

"Sure looks like they left in a hurry," Hicks added.

On the floor their prisoner craned his neck and looked up. He appeared to be trying to communicate though the bandanna was still occupying his mouth.

"Shut up," Cade hissed as he put a boot on Christian's face and forced his head down. "You can do all of your singing to the President and her men when we get back to Schriever."

After panning the FLIR over the entire airport, zooming in on suspect locations, and then making a second pass for good measure, Durant concluded the airport had been abandoned.

"Going in gentlemen, two mikes—lock and load," Ari said.

"Take us to the semi-trucks first," Cade ordered.

"Then we need to top off with JP-8 or we'll be gliding the last two hundred miles to Schriever."

Shaking his head in disbelief, Tice's face tightened and he said, "Helos can't glide."

"Duh *dumbass*... that's Ari's point," Lopez shot back.

Boys will be boys and even though most of the world had died, apparently old rivalries were alive and well. Cade just hoped that when they got back to Schriever the two men didn't come to blows. However if they did, he had already decided his money would be on Sergeant First Class (Low-Rider) Lopez, even though the veteran Delta operator was vertically challenged.

The wheels deployed; seconds later the Gen-3 helicopter flared and Ari settled her down twenty yards from the tractor trailer rigs.

The door opened and the Delta operators piled out. Then with lasers sweeping the ground in front, the men sprinted to the rear of the nearest rig.

The Ghost Hawk lifted off with a blast of rotor wash and hovered near silently five hundred feet above the runway.

Tice strode down the line of trucks, pausing now and again to sweep the Geiger counter around the seals and loading decks of the numerous trailers.

"Getting any readings?" Cade asked.

Tice stopped and turned, fully facing the Delta captain. "Nothing. These trucks haven't been anywhere near a nuke. Nash was right about her bird's imagery... she just didn't know what was contained inside."

"Let's find out."

Tice shrugged off his M4, set the Geiger counter aside and retrieved the miniature bolt cutters, and with an awful impersonation of Bob Barker said, "Let's see what's behind door number one." He snipped the two locks. "Someone give me a hand."

With Maddox's help both doors parted revealing numerous wooden pallets stacked to a height of roughly four feet. Cade grabbed the side of the trailer and pulled himself up, his knees and back creaking in protest. "These go all the way to the front," he commented as he pulled one corner of the heavy canvas covering the cargo. "*Wow!*" he exclaimed as he exposed the entire pallet's cargo.

Tice was taken aback—first from the biggest display of emotion he had seen from the stone-faced operator—then because the most gold he had ever seen in his life was sitting unguarded feet from him.

"Truck's full of gold bars," Cade said, rubbing his dirt and grime encrusted neck.

Lopez whistled, "Must be hundreds of them."

"Close it," Cade ordered. "We refuel and then we're *oscar mike*."

"The gold?" Tice inquired.

"It's beautiful... but it's worthless," Cade said. "Food, bullets, and fuel, those three are the new gold."

"Copy that," Tice said slowly.

Cade swung the doors shut and strode to the helo which had just touched down.

Ari ferried them to the refuel area where Hicks jumped out first. They followed the same routine as Grand Junction. Cade, Maddox and Lopez stood watch while the crew chief checked the fuel trucks.

After a couple of minutes Hicks came loping back to the helo. He stopped and animatedly shook his head and then slid one finger across his neck.

No fuel, Cade thought to himself. Then a cold finger traced his spine as he realized that they had no other choice but to refuel at Grand Junction Regional.

***

3:25 a.m.

Ari kept Jedi One-One close to 189 as they left the valley and the Tetons behind. Along the way they passed over downtown Jackson Hole which had already been overrun by the legions of dead migrating from the southwest. "I've got more bad news from Schriever," Ari said in a funeral voice. "An outbreak occurred inside the wire. The civilian billets were heavily involved."

Except for the humming of the carbon fiber rotors and the turbine's baffled whine the cabin was morgue quiet.

After a few minutes had elapsed and a few dozen miles disappeared behind them, Cade asked the question that no doubt was on everyone's mind. "How many casualties?"

"More than a hundred," Ari said solemnly.

"And a handful in the mess hall," Durant added.

"Did they mention Brook or Raven?" Cade asked knowing full well that Nash would *never* disclose devastating news of that nature during an ongoing mission.

"No sir," Durant answered. "But no news is good news... isn't that what they always say?"

Cade exhaled audibly. Thoughts and memories of Brook and Raven suddenly escaped from the imaginary black box in the deepest recesses of his mind. The knowledge that they had once again been in harm's way, and he had not been there for them, troubled him deeply.

"Mindless rotters, they just roll over everything in their way," Tice muttered.

"Pinche demonios," added Lopez.

"The next waypoint is Grand Junction Airport four hundred and thirty miles to the southwest," Durant informed Ari. Then he switched to private comms to address Hicks directly. "How much JP-8 was left in the tanker at GJT?"

"More than enough to get us home. Five hundred gallons plus."

"Same routine—hot refuel. Let's hope more Zs haven't shown up since yesterday."

"Wishful thinking Durant," Hicks stated.

Cade broke his silence and asked Ari and Durant if they would be at the airport before dawn.

"Negative," said Ari. "This bird will drink way too much fuel if I ride her too hard. You are going to lose the night vision advantage... it can't be helped."

Cade closed his eyes and thought about his family.

***

Grand Junction, Colorado - 6:31 a.m.

"Five mikes," Durant said.

The co-pilot's voice echoed in Cade's headset, bringing him back to the present. Entering the helo from the port side, sunlight filtered through the cabin causing him to squint and rub his tired eyes. He looked out the window at the landscape passing below the helicopter. Standing water in the streets and parking lots reflected the early morning sun, giving the scene a soothing radiance that he knew contradicted the reality of the infested city. Turning his attention to the next task at hand, he swapped the flight helmet for his Kevlar tactical and gave the SCAR the once over.

Full mag? Check.

Round chambered? Check.

Safety? Check.

The weapon went between his knees barrel down and he braced the stock against the side of his helmet. Around him the other men were quietly going through their own personal routines. In his peripheral vision he witnessed Lopez perform the sign of the cross, kiss the ever-present crucifix hanging around his neck, and tuck it back inside his ACUs.

Durant called out time to target. "Two mikes."

"Scratch that," Ari barked.

The closer they got the more dire their situation appeared. Dozens of dead patrolled the runway and hangar area nearest the airport. Over a hundred walkers milled about their last landing spot between the broken fence and the two tanker trucks. And in between the two major concentrations, near the burned out aircraft, a host of stragglers plodded along.

Ari's voice invaded the comms. "What do you think Captain?"

"I think we've got our work cut out for us," Cade answered, craning his head to see out the starboard windows. He paused for a beat and then asked, "How many rounds left in the mini-gun?"

"Twelve hundred," answered Hicks. "Whipper was being a stingy prick so we flew out pretty light."

Ari presented a plan. "How about I bring us in from the east to give you an oblique angle so you can keep any stray rounds away from the fuel trucks. Take out as many as you can. I will put us down quick—same routine as last time. Hicks refuels while the Delta boys watch his six. He gives us a light load of JP-8 and we are out in under five mikes."

"Sound strategy Night Stalker," Cade said, flashing Ari a thumbs up.

"Make them count Hicks," Lopez interjected.

Ari bled airspeed, leveled Jedi One-One, and rotated the bird a one-eighty to present Hicks with an undead shooting gallery.

***

Taryn felt a minute vibration through the carpeted floor. At first she thought it was a small earthquake like the 2.9 from a couple of years back, which was similar only more intense.

Whatever had caused the tremor had also piqued her favorite zombie's attention. Dickless released the door handle, turned woodenly, and then slowly ambled down the stairs.

Taryn was forced to lay flat on the floor in order to see the jet way and landing strip beyond the shattered window. A troubling sight

311

greeted her. The amount of zombies on the tarmac had increased overnight.

Once again she experienced a sensation she couldn't quite place. Some kind of low intensity, low pressure vibration.

She heard glass crunching below as her old boss traversed the concourse to the lip of the missing window where he stood swaying precariously above the tarmac below.

Taryn put her face under the water cooler spigot and drained a few precious ounces into her mouth.

Suddenly a whining jackhammer-like sound reached her ears. She crawled back to her perch and watched the creatures being chopped to pieces. With no idea who was wielding the noisy invisible scythe, she flattened her body and pressed her cheek to the floor in order to see the far end of the runway. To her amazement the noiseless black helicopter had returned and was just touching down. She didn't want this diversion to slip through her hands—she collected her iPhone and solar panel then stashed the pistol in her pocket.

***

The sustained buzzsaw sounding bursts of the mini-gun decimated the walkers nearest the airport.

Hicks swept the fire across the Zs, cutting some in half and rendering many more of them headless.

"Get some," Lopez cried.

Only crawlers and a handful of walking Zs moved on the body part-littered killing field below.

"Save some for the south end," Ari said.

Hicks eased back on the trigger as Ari brought the helo around, and once the Ghost Hawk had regained a steady hover he sent the last of the 7.62 mm rounds chewing into the Zs near the broken fence.

A few seconds later the mini-gun went silent save for its whining electric servo.

"Winchester," Hicks said as he released the trigger, fully silencing the smoking weapon.

"Going in," Ari warned.

Cade's stomach lurched as the helo dropped like a stone. The wheels locked into place and Jedi One-One kissed the earth with a slight bounce.

"*Go, go, go,*" Durant hollered.

Time slowed down for Cade and his vision sharpened as he followed Hicks out the door. He flicked off the safety and bringing the SCAR to bear started dropping walkers. A cordite haze formed and shell casings skittered across the tarmac. Sensing Lopez form up next to him, he looked over to confirm Tice and Maddox were out of the bird. Confident the team had the perimeter around the helo covered, he turned and emptied his mag into the nearest walkers, quickly reloaded and resumed death dealing.

Hicks retrieved the fuel nozzle which was lying on the tarmac where he had left it only hours ago. With rotors whirring feet above his head and gunfire echoing all around him, he began filling the chopper's tank.

"*Maddox, watch your six,*" Durant bellowed over the comms.

Whipping his head around, time slowed further as Cade witnessed the attack. Maddox, with a dozen dead littering the ground around him, was changing mags when the creatures bowled him over. And without uttering a sound the operator rose to his knees and plunged his combat knife into the bloated Z's temple. Dead arms still gripping his legs, he pulled his pistol and struggled to stand.

Tice pivoted and dropped the two Zs approaching from Maddox's left but his reaction proved to be too little too late as the man disappeared under the carrion pile.

"Fuckers!" Lopez shouted as he emptied his magazine into the writhing creatures.

***

Holding herself to her own word, Taryn left solitary confinement and taking the steps two at a time made it to the concourse. She looked past her coffee stand towards the far revolving doors. A handful of walkers including Porkpie stood in her way. Choosing the path of least resistance she turned and ran towards Dickless and brought the black revolver up. The trigger proved much harder to pull than she thought it would be. Likewise, the discharge was exponentially louder than the ones on television. Unscathed, Dickless turned towards her, a hissing sound escaping his dried lips.

This time, anticipating the report, she closed her eyes before pulling the trigger. The .38 boomed. The hollow point struck Dickless center mass on the breastbone sending him sprawling into the bank of plastic and fabric built-in seats.

At a full sprint Taryn went to the ground and slid through the broken glass. She grabbed the edge of the window a second before shooting out into space. Then she looked down to the jet way. A twelve foot drop awaited and at the moment the place she would land was free of walking dead things. She bravely dangled her bare legs into the void and lowered herself over the edge, and as she hung by her tiring fingertips all she could think about were the monsters eyeing her lower extremities.

Let go.

Her fingers wouldn't cooperate.

She heard gunfire ringing out behind her and then a hissing sound started above her. It took her boss's frigid hand groping her arm to make her finally release her grip.

From the tips of her toes to the tarmac the drop was roughly seven feet—more than enough to send her knees into her solar plexus when she hit. As she lay helpless and struggling to breathe on the oil spattered tarmac, Dickless stuck his head through the opening.

Back flat to the ground, Taryn extended both arms holding the pistol steady. She aligned the front sight on the monster's forehead and slowly squeezed the trigger.

Bang.

Dickless slumped as the bullet tore into his eye socket, shredding his brain.

Taryn struggled to her feet, took a couple of deep breaths, and picked her way through the killing fields heading towards the helicopter.

***

"Get in," Durant's voice said over the comms.

Finished refueling, Hicks put the nozzle down and jumped into the black helo.

Tice emptied his magazine into the Zs, dumped it to the ground, and then replaced it on the run.

Cade sensed the rotor speed picking up. Shell casings pushed by the down blast rolled away from the helicopter.

Going to a knee just outside of the open door, Lopez covered Tice's retreat. He fired into the approaching ranks screaming at the top of his lungs, "*Die demonios.*"

Ari's voice came over the comms. "Wheels up."

"We can't leave without his body," Cade bellowed as he waved Lopez inside.

"We have no choice," Ari said as he began to pull pitch.

Reluctantly Cade took an offered hand and boarded the Ghost Hawk seconds before the wheels separated from the asphalt.

Ari took the helo to twenty feet, spun around ninety degrees, and said incredulously over the comms, "Looks like we have one survivor, center of the runway, twelve o'clock."

Cade was fixated on the scene playing out below the helicopter as the remaining zombies attacked Maddox's corpse, their clawlike hands tearing into his flesh and plunging under his body armor. Inexplicably the dead Delta operator's tactical helmet popped off, landing upside down and coming to rest on the still attached night vision goggles. The rotor wash blasted in the cabin and Cade looked away as the helo bolted forward.

***

Waving her arms and jumping up and down Taryn began to cry. Standing in the middle of a sea of pulped corpses she had never felt more alive.

She recoiled against the blowing wind as the helicopter hummed overhead, its black outline blotting the blue morning sky. A man wearing a bulky helmet, his eyes concealed behind a dark visor, reached down and easily hauled her into the craft. Before the door closed she found herself thoroughly scrutinized for bites and under interrogation.

***

A half hour into the solemn flight from Grand Junction to Schriever, Lopez piped up. Speaking to nobody in particular he said, "Besides me... Maddox was the last member of Mike's team. This is a

315

hard one to wrap my brain around. Never, and I mean *never* did I think we would lose this many of our own in so short a time." He took a deep breath and continued to gaze down at the parched desert earth rushing by. "One whole team lost in the White House. More men at the CDC. Desantos... and now Maddox. He was a good man."

A booming chorus of "*Hooahs*" filled the cabin.

Lopez went on, "I want to die just like him."

All eyes, including Taryn's, swept to the operator.

Looking stonily at anyone who would maintain eye contact, Lopez said slowly, "Maddox went out silent—like a true *warrior*. He didn't whimper. There was no wailing for *madre*. He took it to them like a man and he died like a man. When we get back I'm going to build a memorial to him near Mike's grave."

No witty comeback from Tice. Instead he put an arm around Lopez's shoulder. The gesture was received unconditionally.

Lopez hunched over shielding his face. His shoulders shook as deep mournful sobs filled the air.

Robert Christian wriggled up into a sitting position, eyes darting to his hands which had turned a deep shade of purple.

"Down," Cade yelled. He held nothing back as he kicked the waste of skin in the teeth.

"Five mikes," Durant said. Then, craning his head and looking down on the crisscrossing streets added, "Looks like General Gaines's 10th Special Forces boys are mopping up downtown."

Ari slowed the Ghost Hawk and put her into an orbit a thousand feet above downtown Springs.

Looking out the window and noticing that there were far fewer creatures roaming the streets, Cade agreed with Durant, saying, "I wouldn't wish that job on anyone. Kicking doors even when you know there's a Z behind every one... takes a goliath set of balls." He removed his flight helmet and donned his tactical helmet, letting the chin strap dangle.

"You look like shit," Lopez yelled.

"I feel worse than I look," Cade conceded.

As Ari brought the ship in low and slow over the western fence a number of faces turned their way; mechanics looked up, shielding their eyes from the sun, and more than a few salutes were thrown heavenward.

On final approach, fifty feet above the landing pad, Cade looked out over the base. Standing out in stark contrast against the dark muddy ground, a mound of pale white corpses caught his gaze. He said a silent prayer to his God hoping Brook and Raven were not amongst them.

Jedi One-One settled onto the tarmac and not a second later Cade had yanked Robert Christian to his feet. As he ushered the withered man out the door ahead of him he looked over his shoulder and motioned for Lopez to tag along. Instinctively ducking his head under the slowing rotor blades, he prodded Christian along in front of him with the butt of his rifle.

Stopping in front of the dented yellow door outside of Whipper's office, Cade forced his prisoner to sit on the hard ground and said to Lopez, "I want you to personally escort that girl to quarantine and make sure they keep her a few hours extra. The last thing we need is another outbreak *inside* the wire."

"Yes sir, anything else sir."

"Yes Sergeant, as a matter of fact there is. Good job out there. I'm going to talk to General Gaines and get you a promotion."

"Thank you sir," Lopez said quietly.

"And I'm really sorry about Maddox. Didn't need to happen," Cade said, putting a hand on the man's shoulder. "I know you two went way back—ran a lot of ops together. Spilled more blood together. He will be missed."

Lopez removed his helmet and raked his fingers through his close cut black hair. He pinched the bridge of his nose keeping his eyes cast down.

Cade couldn't tell if the man was going to cry or not. Didn't matter. He waited a moment then said, "After you get the girl squared away, why don't you go get a bottle of something strong— pour yourself some—and then spill a little for Desantos and Maddox."

"Hooah sir."

Cade hauled Christian off the ground, making sure to wrench his rotator cuff, just so, causing the delicate aristocrat a well-earned dose of pain. Then he whispered in the prisoner's ear, "It's time to trade you in. The President's men have been waiting very patiently to make your acquaintance."

Robert Christian's eyebrows shot up as he realized what was in store for him. Nothing but unintelligible grunts escaped through the dirty gag as he begged and pleaded for his life.

Chapter 49
Outbreak - Day 12
Schriever AFB
Colorado Springs, Colorado

After leaving the would be architect of a failed new world order with some rough men at the Security Pod, Cade trudged past the civilian tent city. His legs seemed to be honed from granite—every step a monumental effort. He didn't want to go on a fact finding mission. He was afraid of the answer and he hadn't experienced this profound feeling of dread since coming to Schriever for the first time with Duncan, Daymon and the young stuttering soldier whose name—he was ashamed to admit—he couldn't remember. He stopped for a tick to watch as a group of people dressed in white hazmat suits filled black rubberized body bags with the corpses of civilians who had assumed—incorrectly as it turned out—that they were safe inside of the wire at Schriever.

Cade noticed one of the space suited workers peel away from the gory task and shuffle in his direction. With every step the nylon space suit made an irritating swishing sound. The figure, whose white suit was smeared with crimson traces of blood, stopped in front of him and removed the hood.

They locked eyes and the worker said in a soft drawl, "My work here is done."

Cade tried to process the man's words and come up with a reply but said nothing and nodded instead. He started to turn away but found he couldn't tear his eyes from the waist high drift of death.

"It was a bloodbath last night. Screaming and gunshots went on for hours. They think they contained all of 'em. Not before this," the man said waving his hand at the carnage. He looked Cade in the eye adding, "Wouldn't wish this on anyone."

The man perched a ball cap on his head, turned abruptly, and walked away whistling a happy tune.

***

Standing in front of the Grayson billet, a strange feeling of deja vu jumped Cade. Though he wanted this to be his last homecoming he feared it wouldn't be. At least not until the dead stopped walking and the remnants of the Guild were wiped out.

He pushed on the door.

Locked. Good job honey.

He rapped gently.

The door hinged inward and he found himself staring down the gaping barrel of Brook's M4.

"Looks like Annie got her gun," he said to break the ice. He had never had a weapon trained on him by his wife and he didn't know what else to say.

"Just protecting my roost."

"Where's Raven?"

Motioning to the top bunk behind her she said, "Still asleep. We had a long night."

"So I heard," he said propping his rifle near the door.

Lowering her weapon Brook began to cry. "I'm not mad at you anymore," she said softly between sobs.

With a tilt of his head he asked, "What are you talking about?"

"This." She thrust the note at him. "I thought Raven and I were going to die last night. I didn't want *our* little girl to die at the hands of one of those things," she said with the little girl from Fountain Valley still fresh on her mind. "And I didn't want to die mad at you," she went on. "I forgot to ask myself—will any of this matter in twenty years. I stopped doing that two weeks ago after I killed my Mom and Dad... when I didn't even know if I was going to be alive for the next two seconds... let alone twenty years."

After reading the note, Cade responded in a calm voice, "I did not see this."

Brook looked at him with red rimmed eyes and said softly, "I know... it was on the floor. But back to basics, what's the most important thing?"

"Family," Cade replied as he removed his gore spattered helmet and set it aside. Then he unbuttoned his soiled ACU top and tossed it near the door. He gently folded Brook's small frame in his arms, gazed deeply into her eyes, and said, "I like coming home like this... it's much better than the alternative."

Brook smiled, dabbing away a tear. "One more thing," she said.

"Yes."

Eyes brimming with fresh tears she said, "I lost the baby."

"I'm so sorry honey." He squeezed her a little closer and closed his eyes briefly, thinking of the little one that could have been.

"Another casualty to add to Pug's list," she hissed. Then she put both small hands behind her husband's sweaty head and pulled his face closer to hers. They exchanged a tender kiss that instantly threatened to evolve into something more.

"Ewww. Get a room!" Raven cried from on high.

"Hi sweetie."

"Hi Daddy," Raven said as she bounded down and leaped between Mom and Dad. "I love you guys."

In full stereo Brook and Cade repeated the same sentiment.

"Sweetie... do you know what day today is?"

"My birthday?" she said slowly.

Brook led a rousing rendition of Happy Birthday which Cade considered the hardest song to sing (in tune) in the world.

"You're twelve today Raven. Do you know where your mom and I were twelve years ago today?"

"No," she said as a quizzical look crossed her face.

"At the hospital, silly," Cade said playfully.

"Do I get a present?"

Cade tousled her head and said, "Since you are too old for a pony we'll go see the armorer and get you a rifle just your size."

"That's my department," Brook jokingly informed her husband.

"In all seriousness, I have to go find Nash. Before I left for Jackson Hole, she and the President presented me with an offer that I couldn't refuse. Now I have got to go and collect."

Raven asked, "When will you be back?"

"Soon Mister Moon."

***

Schriever Security Pod

Reluctantly Cade relinquished his Glock. Then he unslung the SCAR carbine and handed both weapons to the stoic, stone faced Secret Service agents.

As he made for the inner sanctum, the taller of the two agents said, "Captain Grayson, I have to hold the blade."

"Understood," he answered and removed the Gerber and placed it on the counter.

The man silently nodded and reaching past Cade opened the door for him.

Walking into the conference room Cade was taken aback by the number of people sitting and standing around the expansive table.

Valerie Clay sat at one end flanked by General Gaines, Colonel Shrill, Major Nash, and a handful of soldiers from the 10th Special Forces who Cade had seen before but hadn't yet formally met.

Behind the President, arrayed in a semi-circle, stood her protection detail clad in navy blue combat gear and toting MP7 machine pistols.

Cade took a seat in an empty chair next to Freda Nash, removed his beret, folded it neatly, and placed it on the polished table.

The diminutive Major glanced sideways, nodded, and returned her attention to Colonel Shrill who was going over the information already gleaned from Robert Christian's first session with the CIA interrogators.

After a few minutes the briefing ended and President Clay arose from her chair and moved around the table toward Cade.

"At ease," said the President as she pulled a chair and sat to Cade's right. "Captain Cade Grayson, I was hoping I would get to thank you in person for bringing Robert Christian to justice. He has already confessed to conspiring to overthrow the government. Furthermore he sent Francis here to assassinate me but apparently the man, who is a bit of a loose cannon, decided to take matters into his own hands and did what he did."

"To be honest, Madam President, I had a dog in the fight."

"That's the main reason I agreed to your proposal when Major Nash presented it to me. In light of all of your sacrifice... I think it was the least I could do so that you and your family can finally have some closure."

"I won't have a shred of closure until I hear him confess."

The President pushed her chair away and stood up. She put a hand on the Delta operator's shoulder and gave it a gentle squeeze, then turned and disappeared through the door surrounded by a moving wall of muscle and guns.

Nash poked her head out the door and barked at the man behind the security desk. "*Croswell*, I want you to help Captain Grayson transfer the prisoner. And Cade... this didn't come easy."

"Nothing worth fighting for ever does," he replied, looking directly into the Major's eyes. Then turning to Croswell who had just entered the room he said, "Fill me in."

"Well, he's been hooded the entire time and I've alternated the temperature between extremes as you ordered."

"I just talked to my wife and she mentioned that the doctor administered a larger than normal dose of anti-psychotic meds to the prisoner... has he talked?"

"Your wife's hunch was correct. His demeanor changed drastically after only a couple of hours and now that he's lucid and coherent he has asked us to call him Francis instead of Pug. And to top it all off he says he doesn't remember anything about the killing spree."

"Convenient," Cade muttered.

Croswell went on, "Dr. Keller examined the prisoner yesterday—when he still preferred to be called Pug. The doctor... actually he said he was a psychiatrist. Anyway, he indicated that Pug suffers from acute bi-polar disorder, some form, *or* multiple forms of PTSD, coupled with severe depression. *But...* the fact that he switches between wanting to be called Pug or Francis points to a severe multiple personality disorder... Keller said that would account for his alleged lapses in memory."

Cade sighed and said, "Let's have a chat with Mister whoever he thinks he is at the moment."

Keys jingled as Croswell worked the lock. He pulled the door open and motioned for Cade to enter ahead of him.

Cade squinted from the bright overhead light as Croswell tailed him into the interview room. The A/C was off. The warming air was thick with the dank overlapping odors of sweat and fear.

Chains clinked as the prisoner sat upright in response to the opening door and subsequent footfalls.

Croswell removed the hood. Purple bruising, tinted yellow around the edges, ringed the prisoner's eyes and both ears were encrusted with black dried blood.

Staring directly into the prisoner's eyes, Cade asked, "What is your name?"

"Francis Smith."

"Then who is Pug?" Cade asked.

"I'll tell you the same thing I told them... I do not know who Pug is," the prisoner said forcefully.

"Let's revisit this one more time... sticky footsteps led from the research facility to *your* tent... *your* boots were still wet," Cade said, jabbing a finger into the man's chest. "*You* had the murder weapon in your possession. Hell... Scooby Doo and the gang could have tracked you down."

"Wasn't me..." Francis mumbled, his eyes locked on the table top. "I'll tell you what I told them. I left Breckenridge because of the Omega outbreak. People started eating other people... I met those other people on the road and came here with them. After that fucking quarantine I went to..."

"Where did you go after that," Cade pressed.

"I don't remember. Listen, you have to believe me. I'm sick. I was abused when I was young... and I have always had these *lapses.*"

"Let me see if this jogs your memory. *Robert Christian* is not in Jackson Hole. He's here at Schriever. In fact, he's two rooms down being interrogated as we speak. Listen closely and you might hear him screaming."

Cade paused menacingly.

"He is already on record saying that he sent you here to assassinate President Clay."

Francis's face blanched.

Cade noticed his breathing begin to quicken. "What do you have to say for yourself?"

The prisoner's jaw trembled and he started to say something.

"Too late," Cade growled. He slapped a length of tape over the prisoner's mouth and pulled a handful of flex-cuffs from his cargo pocket. He handed two to the airman and said, "Secure his wrists tightly behind his back." Then, using three of the nylon restraints, he secured the prisoner's legs, leaving just enough slack so that he could take small shuffling steps.

Airman Croswell unlocked the manacles and hauled him to his feet.

"I need a vehicle," Cade said as he scooped up his weapons and hustled Francis toward the front doors.

"Wait one," Croswell said.

Cade stood by the front doors soaking in the warm sun while Croswell brought a desert tan Humvee around. Then, being none too gentle, Cade and Croswell each grabbed an arm and a leg and heaved the hogtied prisoner into the back seat face first.

"I'll have it back before noon," Cade said, suppressing a grin.

***

Francis cried out each time the Humvee's wide tires found a considerable pothole. He could no longer feel his fingers or toes. The inside of the hood that the rude soldier had cinched around his head had become slickened with snot and tears. Two minutes into the trip he had slid from the backseat and was now face down on the floorboard. His head had become a battering ram—hitting the door after each of the madman's sharp turns.

He had been on many journeys like this through the Nevada desert, he thought darkly. Only he had never been the one about to be buried.

After one last bone jarring jounce the vehicle crunched to a halt. He heard the snick and the slam as the madman exited.

Footsteps.

Another click, only near his head.

A tug.

Weightlessness, and then jagged rocks and moist gravel biting into his side as he met the ground hard and lost his wind.

Except for his labored breathing—silence.

Suddenly the hood was off and the blazing sun was eyefucking him.

As he fought to open his eyes, new sounds reached his ears. An emphysemic rasping sound. Rattling chain? No, it was chain-link fence he decided.

More footsteps. He sensed the sun displaced then willed his eyes open. Of course the madman was the shadow's owner and he was holding a black pistol.

Cade grabbed Francis by an elbow and roughly dragged him into the corridor between the security fences.

Eyes finally adjusted, Francis took in his surroundings. He was in a walkway between two very tall chain link fences topped off with razor wire. Half a dozen zombies pressed the fence three feet away. The wind shifted, bringing their stench to his nose. He grimaced, not from the smell but because he had an idea what the madman had in store for him. Then he watched the man stride forward and methodically walk down the fence line and shoot five of the six creatures in the head. The one that was spared growled indifferently at its compadres' demise.

The fact that the tall soldier hadn't said a word since they left the police station was very unnerving. *Say something*, Francis thought, *anything*.

Fight back, Pug whispered. *Head-butt the fucker you pussy.*

Kneeling next to the prisoner, Cade flipped the man over onto his stomach, drew his Gerber and gently tapped it on the trembling man's cheek.

Francis went wild-eyed and squirmed against the flex-cuffs. The madman smiled and reached for the leg restraints.

As Cade drew the razor sharp blade across both of the prisoner's Achilles tendons, the man's primal scream was suppressed by the length of duct tape. Cade waited until Francis's sobs slowed, and then watched his reddened eyes dart to the creature and then back to the blood slickened knife. This went on for a minute as the excited creature hissed and rattled the fence, bony fingers kneading metal.

He knows, Cade thought as he stepped around Francis's prone body. He unlocked the gate and, using it as a barrier, allowed the lone walker access to the meat.

The prisoner belly flopped and tried to inch along the soggy ground like a snake.

Fitting, Cade thought as the creature ignored him and fell atop the bleeding man.

After closing and locking the outside gate he swiftly sidestepped the carnage and repeated the process with the interior gate.

Totally helpless, trussed and face down, Francis ceased fighting and went limp.

The monster went for the neck first; yellowed teeth gnashing, the thing came up with a sizable hunk of bloodied flesh trailing veins and sinew.

Cade let the feeding commence for a moment, then stuck the Glock's muzzle through the fence and put a bullet in the creature's brain.

The prisoner struggled under the Z's dead weight, making a bloody dirt angel as he fought to stay among the living.

For my baby, for Carl, and for the untold others you have murdered, Cade thought sadly. Then he opened the inner fence, cut the plastic restraints from the dying man, reentered the base, and secured the fence once again.

Cade sat on the Humvee's warm hood, gazing at Desantos' grave and the rifle and helmet and pair of now muddy combat boots that had been left there to honor the warrior. He shifted his gaze to Pug's unmoving body and waited.

First a twitch, then he thought he saw the body shift. Soon Omega had run its course through the dead man's body and he had fully reanimated and was the one gripping the fence moaning for meat.

Full circle, Cade thought as he strode to the fence. He drew the black Gerber and plunged the honed blade into the fresh kill's eye socket. He felt the serrated edge grate against the Z's orbital bone as he yanked it free, letting the fresh corpse fall to the ground.

For you Mike.

Epilogue
Outbreak - Day 12
Schriever AFB

A whole day's worth of warm sunshine flushed down the drain, Taryn thought. After being asked to disrobe by a woman soldier, and then, like a prisoner or something she had been thoroughly searched inside and out, she spent twelve hours in quarantine being watched over by grim faced soldiers who in her opinion were just one notch below Dickless. No, take that back, she thought. Dickless was on a pedestal all his own and she was glad she was the one who ultimately knocked him off. Sounds kinda *Sopranoesque* she mused. Knocked him off. Rubbed him out. Made him sleep with the fishes. She snickered.

She needed to find a bed and get some quality sleep minus the door banging, knob rattling and familiar dead faces pressed against the glass.

The soldier who had given her a map of the base had crossed out the civilian quarters in black sharpie and told her to not go there, making it crystal clear that that area of the base was off limits. However, he had pointed out an alternate set of temporary shelters that had been used by the medical personnel and were now empty. "Take your pick," he had said. "Lock your door," he had stressed.

Mounting the steps, Taryn checked the door. *Locked*. She tried the key. *Click*—success.

After heeding the soldier's advice and locking the door behind her, she tossed the new camouflage clothes the soldier insisted that she take onto the desk near the door.

The oblong room held three bunk beds arranged in a row near the rear of the building and as many desks evenly spaced along the right wall. A door beyond the bunks led to a small bathroom. What a luxury, she thought. No more squatting on Richard's carpet.

She rifled through the desks. *Empty.*

Strangely, the prefab building didn't smell anything like a hospital. But then medical personnel, the dwelling's previous tenants, probably didn't take the odor home with them either.

She looked at her iPhone, and noticing that it still held a little charge, plugged in her ear buds. Then she turned off the overhead light plunging the room into darkness. Electricity, another luxury, she mused as she thumbed her phone on and used the soft glow it threw off to navigate her new environs. Then she settled on the bottom bed of the nearest bunk and started scrolling through her vast music collection.

Jimi? No.

Shins? No.

Blue Oyster Cult... perfect.

Engrossed in the tune and far from fearing the Reaper, Taryn noticed the light from the iPhone's display reflecting off of something that had been tucked between the slats and the mattress of the top bed. She reached up and grasped the small brushed metal object, and as she pulled it free the distinct blue packaging and the word Oreo leapt out at her. Forgetting about the device that initially had caught her attention, she extracted the hidden booty and greedily wolfed down the unexpected treats. Brushing the crumbs from the bed, she picked up the thumb drive and turned it over in her palm. On one side the words PROPERTY OF THE CDC had been etched into the aluminum case. On the flip side someone had written FUENTES in bold black letters with a sharpie.

Better have some awesome music on it, she thought to herself. She put the drive aside, rolled over and closed her eyes, then listened for the cowbell.

###

Thanks for reading *A Pound of Flesh*. Look for Book 5: *Allegiance*, the forthcoming novel in the *Surviving the Zombie Apocalypse* series in the summer of 2013. Please Friend Shawn Chesser on Facebook.

ABOUT THE AUTHOR

Shawn Chesser, a practicing father, has been a zombie fanatic for decades. He likes his creatures shambling, trudging and moaning. As for fast, agile, screaming specimens... not so much. He lives in Portland, Oregon, with his wife, two kids and three fish. This is his fourth novel.

CUSTOMERS ALSO PURCHASED:

JOHN O'BRIEN
NEW WORLD
SERIES

JAMES N. COOK
SURVIVING THE DEAD
SERIES

MARK TUFO
ZOMBIE FALLOUT
SERIES

ARMAND ROSAMILLIA
DYING DAYS
SERIES

HEATH STALLCUP
THE MONSTER
SQUAD